Praise for Russell James

"I loved the story so much that I'm eagerly waiting to read more from him. I now have a new favorite book I'll read over and over again." (Five Stars, A Night Owl Top Pick)
    —Night Owl Reviews on *Dark Inspiration*

"A surreal thrill ride of a read! Very reminiscent of Clive Barker at his best."
    —Hunter Shea, author of *Island of the Forbidden*, on *Dreamwalker*

"James has a talent for combining action-packed vignettes into a powerful, fast-paced whole."
    —Library Journal on *Black Magic*

"Surprisingly touching and compulsively readable."
    —*Publishers Weekly* on *Black Magic*

Look for these titles by Russell James

Now Available:

Novels
Dark Inspiration
Sacrifice
Black Magic
Dark Vengeance
Dreamwalker

Novella
Blood Red Roses

Q Island

Russell James

SAMHAIN
PUBLISHING

Samhain Publishing, Ltd.
11821 Mason Montgomery Road, 4B
Cincinnati, OH 45249
www.samhainpublishing.com

Q Island
Copyright © 2015 by Russell James
Print ISBN: 978-1-61922-979-2
Digital ISBN: 978-1-61922-748-4

Editing by Don D'Auria
Cover by Kelly Martin

First Samhain Publishing, Ltd. electronic publication: July 2015
First Samhain Publishing, Ltd. print publication: July 2015

Dedication

For first responders
The police officers who draw that thin line between order and chaos, the doctors and nurses who keep death at bay, the firemen who tame that most destructive of elements. We are all counting on you when this story unfolds in real life.

Part One
Patient Zero

Chapter One

He'd never been so hot.

Despite the plummeting temperature, rivulets of sweat streamed under the wooly mammoth's thick, coarse hair. He felt as hot as on a summer's day, though the cold north wind whipped a dusting of crystalline snow around his feet.

All week, he'd felt abnormal. His joints ached. When he dug for roots with his tusks, shooting pains, like two massive splinters, ran through his skull. In these last few days, he had felt progressively worse. The Siberian plain seemed to bend and roll before his eyes. Waves of rage often crashed within him without cause, and then receded. Sometimes strange sights and colors appeared, and then disappeared as if by magic.

He scanned the endless grayscape through his watery eyes. The overcast sky and the vast open plain met at some invisible point on the horizon, giving the world a haunting uniformity. Save for wisps of blowing snow, nothing moved.

His mother's herd of twenty had fallen as quickly as petals from a dying flower. First his cousin died, dropping without warning as the herd moved south to better grazing lands. Blood poured from her mouth as she twitched on the taiga. The herd gathered around her, unsure why she suddenly fell and went mute. They nudged and prodded her to no effect. As they realized she'd passed, each gave her forehead a caress with the tip of their trunk. By the time mother trumpeted for them to continue, dozens of bloody footprints circled the corpse in the crushed grass. Their heads bowed lower, and with a slow mourning step, the family continued the journey behind the matriarch who knew the way to winter pastures and the sun-driven schedule they had to keep.

By the next morning, three others were stricken. The two youngest and the grandmother were found bleeding in the grasses as the illness struck the furthest ends of his family tree. The tragedy stunned the herd. With such long lifespans, the passing of family members was rare. To see so many losses in such a short time…

Each day dawned upon more dying mammoths, lumps of steaming hair and puddles of congealing blood. His mother balanced the mourning of the herd with the need to survive. She pushed them south, somehow strong enough to carry both the burden of the dead and her responsibility to the living.

On the plague's fourth day, the herd's guiding star went dark. He and his sister stayed at their mother's side as she labored to breathe in the cool morning mist. When her heart went still, his own went numb, unable to understand the loss of what he held most dear. He and his sister spent the day and the night standing, then lying beside her cooling carcass. By morning, the leaderless herd had scattered. That afternoon, his sister fell ill and collapsed.

He tucked his tusks under his sister's body and tried to help her stand. It felt like he was moving a fallen tree. She made no response. He set her back down and caressed her face with the tip of his trunk. He could tell she was dying. Her psychic communal bond with the herd had grown weaker each day, like a tangled mat of ivy, breaking one strand at a time.

The last strand broke. He nudged her eyelids closed. The world wavered and swam. A chill ran up his spine.

Her eyes snapped wide open. His heart skipped a beat with joy at her resurrection then stopped in terror. Her soft-brown eyes had turned the bright, glowing red of a prairie fire.

She rolled up on her feet, and let loose a furious trumpeting. She turned and charged him.

He reacted on instinct with lowered tusks. Before he knew it, his twin ivory spears pierced her side. Blood gushed from two gaping wounds. She fell to the ground, still. No steam rose from her mouth.

Now, for the first time in his ever-shortening life, he was alone. His relief at survival ran tempered by the hollowing sorrow of unbearable loss. As a pounding headache echoed in his enormous skull, he trumpeted a low mourning cry.

The wind picked up. A blast ruffled his thick fur, and a jet of subzero air froze a stream of sweat to his skin. Still, he felt hot beyond anything he'd ever experienced. The fury that had ebbed and flowed since he fell ill rushed in with more force each time. He burned from the inside out. Even the world around him seemed washed in red.

Ahead, the ground sloped steeply down to a small pond. A thin sheet of ice had already formed across the surface. The mammoth saw relief in that frigid water, a gulp to quell the raging fire in his gut and the inferno of anger in his mind.

His aching joints would only move in slow motion. He lumbered forward, trying to make a straight line for the pond as the ground seemed to ripple and sway beneath him.

The hot metallic taste of blood filled his mouth. Time was short. If he could make it to the pond, the water would make everything all right.

He staggered to the pond's edge. The world took a dizzying spin, and his knees buckled under him. With a panicked trumpeted wail, he fell to his side. Tons of dead weight hit the ground like a falling boulder. He slid into the pond, shattering the ice at the surface and sending a shower of crystal shards into the air.

The water ran deep. The pond filled a sinkhole that stretched far into the limestone. The mammoth gave one huge shudder in a weak attempt to surface. He snaked his trunk upward for a breath of air. It tapped against the clear ice that had already re-formed.

The mammoth bellowed out an agonized cry, consumed by the sting of his losses and the pain of his passing. He sank deeper. The world went dark.

He saw one last bright hallucinogenic vision. His mother and sisters stood on a verdant meadow of waving green grass. They beckoned him forward with their trunks. He joined them.

The air temperature crossed minus 30°F. The ice spread downward. In no time, it encased the mammoth's cooling body. It would remain undisturbed for ten thousand years.

Chapter Two

"You're full of shit!"

Stu Balter was fed up with this screwed-up job. He'd been eating vacuum-packed food for three weeks now, and his colon was packed tighter than a sausage casing. The closest thing he'd had to a bath was a pan of melted ice water and a rag. He'd roughed it before, but this was the first time he sickened himself with his own wretched stench. He'd been without alcohol so long he could barely think straight. And now his untrustworthy interpreter was trying to convince him to launch another wild-goose chase.

"No, no," Sergei said. "This is real thing. One hundred percent gold. I know this chief."

Sergei was a master of pleading, his begging all the more convincing when coupled with the little man's eternal hangdog expression. Only in Russia had Stu met so many people with permanent washed-out miens of utter defeat, like a genetically engineered remnant of Communist oppression.

Stu didn't even bother to sit upright to answer. He kept his muddy boots propped up on the homemade wooden table in the center of the small log cabin. He rested his hands across his ample belly. He had no intention of leaving this half-assed command post, except for his helicopter extraction. His watch said that happened in thirty-six hours.

"You told me the same thing last time," Stu said, "and the time before that. None of these people have a damn clue where a mammoth carcass is."

Sergei hopped up and down, then grabbed Stu's parka by the arm and shook it.

"I know is true," he implored. "I seen it."

Stu sat straight up.

"You shitting me, boy?" he said.

"No, no," Sergei said. "A tusk, long as is my arm, sticking out of ground." He held his arm up in an uncomfortable arc to mimic the ancient tusk.

Stu made a mental picture and extrapolated the size of the potential subterranean mammoth. It wouldn't be huge, but his employer was looking for quality, not quantity. If the beast was buried frozen, the quality might be top-notch.

"How far away is this thing?"

"Forty kilometers, not far."

Yeah, not far, but not close. Forty klicks in the wheezy Land Cruiser across open country could take up to six hours, depending on the ground. Stu looked out the window. There were seven hours of daylight left at best. The drive back in the darkness and deepening cold would be torture.

"I don't know…" he muttered.

"The chief extend his offer for only today," Sergei said. "The spirits may not approve another day."

Stu wheezed out an irritated sigh. He'd hunted down some strange game in his years. He'd crossed savannahs and chopped through rain forests. This trip was the first time he'd played vulture looking for a dead carcass. But, no matter the prize, he had to deal with the same bullshit from superstitious dumb-ass locals. He was done having his schedule dictated by some withered idiot interpreting his indigestion as signals from some spirit god. Enough was enough.

But then he considered the payout. His weekly salary barely kept him fed, but his employer had offered a fortune for a choice specimen. He could live like a king for a while on that payday, and after his stretch in this hellhole, he was due. Maybe a pitch-black ride home in the creaky Land Cruiser would be worth it.

"What the hell," he said, dropping his feet to the floor. "But this better not be a waste of time."

Four and a half agonizing hours of rutted caribou tracks and tire-sucking ice melts later, Sergei pointed out through the cracked windshield.

"Over there!"

Two tan, round yurts leaned into the frosty, freshening breeze. A few mangy tethered goats huddled in the lee of one tent. A young man with a face like Genghis Khan and wearing a cast-off Soviet Army jacket eyed the Land Cruiser's approach. He entered one of the tents.

Stu spun the wheel and made a beeline to the camp. At a hundred yards from the yurts, Sergei grabbed the wheel with one hand.

"Here is good," he said. "Stop. Don't frighten livestock."

It was all Stu could do to keep from laughing. The pitiful goats behind the tents didn't qualify as livestock. Even the ASPCA would have had the poor bastards euthanized.

He stopped the Land Cruiser and then slapped Sergei's hand from the wheel.

"Okay, we're stopped," he said.

He zipped his parka up and opened the SUV door. A blast of Arctic wind rushed in and frosted the insides of the truck's windows. Stu shivered and cursed himself for agreeing to this little jaunt.

"Nice day for a little walk," he grumbled. He grabbed a backpack from the rear of the Land Cruiser.

When they reached the yurt's door flap, Sergei stopped Stu one more time.

"Let me speak first to the chief," he said.

The sun was sinking faster than a gambler's dreams behind a pair of threes. Sunset turned the air cold enough to freeze skin on contact. Stu shoved a wad of Russian rubles into Sergei's hand.

"Get it over with."

A revolting mélange of sweat, feces and burned lamb wafted out as the tent flaps opened to swallow Sergei. Stu turned his nose to the wind for relief. Moments later Sergei reappeared and held the tent flap open.

A short, withered old man in a coat of tanned caribou hide emerged from the darkness. Asian features dominated a broad face the sun had weathered into the texture of crumpled newspaper. His gray hair was pulled back into a ponytail, and his dark eyes burned with the determination of a younger man. He pointed a gnarled, crooked finger at Stu. In a cracked and raspy voice, he began to harangue the American in the unintelligible local tongue.

"He warns you," Sergei translated. "He would not give up his ancestors' prize if he did not need medicine for his granddaughter."

Sick granddaughter. Right. Stu knew the old fraud would be soaking in Stolichnaya and puffing Marlboros as soon as he got those rubles into town.

"You must pay respects to the land and to the souls that before you passed," Sergei continued to translate. "He says ill fortune will follow you if the spirits are not appeased."

"Sure, Gramps," Stu said to the chief with a dismissive nod. He turned back to Sergei. "The tusk?"

Sergei looked at Stu as if the American had just tossed his life jacket over the rail of a sinking ship.

"At the base of the hill," he said, pointing to the other side of the yurts.

Finally!

Stu pushed off into the wind and trudged to the designated spot. The ground sloped away to a small depression. The dying sun turned the sky crimson, and the frost and ice forming on the ground reflected the light like puddles of fresh blood. Near the edge pool, a curved, alabaster shaft pointed a jagged edge at the sun. A single mammoth t sk.

Stu let out a whoop and started a barely controlled skid down the steep hillside. A train of loose stone and lichen rolled after him. Near the bottom, he lost his footing and fell face-first onto the rock-hard ground. Too excited to stand, he crawled to the base of the emergent tusk.

It was too beautiful to be ten thousand years old. Windblown ice had polished the mammoth's long upper tooth to a glossy sheen. Stu stripped off a glove, ignoring the needles of pain the frigid air instantly delivered. He ran his fingertips along the slick edge, the first white man to ever caress this creature. It felt like money.

He brushed the blowing snow from the ground around the tusk. It wasn't ground at all, but ice. It was only as clear as the frosted cubes in a drinking glass, but clear enough. He could make out another tusk just below the surface, and something amazing where the two tusks met. A dark, hulking shadow filled the ice, a great oblong mass at the tusks and a larger, humped section beyond that.

The Holy Grail. An intact woolly mammoth.

Stu gave another shout for joy at the thought of how many cheap Eastern European whores his pile of cash would buy him. He pulled a GPS unit from his backpack and flipped it on. The orange latitude and longitude readings came into focus and he hit the Save button. Then he pulled what looked like an oversized lawn dart out of his bag, along with a sledgehammer.

He skittered back to the edge of the hill and found a spot of frozen ground. He balanced the dart on its point. With four swift blows from the hammer, he drove the homing device into the ground. Only a few inches of the fins remained above the surface. He tossed the hammer aside, and pushed a button on the side of the homing device. A red LED illuminated in the homing dart's base. The location was marked.

The sun moved below the horizon and the sky's reds leeched to purple. The LED blinked every ten seconds. Stu lay back against the ground. His breath rose above him in a great ball of steam. He'd be back with a team to excavate this. Winter be damned, this couldn't wait. He'd be rolling in dough.

Chapter Three

Three weeks later

"*Остановитесь! Nyet!*"

The two words were all the Russian Stu knew, but it was most of what he ever needed. Being able to yell "Stop!" and "No!" had saved him enough times that he'd have paid royalties on them.

The two men unloading empty wooden crates from the back of the flatbed truck froze at his commands. Steamy breath curled from their mouths in the still air of the unheated warehouse. But it was the third man, the one lifting the tarp off the big mass on the floor, whose attention Stu really wanted. Of course, that one had missed the message.

"Goddamn it! Don't touch that goddamn tarp!"

The man looked over at Stu. Either the English or the furious tone had made an impact. Stu didn't care which. He waved the man away with a few frantic gestures. The man shrugged and walked back to the truck.

Stu pointed at the two remaining crates and gestured for the men to unload them. As they placed them in a pile with the rest, he handed the burly leader a wad of rubles. The crew muttered a few curt words of Russian to each other, got back in their truck and drove off.

At American rates, the crates were a bargain. The lids fit with a precision that spoke of Old World craftsmanship, a rare commodity in socialist-shoddy Russia. He popped one off and revealed the interior lined with sprayed foam overlaid with protective insulation. Once he dropped in the chunks of dry ice, the sealed crates would keep the mammoth frozen until opened at its New York destination.

Black market meat meant big money. Ex-pat Africans wanted monkey, for some unknown reason. Asians thought that rhino horn made your cock permanently hard and that a rhino steak did damn near the same thing. Tiger. Lion. Ridley's sea turtle. If it breathed, someone on Earth longed to eat it. Depending on the buyer and the product, the stuff sold for more per pound than uncut heroin, and you didn't get life sentences for smuggling some mystery meat across a border.

But this find would set him up with a year's pay. One man with more money than brains wasn't content to have eaten almost anything that roamed the earth. He wanted to sample what *used* to roam the earth. He'd read about a frozen mammoth found above the Arctic Circle, and called to offer a fortune for mammoth steaks. He dangled enough cash to finance this entire ridiculous expedition, plus a bonus finder's fee.

Stu had promised fifty pounds, and figured the remainder of the mammoth was gravy. He'd sworn his client to secrecy, just to ensure there would be word of mouth. Once the news leaked out through the bizarre bush-meat community, clients would be beating down his door for the rest of this thing safely stored in his own private walk-in freezer.

He threw back the tarp, and exposed the frozen remains of the mammoth, severed with a diamond-tipped circular saw into rough blocks, bones still embedded and furry hide intact. He'd left the inedible parts in case someone needed proof that their meal was worth five digits per pound.

He hand packed each crate, then filled the corners with steaming, sublimating dry ice. He screwed each lid shut with an electric screwdriver. With the last box sealed, one small slab of meat remained. Stu tossed it on top of the crates. The frozen mammoth hit with a whack, like a ceramic plate on a countertop.

He'd never sampled any of the exotic meat he'd procured. It wasn't like he had some version of a drug dealer's code about not sampling his own product, or that he had suppressed, subliminal vegan leanings. He just had no desire to eat hippo, Gila monster or wombat. But mammoth…well, that really was a once-in-a-lifetime opportunity. At the prices he was going to charge, he'd be asked what mammoth tastes like, and he'd need an answer. He wrapped the spare slab with aluminum foil.

Later that night, alone in his crumbling Soviet-era hotel, he'd see what Neanderthals used to risk their lives for.

Chapter Four

Four days later

Stu nosed his cabin cruiser toward the white light at the tip of the mansion's private dock. Just two windows in the house beyond were lit. The inlet near Napeague, out on Long Island's tony East End, was black as an abyss, the water smooth as glass. He cut the engine to Idle and coasted at a slow rumble towards the dock. He killed the running lights.

While his cargo was clandestine, the cloak-and-dagger delivery wasn't necessary. It wasn't like Federal agents had been tracking him since he arrived in the States. This deserted stretch of the bay harbored no threats. But Stu thought a touch of the theatrical wouldn't hurt. Old Man Chadwell ought to get his money's worth. It might pump up the story he told his friends, and that was the kind of advertising money couldn't buy.

Stu would have relished his role if he felt better. The rolling chop to the water outside the inlet had sent his stomach into an unusual bout of mild seasickness. He blamed it on the night's erased horizon.

Closer in, the old man appeared under the umbrella of light at the end of the dock. Even at one in the morning, he wore pressed tan khakis, black-leather loafers and a button-down shirt.

Stu groaned. The silver-haired geezer wore a red cravat. Seriously? Apparently that was his secret-rendezvous outfit, the dashing world-spy look he imagined fit this special moment. Well, Chadwell paid the bill, so whatever made him happy. The wrinkled old man beamed a smile of perfectly capped, white teeth.

Stu dropped the engine into neutral and coasted into the dock. A quick surge of reverse brought the ship to a halt. He killed the engine. Mr. Chadwell tossed him a line to secure the boat.

"Ahoy, Mr. Balter. Right on time."

"With a delivery ten thousand years late," Stu said.

He bent and clean-jerked a crate up from the cockpit to the deck alongside the pier. Chadwell rolled a cart over to the gunwale of the boat. Stu hopped off, and he and Chadwell transferred the crate to the cart.

The giddy look of a child at Christmas filled Chadwell's eyes. "So heavy!"

"A lot of that's crate. Your quantity is just what you ordered."

"And what does it taste like?"

Stu smiled at his ability to anticipate a customer's response.

"It's sublime," he said. "Gamey, with a similarity to venison."

That was a lie. It was passable, but it was certainly no Kobe beef. A bit freezer burned, actually. He'd tried it four days ago, the night before he and his cargo jetted out of Russia. He'd probably undercooked it.

"The other half of your payment will be wired to your account within the hour," Chadwell said.

They shook hands, and Stu returned to his boat. He cast off and started the engines. Stu spun the boat in a tight reverse circle and slammed the throttles forward. The boat's tail dug in, and Stu rocked back in his seat. The bow cut a fierce, glowing white wake across the water.

For the third time that day, the outside world went a bit wavy, and Stu's stomach did a disquieting backflip. He wondered what kind of medicine he had below in the head.

He snapped on the autopilot, and set it to backtrack the course he'd taken on the way in. He'd sail out between the long fins of Long Island's eastern fishtail, and then skirt the Atlantic's edge on the way to Martha's Vineyard and a well-earned rest.

A bead of sweat rolled down the side of his face. He wiped it off and his cheek felt like it was on fire. He touched his forehead. He was burning up! He wasn't seasick. He'd probably just caught the goddamn flu somewhere.

The cabin's darkness masked the creeping transformation on his arms, the steady alteration of blue veins to slate gray.

Chapter Five

Twelve days later

The Coast Guard cutter *Escanaba* pulled alongside Stu Balter's sinking cabin cruiser. The cruiser's bow rode low in the water. Waves licked at the forward cabin. The cockpit sat high and angled. Dried blood splattered the transom.

On the roof lay a collection of dead animals, seabirds, fish, none of which had died of natural causes. Their bodies lay ripped open, some shredded beyond recognition. Sunlight flashed on fish scales embedded in the blood-washed deck. Stray feathers fluttered in the breeze, stems glued to the deck, as if trying to take flight from the grisly scene.

Stu Balter lay in the cockpit, naked and faceup in the sun. His arms stretched overhead, locked in rigor mortis. Blood covered his hands and arms like hellish evening gloves. More blood coated his mouth and sent trails from each side down his neck. From a distance, it looked like a clown's painted frown. The sun had already shrunk his opened eyes into two shriveled grapes.

The cutter captain ordered a team to board the vessel, but no sooner had the command been given than the sinking ship nosed over and began a slow dive beneath the waves, like a dying man who'd held on to make sure his last story was told. The stern slipped under the sea and left Stu on the surface, faceup. He rolled over onto his stomach. The suction of the sinking ship caught him and pulled his feet down. His stiffened arms snapped out of the water like a Pentecostal praise to Jesus.

His blackened eyes stared at the cutter. He flashed his horrid clown smile at the crew and then sank into the sea—first, face; then, arms; and, finally, bloodstained fingertips.

The crew would run the registration and then record that location as the last resting place of Stu Balter, but never know him by the name the CDC would try, and fail, to assign him: Patient Zero.

Part Two
Outbreak

Chapter One

Lucian Chadwell rose as he tapped the side of his crystal wineglass with a pastry fork. The staccato *tink* of silver on crystal ushered a hushed silence over the dozen seated at the long dining table. All eyes turned to their dinner host.

The dinner setting put kings' tables to shame. Tapers burned in silver candelabras set on a starched, white tablecloth. A squad of specialized silverware surrounded each place setting, ready to do combat with the evening's meal. Pure platinum ringed the edge of each gleaming, bone-white plate. The guests had dressed for the event in tuxedos and gowns, and had adorned themselves with diamonds and gold.

A dinner with the group that called themselves the Wild Ones (and they were the only ones who did) was always an upscale event, but this level of formality was a first, as was the meal they were about to share.

Lucian's tuxedo fit with sartorial precision, hand-tailored and taken in twice over time to fit his age-diminished frame. His silver hair was swept back in the pompadour style he'd favored since he turned eighteen. He claimed the skin that still stretched tight over his high cheekbones was the result of their group's dietary regimen, but trace scars along his neck begged to differ on that account. Candlelight flickered in his dark eyes as he began to speak.

"My friends, my Wild Ones. For two years now, we've rotated hosting these dinners, and our taste buds have traveled around the world. We've sampled wild animals from every corner of the globe, like wildebeest at Gwen's, or gazelle at Rick and Rachel's. A few endangered species may have stretched the limits of the law on some nights. Then there was the alleged snow leopard at Vincent's…"

A discontented murmur rumbled through the room. Vincent, a portly, bald man in a double-breasted tux raised a hand in protest.

"See here, I had on absolutely rock-solid authority that meat was snow leopard."

"More like NO leopard," Gwen Albritton, a frail older woman in a green velvet dress, said. "It tasted like chicken!"

The room broke into laughter. Lucian tapped his glass again.

"But, tonight, we have something special," he continued. "A meal we will never see again, a meal no one has seen for ten thousand years."

Lucian nodded to a servant who dimmed the lights. The candelabras transformed everyone's face into a yellow, deathly pallor. The women pointed and laughed at each other's sickly appearance. Lucian moved a candle in a glass candlestick closer to him. The light cast insidious shadows up along his face.

"Early man walked the Earth," he said, summoning the bass CEO voice he'd used decades ago, "hunting and gathering to survive. He left little to record his life, only selecting the most momentous events."

The wall behind Lucian lit up with the projected picture of a primitive cave drawing. A group of spear-wielding stick figures surrounded a shaggy representation of an elephant. Spears protruded from the creature's side. Its trunk was raised in a trumpet of distress.

"Imagine the courage of the clan to face the mighty wooly mammoth, largest land mammal to ever walk the planet, the warriors armed with nothing but stone-tipped spears. The feast this creature could provide would feed the clan for weeks. Imagine how amazing this creature must have tasted, that the members would risk their lives for it when easier prey abounded."

Lucian paused. "Tonight, you won't have to imagine it at all."

The lights came up and the picture behind him faded away. Two waiters entered carrying covered silver platters. They placed one at each end of the table and stood next to it.

"My man has scoured the world for the exotic, the rare." Lucian tapped the cover on the platter before him with a perfectly manicured nail. "He insists I spare no expense."

The room laughed.

"So tonight I bring you a treat straight from the icy tundra in Siberia, locked deep within a frozen lake since before *Homo sapiens* evolved. The most sought-after meat of the Neolithic."

On cue, the two waiters removed the silver domes from the platters and retreated from the room. On each platter was a low pyramid of tiny cubes of raw, red meat, each piece with just a hint of marbling.

"Wooly mammoth," Lucien announced. "*Tartare*, of course, as we savor all our dinners."

A few people gasped. The rest just stared.

"See here," Vincent said. "My leopard is questioned, but you expect us to believe this is a species extinct for millennia? Really, Lucian."

"My friends, my source is unimpeachable. And the shaggy skin was intact when I received the meat. I had the hair tested by my own lab, and the DNA matched no living creature in the database. So unless it's a yeti…"

Nervous laughter.

"…my paleobiologist says it's mammoth."

No one made a move.

"People, please!" Lucian said.

He reached over and speared a piece with his fork and popped it into his mouth. He chewed and swallowed.

"It's wonderful. The chef prepared it with five different marinades, so don't stop with one taste."

Gwen Albritton smoothed her green dress, reached over and speared a cube of mammoth with her fork. "If eating moray eel didn't kill me, an elephant sure won't. C'mon, people, don't let Lucian go on this adventure all alone."

She plucked the cube from the fork's tines with her teeth, and then tossed the morsel into her mouth with a snap of her neck. Gwen swooned with exaggerated pleasure.

The rest of the guests dove in.

Chapter Two

One week later

Melanie Bailey slapped off the alarm, and rolled over in the darkness to an empty bed. Nothing abnormal there, but the light in the master bath wasn't on either. She sat up in fear then relaxed as she remembered. Her husband, Charles, had spent the night in New York City. Again.

Truth be told, he wasn't much help in getting their son, Aiden, off to school in the morning anyway. On a normal day, Charles was out the door long before Aiden left for Brock Academy. But the house had an empty feel with him gone for the night. No matter how busy the day, she needed all three of them reeled in each evening to reassure her that this house was indeed their home.

Melanie slipped out of bed and onto the cold floor. The snooze button wasn't an option in the Bailey household. The Routine was king, and from the stroke of 5:12 a.m. each morning (for she'd timed it to extract every minute of sleep possible), the sweep of the clock's second hand brought on the Routine.

Every normal family made concessions for each individual's needs, but when one member had autism spectrum disorder, his needs trumped all others. The disorder had Aiden in a bear hug. Autism skewed the victim's perception of the world, and one of its manifestations was often an overwhelming need for repetitive predictability.

Melanie thought Aiden was trying to compensate for being unable to make sense of the world, like he was navigating his way through a foreign country, incapable of reading the street signs but just using the same daily route. His pediatrician didn't endorse her explanation. She didn't care. No matter the reason, Aiden needed to do everything the same way each day, starting when she awakened him at 5:15 a.m..

She slipped on a robe against the morning chill and cinched it tight around her narrow waist. One child into motherhood, she still had a petite figure, though her time-consuming, long, brown locks had been sacrificed on the altar of maternity.

She padded down the hallway of their Long Island condo and cracked open the door to Aiden's room. A shaft of light from the doorway lit the six-year-old's bed. He threw the covers up over his head and moaned, one of the few noises he made at all.

"Aiden, time to get up." She closed the door most of the way in deference to his light sensitivity. He'd be up. The Routine demanded it.

Melanie returned to the kitchen and assembled the elements of a fresh pot of coffee with the precision of a sniper snapping together his rifle. The ritual was just as automatic, just as perfunctory, just as serious. Starting a day without coffee hadn't been a good idea for years.

She opened Aiden's backpack to load his lunch. She pulled out sheets of drawings, stick-figure scenes Aiden drew throughout the day. What they were scenes of, she never knew. The places and people he created in his drawings rarely matched the real world. The doctors said kids drew what they saw. God help her son if these drawings were how he saw life.

She popped her phone to Speaker and dialed Charles's cell. He picked up on the fourth ring.

"Your work night turned into day again, didn't it?" she said.

"You have no idea," Charles said. The rasp in his voice said he'd just woken up. "Did I mention that the couch in my office can double as a CIA interrogation device?"

Melanie placed twelve squares of shredded wheat in a bowl, sugared side up, and put the bowl at Aiden's place at the table. She put two pills in the spoon.

"There's a soft bed right here at home, you know," she said.

"Two words. Global economy. Gold stocks started a run for the sky in the Hang Seng last night. We began moving clients' positions about 7:00 p.m. and never stopped 'til it peaked. By then, the last train to the island was long gone. But we locked in millions. Here's hoping the clients appreciate the effort."

The coffeepot chugged and spit on the countertop. Melanie raised an empty mug in a mock toast to no one. "To appreciation."

"I know our banker will have some," Charles said. "Major commissions."

"That's great." And it really was. Autism didn't come cheap. Aiden had therapists and specialists that exhausted their insurance coverage in the first few months of each year. Charles made good money at his brokerage firm, but financially the family treaded water, even with a small condo and him driving a nine-year-old Ford to the LIRR each day. She took the blame for their financial situation.

"I've gotta hit the gym for a shower and change of clothes," Charles said. "See you tonight."

"I love you," Melanie said as Charles hung up.

She didn't hear "I love you" that often from her husband, and she understood why. Charles was a decade older and mid-divorce when she started as an admin temp in his office. Gossip painted her as the "fling that got pregnant" and hinted that the firm forced Charles to marry her for appearance sake. The ex's divorce lawyer certainly played up that angle for the alimony settlement.

But Melanie knew Charles loved her, even with the stress she and their son added to his life. His extra hours at work would get him a promotion, their finances would stabilize, he could spend more time at home, and the Charles who'd swept her off her feet would be back forever.

Aiden walked into the kitchen. He had an odd gait, with his upper body upright and motionless, his eyes invariably cast to the ground, hands glued to his sides. The left side of his black hair stood up on end, like someone had severely scared it overnight. He shared his mother's fair skin, but with no extended time outdoors, it remained unnaturally pale. He took his seat without speaking. He spooned the pills into his mouth and swallowed. He picked up one shredded-wheat square with his fingers and put it in his mouth. Pause. One count, two counts, three counts. He chewed and swallowed. He'd be done eating at 6:31 a.m.

A knock sounded at the door. Melanie checked and saw her neighbor Tamara Drake through the peephole.

"Tamara!" She turned the key in the front door's upper deadbolt, another precaution to make sure Aiden couldn't leave the house without her knowing. She opened the door.

Tamara was her age, stout with short, blonde hair. She wore her dark-blue nurse's scrubs. "Hey, Mel."

"I haven't seen you all week," Melanie said.

"Swung to nights for a while, so I kind of turned vampire."

"Did Jennifer call you about the Range Rover?"

Tamara's broad face screwed up in disgust. "That fu…" Tamara looked past Melanie's shoulder at Aiden, "…that damn truck. Why did I ever fight for that stupid thing in the divorce?"

"Because your ex wanted it."

"Well it's been a year, and I can't get rid of it. Jennifer thought all the off-road accessories a bit much to drive to Target. So it's still sucking up my storage unit out back. Anyhow, I'm running late and I'm here with bad news. Someone dinged your car."

"Oh no." The Ford Escape was only a few months old, Charles's begrudged purchase out of his annual bonus.

"Hit up Mario today when he comes on duty. He'll review the security feed with you, find out who we need to string up at the next condo meeting."

"I'll do that," Melanie said. "Thanks for bringing such joy to my morning."

"You mean that sarcastically, but I'll pretend you don't. I gotta go."

Melanie closed and relocked the door. It seemed like Tamara always had her back. Tamara understood Aiden. Her neighbor had developed a pretty tough exterior, especially after her divorce, but had a soft interior she seemed to only share with Aiden and Melanie. Melanie wished Jennifer had bought the Rover. She could have helped Tamara out, instead of it always being the other way around.

Aiden's chair scraped the kitchen floor. Without checking the clock, Melanie knew it was 6:31 a.m.

The coffee machine spit the last of the morning's brew into the pot and wheezed. The rising sun backlit the kitchen curtains in ruby. Another day cranked up in the Bailey household.

An hour later, Melanie buckled Aiden into the backseat of the Ford. Rare were the mornings he did it himself. She snugged the belt over his red, hooded sweatshirt. The doctors said that the soft, thick folds gave him a sense of security. He wore it almost every day, even during Long Island's sweltering August. He didn't have the hood up, his last line of defense against an incomprehensible world, so there was hope for a good day today.

She closed the door and sighed at the dent in the front fender. She could already hear Charles berating her. He'd warned that a new car wouldn't be new for long between New York drivers on the outside and a kid on the inside. She'd taken such good care of it to prove him wrong.

After a short drive, they arrived at the well-landscaped campus of Brock Academy. Brock Academy was the premier school for special-needs children, ranging from learning disabilities to severe dysfunctions. On a public playground, Aiden stood out like a Red Sox fan in Yankee Stadium. But here he was the median. He didn't require the constant attention of the heartbreakingly handicapped or the mind-numbing repetition of the severely mentally challenged. In fact, he tested borderline genius when the school found an examiner who could get Aiden to finish the tests. Aiden just needed structure in his world, and then he could complete most schoolwork within that structure.

She opened the door, and Aiden got out. He left a new drawing on the backseat, yet another part of the Routine. It varied little from the others. Stick figures, boxes, squiggles. Petroglyphs made more sense.

She walked Aiden to the front door. She mentally double-checked that she'd packed all his books and his lunch in his backpack.

"See you this afternoon," she said.

He didn't answer, didn't even look up. He just marched through the school's front door and disappeared down the hallway.

The irony of having two distant men in her life wasn't lost on her. She went back to the Ford and wondered how much fixing the fender dent would set them back.

Chapter Three

Dr. Samuel Bradshaw preferred morning rounds at St. Luke's, the earlier the better. The hospital was calmer. The staff was at the start of their day. Best of all, the patients were less cranky since they hadn't waited all day to see their physicians. He had learned something after practicing medicine for over forty years.

Another reason he preferred the a.m. was that he was already awake. Sleep had become more elusive over the last few years. Five seemed to be the magic number of hours his body had determined he needed, way down from the seven and a half that had worked ever since the end of his internship. His wife, Brenda, claimed that was an indicator it was time to retire, but he thought it meant just the opposite. What would he do with all the extra waking hours?

Besides, he didn't feel old enough to retire. Maybe he had a little stiffness in his lower back each morning before he stretched it, but other than that, he looked years younger than he was. He still had a full head of hair that modern chemistry kept a chestnut brown, and a regimen of cycling and rowing-machine workouts kept him as fit as ever. Well, as fit as forty, perhaps, if he was going to be realistic.

He greeted the ward clerk at the station on the eighth floor, his last stop. He didn't recognize the slight twenty-something nurse with the pixie haircut. That didn't surprise him. Every year there were more new faces than old, and more faces that looked like they still belonged in high school. In addition, the current generation of nurses had lost the site loyalty he'd grown up with. RNs swapped locations on a whim for different hours or slight changes in benefits. He'd given up keeping track of them and thanked God for the name tag this one wore that read *Bethany*.

"How's Gwen Albritton doing?" he asked.

Bethany shook her head in wonder. "She was up all night, filling up a notebook with poetry. The fever she had yesterday broke. She woke up feeling fine, vitals all normal. Then she grabbed a notebook from her bag and started writing. She didn't quit until about two hours ago."

"Well, good for her," Samuel said. "When she was younger, she was a published poet. She told me that after she got married and had children, the muse departed her. She must be feeling better if she's taken up writing again. What about her physical symptoms?"

"No change there, Doctor."

That tamped down his relief about her rebound. She'd presented yesterday with what looked like symptoms of sepsis, or blood poisoning to the layman. Fever, bloodshot eyes, pounding headache, red streaking along ashy skin, and bulging, darkened veins. He couldn't identify a specific infection, but had prescribed antibiotics Rocephin and Levaquin until he could come up with something concrete. It appeared that part or all of the chemical cocktail had worked.

Samuel strode into Gwen's room. The diminutive woman lay fast asleep, her silver hair fanned across the pillow behind her. Her face looked calm, though a bit drawn, but at seventy, people didn't have a lot of facial fat left. The red striations and the darkened veins remained. He looked up at the monitors. Blood pressure, oxygen and pulse registered all damn near perfect. By lunch, perhaps the other symptoms would pass as well, and he'd be able to send her home. Decades in, it still felt great to make someone healthy.

Samuel picked up the notebook by her bedside, a tattered, spiral-bound volume with a blue cover. Shafts of paper shreds lay inside the steel coil, linear tombstones for the failed pages torn out and tossed away.

He flipped it open to the first page. Gwen's elegant handwriting hearkened back to the time when penmanship was a graded school exercise. Perfect sweeping loops kissed the page's blue, horizontal lines. The dot of every letter *I* fell dead center. The page contained a single poem written with no corrections.

The Tender Passage

In gentle, rolling springtime land,
Is beauty found on surfaces smooth.
As beg a tender caress by hand,
An area unmarred by a single groove.

But deep within canyons and cracks,
Alone reside the thoughts so sage.

In faults that a spring youth lacks,
Is the true beauty found in age.

Gwen always said she was proud of her past as a poet. If she was inspired to write something so lovely lying in a hospital bed, she had to be feeling much better.

Gwen's eyes snapped open. Samuel jumped back. Her irises, which he remembered as pale blue, were a wholly unnatural dark red. Though her eyelids were wide open, she was not awake.

He whipped out a penlight and checked her eyes. No reaction at all. That was odd. When she woke up she'd be seeing the world with a decidedly reddish hue and would want an explanation. Her eyelids slid closed on their own. The monitors continued their steady backbeat of pulse and oxygen levels.

Tamara Drake entered the room. He welcomed the familiar face. He'd worked with the nurse for years, and liked her professionalism and skill. She wore an open long, blue cardigan over her scrubs and carried a saline IV bag in her hand.

"Tamara, I haven't seen you in a while. Where have you been hiding?"

"Swung over to nights for a while for the pay bump. Everything okay here?"

"Amazingly okay," Samuel said. "Except for her irises and the skin discoloration. Can you draw a new 10 cc blood sample from Ms. Albritton for a culture?"

"Absolutely."

She stepped to the treatment cart and pulled out a butterfly needle and a blood vial. Samuel returned to the nurses' station.

"Didn't I tell you she was doing better?" Bethany said.

Behind Samuel, the elevator doors opened to reveal a nursing assistant named Manny and a sleeping man on a gurney. The orderly, a well-muscled black man in a set of scrubs one size too small, maneuvered the gurney into the hall with one hand. Samuel went to the medical-records terminal and called up Gwen's records.

A scream pierced the air.

Tamara staggered backwards out of Gwen's room. The nurse stumbled and fell on her back. Her hands covered her face. The blood sampling needle protruded from her left eye and between her fingers. Blood ran down from under her palm.

Gwen Albritton stood in the doorway, though Samuel wouldn't have recognized her as the woman he'd checked in the day before. Her eyes burned a solid, bright red. Rage contorted her face into a gargoyle's visage. Her bony legs stood spread shoulder-width apart, knees flexed like a sumo wrestler before a bout. The hospital gown, wide open at the back, hung in front of her like some reverse cape. The morning sun backlit the shadow of her frail body. Her white knuckles gripped the IV stand like a medieval battle ax. Her IV bag lay on the floor behind her, bleeding its clear contents across the floor.

"I said don't touch me, bitch!" Gwen screamed.

Tamara pointed up with her free hand. Blood covered her index finger. "She's gone crazy!"

Bethany slammed an alarm button at the nurses' station and bolted toward Gwen. Three steps behind her, Manny came around the hallway corner at a run, like a wide receiver on the way to the end zone,. They filled the narrow hall like a wave of blue-cotton scrubs.

Together, they outweighed Gwen three to one. She didn't flinch. Instead, she charged.

Gwen spun the IV stand in her hand like a Texas baton twirler. She snapped it to a stop with the top pointing forward. Gwen lunged and drove the stand into Bethany's gut. The stand ripped through flesh and organs until the tip punched through her back.

Samuel froze in shock. Gwen lifted the impaled nurse like a pitchfork full of hay and slammed her through the false ceiling. Tiles exploded in a fibrous dust storm, and the light above her flashed and popped. A sadistic, victorious grin grew on Gwen's face.

Manny swept in from her side, curled an arm around her waist and threw her back down the hallway toward her room. Bethany fell to the floor with a lifeless thud and the clatter of the IV stand on tile.

Normally, Gwen's ninety-two pounds would have smashed into the wall after Manny launched her across the floor. But nothing here was normal. Gwen crouched and dug her bare feet in as she slid backwards. At the wall, she skidded to a stop and stood straight up. Her eyes narrowed.

"Is that all you've got, sonny?" she said.

Samuel joined the orderly, and the two charged Gwen. Each grabbed one of her arms.

Gwen nearly lifted him off the ground with the arm he'd clamped under his armpit. Her muscles felt like steel cables across his chest.

"Get her to the floor," he ordered.

Manny swept one leg under Gwen's in some kind of martial arts move, and the two men followed her down to the ground. Gwen snarled. Her head darted at the orderly. She clamped her teeth on his ear, bit away a chunk and spit it out.

Manny screamed and pulled back. He put a hand to his damaged ear. He realized his loss, and his face went red with rage. He hauled back and nailed Gwen across the chin. Her head bobbed, stunned. Her body relaxed.

Samuel reared back. The orderly looked shocked and scared.

"Doc, sorry! I didn't even think. I mean, the bitch bit off my ear!"

"I understand." Samuel checked her pulse—strong and racing. "Get her back in bed. And in restraints. I'll reset her IV with a sedative."

The orderly picked her up as if she were weightless. Samuel went to Tamara. She was on her feet by a treatment cart, left hand pressed against her wound. Gauze peeked out from beneath her palm. Clear ocular fluid dripped out of the end of the needle's tube. The nurse had guts to follow protocol and not remove the needle.

"Shit," she said. She plugged the end of the tube with a finger.

"Let me get the EMTs up here for you," Samuel said.

"I'll just go to them," Tamara answered. Pro that she was, she'd apparently reverted to her role as a nurse and assessed herself as a patient. "It'll be quicker."

She headed for the elevator. The doors opened and two security guards exited at the ready, weapons drawn.

"In there," Samuel said.

The two guards rushed into Gwen's room. Samuel bent beside Bethany's impaled body to check her vitals. But the growing pool of blood beneath her telegraphed what he'd find.

"Hey, Doc!" called Manny from Gwen's room. "You better get in here."

Samuel ran in. The two guards bracketed the door, standing as far from Gwen's bed as they could get. The orderly stood facing Samuel, hands up at his sides.

"All I did was lay her down. By the time I tightened the straps, she was dead."

That made no sense. Seconds ago, she was strong enough to harpoon a nurse like a Nantucket whaler and then give two men a tough fight. Samuel went to the side of her bed. Gwen stared up at the ceiling with glazed, red eyes. Her vitals ran flat.

"Get the crash cart!" Samuel started chest compressions.

A security guard ran out and rolled one in. Samuel charged the paddles and pressed them against the shell of Gwen's body. The woman who'd nearly thrown him across the room felt as insubstantial as a paper-and-balsawood kite.

"Clear!"

He sent 200 joules through Gwen's static heart. Her body jumped, then went still. He checked again for a pulse. Nothing. Two more rounds produced the same result. Samuel tossed the paddles back on the cart in frustration.

"Doc...it wasn't because I hit her, was it?" Manny said.

"No, I'm sure it wasn't." In fact, he wasn't sure at all, but the guilt-ridden orderly didn't need to know that. Samuel closed Gwen's blood-red eyes. Then her face looked normal again, like someone's great-grandmother, except for the gray streaks.

The autopsy would have to discover what really happened. And Samuel would be waiting for the results.

Chapter Four

Two hours later, St. Luke's eighth floor had transformed from a working part of the hospital into a crime scene. The police had taken Dr. Bradshaw and Manny, whom one cop had taken to calling Van Gogh, down to the police station to fill out statements. Tamara was hospitalized across town at Smithtown General to be treated by Dr. Norton, Long Island's acknowledged ocular maestro. The cops tried to sort out the story of how a near octogenarian killed a healthy woman in her twenties. They took hundreds of photographs. The evidence bags included a chewed-up chunk of the orderly's ear on ice.

Inside the hospital room of the late Gwen Albritton, Reynolds and Bevers, two coroner's technicians in dark-blue coveralls, had already removed Bethany's body. Reynolds zipped Gwen's naked corpse into a black-plastic body bag on a gurney. Her gown had been bagged as evidence.

"Two for one today," Reynolds said.

"A full day's work before noon," Bevers answered.

They rolled her out to the hallway. A pool of Bethany's dried blood stained the hall floor. The other crime scene investigators made way for them as they pushed the stainless-steel gurney into the elevator. Bevers pushed the button for the basement parking where the coroner's van waited.

The body bag moved.

"Oh hell no," Reynolds said. "She was pronounced hours ago."

The elevator door slid shut.

"I've had docs screw up before," Bevers said.

The bag moved again. This time it swelled at the center like a rising muffin.

" For the love of Christ?" Reynolds said.

He unzipped the bag. Inside, Gwen's scrawny corpse had swollen like a summer sausage, every wrinkle in her skin erased. Her arms and legs looked like they belonged to a balloon animal. Her abdomen had expanded into a mottled beach ball with two desiccated breasts.

The elevator headed down.

Bevers peered closer at the taut, still-stretching skin. "Have you ever seen—"

Gwen's abdomen exploded with a bang. Blood and shreds of oil-black organs splattered both men and the inside of the elevator. The air filled with a dark, dusty mist. The technicians screamed obscenities and fruitlessly wiped with slickened hands at the greasy goo on their faces. The sickening goo stank like rotted meat. More black spores drifted up from the yawning cavity in Gwen's abdomen.

The door slid open to the seventh floor. The three people waiting for a ride down screamed and backed away. Newborn spores drifted out and settled on the onlookers. Behind them, the charge nurse grabbed a phone and dialed. The doors slid shut.

The scene repeated seven more times, the doors opening and closing like some recycling horror peep show. Panic and spores spread throughout the hospital. The doors opened the last time to the basement garage. Reynolds, Bevers and the black mist exited into the unprotected outside world.

Chapter Five

Waking up in jail sucked. Jimmy Wade had done it enough to know. Hard, cold surfaces. The trifecta stench of stale sweat, vomit and piss. The never-dimming fluorescents that made time stand still. They all combined to make a room in the Bates Motel seem cozy by comparison.

But the worst part was sharing a room with several newfound friends. This night's fellow travelers included a shivering, skinny meth head sitting in the middle of the floor and a blood-encrusted biker on the opposite bench. The meth head was just in for B&E.

But the biker had proudly earned his room and board with attempted murder. Apparently a bar patron had questioned the legality of the biker's parents' union at the time of his birth. The biker wore a Harley Davidson T-shirt with shreds for sleeves that allowed his prison gang tats fresh air and the chance to intimidate. He weighed in at over 250, with all of it muscle.

Jimmy was just shy of five feet six, a height too tall to be written off as nonthreatening, but way too short to ever command any respect. His body was toothpick spindly and topped with a head the shape of a light bulb, an unfortunate shape accented by his receding hairline. His beady eyes were close set enough to give him the untrustworthy look of a weasel, a look he frequently lived up to.

He'd gotten himself a corner last night and had tried like hell to stay tucked in its shadow. He'd succeeded in that and in not using the seat-free toilet in the opposite corner. He'd gotten a solid fifteen minutes of sleep since the Suffolk County Police booked him.

"Wade!" shouted a cop outside the holding-cell bars.

Jimmy's bleary eyes brightened. With a creak, he stood up for the first time in hours. The biker looked at him like he'd just materialized out of thin air. His eyes narrowed with the "I've found a victim" look that Jimmy had known all his life. Jimmy nodded like a low-ranking dog to an alpha male and skittered sideways to the cell door.

"Wade?" the cop said. "You're free to go."

Jimmy puffed out his insubstantial chest as far as it would go. "See, they had nothing on me."

"No, they had everything on you," the cop said. He rolled open the cell door. "Shoplifting a six-pack just isn't worth the hassle. The shop owner said she wasn't pressing charges since she recovered the beer when you dropped it."

The biker grumbled like a plugged volcanic vent. Jimmy had just slipped down below the meth head in the prisoner pecking order. He squeezed through the door as soon as it was open enough to let his skinny body escape.

He followed the officer to process out. The property cop at the window opened and dumped a brown-paper envelope. He passed Jimmy his faded, fake-leather wallet. Jimmy didn't bother to inventory the contents. There wasn't anything inside worth stealing. Next, the cop slid over a cracked flip phone. The low-battery light flashed three times and then faded to black.

"That had better still work," he threatened the cop.

"Yeah, right," the cop said. His forefinger flicked another baggie through the window opening. Inside was a single condom in a hopelessly battered wrapper. "Live large, Romeo."

Jimmy almost flicked the condom back at the cop. He shoved the phone and condom in his pocket and headed for the door.

Outside, the morning sun battled in vain against low-hanging clouds. Jimmy turned left for the bus stop, to catch a ride back to his apartment.

"This is all bullshit," he said. "One hundred percent Grade A bullshit. World's rule number one: Jimmy always gets screwed."

Things never broke his way, not even last night's spur-of-the-moment decision to lift the six of Michelob. He couldn't remember the last time he didn't get the dirty end of the plunger. Everything he tried seemed to blow up in his face. At best, he got penny-ante results from penny-ante plans. He needed to think bigger, he needed to do bigger. There was money out there for the taking, if only he'd step up and—

Staring at the sidewalk, lost in his plans, he ran headfirst into a massive chest that made his cellmate biker look wimpy.

"Well, if it ain't the one and only Jimmy Wade," a rough voice said.

Jimmy's mouth went dry as he recognized K-Dogg, Mozelle's favorite enforcer. K-Dogg had a coal-black bullet of a head and shoulders wide enough for vultures to perch on.

"K-Dogg," Jimmy croaked. "Whassup?"

K-Dogg grabbed Jimmy's shoulders with hands the size of phone books and lifted him off the ground. "Looks like you are."

Minutes later, a midnight-black SUV crept through a rusted-steel roll-up door and into a warehouse in Wyandanch. Jimmy dripped with sweat in the SUV's leather backseat. He hadn't said a word during the trip. He didn't have to. He already knew the plotline of this story, and it wasn't going to have a happy ending. The SUV stopped.

"Get out," K-Dogg said.

"Yeah, yeah, sure." Jimmy swallowed and opened the door.

He stepped out into the warehouse. He passed between aisles of boxes stenciled with Chinese cities of origin. The passage widened where two open, long wooden crates sat in front of a table. Strands of packing material escaped around the edges. The black barrel of a Kalashnikov AK-47 peeked out of one like a periscope. Two muscle-bound enforcers in mirrored sunglasses and black wife-beater T-shirts stood like bookends at the table.

Mr. Antoine Mozelle sat in a swivel chair at the center. The mob boss would never have made a Hollywood casting call for his own job. Short and fat, he had the kind of weak chin that commanded zero respect. He wore a bad black toupee that no one dared question. A pair of bushy eyebrows could have used a trim a decade ago. He chomped a thick cigar at the corner of his mouth.

But Madman Mozelle didn't need to look the part. The rest of the world knew he lived it. He'd advanced to the top of the ranks over the corpses of rivals, fools who'd taken him at face value and underestimated the guy with the reedy voice. Word was that he'd decapitated a man with a hacksaw, alive, over the course of a day, until nothing kept his living head attached to his body but a spine, a vein and his carotid artery. He ran drugs, prostitutes and, unfortunately for Jimmy, made a little book.

K-Dogg shoved Jimmy from behind. The petty thief staggered to the front of Mozelle's desk.

"Mr. Mozelle," Jimmy said.

"Jimmy, Jimmy, Jimmy," Mozelle said. "When one man owes another money, the debtor should seek out the creditor, not the other way around. Yet I have to have my associate pick you up."

"I know I owe ten grand—"

"Eleven now with the juice."

Jimmy blanched. "Yeah, okay, eleven, right. But see, I was in jail. I can't make any money in jail."

"It seems you can't make any money out of jail. You certainly can't make any money gambling. You missed the point spread with me on three games on the same weekend. That was a month ago."

One of the enforcers stepped forward and pulled a crowbar out from under the open lid of one of the wooden crates. He lobbed it past Jimmy to K-Dogg. Jimmy flinched as the metal bar sailed by his head. K-Dogg caught it with one hand like it was made of bamboo.

Jimmy's stomach roiled like a ship in a storm. Sweat formed on his upper lip.

"Well, Mr. Mozelle, I ain't got nothing. I respect you, and I'd give you everything I have. There's just nothing to give."

Duct tape ripped behind Jimmy. K-Dogg unwound a roll and strapped a dirty towel around the crowbar.

Mozelle broke into a serpentine smile. "I know that, Jimmy. I knew that when you made the bets. And given what you were betting on, you were a sure loser. But advertising costs money."

"I don't get it."

"You see, Jimmy, I've got a rep to keep up. Every now and then, my clients need to be reminded that missing payments brings consequences. Heavy consequences."

The crowbar whizzed through the air behind Jimmy as K-Dogg warmed up like he was in a batter's box.

"Now, I can't hospitalize a normally paying client, a regular. Bad for business all around. But you, you're expendable."

The crowbar came around and crashed into Jimmy's arm. He screamed. Bones fragmented, and pain ran up and down his arm like lightning bolts. He pitched to his side and collapsed.

"Now, K-Dogg's going to work you over good, you understand. He's got a rep to keep up too."

Jimmy was down on his side, his arm facing in a fundamentally wrong direction. The crowbar came down on his hand. Blood splattered, and a new wave of pain arced up his arm. He whimpered a plea to stop.

"But the good news is he won't kill you. Better to have you be a kind of walking advertisement, well, more limping, really."

The crowbar swung low and pounded him in the gut, did a snap reversal and hammered his back. Jimmy begged God that he'd pass out from the pain.

"The bad news is your debt will go up to eleven-five. This comes from a service charge, because someone will have to pay to clean the blood out of the back of my Lincoln."

The crowbar came around for another swing. It hit Jimmy in the head, and his prayer was answered. He passed out.

Chapter Six

"Brenda?" Dr. Samuel Bradshaw called as he entered his upscale Northport home.

It was nearly 6:00 p.m. His statements at the police station had taken forever. He'd had to go over Gwen's medical history, first with the detectives and then again with the medical examiner.

Then came word of the aftermath, of Gwen's body exploding postmortem. He'd never heard of anything like that before, and he'd investigated some strange stuff in his first medical career.

He'd started out in infectious-disease research, HIV, Ebola, influenza and a host of less famous also-rans. He'd settled on polio, a disease near eradication, but not quite there yet. He'd alternated lab work at Brookhaven Research with fieldwork around the globe. Before switching to private practice, he'd won enough recognition to be offered a slot with the CDC in Atlanta.

"Samuel!" Brenda called from the kitchen. "It's about time!"

She turned the corner in her wheelchair, one of the expensive, lightweight models the permanently disabled rated. Brenda was still a beauty from the waist up, svelte as she'd been when she used to run marathons. Now she favored long skirts to cover the atrophied damage from the waist down. Her long face remained elegant and beautiful against the attrition of age and the ravages of her disease. Or, as Samuel always thought of it, *their* disease.

Samuel knelt down and kissed her forehead. He ran his fingers through her shoulder-length brown hair. "This has been one long day."

She pivoted her chair in a flawless zero turn, and Samuel followed her into the kitchen. The countertops were all a foot lower than normal, the kitchen table a shade higher, with only one chair. The table was set for two. A large bowl of salad doubled as a centerpiece. She used the Grappler, a long stainless-steel gripper Samuel had bought her, to pluck two glasses from an overhead cabinet. She brought them over to the table.

"Any idea what was wrong with Ms. Albritton?" she asked as she filled plates with steamed vegetables and sausages.

"I have a good idea what it wasn't, but that's about it. It presented as an infection, and it looked like we'd gotten a handle on it, but we didn't. When she attacked us, she was incredibly strong."

"Adrenaline surge?" A lifetime married to a doctor had given her an MD by osmosis.

"No doubt about it. She was completely enraged. It was like the time that Bellevue patient was convinced that the orderlies were aliens trying to abduct him. He ripped his bed from the concrete floor anchors."

Samuel took a seat, and Brenda rolled over with one plate in her hand and one on her lap. He'd stopped asking if he could help her about a week after she returned home in the chair.

"The news was vague on what happened next, why they locked down St. Luke's," she said.

"I can understand why. The nurses who witnessed it said her body looked like it had exploded. There were shoulders, arms, legs and a cavity in between."

Brenda popped a broccoli floret in her mouth. Infectious-disease fieldwork had bumped their repulsion thresholds for mealtime conversation pretty high. They didn't get a lot of dinner-party invitations.

"The autopsy should be revealing," he said. "The preliminary results should be available soon. And how was your day?"

"Two conference calls with the new schools in Sudan. Rumors we are sterilizing the girls have started again."

Brenda's foundation sponsored Third World schools for girls. She sought out the kinds of places where child brides and genital mutilation were the norm. Women's education had become her passion as soon as polio robbed her of her legs..

The disease was in its death throes. Pockets of the wild virus in Nigeria, the Horn of Africa and the tribal regions of the Afghan/Pakistan border were about all that had survived against the onslaught of childhood immunization. He had to go to the ends of the world for his research.

Tired of their long summer separations, Brenda had opted to join Samuel during a polio research trip. Samuel quickly agreed, forgetting about the risks he took for granted and selfishly focusing on alleviating his loneliness. Once she arrived, she'd pitched in to assist at the overwhelmed clinic. Six weeks later, she'd contracted the disease.

Maybe her vaccine had been defective. Maybe she'd never been vaccinated. Perhaps her natural defenses… The reason polio infected her didn't matter, just the result.

But the infection's source mattered. She believed she caught it in the clinic, through some slip she made in the protocols. Samuel never bought that excuse. None of his clinic techs had ever contracted the disease, and Brenda was religious in taking the proper protective measures.

Samuel was certain he'd infected her. He was the one dealing with the live virus every day. Human-to-human transmission was a lot tougher to do than raw virus to human. He'd probably gotten sloppy, content that his immune system would slay polio on sight, never considering that Brenda's might not. He'd brought her to the danger zone without a second thought. Then he'd infected her due to his own negligence. And polio, the scourge he was locked in mortal combat with, got the last laugh, for while there was a vaccine, there was still no cure. His wife, who ran varsity track in college, would never even stand again,.

They returned to the States. He told polio it won, and went into general practice. They never discussed the reason. They just installed ramps at the house and made the transition. She insisted on her own bedroom, she claimed so she wouldn't take all his space with the wheelchair and the harness to get in and out of bed.

Devotion filled her voice each time she spoke of her foundation and the schools. But Samuel remained convinced they were an outlet for the anger she had to feel at him for leading her to an early grave. He knew he'd feel that way if the situation were reversed. He saw her crusade as a way for generations of girls to fend for themselves and not follow men who put them second to anything else.

"Anything we can do for the schools?" he said.

"No, it's the usual. Religious zealots whip up the men with emasculation terror tales. They take it out on our teachers."

They ate in silence.

"Are you planning on turning in early?" Brenda asked.

"I don't know. Why?"

"A DVD came in the mail today, a Myrna Loy/William Powell comedy from the '30s, a little escapist entertainment."

It would have had to come in the mail. Her modified van had its transmission spread out all over Canuto's Auto Repair.

"Sounds great."

They sat side by side that night, wheelchair to recliner, and laughed at all the right places. He wanted the movie to help him mentally escape a long list of problems.. He could never shake the feeling that Brenda's list also included him.

Chapter Seven

Samuel picked up his cell phone later that night on the third ring. It was Dr. Chase Harwell, the county medical examiner.

"Chase, you're burning the midnight oil."

"Your late patient will keep us all here awhile. What exactly did you witness?"

"She was incredibly violent and incredibly strong. Then, she just died."

"No doubt about that. I found what was left of her heart. Her aorta had an inch-long rip in it. The rest of her was a mess, but I'd place that tear as the proximate cause of death, not whatever infected her."

"You think something infected her?"

"What blood I could sample was full of adrenaline, corticotropins, orexin and a half-dozen others. I've never seen a mix like that. I doubt you shot her up with them, so something had to send her body into overdrive producing them."

"Her initial symptoms resembled sepsis, but she was much better just before she went wild."

"You don't even know the strangest part." Harwell's words came out rapid-fire. "I called a few other hospitals on the island, checking for any ideas from other colleagues. Mather Memorial in Port Jefferson and North Shore University in Manhasset both had similar cases, with the same postmortem reactions."

Alarm bells rang in Samuel's head, alarm bells tuned by years working with infectious diseases.

"Chase, have you called the CDC?"

"Just before I called you. I thought it was right to keep you in the loop as well, in case her family contacted you."

"Thanks, Chase."

Samuel hung up. He rifled through a drawer in his desk. He pulled out an old foldout map of Long Island and spread it out over the blotter. Oyster Bay, Port Jefferson,

St. Luke's. In the movies there was always a central point equidistant from the reported points of infection, a location for Patient Zero, the initial source. In real life, that never happened. This was no exception. All three locations were strung out in a row along Long Island's North Shore.

These were also the only three Harwell had found. Were there other hospitals with sick patients who hadn't gone berserk yet? Were there other people sick, but not hospitalized? Were there other people infected, but not yet symptomatic? The situation could be far worse than they knew.

Samuel had one ace up his sleeve at the CDC. His assistant on several African sojourns had been Dr. Vanessa Clayton. Samuel might have retreated from the field of epidemiological battle, but she never had. She'd signed up full time with the Centers for Disease Control in Atlanta and had been a director or something the last time he checked. If this outbreak was as dangerous as he thought, she'd be in the heart of the action already. If she wasn't, he'd convince her to get there.

Samuel picked through the faded business cards in his center desk drawer. Most belonged to pharma reps, always quick with a flashy card and a hundred free samples. He flicked through one card after another until he came upon a plain, white one. Dr. Vanessa Clayton. East Coast Operations Director. Centers for Disease Control.

He never doubted she would go on to something big. On every research trip, she demonstrated a strong combination of drive and intellectual curiosity, the kind that generates the heat that makes careers rise. When she worked in the small villages in Africa, she was the instant center of attention. Little girls always approached the statuesque woman whose skin tone matched theirs, awestruck that indeed she was a doctor. She tried hard to keep him at his research after Brenda's illness. But he was in no shape for it. The CDC had scooped her up in two days.

He hadn't spoken to her in so long. Nothing acrimonious, just the natural drift of two lives on different trajectories, one downshifting to first gear, the other upshifting to overdrive. He dialed the number.

"Director Clayton's office, this is Jared. How can I help you?"

It took Samuel a moment to adjust to the unexpected young male voice and to the fact that Vanessa rated an office assistant. Of course she would.

"Dr. Samuel Bradshaw from St. Luke's Hospital in New York calling for Director Clayton." He figured a formal introduction would give him more of an edge in getting connected. Certainly better than saying it was her old boss Sam calling to chew the fat.

"Hold please."

Vanessa's voice cut in almost immediately. "Samuel, how are you?"

"Great, Vanessa. Yourself?"

There was a pause. Busy voices filled the background. "Swamped. I was just thinking of you. Can I call you right back?"

He acquiesced. The return call came a few minutes later. Caller ID indicated it came from another phone. The background noise was gone. Vanessa's voice was softer, lower, as if trying not to be heard. "What sparks your call, Sam?"

"Have you been notified about what's going on here on Long Island?" he asked.

"What do you mean?"

Samuel knew this word-game trick. He'd used it a thousand times to keep from admitting something to a third party that they may know nothing about.

"Three hospitals here report the same strange disease. It starts like sepsis, goes into latency for a while and then turns the victim psychotic."

"We're aware of it. More than aware."

"You have some samples?"

"That's why I was thinking of you, *Bosi Daktari*." She'd affectionately started calling him the Swahili translation of "boss doctor" after the children in one village hung the name on him. Her voice dropped to a whisper. "It's a new pathogen."

"A mutation of what?"

"That's just it. Of nothing. The genome is unique. But it has some similarities to our old nemesis, poliomyelitis."

That sent a cold shudder through Samuel. Polio had almost every awful pathogen attribute: person-to-person communicability, no initial infection symptoms, permanent or fatal aftereffects. All the thing had to do to be worse was become airborne transmittable. If this new pathogen was polio's sister, it might take decades to take it down.

"That's why I was thinking of you," Vanessa continued. "I've been on the inside of the CDC now. We have great people, the best in the world. But when it comes to polio we don't have anyone with your understanding of it, your ability to see the virus from a different angle. As far as CDC is concerned, polio has a vaccine. We focus our limited resources on pathogens that don't. Can you get the next plane to Atlanta and give us a hand here?"

Decades ago, the offer would have made him ecstatic. He'd have been at the airport in an hour flat, with nothing but the shirt on his back.

"I wish I could, Vanessa," he said. "It's not easy to just up and jump across the globe anymore, what with Brenda's condition."

"I was afraid that would be your answer, but I had to ask."

"You can send me any data you have, sample analyses. I can look it over here."

"I can't let secure materials out of the building."

Samuel nearly dropped the phone. "It's that bad?"

Vanessa paused. "You know that place you always bragged about in the Poconos?"

"Silver Lake."

"That's the one. You and Brenda deserve a break from all the stress on the island. You should really give that place a visit again. Look, I have to get to a meeting. My offer stands if you change your mind."

She hung up, but Samuel just sat there with the dead phone to his ear, jaw slack. Did she really just tell him, in her own way, to get off of Long Island?

Brenda rolled down the hall and stopped at the open door to his office. They hadn't widened it with the other doors in the house. Brenda had told the contractor to skip spending the money on a room she didn't need to get into. Samuel thought it was more like a room she didn't want to get into, a way to keep more distance between her and his work, the work that had condemned her to having wheels for legs.

"You look a bit disturbed," she said. "Everything okay?"

"Yes, fine. Just the usual St. Luke's stuff."

She nodded, though she obviously wasn't buying his line of bull. What was he going to do anyway? With the modified van out of commission until the day after tomorrow, that left them with using his car, a car too small to accommodate the wheelchair. If they used his car, what would they do when they did get off the island with no wheelchair or, worse, if something went wrong along the way there? A potential escape plan could wait a couple of days. No disease spread that fast.

He'd have to let Vanessa and the CDC do the work in Atlanta. Starting tomorrow morning, he'd do his own work at St. Luke's, at the infection's ground zero.

Chapter Eight

Tamara awoke in the dark and screamed.

Her first, panicked thought was that she was blind. Something had happened to her remaining good eye: retinitis pigmentosa, optic atrophy, cytomegalovirus or some other rarity only a nurse would know to worry about.

She reached out of bed and slammed the desk lamp switch. Nothing happened. Her pulse rate soared.

Then the stupid energy-saving bulb finally blinked itself awake. Her paranoid fears skulked off to the bedroom shadows. She sighed in relief and dropped back onto the pillow.

The clock read 7:15 p.m. The blackout curtains, a necessity with a nurse's rotating-shift schedule, had kept the sunlight at bay for hours.

She'd slept ten of them, or about two normal days' worth. A little bit of Dr. Norton's sleep-inducing narcotics went a long way. Her arms felt heavy as lead.

Her bedroom door creaked open a few inches. A whimper sounded from the hall.

"C'mon, Mallow," Tamara called. "You know I'm up."

The door flew open. A huge German shepherd bounded into her bed with fifty pounds of happy. His wagging tail thumped the sheets, and a wet tongue took a swipe across the unbandaged side of Tamara's face. Mallow looked like a police dog, but was a big, cuddly puppy with his owner. Brown and black on the tough-looking outside and soft on the inside, she'd named him after a roasted marshmallow.

Most pets had an internal clock, waking their owners at a precise hour for a meal or pestering them for a walk. Mallow somehow understood that Tamara didn't have a set schedule, and always waited with uncharacteristic canine patience, even on the days when Tamara was too exhausted to remember to refill his food bowl. This compassion was a trait Tamara had been unable to cultivate in her ex-husband.

"C'mon, boy, let's get some breakfast."

Mallow yelped and bounded into the kitchen.

Tamara reached up to sweep some hair back from her face. Her hand hit the wad of bandages that covered her left eye. Her heart sank as yesterday's memories returned like a dark, high tide.

Dr. Norton's prognosis had been guarded, the usual ass-covering routine the medical profession employed, though she herself eschewed it in favor of honesty and decency. Dr. Norton had said she might see again, or she might just be able to discern shapes, or she might end up blind. The needle might have grazed the optic nerve, it might not have. If blinded, her eye might cloud over, it might not. In the ray-of-sunshine department, the doc was an underachiever.

She rolled out of bed to a piercing headache, like someone had driven a hot nail into the back of her head. She imagined her occipital lobe scrambling to process the sputtering synapses that relayed the short-circuited inputs from her left eye.

She went to her condo's small kitchen and began her wake-up routine on autopilot. Load and start the single-serve coffeemaker. Pour a bowl of food for Mallow, grab his water bowl for a refill on the return trip. Pull a breakfast burrito from the freezer, toss it in the microwave and hit Start.

On the countertop sat the two mucous-yellow prescription bottles Dr. Norton had prescribed, one antibiotic and one painkiller. The throbbing in her brain demanded the latter. She reached for it then swerved for the antibiotic instead.

Her last painkiller had been twelve hours ago, long enough to clear her system. And she needed her system clear.

The good doctor hadn't written her out of work. Probably just an oversight, a skipped step while working with a fellow medical professional. Tamara was going to leverage that.

Staying home all day with Mallow would be a nightmare. She'd obsess about her eye all day. Her subconscious had already telegraphed that loud and clear as she awakened. She needed more mental distraction than a German shepherd could provide. She needed to go back to work.

Back in her bedroom, she checked her closet. Seven pairs of scrubs with the St. Luke's hospital logo hung there, like a squad of soldiers awaiting orders. A few dresses, years out of style, hung bunched at the closet's edge. Dust blanketed a few fashionable shoe boxes underneath them. She laid a set of scrubs on her bed.

Down the hall, Mallow crunched his breakfast loudly enough to wake the dead. The coffeemaker began to hiss and drip. The microwave dinged like the bell at the start of a boxing round.

An hour later, on her way to her car, she passed Paul Rosen at the mailbox. Paul was about her age, tall and pear-shaped with a head of disheveled dark hair that always looked a day late for a shampooing. Whatever work he did, he did out of his condo. She assumed it was some sort of IT support. He pushed his oversized glasses back up his nose and then unloaded with both hands a bundle of mail from his box.

"Back from Saranac Lake, I see." She had a passing acquaintance with Paul, who lived in the condo down the street from hers. He'd told her he'd be gone for his annual hunting trip and asked her to watch his porch for any packages.

"Yes," he said. "I got an eight-point buck and… Wow, what happened to your eye?"

She raised a hand to her bandage. "Oh, a little work accident. No problem." There was no way she was explaining her encounter with Gwen to a near stranger.

A few envelopes in his pile slid sideways, and he struggled to keep them all together. "That's terrible," he said without looking at her.

Tamara had noticed he always seemed uncomfortable around her. He was near tongue-tied asking her to monitor his porch. She wondered if he was that way with everyone, or just women, or just her.

"You didn't get any packages while you were gone," she said. "I checked every day."

"That's okay," he said. "I wasn't expecting any."

Tamara arched an eyebrow. His face reddened.

"It just pays to be prepared," he said, "for all eventualities. Something might have come, and then it might have rained and ruined it."

"Well, yes, I guess you're right." Now their bizarre pseudoconversation made her the uncomfortable one. "Gotta get to work. See you, Paul."

She was halfway to her car when he called after her. "Say, I brought back some venison if you'd like some, you know, for minding my porch."

"Vegetarian!" she called back over her shoulder. She wasn't, but the last thing she needed was Paul Rosen on her doorstep with an armful of dead deer. Paul was a kind of reminder that being single wasn't so bad.

On her way out the Cedar Knoll Condos gate, she had her first cue that she was half-blind. With her monocular tunnel vision, she crept her car through the gate, swinging her head both ways to clear the posts. Having plenty of room didn't make it any less nerve-wracking.

"And you're going to care for patients like this?" she muttered to herself.

Close-up work would be okay, she rationalized. No problem. At least nowhere near as big a problem as a full, unproductive day in her condo, spent worrying about her healing process.

Chapter Nine

"Tamara, what are you doing in today? Julie is supposed to fill in for you."

Tamara stood in front of the charge nurse's desk as Ruth Clavell eyed the unfashionable addition to her nurse's uniform, the left-eye bandage.

"Dr. Norton didn't specifically write me out of work," Tamara said. "So I could stay home and worry, or come in and work and keep my mind off it. I called Julie off."

"You did what?" Dour old Ruth bore an uncomfortable resemblance to Oz's Wicked Witch of the West, and she was a stickler for doing things by the book. "I don't see how, with only one eye, you could—"

"I'll let you stick any needles, and handle all the depth-perception tasks, okay? I'm off all painkillers. You know me. I really need this."

Tamara sent up a silent prayer. Her work ethic had always made her one of the few Ruth didn't ride like a lazy mule. Maybe that would count for something...

"One workaholic to another," Tamara added.

Ruth broke into what, for her, passed as a smile, just a slight twitch at the corners of her mouth. "Fine."

"Thank you so much!" Tamara would have hugged any other nurse.

"You're lucky we're even open. There was talk of transferring all the patients out."

"I don't get it."

"That patient who stabbed you and killed Bethany, she, well, exploded."

"Exploded?"

"Right after she died. Like necrotic bloating on steroids. No one had ever seen anything like it. The two morgue attendants were coated in the woman's internals. The elevator was out of service for the rest of the day for cleaning. The whole thing was so unexplained that several department heads asked the board to, at least temporarily, close the hospital. The board weighed whether insurance companies would cover the transfer expenses, then decided evacuation would be an overreaction."

That news didn't sit well with Tamara. It was bad enough that Ms. Albritton had gone homicidal, but then to have her body explode said there was something more than a mental snap going on. There had been some underlying medical condition, something she'd never heard of.

Behind them, the elevator doors rolled open. The antiseptic smell inside was twice as strong as usual. Manny, the orderly from her experience yesterday, rolled a restocked supply cart out and into the hallway. A heavy-duty bandage covered his ear. It looked like he wasn't ready to take a day off yet either. Tamara followed him to the end of the hall.

"Manny, how are you?"

He looked up, his face ashen. "Not bad." His fingers grazed the dressing on his ear. "The doc reattached it. Lots of stitches, but they think it'll take. Ain't bad enough to get out of work, though. Looks like you neither."

Tamara touched just above her bandaged eye. "Better to work and worry about others, than to sit home and worry about myself."

"You ain't the type to miss work."

His collar rode high and uneven beneath his bandaged ear. Tamara reached up to straighten it. His hand flew up and blocked her.

"It's just your collar," she said. "It's all—"

There was something wrong with his neck. She grabbed his hand and pulled his collar down. Whitish lines like a cracked windshield radiated down from under his bandage to under his shirt. Darker veins bulged within them like polluted streams. Just like Ms. Albritton.

"Manny, how long has this—"

Manny slapped her hands away then shoved her back against the wall, hard. His irises turned a thick bloodshot red. The color spread like someone had poured red paint in a pool.

"Get your hands off me," he yelled. "All of you! Trying to make out there's something wrong with me. Well, there ain't!"

The shouting brought Ruth out from behind the main desk. Manny spied her and went red with rage.

"You gonna join in too? Try and lock me up like my brother? Crazy bitches, the bunch of you!"

He reached into his scrub pants and pulled a large surgical knife from his waistband, the model used in amputations. The blade flashed as he waved it between the two women, like a lion tamer keeping a chair between him and his cats.

"See," he said. "I'm prepared for this. Knew it would happen." His voice rose to a panicked pitch. "One goddamn step closer and I'll slash you two. I swear to God."

He charged down the hall at Ruth. She backed into the nurses' station, metal clipboard raised like a tiny, useless shield. But Manny rushed past her to the emergency exit at the hall's far end. He slammed the door open so hard that it cracked cinder blocks in the wall behind it. He rushed down the stairs. The door swung shut behind him.

"Dear God," Ruth said. She dialed security and repeated what happened.

Tamara ran to the window by the stairwell. From this eighth-floor vantage point, the tree-lined parking lot was in full view, the stairwell exit door right below her. From the look on Manny's face, he was heading for the great outdoors ASAP and wouldn't be stopping at any floors along the way.

In the lot below, a silent movie began to play. A black-and-white hospital-security SUV pulled up in the parking lot by the door. Its yellow emergency lights flashed to life. The guard stepped out, head cocked as she talked into the mic attached at her shoulder. She crossed the nose of the idling vehicle and approached the exit door.

The door burst open. The startled guard's eyes went wide as she saw Manny with the huge knife in his hand. She dropped her mic and went for her sidearm.

Manny moved faster, inhumanly fast. In one leap, he was at the guard's side. With one powerful swipe of the blade, he slashed the guard's neck. She gripped the gaping wound and dropped to her knees. Blood spurted between her fingers. Manny kicked her in the chest, and she fell on her back. She mouthed meaningless, terrified words.

Tamara caught her breath and raised her hand to her mouth.

Manny plunged the knife into the guard's chest so hard that he buried it to the hilt. The guard's scream penetrated the thick glass as a distant, muffled yelp. She jerked and then lay still. Her hands fell from her neck to reveal a raw ribbon of slashed meat.

Manny grabbed the pistol from her holster and jumped into the security SUV. He slammed it into reverse and backed it into a car with a muted crash of plastic and steel. The car's alarm sounded, and its lights began to flash. The security SUV peeled out. It hopped a landscaped barrier to the main street and raced away, red lights blazing.

Seconds later, the morgue van came flying into the hospital complex. The enormous beast of a vehicle usually blocked traffic. Now the truck cleared it. It entered the traffic circle in the wrong direction. Oncoming cars crested curbs to escape head-on collisions. One lumbering Lincoln took evasive action a second too late. The big van nailed it in the rear wheel well. The car spun and sideswiped the van before jerking to a steaming stop.

The van barreled straight at St. Luke's main, covered entrance. Tamara gripped the windowsill. The van accelerated. Cries sounded from outside. The van disappeared under the entranceway roof.

The stereo sound of a crash rolled up both outside the window and through the floor, a combination of the shriek of shattered glass and the grind of crumbling bricks. Gunshots popped, distant and disconnected, like a child's cap gun. Screams followed.

The hospital-wide alarm sounded. Tamara ran into the hallway.

"Lockdown," Ruth said. "Check that the doors are secure."

The hospital had practiced the lockdown procedures, planning for the event of a stolen baby. Tamara could never think of what other realistic situation would make one necessary. Now she knew. The elevators froze without the override key, all building exit doors locked without an employee badge and ID. Airtight doors sealed certain sections of the hospital off from the rest, like a cruise ship ready to keep a flood of seawater at bay.

Tamara yanked at the exit door to make sure that it had closed behind Manny. Behind her, the elevator dinged and the doors rolled open. Two security guards stepped out.

"Praise God," Ruth said. "You're a minute late. Manny just went crazy and…"

Her voice trailed off. Tamara watched from the far end of the hall with a growing sense of dread. A career spent around the sick gave a nurse a special insight, an innate sense when something was wrong. The two guards set off every warning. They both wore the same malicious grin, a bully's gleeful, gruesome look. Then she noticed the darkened blood vessels that rippled up their arms, the irises that flashed Ferrari red.

The two drew their weapons with a spray of wild laughter. One aimed at Ruth and fired.

The back of her sweater exploded in a misty, red cloud. The impact sent her flying against the wall. She slumped to the floor. A wide, red, glistening skid mark marred the wall in her wake.

Tamara ducked behind the supply cart. The two guards laughed like rowdy drunks in a bar. The shooter waved his partner left. They split and attacked the circular hall in opposite directions.

The shooter in Tamara's line of sight disappeared into a patient's room, an old man a day out of surgery for a pancreatic tumor.

"Who are you?" drifted a feeble, detached voice through the open doorway.

A gunshot rang out. The guard stepped out of the room, sporting a wicked, twisted grin. From across the hall, another gunshot echoed.

Seventy-two-year-old Alva Bishop tottered out of her room with her IV pole as a crutch. She was a day from release after treatment for pneumonia. Her free hand clutched her gown closed behind her.

"What's going on out here?" she wheezed.

Before Tamara could rise and warn her, the guard leveled his pistol and fired. The headshot sent the frail little woman reeling back into her room. She and her IV stand crashed to the floor.

Tamara shrank back behind the cart. Random gunshots sounded right and left, each one closer than the one before. It was just a matter of time before one of the guards discovered her cowering at the hallway's end.

Her bandaged eye created a claustrophobic, tubelike perspective of the world, made worse by the narrow alley of a view she had from either side behind the cart. She whipped her head from side to side, dreading her discovery.

One more shot barked in the last room on her left. She held her breath. The guard rounded the corner of her cart. He gazed down at her and cocked his head, like he'd just seen a cute kitten.

"Aw, now look what we have here. Someone who can make a run for it, like actual prey. No more shooting fish in a barrel."

He lowered the pistol at Tamara.

She flung the cart in his direction. He dodged away. His gun fired, the bullet sailed high and wide. The stray round zinged down the hall and impacted the wall a few inches from the second guard's head.

"What the hell!" Furious, the second guard brought his pistol to bear and fired. The first guard took a shot to the shoulder.

Tamara hit the ground and closed her eyes. Gunfire filled the hallway from both sides. Bullets sang overhead.

Silence. She raised her head.

Both guards lay in moaning heaps on the floor. Blood pooled under each one.

Her nursing instincts demanded she rush to apply first aid. Self-preservation said otherwise. She scrambled for the stairway door.

The stairs were a madhouse. Employees and patients jostled each other in a packed rush for the bottom floor. The herd swept her forward. The air stank of fear. Crashes and screams came from the floors above and below. The whole hospital seemed to be imploding.

The stairwell crowd swelled. The seething mass pinned her arms to her sides, lifted Tamara off her feet and carried her helpless down the last full flight to the lobby. Bodies clogged the open doorway. Four steps from freedom, forward motion ceased. Gravity and momentum pressed the panicked in from behind her. Her chest compressed, air whooshed from her lungs. She pressed outward to get the space to inhale. It was like pushing against a brick wall. She sucked in a tiny, gagging breath.

This was not how she wanted to die.

Chapter Ten

Samuel slammed on the brakes. He barely missed a fleeing patient in a hospital gown. Dozens more people followed him through the intersection at the entrance to St. Luke's. Cars barreled out of the parking lot any way they could, against the light, out the entrance, across the grass. Muffled gunshots popped in the distance.

He hadn't expected this kind of a reception this morning. Yesterday had been traumatic at the hospital, but no one told him the complex had gone insane.

As soon as a gap in the exodus opened, Samuel zipped into the parking lot. The place was a disaster. The crumpled morgue van lay impaled in the main entrance, part of the overhang collapsed onto it. Patients littered the lot, exhausted, many bleeding through postop bandages, medically unable to complete their escape. A number lay still on the ground.

Samuel's first instinct was to tend the patients. But his old researcher's mind-set kicked in like a bad case of déjà vu. He'd returned to investigate the disease that had claimed Gwen and possibly others across Long Island. He was here to eliminate future deaths, not to ameliorate current suffering. His cold, rational excuse didn't sit as well as it used to.

He left the car and went straight for the main entrance. The gut-wrenching callousness of his researcher past rushed back with a vengeance. He avoided eye contact with the people on the ground. He wasn't in a lab coat, didn't have his ID pinned to his belt. The anonymity of his street clothes got him inside without having to deliver the heartbreaking phrase "I don't have time to help you".

Splinters of glass crunched under his feet in the frantic main lobby. A jam of people clogged the stairwell exit. One popped free like a champagne-bottle cork and fell to the ground. A crush of frightened humanity surged over and around him. Tamara's head bobbed in the crowd, her damaged eye still bandaged shut. She smiled in relief as she saw him. She approached, gasping for breath. He pulled her aside to a corner in the lobby.

"That was seconds from becoming a catastrophe in there," she said.

"What are you doing at work?" he asked.

"No rest for the wicked," she said. "I couldn't stand the idea of doing nothing at home. I didn't expect the place to turn into a war zone." She gave her head a quick shake. "But what are you doing here?"

"Looking into Gwen Albritton's postmortem. What's happening? The streets are full of fleeing patients."

"Insanity," Tamara said. "Guards on shooting sprees. Manny the orderly went homicidal. All of them with Gwen's red eyes and dark veins."

"How long ago?"

"A half hour ago everything was normal."

Samuel checked his watch. "Less than twenty-four hours after Gwen. That's bad. Very bad. Even the Ebola virus doesn't present for at least two days."

"She did bite Manny, and he had all her symptoms."

"Did you have any contact with his or anyone else's body fluids?"

"No."

The hospital exodus slowed to a trickle and the hallway from the lobby emptied. An unnerving silence descended around them.

"This hospital is ground zero plus one," Samuel said. "I had a career doing infectious-disease research. This place is a trove of primary information right now. I need to gather some of that information."

Tamara put a hand on his chest. "This place may still be full of crazies."

"The samples degrade every minute I wait. I don't have a choice."

"If you're going to be that way, then how can I help?" Tamara said.

"This hospital and the parking lot out there are filled with the sick and people who need help now. I could use your assistance, but it would be at their expense. Later, you'll feel a lot better about yourself for helping them."

Tamara looked through the windows behind him. Outside, one by one, doctors, nurses and orderlies filtered back into the parking lot, asking questions, checking pulses and starting triage.

"The cavalry has arrived," Tamara said, "or returned. Let's drop this thing in its tracks. I'm with you."

Samuel was half-elated, half-unsettled with Tamara's commitment to work for the greater good. It had taken him much longer to accept that trade-off. The last person he'd seen dive into it like that had been Vanessa.

With his hospital ID, Samuel scanned them into a supply closet. Full biohazard suits would be the right call, but he didn't have the time to track them down. He passed rubber gloves and a face mask to Tamara.

"I have a bad feeling this thing has an airborne component. Manny might have been bitten, but he was the only one. You and I don't have symptoms, so I'm going to assume we aren't infected. We still need to watch each other, just in case. Who knows what this thing does."

They both pulled on a pair of gloves.

"The crazed security guards you saw," Samuel continued, "their infections happened some other way. That's the mystery we need to solve. And we need to take some reasonable precautions while we do."

They tied on face masks.

"First stop?" Tamara said.

"The morgue."

On the way to the morgue, Samuel grabbed an abandoned lunch cooler from the cafeteria to transport his samples and packed it with ice. Once inside the morgue, he pulled up Gwen's report on the desktop computer. Dr. Harwell had been pretty thorough in his description over the phone. Samuel cross-referenced the corpse's location and led Tamara to the correct insulated door along the rear wall. The soft neon lighting gave everything a ghostly appearance. He pulled the door open. A blast of colder air rushed by. He rolled out his former patient.

Gwen was as described. Her face was oddly calm and complacent, shrunken but with a relaxed look, as if she were happy to be gone. That was believable when he looked at her from the neck down. It was as if she'd swallowed a live grenade. Her shattered rib cage bent outward. The skin between her breastbone and waist was nothing but shreds. The soupy remnants of her internal organs gelled black and gooey in the cavity.

"No way she should be that decomposed," Tamara said. "Not so quickly."

Samuel strapped on a pair of binocular medical magnifying glasses from an adjacent equipment cart and flipped them down. He inspected the edges of the body cavity.

Black flecks peppered the tips of the corpse's desiccated, white skin.

"Can you get me some sample bags and a scalpel?" Samuel asked.

Tamara returned with both.

He put samples of what was left of Gwen's liquefied organs into a bag. Then he scraped some of the black flecks into another bag and sealed it shut. He lay down the scalpel, held the sample up to the light and peered through the magnifying glasses.

"This looks a lot like—"

The doors to the morgue burst open. A man wearing a hospital maintenance shirt stood there with a red fire ax in his hands. The ax matched his eyes. Blood splattered the patch on his chest, which read *Dean*, into near illegibility. A road map of black veins covered his face and neck.

"This is where they're at, isn't it?" Dean screamed. "Well, you can't hide 'em here anymore. And you're going to pay for trying to do it!"

Dean raised the ax over his head and charged at Samuel. Samuel dodged just in time. The ax came down and hit Gwen on the metal slab. The blade sliced through her leg with a clang. Her limb rolled off onto the floor.

Samuel scrambled across the floor on all fours. Dean yanked the ax from Gwen's corpse. Blood and black ooze coated the blade. He turned toward Samuel and raised it for a second attack.

Tamara grabbed the scalpel from the table. She leapt on Dean's back and sliced the blade across the right side of Dean's throat. Blood exploded from the slashed carotid artery. Dean wheeled, ax extended, in a clumsy pirouette like a gory, murderous ballerina. Violent gushes of blood sprayed across Tamara's chest and face. Dean staggered and collapsed to the floor. Tamara rode him down and then rolled off his shuddering body. The blood gusher from his neck pulsed weaker with each beat of his heart. It wound down to a dribble, and Dean lay still.

Samuel used the back of a chair to pull himself up to his feet. He stepped around the widening puddle of contaminated blood under Dean. Tamara lay panting on the floor. He reached down and helped her up.

"That was quick thinking," he said.

"There was no thinking about it," she muttered. "He attacked you and I reacted completely on instinct. A rational woman with just a scalpel in her hand wouldn't take on a man with an ax."

"Then pass my thanks on to your instincts."

Dean's blood had soaked her mask. Samuel ripped it off her face and examined around her mouth and nose through the magnifying glasses. They looked clean. The rest of her though…

"We need to get that blood off you," he said. "Now."

He didn't say it because they both knew. One open nick to her skin or one drop into her eye, and she'd be another victim. Samuel sealed his samples in the cooler, and they ran to the emergency shower in the ER.

Tamara dashed straight in and pulled the handle under the showerhead. She faced the stream of cold, clean water with her good eye closed and her mouth clamped shut. She ripped off her scrubs. They splatted on the tile floor.

Samuel grabbed antibacterial soap and a scrub brush from the sinks nearby, and handed them to Tamara. He grabbed a clean pair of scrubs from a rack nearby, and left them on a counter beside her as she scrubbed her skin red.

Dead bodies packed the ER. Gurneys and beds were double-parked like Manhattan streets on a Monday morning. A system designed to meet the needs of the fundamentally well could not handle a population profoundly ill. Samuel held the sample cooler tight as he checked out the nearby bodies. Several showed the blackened veins of the infected. The rest were collateral damage of the plague. Gunshot wounds. Traumatic accidents. He wondered which would kill more people, the disease or the people themselves.

Tamara came up behind him, rubbing her hair dry with a towel. She wore clean scrubs and a new mask over her face.

"And?" Samuel said.

"No cuts, no scrapes. I think I'm good."

Samuel looked into her good eye for any sign of deceit, and saw none. He checked the bandage on the other. It was wet. The tape hung loose.

"Let me replace that bandage."

He gathered what he needed and removed the old bandages. A milky lens stared sightless from the swollen socket. He was no ocular expert, but it looked to him like the damaged eye might be beyond saving.

"Your bedside poker face needs work, Doc," Tamara said. "It looks bad, doesn't it?"

"I'm afraid so." He cleaned the area and reapplied a dressing. "But I'm not a specialist. It could pull through."

"Yeah, sure."

To their right, the sheet covering one of the corpses began to rise like an inflating white balloon.

They approached the body. Tamara yanked the sheet away like a magician's reveal.

A Hispanic man in his twenties lay there in his boxer shorts. Black veins crisscrossed his entire body. His stomach swelled to the soundtrack of stretching skin.

Samuel remembered Gwen's corpse and Dr. Harwell's description of a chest cavity explosion. He reached out to touch the distended belly. What gasses could be building up so quickly that—

"Doc, no!"

Tamara grabbed his arm and yanked him back. The man's stomach twitched. Samuel and Tamara beat a retreat to the ER entrance. Samuel scooped up his sample cooler on the run. The stretching noise reached an unsustainable high pitch. The corpse burst open. Black goop sprayed for several feet in all directions. A cloud of black dust specks arose from the cavity like fumes from an erupting volcano.

They both ran for the exit doors, each throwing one wide open as they entered the parking lot. They stopped well clear of the building. This side of the hospital was empty. Samuel turned and looked back. Paranoia cried out that the black, dusty cloud was sentient enough to follow them.

"This is bad," he said. "Apocalypse bad."

"What was that?"

"That dust looks like the same thing that was on the outside of Gwen Albritton's corpse. This virus looks like it mutates dramatically. No, not a mutation. More a metamorphosis, like a tadpole becomes a frog, or a caterpillar becomes a butterfly. When the host dies and the likelihood of transmission drops, it goes from blood-borne to airborne. It's a perfect Darwinian evolutionary step. Bad news for potential hosts."

"That's why it isn't contained," Tamara said.

"And maybe why it can't be."

A Nassau County police chopper screamed by overhead. A dark-green, twin-rotor Army Chinook followed behind, adding its deeper thunder of rotor noise.

"Find every doctor and nurse in the lot and warn them about what you just saw," Samuel said. "Warn them not to enter the building, not to approach any infected corpse."

He whipped out his cell phone and dialed home. A message flashed up that the network was busy. Of course it was. Millions of people at ground zero of a global pandemic were trying to call loved ones.

"I need to get home to a landline," he said. "I have a contact at the CDC who needs to know this."

Samuel had war-gamed pandemic scenarios in dozens of different ways in his old job. They all ended badly, and none had started with parameters this dire.

"You need to get home and hunker down," he added. "This is going to get ugly fast."

Chapter Eleven

The news had an item each day that was supposed to terrify Melanie—invasive plant species, pesticides on fruit, asteroid collisions. Advertising space had to be sold, and more panicked viewers meant more advertisers. Melanie had long ago learned to keep the products of the fear factory out of her mental shopping cart. When a real disaster loomed, a more honest harbinger would probably warn her.

A phone call did just that. School would close in an hour, and she needed to pick up Aiden.

She couldn't ask the automated message for details. For now, she didn't need them. She just needed to get to Brock Academy. A deviation from the Routine as large as leaving school a half-day early would send Aiden into a chaotic spiral. He'd need a rock to stand on, and she'd always been that rock.

From the moment she left the condo gates, it was clear the neighborhood was wrong in a big way. The light midday traffic today ran heavier. It also ran…tenser. The cars did more jockeying for position, had more jackrabbit launches through yellow lights. Melanie got a sense of psychological strain pulling the very air taut.

She popped the car radio over to the never-used AM band and scanned over to 880 to see what WCBS could tell her.

A live announcer had superseded the usual programmed rotation of taped news segments. A hint of nervous excitement ran through his voice. Papers shuffled near the mic, and he vamped for time with filler sentences as new notes were handed to him. Voices muttered in the usually silent background.

He spoke of a vague dangerous-disease outbreak. He didn't say plague, but Melanie could fill that in herself. Symptoms included dark skin discoloration along the veins, followed by violent outbursts. Transmission methods were unknown now, but as a precaution, schools and government offices in the affected areas were being closed.

Areas? she thought. *How widespread is this?*

A block short of the school, Melanie jammed the brake pedal to the floor. Cars crammed the half circle in front of the school and the parking lot. Vehicles idled in the grass and on the road. Drivers' doors hung open, front seats empty. Parents streamed from across the front lawn to the main door like ants converging on dropped watermelon. A smattering of parents with children in tow bucked the incoming waves.

This was bad. Too much noise, too much motion, too much confusion. She imagined Aiden cowering in a corner, tears in his eyes, rocking in that upright fetal position she'd seen way too often. The maternal imperative to rescue took over.

Cars filled the road behind her. She didn't want to get blocked in the growing Gordian knot of steel in front of the school. She spun the Ford into a U-turn and parked across the end of someone's driveway. She ran for the school entrance as the engine coasted down.

Ashen-faced, wide-eyed fear filled every person she passed. She could smell it in the air, a sour odor of adrenaline and sweat that grew stronger as the people converged. Four across, they tried to breach a doorway built for two. Shoulder to shoulder with them, Melanie wedged herself into the hallway.

The normally quiet school resounded with raucous chaos. Melanie shuddered at the disappearance of the usual regimented sign-in security process. Parents shouted for children. A few confused youngsters cried, some with their parents, some without. All of it echoed and amplified along the red-brick walls and the polished linoleum, a wall of sound to match the wall of bodies.

A trio of middle-school boys snaked through the crowd. Their faces, far from fearful, were alight with excitement. Each had a bulge under his shirt and an anticipatory smile that promised evil was on the way. The three gave Melanie a chill.

She wondered who'd released them from their classes. In an emergency, teachers were supposed to stay with their children until a parent picked them up. There were kids in this school who could turn dangerous in an instant without strict supervision. If a teacher had abandoned the class these boys were in, what about Aiden's?

Aiden's room was at the corner. She swam through the surging crowd, alternately crushed and jostled as she tried to keep forward momentum. She reached the open doorway to Aiden's room. The pressure of the crowd practically spat her inside.

The room was almost empty. The teacher was gone. Three kids stared out the window with longing, distraught looks. None of them was Aiden.

Fear clamped itself around her heart so tightly she could barely breathe. The idea of separation from her son turned her hollow.

"Aiden? Aiden!" Her voice screeched so high it startled her.

She began a frenzied search. She threw open the door to the empty bathroom. She looked under children's desks, behind the shelves. She threw the teacher's rolling chair across the room to check her desk's footwell.

The three kids at the window ran for the hallway, apparently feeling safer in the crazed crowd than alone with one madwoman.

Melanie tore jackets from their hooks in the closet. She deconstructed a pile of backpacks, searched anywhere large enough for Aiden to hide. Nothing.

Melanie began to hyperventilate. Sweat stippled her upper lip. She clenched her fists against her racing pulse. She had to calm down, to think.

Aiden would not leave the school. The confusion within the walls would be scary, but the outside world would be terrifying. He wouldn't run away to a bigger place, he would retreat to a smaller one, one where he felt more secure. At home, he sat under the pine tree in the backyard, shaded and secluded by the great drooping green branches. Here he'd...

She braved the hall again. More parents screamed their children's names. Sobbing boys and girls clung to the waists of rushing parents. A fuzzy voice came over the intercom in a plea for calm, but snapped off halfway through the sentence.

Melanie worked her way down along the wall, past the closed door of another vacant classroom. She stopped outside the janitor's room, a windowless space about three closets' size. It always smelled like Pine-Sol.

She braced herself against the crowd and pulled the door open. The artificial pine scent rolled out the door. The hallway light lit a sliver of the room. A boy seemingly swallowed by a sweatshirt sat on a yellow, upturned mop bucket. His hands wrapped around his legs, his forehead touched his knees.

Aiden looked up and blinked against the light.

Melanie rushed inside. The surging crowd slammed the door behind her. She went to her knees and chased the fading afterimage of her son into the closet corner. In the dark, she felt his lambskin-soft arms, then his bony little shoulders. He made a moaning, unhappy sound at the contact. She pulled away. Outside, humanity swarmed through the hall, a pulsing, panicked, terrified mass.

"C'mon, Aiden," she whispered near his ear. "We're going home."

She cracked open the door, and guided him to his feet. His hood was now pulled so far down over his head that the sweatshirt's shoulder seams touched his ears. He held his backpack tight against his chest.

"It's very crowded out there," she warned. "But we'll only be in the crowd for a minute, then outside, to the car and home. Stay with me."

Aiden reached out and grabbed her belt loop, a rare move. Whether driven by love or fear, Melanie didn't care.

They stepped out into the crowd. Aiden pulled at her belt loop.

One of the trio of unsettling middle-schoolers stood in the hall between her and the main entrance. He pulled a can of spray paint from under his shirt. Melanie thought that the worst thing for the school right now was a kid with a demonic grin and a can of spray paint.

She was wrong. There was something worse.

The kid pointed the spray can to the ground. He pulled out a lighter. He pressed the can's nozzle, and the can sputtered out a fan of blue-lacquer mist. With a flick of the lighter beneath the nozzle, the spray erupted into a stream of flame.

The crowd's riverine flow in both directions transformed into a one-way tidal surge, away from the main entrance and the boy with dragon's breath in his hand. The press of the bodies nearly knocked Melanie over. The surge pulled Aiden from her side as it propelled them down the corridor. One of his fingers slipped from her belt loop.

Her heart pounded. The trilling bell of the fire alarm sounded. Red strobe lights flashed. Then the bell cut out. The ringing returned, but this time wound down like a deflating balloon. Melanie's hope of sprinklers spraying their rescue route disappeared with the bells.

The boy in the hall, now with room to work his art, sprayed an arc of fire across the paper decorations on the wall. They burst into flames that then raced for the ceiling.

She pulled Aiden back from being bowled over. She wrapped an arm around his waist and lifted him off the floor. He wailed and struggled against her. Shoulder first, like a football player, she barreled through the crowd and back through the door of Aiden's classroom.

Screams in the hallway turned up an octave. The boys who'd been in the classroom before were gone. Melanie locked the door behind her and dragged Aiden to the window. Outside, a police car locked wheels to a smoking stop, red lights blazing. She pulled at the window sash. It didn't move. The window was screwed into the frame.

A twisted, high-pitched laugh came from the hallway. The smell of smoke filled the air.

Melanie glanced at the other three windows. All sealed.

"Who's in there?" the boy yelled from the other side of the window in the classroom door. "Aiden the mute? You could use a warm-up."

Blue paint shot under the door and into the classroom. Then it burst into flame. Ribbons of fire swept across the floor. Papers inside a student's desk ignited in a fireball.

A small fire extinguisher hung on the wall by the teacher's desk. Melanie plucked it from its mount. By the time she turned to face the flames, they'd consumed six more desks. The room was already lost.

She ran for the window. She raised the extinguisher over her head and let it fly. It shattered the window dead center and flew out into the yard.

"Aiden! Go through the window!"

The boy in the hallway laughed. His face glowed gold in the fire's light. Aiden stood frozen.

Melanie picked up her son at the belt and collar, like a barkeep tossing a drunk. She hurled him through the open window and onto a landscaped bush outside. Melanie scrambled for the window frame. She grabbed the edges. Glass shards sliced at her palms. She catapulted herself out the window.

She landed on the ground with a thud. A fire truck pulled up outside the school. Men in heavy, yellow coats jumped out and began to slither hoses from the truck.

Melanie scrambled on her hands and knees to her son, who had rolled off the bush, onto the ground and into a fetal position. He stared off at nothing. She crawled beside him.

"Aiden, are you all right?"

He sat up and nodded.

Parents now ran from the school, kids carried or in tow. Smoke roiled from broken windows. Car horns blared. Several vehicles rammed their way through the parked cars and back to open roads. Another police car pulled up out front.

Melanie pulled Aiden up. "Now we run." They made a break for her car. When they got there, he jumped into the back and strapped the seat belt on with no prodding. Melanie climbed in the front seat. The key slipped between her bloody fingers as she twisted it in the ignition.

"Hang on, honey," Melanie said. The engine roared to life. "We're going home."

Chapter Twelve

Melanie had a rough ride back to Cedar Knoll. Several accidents snarled traffic and her internal GPS had to do multiple recalculations. The trip was so hectic that she didn't even call Charles until she had Aiden safely back inside the house. The call rolled to voice mail anyway, as did the next one to his cell.

He called back fifteen minutes later. Yelling traders filled the background.

"You called?" he said.

"Of course I did! Have you seen the news?"

"Have I? Rumors are running rampant about quarantine zones for some infectious disease." His voice went muffled and distant as he spoke to someone else. "Yes, sell order. At 102." He came back to the phone. "You should see what this is doing to the markets. We're about to sell short and rake in millions."

"We're fine, thanks for asking."

"Of course you're fine. You would have told me first thing."

"I just pulled Aiden out of school," she said. "The place was insane, kids set it on fire. We jumped out a window! The drive home was nuts. There were lines out the door when I just passed King Kullen. People are stocking up—"

"No, no!" Charles said to someone else. "All of it. Dump it all!" He returned to the phone. "Hon, you'll need to hold the fort there. This'll keep spinning out after the closing bell, and we need a solid strategy for overseas markets and the opening. This one's definitely an all-nighter. I'll call you back."

He hung up before she could answer, before she could tell him what an unfeeling bastard he was at this moment.

She flipped on Channel 7. Live news had preempted the afternoon soaps. The invasion of Iraq hadn't done that. Her stomach sank.

"The governor has just finished a news conference in Albany," the announcer said. She looked more harried than reading a teleprompter usually warranted. "He was quick to emphasize that the residents in the affected areas should not panic. To summarize, the nature, extent and lethality of the disease is still unknown. The number of confirmed cases is small, and they are isolated. The State of New York is working with the CDC to find out the cause of this strange disease." The anchor turned to someone out of camera frame. "Have we gotten in touch with the CDC? What do you mean they don't answer?" She touched her earpiece. "We have live footage now from our News Copter 7 and Danny Raymond. Danny, where are you?"

The screen switched over to an aerial view of the smaller harborside town of Port Jefferson. The town sat at the base of three hills, with the north side of it against Port Jefferson Harbor. Route 25A ran into town from the east and out to the south. All the lanes now traveled outbound, filled with cars trying to get away. Police lights flashed from all over the scene.

"Maria, it's chaos down in Port Jefferson. The morning started with the shooting we reported at the harbor, initially believed to be a terrorist attack related to the ferries that cross the Sound here. We soon had confirmation from Homeland Security that it was not an act of terrorism, just a lone gunman. By noon, there were reports of several other incidents around town, a knifing at a local supermarket, an SUV running down a score of people along Main Street. Then things went out of control at St. Charles Hospital. We can't get in there against the flow of traffic to uncover any details, but we were able to pull some unconfirmed video from purported witnesses at the scene."

The shot cut to a shaky cell phone video. In a close-up, a young, harried black man stared straight into the lens in panic.

"I don't know what's going on. The hospital's gone crazy. There's gunshots and screaming. I gotta stream this so everyone can see."

The camera swung in a dizzying arc to point at the hospital. Smoke billowed from the shattered upper windows of a newer all-glass addition to the older brick structure. Out of the doors streamed doctors in lab coats, nurses in scrubs, people in street clothes, even barefoot ambulatory patients clutching closed the backs of their hospital gowns.

"I was just delivering flowers when everything went bat shit," the man voiced over the scene. "Lots of screaming. I saw two people in the hallway, stabbed. No, not stabbed, they were *opened*, like top to bottom, still alive, trying to pull their skin together like they were buttoning a shirt. I dropped the flowers and ran. There were gunshots from somewhere. No one knew what was happening, just that they wanted to get the hell away from it."

He flipped the camera back around to himself. "I'm going home. Screw this. I'm streaming this in case I don't make it. I'm Marcus Lenore from Patchogue. Tara, I love you if you see this." He waved.

The view cut back to Maria at the anchor desk. She stared agog at her monitor. She tapped her earpiece as some off-camera director reminded her she was on the air. She jerked up to face the camera.

"Several hospitals around Long Island have had similar reports of violence. Again, the Department of Homeland Security reassures us that these are not widespread terrorist activities, though compared to some of the reports I've seen, I'd be happier if they were. Most of what we're getting is from viewers, so keep sending in those reports and videos. Everyone needs to follow the government's instructions to stay in your homes. Stay tuned here at Eyewitness News as we bring you the latest developments."

The station cut to a commercial for toilet paper with softness claims bold enough to make someone look forward to taking a dump. Apparently, even in a crisis, the station's bills needed to be paid. Melanie went to her desktop and called up her Socialize website page. She didn't spend much time on the Internet, but this site had been a boon for access to forums about Aiden's autism and to keep in touch with the other mothers at Brock Academy.

Her news feed overflowed. Postings and shares and links to more postings. She would have dismissed the more unbelievable stories, except that her personal experience and what she'd seen on the news made them all somehow credible. She hadn't seen anyone infected, but that didn't matter. Even rumors about it were enough to make people act crazy, and that was scary enough.

She made a frantic sweep of the condo's ground floor. All the windows were locked, the front door bolted. Cedar Knoll's front gate would keep any nonresidents out. What if one of the residents became infected or went off the deep end? The gossip was that Paul Rosen was a survivalist nut. He definitely had guns in his condo. She'd seen plenty of tragic examples when guns got into the hands of the wrong people.

She shook her head to clear that thought away. Too much to worry about too soon. Tamara was a nurse. She'd get her to overlay some medical sanity onto the situation. Later.

For now, she entered Aiden's room. He sat at the head of his bed, knees tucked to his chin, arms wrapped around them so tight his elbows were white. He rocked back and forth, eyes closed.

Melanie sat at the foot of his bed. She wanted to hold him, to envelop him in her arms, calm his fears and tell him everything was fine, that they were safe at home. She wanted to feel his warmth as well, to revel in that feeling only a mother can have with her child, that amazing sense of completeness when rejoined with the life she had created.

But the foot of his bed was the best she could do, the best she'd been able to do since Aiden had first rejected her touch at just months old. A yard of physical distance separated them, but it felt like an emotional mile.

"Everything's going to be fine," she said. "Your father will be home soon. In no time, school will reopen. We'll be back to normal."

Aiden kept rocking.

She guessed that the lies didn't make either of them feel any better.

Chapter Thirteen

Dr. Samuel Bradshaw went straight home from St. Luke's for a number of reasons. The streets were only marginally safe, and public landlines were as scarce as honest politicians, but mostly because Brenda was home alone. She'd have been watching the news and connected the same dots he had. She was bound to be worried. He'd have been surprised she hadn't called, except cell phone service was nonexistent.

The neighborhood lay quiet as he drove up to his house. The upscale enclave of older homes along Long Island's North Shore had large lots wooded enough to obscure your neighbor's home. The stillness was not unusual at this time of day. He'd check on Brenda, call Vanessa at the CDC. He looked at the cooler in the floorboard of the passenger seat. He was certain those samples were critical to finding a cure.

He reached for the cooler and stopped. Bring it inside or leave it here for now? Risk exposing Brenda if the cooler opened or risk the neighborhood? He thought of the wheelchair he'd condemned her to and left the cooler in the locked car for now.

"Brenda?" he called as he entered.

The house answered with silence.

She'd still been asleep when he left for the hospital, but she certainly would have been up by now. But Brenda always had the radio on…

He rushed to her room, and threw open the door. Her covers lay wadded up at the foot of the bed. She lay on her side, arms and legs uncomfortably askew, the sheets beneath her damp with sweat. Her soaked pajamas stuck to her body. Damp hair clung to her face. The air smelled of adrenaline and fear.

"Oh God, no," he whispered.

In a flash, he was at her bedside. He slid up the sleeve of her pajamas. A network of black, throbbing veins covered her arms.

He rolled her onto her back. Her body felt lifeless, limp. He lifted her eyelid and revealed a bloodshot sea of red.

Denial kicked in. This nightmare could not be real. He had to be dreaming or hallucinating. The stress, the shock of the day.

The doctor in him rejected the lies.

He checked for a pulse. Strong, steady. He remembered Gwen's progression and estimated Brenda had been infected for a day. She didn't leave the house, so how could she have been infected with the virus? His heart skipped a beat.

"Not again."

He had to have brought it home, brought it home from Gwen. How else could she have gotten it? Damn it, it wasn't enough he had to paralyze her, now he had to kill her as well?

He swept her wet hair from her forehead and laid his palm against her clammy skin. She didn't feel hot. The fever may have already broken.

His first thought was to call an ambulance. But where would they take her? If St. Luke's was a disaster, the rest of the hospital system wouldn't be far behind. Thank God, a decade plus of family practice had stocked his house with a decent cache of medical supplies and equipment. The pantry had been converted to a mini medical storeroom. He caressed her pallid cheek with his fingertips.

"Be right back."

In the kitchen, he threw open the pantry door. He found the digital thermometer, the blood pressure cuff. He rooted through the bottles of pills for a quick inventory of the weapons he had at his disposal.

Something metallic snapped in his wife's bedroom. He went to the hallway and froze.

Brenda stood in her bedroom doorway. Stood! Wet pajamas clung to her thin body. Stands of hair plastered across her face. Blackened veins crept up her exposed neck. Sandstone-red irises burned holes in Samuel.

"Brenda?"

She held the Grappler at her side. She swung it up and gripped it across her chest like an infantryman's rifle. She'd snapped the cushioned, gripping ends away and left two jagged metal points.

"You bastard," she said. "You self-centered bastard. I'm going to make you eat that chair you stuck me in."

She staggered forward with the Grappler pointed like a mounted bayonet. The twin shock of his wife walking and turning homicidal nearly incapacitated him with its combination of elation and horror.

"Brenda, you're—"

"You prick. Do you know what it's been like being in a wheelchair? Viewing the world from four feet tall? The frustration of seeing even one step up as an insurmountable obstacle?"

She took two halting steps forward. Samuel took one step back. He hit the kitchen table. Brenda raked a gouge into the wall with the Grappler's ragged tips.

"I'm going to return this frigging gift you gave me, this reminder of my inadequacies, this pathetic apology for ruining my life. I'm going to give it to you in the back, sever your spine between the fourth and fifth vertebrae and see how you like a life as hell on wheels."

She charged him, Grappler point first. Samuel rolled up and over the kitchen table. His old back screamed in pain at the maneuver. Plates and silverware crashed to the floor. Brenda thrust the Grappler after him, missed by an inch, and the tip stuck in the tabletop.

Samuel hit the floor. Brenda yanked the Grappler out of the tabletop. Samuel saw her legs on the other side of the table. Her pajamas stuck to them like the rain-soaked cloth over collapsed umbrella ribs. Somehow, the disease returned control of the neural pathways, but it couldn't make muscle reappear.

Her legs were weak. Years of sitting had numbed her sense of balance.

He reached up and shoved the table into her at the waist. Her arms flailed as she staggered backwards. One foot slipped out from under her. She slammed the floor flat on her back.

Samuel leapt up and over the table. He landed straddling his wife and pinned her wrists to the floor.

"Brenda, listen. You've been infected. You aren't thinking clearly."

Her face burned with rage. Dark veins spread along her upper chest. Spittle danced on her lips.

"Screw you. This is the clearest I've thought since you poisoned me and left me next to useless. You're going to feel the same way."

Her legs might have been weak, but rolling a wheelchair had kept her arms toned, though not enough to explain what she did next. She swung them up with overpowering force and slammed her fists into the sides of Samuel's head. Stars sparkled his vision. He dropped her wrists.

Her fist shot out like a crossbow's arrow and hit his throat. His windpipe collapsed. He gasped and rolled off her. She crawled forward and grabbed the Grappler off the floor.

Samuel pulled himself to his feet. Brenda turned to face him, Grappler brandished, murderous intent in her red-stained eyes.

"Now you pissed me off," she said. "I'm just going to kill you."

She started to lever herself up with the help of a chair, eyes locked on Samuel every moment.

He searched the kitchen for a weapon. A cast-iron pan sat on the stove. He could smash the coffeepot and use a shard to...

To do what exactly? Kill his wife? Slash her throat, stab her heart, crush her skull? He'd spent his life healing, and now he'd take life and start with the woman he loved? She wasn't in control of herself. The disease was.

Brenda stood straight up. One arm steadied her against the kitchen table. Her lips twisted in a grin so demonic it made the hair on Samuel's arms stand on end.

"I'm sorry, hon," he said.

He grabbed a chair and skidded it along the floor at her. It bowled into her legs and sent her flying backwards into the refrigerator and down to the ground.

Samuel bolted for the front door. He jumped into his car and locked the door behind him. He pulled his keys from his pocket. They tumbled out of his shaking hands and fell between the seats.

His heart stopped. He shoved his hand between the cushions and groped blindly for his only ticket out of here. His fingers found only carpet.

The door glass thudded beside his head. Brenda stood next to the car. She slammed her hand against the window again.

"Come out and get what you deserve, you bastard!"

His groping fingertips grazed something cold. He pinched and fished up his keys. He jammed them into the ignition.

Brenda switched from her hand to her head and pounded the door glass again. The glass cracked. She punctuated each bash into the door glass with another furious shout.

The car roared to life. The door glass disintegrated in a sharp crystal mist. Samuel slammed the car into reverse. Brenda's hands shot through the open window frame and clamped around his throat like a vise.

He stomped the accelerator. The car lurched back. Brenda lost her grip. The car pulled away and she rolled down the side of the front fender, arms flying out from her sides like a giant top. She spun past the bumper and landed on the ground.

Samuel backed the car onto the road. He shifted gears and paused. He stared at

Brenda's prone body. She moved one arm, then the other. She rose to her feet, unsteady and furious. Blood from a gash on her forehead ran down into her eyes.

"I'll find you!" she yelled. "Don't think I won't."

Samuel drove off. He kept his eyes straight ahead, afraid to see what he knew was in the rearview mirror.

Chapter Fourteen

Samuel had nowhere to go. Insanity had taken over his home and his work. During his visit to St. Luke's, he'd had a good taste of how dangerous the streets could be. The roads were near deserted now, but that made him feel more uneasy, knowing that if the well were smart enough to stay inside, only the infected were out here. His receding adrenaline rush left him hungry and tired.

A police cruiser sat at the entrance to a packed CVS pharmacy parking lot. Samuel steered to the subconscious promise of safety the black-and-white Charger offered. The car was empty. Samuel wondered if it was a decoy, like the empty cruisers always parked in construction zones.

He parked the car in the grass. He tossed a coat from the backseat over the cooler, and locked the doors as he left the car. He entered the store to buy something to eat. The line to fill prescriptions stretched all the way down the aisle. Bare spots dotted the shelves where some of the higher-demand items had already disappeared. Two cashiers worked full speed, but people were backed up from the registers, anxious but orderly. The shotgun-toting cop at the door probably had a lot to do with that, assuring customers that they were safe both from people on the outside and from anyone who got any stupid ideas on the inside.

Samuel's appetite disappeared. He returned to his car. A National Guard Humvee rolled in and parked across from the CVS front door. A helmeted gunner in a flak jacket stood behind a turret-mounted .50 caliber machine gun. The shining tips of the loaded band of ammunition snaked down the weapon's side. The cop stepped out and exchanged a few words with the Humvee driver. He made a call on his radio. He nodded to the soldiers, returned to his cruiser and left.

Samuel needed a next move. Carrying these samples around was like carrying a biological weapon. He was a car accident away from starting a new hot spot. Home was out, the hospital was a shambles. His cell phone rang. He'd written off its functionality, and it took a second to recover from the shock. Caller ID was blocked. He answered.

"Hello?"

"Dr. Bradshaw?" said a stranger's voice.

"Yes?"

This time there was barely a pause before Vanessa picked up. "Samuel! Glad I caught you. I guess you didn't opt for that vacation I recommended?"

"I'm afraid not." How he wished he had. If he'd gotten off this damn island, maybe Brenda would be…

"Good news for me," Vanessa said. "How about we meet to discuss this outbreak? I pick your brain a little."

"I gathered some samples from my hospital right after an outbreak there. They could use some detailed analysis."

"What kind of samples?" Excitement filled her voice.

"Blood from our Patient Zero, samples from what looks like a secondary infectious stage."

The conversation paused. The background noise disappeared for a moment, like Vanessa's line was muted, then returned.

"I can get those samples analyzed," she said. "Bring them in."

"I don't think I can make it to Atlanta anytime soon."

"I've already come to you," she said. "Head to JFK Airport. Take the Van Wyck. The JFK Expressway will be closed by then. Head to Terminal One."

"How will I find you?"

"It won't be hard. See you in about thirty minutes."

She hung up before he could ask even one of all the questions he'd amassed. How was he going to find her at the airport? Why would she want him to bring infectious-disease samples to such a public place? How did she know he was less than thirty minutes away? How did her call get through to his cell phone?

A half hour later, Vanessa seemed prescient. The JFK Expressway exit was closed. Actually, more like sealed with waist-high mobile concrete barriers blocking the road and New York's Finest manning them with shotguns. The exit was another story, with cars jammed up as far back as he could see.

He flipped on the radio to 880 AM.

The announcer began to discuss train, subway and airport cancellations. Bridge and tunnel traffic was restricted. Samuel recognized the first steps toward quarantine. It was hard to imagine the government doing the whole island.

Samuel turned south on the Van Wyck Expressway. He was about the only car on it, though the northbound lanes were jammed. Short of the airport property, soldiers were digging fighting positions and filling sandbags along the side of the road. Armored personnel carriers flanked the entrance. The gunners on each kept their machine guns trained on Samuel throughout his approach. All the soldiers wore surgical masks. On the highway median, a main battle tank with a turret gun that seemed to stretch out forever clanked down and off a flatbed's ramp.

Samuel pulled to a stop at the hastily erected concrete barricades that blocked the entrance. An MP with his hand on his pistol and wearing a surgical mask approached the car. The MP's eyes were all Samuel could use to judge the soldier's mood, and he didn't like what he saw. Fear and suspicion. A bad combination for a man with his hand on a gun.

"Sir, the airport is closed. You'll need to turn around. There are no flights today. All workers are being evacuated."

"I was told to come here. I'm supposed to meet Dr. Vanessa Clayton of the CDC. I'm Dr. Samuel Bradshaw."

The MP's eyes narrowed. "Let me see some ID, sir."

Samuel dug out his license. The MP took it away and spent some time talking into a radio. He returned and handed Samuel back his license.

"Sir, head straight to Terminal One and park there. Inside go to gate ten."

Samuel stopped himself from sarcastically telling the guard he wasn't trying to catch a flight. He nudged his car through the S-shaped barrier maze and headed to the terminal, passing vacant parking lots. Overhead, a steady stream of airliners took off, practically nose to tail, from multiple runways, one long scream of full-throttle turbine engines. Delta, American, Aeroflot, Air France. If the parking lots were empty, so were those aircraft. Each plane was a potential escape route to elsewhere, but none were sticking around. An uncomfortable simile of rats deserting a sinking ship came to mind.

The empty parking lot outside the terminal filled him with foreboding. What cars remained were airport vehicles or military. He picked a close spot. He laughed at himself for habitually locking the doors as he left his car. Could he be someplace more secure?

A mean-looking Black Hawk helicopter flew overhead along the perimeter fence line. A gunner in a green flight helmet scanned the ground behind a door-mounted machine gun. A smoked plastic visor covered his eyes. A blue surgical mask covered his mouth.

Samuel grabbed the sample cooler and left his car. He passed by a dozen soldiers setting up yet more defensive positions. As the helicopter flew off, the air went still, the passenger aviation exodus apparently over.

The doors to Terminal 1 slid open. The vast, airy lobby was a sea of military and civilians moving between folding tables, tapping on tablet computers and consulting maps, all too busy to notice his arrival. Surgical masks hung from all of their necks.

Samuel went straight to the security checkpoint for the departure gates. The TSA agents looked tired and agitated. A short, fat black agent stood beside the scanner. His shirttail was untucked. His mask hung around his neck. He hadn't shaved in a while and his eyes were bleary. He made Samuel empty his pockets, take off his shoes, the whole air-travel routine. Samuel sent the lunch cooler of infectious samples through the X-ray machine, explaining what it was and not to open it. Samuel passed through the personal scanner and reassembled himself on the other side.

Vanessa met him there. Still a towering beauty, she'd replaced the natural kink in her hair, that she'd favored in rural Africa, with a short, straight style that accentuated her high cheekbones. She wore a medical lab coat with a CDC patch on the breast, as did most of the others on this side of security. She looked relieved.

"Samuel! Thank God you made it. All I could think about was the thousand things that could go wrong on the way here." She eyed his cooler. "Samples?"

"You bet."

She waved a technician over to get the cooler and told him to process all the samples per protocol.

"They're all properly labeled," Samuel said.

"I knew they would be," Vanessa replied.

She led him down the main hallway.

"Are you considering quarantining all of Long Island?" he asked.

"It's a worst-case-scenario," she answered. "It was a tough sell until I hit the President with the outbreak projections if we did nothing. Then the economic impact of sealing Long Island paled in comparison."

She walked him back to gate 10. All the seating had been piled in one corner. CDC people milled around folding tables and punched at laptops plugged into an octopus of extension cords. She led him to the table in the corner that was her desk.

"This happened so quickly," he marveled.

"That Ebola scare woke everyone up. We now have contingency plans for every major metropolitan area in the country. We use natural barriers like firebreaks to stop the spread of a disease: rivers, valleys, interstate highways we can patrol. As soon as our computer models detected a potential outbreak, the plan geared up."

"Computer models?"

"With health care mandates for computerized records keeping, our CDC mainframe is tied into every sneeze and cough across the country. The system looks for patterns, and it painted Long Island red days ago. Once the governor activated the National Guard to tighten security, we started the process."

Samuel remembered the soldiers outside the pharmacy relieving the police.

Out the window, several gray US Air Force cargo jets taxied to gates around gate 10. Rear ramps lowered and soldiers disembarked like dandelion seeds in a breeze. Farther back, a flight of three Apache helicopter gunships hovered by at ten feet off the ground.

"It's about time they arrived," Vanessa said. "We can send the TSA people home and seal the airport completely."

"Those aren't National Guard soldiers out there," Samuel said.

"Tenth Mountain Division out of Upstate, Fort Drum. The Guard won't be able to control the whole island by itself."

"They brought gunships?"

"As a show of force," Vanessa said. "Hurricane Katrina showed us that if people believe all hope of safety is gone, society's fabric breaks down in hours. We plan to make a strong visible show of security."

"Those are all combat veterans out there, used to dealing with a very different population in the Middle East. Should they be in charge—"

"The CDC is in charge, Samuel," she cut in. "Not the military. They report to me. I report to the President."

Samuel could tell he'd struck a nerve, and backed off this line of questions. Vanessa slid a map of Long Island on her desk in front of Samuel. He recognized the coding immediately. Red dots signified outbreaks. There were more than he'd imagined, more than the news had reported. Some of the dots were more like blots, especially around St. Luke's. Port Jefferson looked like a spilled wine stain. Samuel grimaced. Vanessa touched his hand.

"Is Brenda with you?"

"No."

"Is she okay?"

Infected, on her feet and homicidal, he thought. "Yes, she's fine." He shifted the subject. "You have some people wearing surgical masks here."

"We're not certain about the airborne manifestation of the virus. Range, lethality. For those on the perimeter, better safe than sorry. It also gives them a sense of security."

A sense of security. Not the same as the actual security a full, filtered protective suit would give.

"JFK is like our beachhead here, so we have fast access to the zone, with minimal risk. We administer in Terminal One. Research is in Terminal Two. Terminal Three is CDC housing. Teams are prepping all three as we speak. I want to tell them to make a place here for you."

"Vanessa, I'm just a GP now. I haven't done research in ages. I'm not up to date on the new technology."

"But my technicians are. I don't need you spinning a centrifuge. I need you leading the team, providing the insight."

The temptation was strong. As much as being a GP helped so many individuals, he'd missed the rewarding idea of his polio research curing the masses. And this epidemic could make polio look like the common cold.

"You can bring Brenda in with you," Vanessa said. "Call and have someone drive her over. I already added her to the access list at the gates."

The memory of Brenda in her infected state gave him a shiver. What he could do for the multitudes meant less than what he could do for his wife. Here he could find a cure for the virus and reverse its effects. Perhaps he could even engineer a cure that kept her regained ability to walk intact. He could erase not one mistake, but two, the two that destroyed her life twice over. For that, he'd need to stay inside the airport perimeter.

"I'll do it," he said.

Vanessa rolled open a drawer in a cabinet against the wall. She fished out an ID badge. It already had Samuel's name on it and a copy of his driver's license picture.

"I had a feeling you'd say yes. Do you want me to send an escort to get Brenda?"

"No, she's safe with family."

Vanessa pointed to a phone on her desk. "Call and let her know you're staying here."

"It'll go through?"

"We have priority. Civilian access to telecommunications is being restricted to make sure the government has clear access when we need it. How do you think I got hold of you?"

She stepped away to give him some privacy. He stared at the phone, then dialed his home number.

It rang four times. The answering machine picked up. His own voice asked him to leave a message. He cupped his hand over the receiver and spoke softly.

"Brenda, I don't know if you'll listen to this or understand it if you do. The CDC has converted Kennedy Airport into a secure lab. I've signed up to help them. We'll find a cure, and I'll bring it back, and then I'll bring you back. I promise. So whatever part of you is still awake, hang on. I will fix this or die trying."

Chapter Fifteen

Tamara tripped the automatic gate as she returned to Cedar Knoll. Paul Rosen stood watch on the other side, outfitted for the occasion. He wore a set of hunter's camouflage coveralls. With his paunch, he looked a bit like an underripe pear. He cradled a .308 Winchester rifle in his arms. He flipped Tamara a self-conscious, two-fingered salute from the edge of his glasses.

Tamara stopped the car beside him and rolled down the window.

"Paul, what the hell?"

"Best to be prepared for all eventualities, right?" he said. He sounded almost apologetic. "The news is full of crazy stories, crazy people. We've got one way into Cedar Knoll and one way out. If a nonresident tries to get in through that gate…" he patted his rifle like a baby, "…this ought to scare them off."

There was something unnerving about an armed civilian at the gate to her home, especially Paul. But St. Luke's had gone insane. If Paul wanted to dress up and play one-man neighborhood watch to scare off any trespassers, more power to him.

"The condo board always gave you such a hard time about having your rifle on the property," she said. "What will they think of this?"

"It was Bill Meyers's idea," Paul said. "If the condo board chairman asks me to take out Winnie here, then he can't complain about her."

She couldn't count the number of times she'd cursed waiting for the gate to grind open so she could get home. Now she was thrilled to have it, that barrier between the chaos outside and the calm within. She was glad Bill put Paul there to back it up.

"How are things out there?" Paul said. "As bad as it looks on the news?"

"The hospital imploded. A combination of the infected and the terrified turned the place into one of Dante's outer rings of Hell."

"Where has the National Guard set up?"

"National Guard?"

"The governor declared martial law a few hours ago. All guardsmen were ordered to report for duty to the nearest armory. Mandatory sundown curfew."

"Jesus."

Paul pointed at her eye bandage. "I've some medical supplies set aside. If you need to change the dressing or something, let me know."

"Thanks." She realized all the activity hadn't helped her condition at all. The doctor had recommended taking it easy. The left side of her head had turned into one big, low-level ache.

Tamara thought how the oddball deer hunter didn't seem so odd now. Maybe it was because the facts of his humanity were overriding her preconceptions. Maybe he was rising to the occasion. Maybe she was just ignoring her misgivings in a blind search for security.

An hour later, over a hundred bodies packed the condo dayroom to overflowing. Folding chairs filled the room with just the narrowest of aisles down the center. A table and chair sat empty at the front of the room before a bay window. A small sign on the table read *Board President*. The air turned stifling as the mass of body heat overtaxed the air-conditioning. The low rumble of dozens of conversations made each one unintelligible, but the same cadence ran through all—the short, sharp tang of fear.

Nearly two hundred resided at Cedar Knoll. Tamara and Melanie were close, but, past that, she knew maybe six by name, another twenty or so by sight. She always blamed the long hours of her job, the rotating shifts. But that probably wasn't it. Most people in the room gave the crowd of strangers a blank look of inspection. Apparently, most of them were as isolated as she was.

The children were all outside by the closed, covered pool, under the supervision of a few volunteer spouses attending the meeting. There wasn't any need to expose them to more of this unfolding disaster than necessary. Only Aiden was in the room at the far corner. Leaving Aiden with unfamiliar kids in an unfamiliar place would be courting disaster. Instead, Melanie stood beside him, positioned to keep a bit of space between her son and the crowd.

Melanie usually looked a bit harried, but today she looked spent. During Tamara's medical training she'd studied all about autism. The nurturing-nurse side of her felt for the boy the first time she met him. Tamara couldn't imagine Melanie's stress level now, with caring for her son added to what felt way too much like the world falling apart.

She caught Melanie's eye and waved. Melanie returned a weak wave and a halfhearted smile. Band-Aids flapped at her palm. She adopted a look of concern and pointed at Tamara's bandages. Tamara mouthed that she was okay.

Bill Meyers entered from the back of the room. The condo board chairman always entered the room with a near-regal air, his full head of silver hair always in perfect place. Imperious and overbearing, the diminutive septuagenarian ran a ruthless meeting. Able to quote bylaws to the paragraph, he was quick to assess for infractions, slow to permit change. Retiring from his accounting position and assuming the presidency had allowed his unrealized Napoleon complex to blossom.

The room hushed as Bill approached his table, his throne from which he held court once a month. But the crowd wasn't silenced the usual way, by implied intimidation. Instead, they fell still in shock. The majestic President Meyers was disheveled, hair hastily combed, golf shirt wrinkled. His normally steely blue eyes were more faded gray. The crowd took their seats.

"Fellow residents," Bill began. He always opened with the same two words, always with an air of condescension. "Our town, our whole island is experiencing a lot of confusion. Some members asked that we meet to talk events over."

"Oh, Bill, for the love of Christ." Mickey Reynolds stood up, though it made only a marginal improvement in the ability of the others to see and hear the stout little plumber. The light reflected off his shaved head that seemed perpetually polished. He gave his goatee a tug, his signature nervous tic. "No time to beat around the bush, here. I wanted this meeting, and not to chitchat, but to take some damn action."

"Now, Mickey, we should follow the rules for addressing the group, by having me first recognize you. There's no need to get agitated—"

Mickey's face went red. Tamara sighed. The man's personal feud with Bill went back three years to when Bill cited chapter and verse of the condo regs to force him to take down his American flag, and then later acted like it was a big favor to let him fly it on the Fourth of July. Petty citation after petty citation had followed ever since.

"No need?" Mickey said. "Have you watched the damn news? It's looking like New Orleans after Katrina out there. I've been out doing calls. People are looting, women are getting raped."

A gasp rippled through the group.

"I'm sure that those stories are overblown," Bill offered.

Tamara wondered what planet Bill had been living on the last two days.

Mickey stepped into the aisle. "You calling me a liar? I know what I seen!"

"Calm down. As a precaution, I agreed to Mr. Rosen's request to keep an eye on the main gate…"

Tamara's brow furrowed. That was a bit different from the way Paul painted the picture, where Bill had sought *him* out.

"…but security is really the realm of law enforcement."

"Law enforcement?" Mickey said. "The cops are stretched so thin the National Guard needs to reinforce them. And do you think the infected are going to listen to a cop? Can one cop stop a gang of six like I saw by the Quick Stop? We need more than just Paul watching the gate."

A murmur of strong assent filled the air.

"Admiral Security is on-site," Bill said. "As always."

A few groans rose from the crowd. Mario Walsh was Cedar Knoll's sole representative from Admiral Security. The old man sat in a room monitoring security cameras and punching open the main gate for visitors with plausible access excuses.

"Old Man Walsh?" Mickey said. "The guy must be pushing ninety! He hasn't been in his prime since he landed during D-Day. He isn't even armed!"

A few people openly voiced support for Mickey. Bill fished a worn pamphlet of the condo regulations from his pocket, the Bible he referred to for years, his ultimate authority. He thumbed back and forth looking for a page.

"The regulations are clear on such vigilantism," Bill said. "No such steps can be taken without the consent of the full board and giving the motion three readings. Two of our board members are absent so—"

Two rifle shots split the air outside the dayroom, followed by a scream. Bill Meyers spun in his chair and looked out the window.

"Sweet Lord," he whispered. He stood and addressed the group, "Everyone stay calm."

His admonition had the opposite impact. The attendees surged past him toward the window. Bill worked his way, salmon-like, down the main aisle to the exit doors.

The person's scream outside kicked Tamara's nursing instincts into high gear. She fell in behind Bill. He looked over his shoulder at her, sized up her scrubs and looked relieved.

"Yes, splendid idea. Y-you may be needed."

They passed through the double doors and headed for the front gate at a run. A man lay on the pavement inside the gate, facedown. Two gaping exit wounds bloomed from his back. Blood from the expanding puddle beneath him spread up the sides of his tan T-shirt.

Paul stood on the sidewalk in the same place Tamara saw him when she got home. He still pointed his Winchester at the corpse on the ground. Smoke drifted up from the barrel. Bill and Tamara froze.

"Paul?" Bill said. "Paul!"

"He scaled the gate," Paul said. His eyes never left the dead intruder. He jerked the rifle barrel once to the right. "Flip him. He's infected."

Bill's mouth hung open in shock. Tamara dashed to the body and rolled him over. The victim was in his early twenties with his blond hair slicked back. His glassy, blue eyes stared half-open. A mass of blackened veins coated his neck and arms. His chest had two holes center of mass. A large hunting knife lay beside the body, pointing towards Paul. Paul pointed the rifle away from Tamara.

"He climbed the gate and came at me, crazy," Paul said. "It was him or me."

A chorus of gasps filled the air. A knot of people from the meeting now stood behind Bill, who remained uncharacteristically speechless, seemingly fumbling for thoughts. Paul noticed the crowd forming behind Bill.

"I mean," Paul corrected, "it was him or us. He was out for blood. Look at that knife."

A general consensus of assent rumbled within the crowd. Tamara could practically smell a mood shift.

"See, I told you," Mickey said. "We have to defend ourselves. The world is going to hell. Bill?"

Bill just gave his head a few shakes, his eyes locked on the dead man. Paul slung his rifle over his shoulder and stepped toward the group.

"We can, and will defend ourselves," Paul said. His voice rang out over the people's heads. "Show of hands of who has weapons. Guns, bows, anything."

A few residents raised their hands.

"Good. Gather them and meet me in the dayroom. We must be prepared for every eventuality. We'll set up a security schedule. Everyone else should do two things. First, go home and take inventory of provisions—food, water, medicines. Then I need glass, broken glass, at least two shopping bags full from everyone."

"What for?" someone asked.

"The top of the wall. We need to make that space a minefield for any more hands that try to climb over it."

Bill roused a bit from his stupor. His eyes stayed fixed on the corpse. "We can't litter the wall. The association rules—"

"Screw the association rules," Mickey shouted.

"Mickey," one woman admonished, "Bill's the chairman."

"This ain't no time for someone who figures out whose dog crapped in the petunias," Mickey said. "We need someone with the balls to take action." He pointed at Paul. "I nominate him as chairman."

Paul looked startled. A few shouts of support rose from the crowd.

"Now you heard the man," Mickey said. "Weapons and glass. Get to it before we're overrun."

The crowd dispersed. Bill stood still, staring at the dead man. He twisted the condo regs into an ever-tightening tube in his hands.

Tamara didn't need to check the victim for vitals. Given the wounds, he was likely dead before he hit the ground.

"Bill," she said, "we need to get this body out of here. Bill?"

Bill just stared through the corpse. "My daughter lives with her daughters in Port Jefferson, a block from the hospital. There were riots. I can't get in touch with her…"

Paul stepped between Bill and Tamara. "Tamara, why do we need to get rid of the body?"

"Something happens to a corpse later. It explodes. A doctor I know is pretty certain it's one of the ways the infection spreads. We can't take the chance."

"Agreed."

Paul pulled a remote control from his pocket and hit the button. The main gate ground open. He grabbed the corpse's ankles.

"Whoa," Tamara said. "What are you doing? We need to call an ambulance, the police."

"The living can't get help. You think someone has time to respond to the dead?"

He was right. Society was in the midst of a horrible paradigm shift.

Paul dragged the body on its stomach down the driveway. Its chin caught on the gate's track in the pavement, and its head snapped back with a crack as it released. The corpse left a wide, wet, red trail down the dark asphalt, all the way to the sidewalk. Paul left the body along the gutter. The head faced up the driveway. Its dead eyes looked up the accusatory crimson trail that stopped at Tamara's feet.

Paul walked back. He trod in the blood trail and left one smudged, red heel print every other step. He crossed the gate and clicked it closed with the remote, without looking back.

Mario Walsh, daytime security guard, appeared from between two buildings. He headed for the main gate at a gimpy half jog. A bundle of keys jangled from the belt loop of his gray pseudomilitary uniform. The old man had his eyes on the prize of the main-gate exit. As he passed Paul, barely looking at him, he pulled the keys from his belt loop and shoved them against Paul's chest.

"Here, son. They're all yours. I got my own place to keep secure. I don't want anything to do with what I just saw on the security camera, and I don't want to be stuck in here when this town goes all hellfire crazy."

Paul gave him a bemused look. Mario stabbed the code into the main-gate keypad with a gnarled, shaking index finger. He rushed through the gate as soon as the lock buzzed open.

"And there goes Bill's vaunted line of defense," Paul said.

And, Tamara realized, that was it. Between the mob's acclamation and the guard's abdication, the flag of command had passed to Paul. Simple as that, Cedar Knoll was under the protection of Paul Rosen and a .308 Winchester.

Chapter Sixteen

Tamara had the key in her condo door lock when Melanie's voice made her whirl around.

"Tamara, I took Aiden back to the condo as soon as I heard the gunshots. What happened out there?"

"An infected intruder came over the gate. Paul Rosen killed him."

"Killed him? My God. I barely made it home with Aiden from school. We had to jump out a window! But the chaos seemed created more by panicked people than the infected."

"St. Luke's had plenty of both." She looked at the slipshod bandages on Melanie's hands. "How badly are you hurt?"

"It's nothing, just scratches." Melanie pointed to Tamara's bandaged head. "What about you? Did you get hurt at the hospital?"

"No, earlier. Nothing to worry about. I just need to keep it out of the light for a few days."

"Why would one of them try to climb our gate?" Melanie's voice had an air of panic, as if the idea of a violation of the little Cedar Knoll enclave was inconceivable.

"From what I've seen, their individual acts are rational, but their overall course of action isn't." She thought of the two guards on a rampage. "They're hell-bent on insane destruction, but can still think through how they want to do it. Not a good combination for the rest of us."

The front door to Melanie's condo across the sidewalk stood open about a foot. Aiden peered through the gap. His hood hung forward, the opening pulled to half size with the drawstrings.

"How's Aiden doing?" Tamara said.

"Pretty good, considering. But the medications he's on, Risperidone and Fluvoxamine, help. I'm so worried about running out. What was it like at the hospital, at pharmacies?"

Tamara tensed. This situation, this outbreak, was apparently going to pose one moral dilemma after another. First, what to think about Paul's ascendancy by acclamation; now, whether to sugarcoat the truth for her friend or lay it out on the line. Melanie's eyes were alight with fear.

Honesty overwhelmed sympathy. Tamara was pretty sure that the world was going to get worse before it got better. No point in delaying that realization for Melanie.

"The hospital was a shambles when I left it. People out there are turning a bit panicky. The cops seem to be staked out at pharmacies and liquor stores, the easiest targets for looting. The pharmacies seemed to still be open. As long as they stay open, I don't think any pharmacist will think twice about refilling your son's prescriptions, even if you burned through the refills. How many days' supply do you have?"

"Ninety days or so."

Melanie pronounced this like it was the countdown to an execution date. Tamara immediately regretted her decision to be forthright about the situation.

"I'm sure all this will be back to normal by then," Tamara said. One lie wouldn't be so bad.

"You think so?"

"Absolutely." In her head, she added an emphatic *not*.

Melanie seemed to relax a bit. Mission accomplished.

"I'm always right across the sidewalk if you need me," Tamara said.

"You're the one injured," Melanie countered. "Let me know what we can do for you."

"I'm doing fine. Thanks, though." Two lies in ten seconds. A new record.

Melanie ushered Aiden into their condo. Tamara entered hers. The left side of her head felt like a glowing lump of lead.

Mallow came bounding up, a big, black-and-tan bundle of pent-up affection. She closed the door just in time for the assault. He rose on his hind legs, and pinned her to the door with his front paws. His big, warm tongue licked the undamaged side of her face with enthusiasm.

"Okay, boy! Looks like you're in the mood for some affection."

Mallow dropped to all fours. Tamara knelt and buried her head in his warm fur. She always thought that anyone who sought comfort in the false pleasure of drugs needed to just experience the real fulfillment of a dog's unquestioned affection. They'd swear off drugs forever.

"Go get your leash, boy!"

Mallow bounded off. Tamara hoped that one normal activity would calm the spin of this horribly abnormal day.

Her cell phone rang. *Caller ID Blocked.* She answered and heard Doc Bradshaw's voice.

"Tamara, I was just making sure that you got home okay. I saw some hairy moments out there on the way from St. Luke's."

"I had some hairy moments in the condo complex as well, but everything has calmed down. Is your neighborhood okay?"

Uncomfortable pause. "Sure, everything's fine there."

"We're pretty secure here, behind the condo walls." Tamara opted to leave out the recruitment of their internal security. "If you and Brenda need a safe spot, my spare bedroom is yours, and I'm on the ground floor."

"We both appreciate that offer." Pause. "Look, thanks for your help today. But don't go back to the hospital. Not in general, and especially not with your injury. Let's baby that eye back to health."

"I will. And thanks for nagging."

Doc Bradshaw forced a laugh. "My pleasure. Now, I want you to know that the CDC has turned JFK Airport into a secure medical facility. They want me on their team there. They think my background in polio research may make a difference."

"That's good news."

"Stay home and recover. I'll keep you up to date on anything we find if I can get a working phone again. Okay?"

"You got it, Doc."

"Talk to you soon." He hung up.

Mallow loped up and sat at her feet. His leash dangled from his panting mouth. She patted his head.

After the situation at the hospital, she thought things were bad. But if the CDC had arrived in force, then that could only mean things were even worse. The newfound Cedar Knoll militia didn't seem like such a bad idea after all.

Chapter Seventeen

Jimmy Wade swam back to consciousness with no idea where he was. The last thing he remembered was the tip of K-Dogg's boot smashing the side of his head and Mozelle laughing from somewhere that seemed very far away.

The dark room was all shadows and gloom, but he knew it wasn't his decrepit apartment. First off, the bed was canted up at the head. Second, it smelled clean, not his apartment's usual combination of roach spray and decayed food.

He tried to sit up. His head pounded him back down to the mattress. A bandage covered his cranium down to his ears. He reached up to touch it but only his right arm moved. A plastic compression cast sheathed his left. His whole body felt sore, no it felt *pummeled*, like tenderized meat.

His last conscious moments came back to him. Mozelle's goon K-Dogg swinging a crowbar. Over and over. Him curled up on the cold concrete floor in a warm, coppery puddle of his own blood. Ah, the good times.

A controller lay on the bed by his right hand. He pressed a button and the light over his bed blinked on. He lay alone in a two-bed hospital room. The sheets on the other bed were thrown aside, the pillow on the floor, an IV stand against the mattress. Maybe the other guy went to the can.

He pressed the red button on the controller. A bell dinged far away in the hallway outside. It was the only sound in the whole wing. Shouldn't there have been someone doing something in this hospital?

Two more attempts to summon a nurse failed. Jimmy opted to take things into his own hands. He slid around to the side of the bed. His head felt like someone was beating it with a bat in time with his heartbeat. He grabbed his IV stand as a crutch. The bag on it was bone dry. He took a tentative step on his unsteady legs. On the little table by the bed stood three white prescription bottles. He scanned the labels in order.

Antibiotic. Antibiotic. Morphine!

"Hallelujah, Jesus!"

The warning label spoke of potential addiction.

He laughed. He popped the top on the last bottle and downed two.

He hobbled to the door and looked out into the deserted hallway. No nurses. No orderlies. No announcements on the PA. The fluorescent lights gave the place an ethereal glow that only added to the creepy vibe. He shuffled over and looked out through the first-floor window.

Night had fallen. He wondered how long he'd been out. The place looked as deserted outside as it was in. The harbor lights twinkled in the distance. That put him in Mather General in good old Port Jeff. Mozelle must have dumped him here, walking distance from his own apartment. What a bighearted guy Mozelle was.

His mind was fuzzy, but the cast told him his memory of watching his arm snap in two wasn't a hallucination. Despite the damage he'd sustained, he could get around on his own. It didn't look like there was anyone here to treat him. Since there was no way for him to pay the bill anyway…

The painkillers were kicking in, and if he was going to sleep off this beating, he might as well do it in his own bed with a few cold beers.

He pulled the dry IV needle from the top of his hand and thanked the morphine for taking the sting out of it. He noticed something seriously wrong with his arm. All his veins had turned black. He pressed against his skin. It didn't hurt. He touched the bandages across his forehead. Even through the gauze, he felt a low fever.

A clear-plastic bag at the base of his bed held his clothes. His missing roomie's were at the base of the other. That loser might not mind taking off in a half-assed nightgown, but Jimmy had more pride than that. In fact, more pride than to put his own bloodstained, night-in-jail, rarely washed anyway threads back on if a better option presented itself.

He poured out the other bag of clothes. A pair of jeans with two extra inches in the waist. He could make that do. A button-down shirt with a Port Jefferson Yacht Club logo on the pocket. Jeez, who was this guy?

He pulled a wallet from the jeans pocket. Michael V. Quinn. Ritzy Belle Pointe address. A picture of the guy with a smoking-hot trophy wife. A black American Express card. Upwards of $300 in cash. This guy should have rated a single room.

Jimmy slipped on Mr. Quinn's jeans, no mean feat with one arm in a cast. A set of keys made a lump in the front pocket. He picked up the shirt and knew it wouldn't go on over the cast. Pulling the IV was one thing. Shedding the cast was something else. Jimmy guessed he'd be better off letting that bone set properly.

He bit the shoulder seam of the shirt's left sleeve and tore it free. Now half vest, the shirt passed over the cast with ease. He fastened a few buttons. He reached down to retrieve his own wallet from his bag and stopped. It was a sorry excuse compared to the one he had now. It held a tattered, suspended license, a debit card to a closed bank account and a few crumpled dollars. Nothing there he needed. He'd try walking out of here as Michael V. Quinn and see how that worked for a while. It had to be better than being lowlife Jimmy Wade.

He stuffed his prescription bottles into his pockets, then entered the hallway and went for the lobby. A body lay across the floor. From the formerly white coat, he had probably been a doctor. It looked like a land mine went off in the man's rib cage. Flies buzzed around the gaping hole. Black goo splattered the floor and walls. Jimmy's mind tried to connect the spray on the wall with the dark matter that discolored his veins, but he couldn't face that right now. He stepped over the body.

He passed two more gut-grenade victims on his way to the lobby. The scene there looked like the aftermath of a spaghetti-western shootout. Corpses lay everywhere, but they hadn't exploded. These were all gunshot victims, cut down as they tried to get out of the building. The bodies had gaping holes, some with arms or legs blasted off to jagged stumps. All the blood was dry.

One body lay on its back and blocked the inner set of automatic sliding glass doors. The middle-aged man wore a white shirt and a blazing-blue tie. An AK-47 lay at his side, a collection of empty magazines at his feet. A knife protruded from his chest. The door kept sliding closed, smacking his head and reopening, like the building wanted to wake him so he could leave.

This scene was all kinds of screwed up, a crime scene that would make national news for a week. But there wasn't anyone here. No cops, no CSI, no crime tape, no reporters. That meant the rest of the world outside the hospital had to be even *more* screwed up than this.

That thought made him consider taking the dead man's AK with him, but he'd never fired anything bigger than a .38 pistol, and he didn't trust his one-handed aim with an assault rifle. Shit, it would probably just make him a shoot-first, ask-questions-later target for the first cop he came across.

He slid sideways past the dead man and out the front door into the cool night air. He paused to get a bearing to his apartment.

"Freeze and raise your hands!"

That first cop encounter didn't take long at all. It only made sense that if none were inside, at least one would be outside. Jimmy raised the one arm he could.

"Both of them!"

"The other one's broken." He bit his tongue before adding *you moron*.

A uniformed cop approached him, weapon drawn. This was going to go down as the world's shortest time on bail. He was barely a day out of county. This cop wouldn't believe a thing he said. Playing dumb would at least gain time.

"I just woke up," Jimmy said. "What happened?"

"Just stand still. What's your name?"

"Jim…Michael Quinn. I have ID in my back pocket."

"Slowly take out your wallet. Then sit down, feet crossed at the ankles, and set it down on the ground."

Jimmy followed the familiar instructions. The cop approached and flipped open the wallet. He stared at the driver's license in the plastic window then angled it for a better view in the parking-lot lights. Jimmy knew he looked nothing like Quinn. The cop squinted at it.

It's dark, he thought. *It's hard to see. Fuzzy through the plastic. My head's all bandaged. Just let it go. The picture's me. Just lost a few pounds. Whatever. Please. The picture's me.*

Jimmy's head pounded out a speed-metal bass line that made him close his eyes.

The cop holstered his weapon and handed the wallet back to Jimmy. "Sorry, Mr. Quinn. We're on the lookout for looters."

Jimmy nearly dropped dead with relief. Bad lighting, bad eyesight, mental exhaustion—he didn't care which one he had to thank, so he mentally thanked them all. He put the wallet back in his pocket. "So what happened here?"

"Some nut came into the lobby and started shooting, but he wasn't the only one. It was like homicidal maniacs started coming out of the hospital walls. And not just here. All over town. If you feel well enough, you need to get home. There's a curfew, so stop for any officer who flags you down. You can drive with one arm?"

Jimmy was about to tell him his apartment was only blocks away, then realized the cop had read the Belle Pointe address off the license.

"Sure I can drive. It's not far."

"Well get home and stay home."

"Thank you, Officer."

The cop walked off to check the hospital perimeter. Jimmy stepped into the parking lot like he knew where he was going. He remembered the keys in his pocket. He pulled them out and pressed the Unlock button. A car one row over chirped, and its lights popped on. He approached it and stopped at the trunk.

He won the lottery again. A shining, black BMW M3, a combination of luxury and performance for people about ten tax brackets higher than he'd ever been in. He slid inside and relaxed into the deep leather seats. The engine fired up with a smooth, throaty rumble. He dropped it into gear. The tires chirped with the brake depressed.

Jimmy smiled. This was the best end to a hospital stay he'd ever had. Except for whatever kind of apocalyptic episode the town was going through, but, hey, it worked to his advantage.

He was on a lucky streak at the table Fate had assigned him tonight. He might as well double down on the next bet.

He pulled the BMW out of the parking lot and headed for Belle Pointe.

Chapter Eighteen

The town of Belle Pointe jutted out into Long Island Sound along a rising peninsula that appeared to give Connecticut the finger. Just one road led in past the guardhouse and wound its way north to the coast. Old-growth forest shielded secluded mansions from the main road. Most homes had breathtaking cliffside views of the harbor or the Sound. Private trash pickup, private security and private beaches made this exclusive enclave the favored neighborhood of the ultrarich.

Jimmy crawled the BMW up to the guard shack. The gate was down. The car's windows were smoked, but he'd need to roll them down and expose himself to get past the guard. He spooled up a crock of a story about delivering the BMW from the shop after repairs. Transmission work. Very expensive. The more detailed the lie, the more people believed it. He'd wing explaining his bandages. He hit the window's Down button.

As he coasted to a stop, he passed a laser scanner just before the shack. It painted a red line of light across the side of the car. The gate rose. Inside the guard shack, a gray-haired lady gave him a wave without looking up from her paperback novel.

Jimmy looked over his shoulder at the decal on the lower corner of the rear window. Well, three damn cheers for technology and an elite too self-important to stop for identification. He hit the Up button on his window and punched the accelerator. The rising gate missed the BMW's roof by millimeters.

A mile up the road, he turned left at the address on Michael Quinn's ID. Twin stone lion statues guarded the entrance. He looped up through the woods to an expansive, modernistic mansion. He rounded the lit circular fountain in front and parked beside the front door.

The two-story building was all glass and sharp angles, with a soaring entranceway designed to impress upon arrival. It worked. Jimmy shook his head in wonder. The mahogany front door probably cost more than every stick of furniture in his roach motel of an apartment. He exited the car and approached the brilliantly lit entrance.

A reassuring darkness filled the house's windows. Jimmy tried keys until one fit the lock, and opened the front door. A split second after it opened, he worried an alarm might have been set. The house remained silent. He flicked on the lights and was near blinded by the foyer's dazzling-white marble floor.

Apparently, Michael Quinn's taste bordered on the baroque. Red velvet and gold seemed the house's theme. "Mexican whorehouse" was the first phrase that came to Jimmy's mind. The few incomprehensible, gaudy modern-art paintings didn't help the place at all.

"Beggars can't be choosers," he whispered. Besides, the plunder here was the real prize.

He entered what looked like an office down the hall. Through the open drapes, the enormous picture window framed the harbor lights. He flipped on the light. Everything in the room seemed made of glass and chrome. The tabletops, the desktop, the backs of the chairs. Even the frames around two diplomas on the wall. An oil portrait five feet tall hung on the wall in yet another flashy frame. Based on the borrowed license in Jimmy's pocket, this had to be Quinn himself, positioned so the egotistical bastard could gaze upon his own likeness from the comfort of his desk. Jesus, what a prick.

Behind the glass doors along one wall resided the mother of all alcohol reserves. Bottles of booze he'd only seen in advertising stood shoulder to shoulder, lined up to quench his thirst. Aged scotch, bourbon, vodkas with Cyrillic lettering. Dear God, he'd died and gone to alcoholic heaven. And a little hair of the dog might be what he needed to squash his pounding headache.

He poured himself a glass of Johnny Walker Platinum, aged 18 years, older than most of the kids he'd peddled pot to. He downed the glass in one shot. It burned with sweet fire all the way down. His headache didn't feel better, but the rest of him did. He poured a second glass and slammed it home.

"Hey, who are you?"

Jimmy spun around to face the voice from the doorway. A narrow-faced man in his forties in rough gardener's working clothes stared him down, angry. Jimmy's heart skipped a beat.

He struggled for a moment against the euphoria of the alcohol. Who was he, or who was he supposed to be? He tried to picture the license in the stolen wallet. He saw the face, the same one on the wall. The name came into blurry focus. His brain pounded inside his head.

I'm Michael Quinn, he thought. *That's it, Michael Quinn.*

Before he could say it aloud, the man's face relaxed. "Mr. Quinn, jeez, sorry. I didn't recognize you at first. My eyes must be tired. From my place, I saw the light go on here. We thought you were still in the hospital, so with everything going on and all, I thought it was a thief, you know? I'm so sorry."

Jimmy couldn't believe it. The gardener thought he was Quinn. No, the gardener *knew* he was Quinn. Even with the head bandages, at this range, any employee should know he was an imposter.

Jimmy had mentally sent him the picture of Quinn and the name, and through some Jedi mind trick, the guy was now convinced he was Quinn.

"Yeah," Jimmy said. "The hospital just released me." He held out his empty wrist. "They didn't even remove my ID bracelet. Can you give me a hand with cutting it off?"

He sent a picture of a hospital ID wrapped around his wrist to the gardener's mind. A throbbing pain accompanied the effort.

The gardener nodded and pulled a small knife from his pocket. He flipped it open. At Jimmy's wrist, he grabbed an imaginary bracelet, laid the knife against it and swept the blade upward. The knife even paused part of the way through the stroke, where it would have slowed against the pressure of cutting. The gardener finished the stroke.

Jimmy cut off the image. The pain in his head spooled down to a dull ache.

"Well, thanks there," Jimmy said. "That'll be all."

"Sorry again, sir, for the interruption."

The gardener left. Jimmy let loose the smile he'd been struggling to suppress. This setup was a dream come true. Now he understood why the cop let him walk away. He left that hospital with more than just a cast on his arm. He also got himself a regular superpower, like he was one of the X-Men or something. Maybe it was that knock on the head. Maybe it jarred something special loose. Maybe it was whatever had made his blood run black beneath his skin.

The Johnny Walker and the painkillers joined forces and summoned the deep comfort of sleep. Jimmy staggered over to the couch and collapsed into the thick leather cushions. His broken arm sent a bolt of pain up through his shoulder. He rolled right and rested his back against the couch. He kicked his shoes to the floor. He barely had time to register how uncomfortable he was when he fell fast asleep.

Chapter Nineteen

Two eyefuls of sunrise blasted Jimmy awake well ahead of his usual midday arousal. It took a few moments to remember where he was, but when he did, he smiled.

"Good morning, Michael Quinn," he said.

He rolled upright far too quickly, and his head swam like he'd left it tethered behind on the couch cushions. Pain shot up his left arm as he bumped it against the armrest. His head thrummed underneath his soiled skullcap of bandages. The smile left his face as he remembered how badly damaged he was. His empty stomach rumbled that a meal was damn near a day overdue. The stink of his ripening body told him a shower was in the same category. Food first.

He padded into the kitchen. Light reflecting off the yards of stainless steel made him wince. High-end coffeemakers, brass pans hanging from the ceiling. Quinn had to be a regular Martha Stewart, or have one on the payroll.

Jimmy rummaged around for supplies and found the elixir of life, coffee. He wondered what the hell made these beans "organic" and who in Colombia certified that process. He started a pot. He pulled a box of granola from a cabinet and tore open an end. He flipped on the countertop television and poured granola straight into his mouth. Several chunks missed their mark and bounced on the hardwood floor.

The local news carried a banner that read *Mystery Plague Strikes*. Jimmy's chewing slowed to a near stop as the anchors relayed the growing number of outbreaks across Long Island. Footage rolled of running crowds and burning buildings. He recognized aerial shots of Port Jefferson.

The anchors reiterated what doctors knew about the plague. The living transmitted it through any body fluid: saliva, blood, urine, possibly even tears and sweat. The dead bloated and exploded. When they did, they released an airborne version that infected upon inhalation. The infected manifested sociopathic and often psychotic tendencies. There was no stable timeline between infection, manifestation and death. Sometimes it happened rapidly, sometimes not.

But they did know the symptoms of infection. Darkened veins like having blood poisoning. High fever. Delirium. Red irises. Then sometimes a time of normalcy before the psychosis set in.

At the description of darkened veins, Jimmy checked his right arm. He hadn't dreamed it. His veins looked like they were pumping coal dust. He checked his reflection in the refrigerator. No marks on his face or neck. He looked down through his shirt at his chest. Black veins pulsed beneath his sparse chest hair.

"Son of a bitch!" He threw the box of granola across the room.

Infected. His heart raced, and a dull ache returned to his head. It must have happened at the hospital. One of those exploded bodies he saw on his way out the door had probably infected him while he slept. Damn it. Just when shit gets good, it turns back into shit. Damn story of his life.

He tried to calm himself down. Sure, he was infected. His arm proved that. But he didn't have a fever anymore. He didn't feel psycho. In fact, except for the goddamn headache, he felt better than he ever had.

Speaking of headaches, he really needed to check his head. The bandages felt puffy and oozing. He let the TV continue as background noise and found his way to Michael Quinn's bedroom. The guy knew how to live. The bedroom was bigger than Jimmy's apartment. Twin bathrooms on either side and a walk-in closet full of high-end fashion said Old Mike shared this room with his thankfully absent wife.

The thought crossed Jimmy's mind that if he could convince the gardener he was Quinn, he could probably convince Quinn's hot wife the same thing, at least long enough to get her in and out of bed.

He entered one of the bathrooms. The countertop paraphernalia tagged it as Mrs. Quinn's. He checked the mirror and didn't make it to a bandage inspection.

His irises glowed red.

Not a fire-engine red, but a softer rosy hue. A stranger might not even notice, but with a lifetime of looking at his own brown eyes, Jimmy sure noticed. He also noticed the black veins at the base of his neck. At least his face was clear.

He focused on the bandages around his head. They didn't look promising. Blotches of umber blood and ocher pus stained the gauze. With his good hand, he picked up a tiny pair of scissors from the countertop. From the bottom up, he snipped away at the bandages until he'd cut a slit to the top of his head.

He gripped the edge of the bandages. He pried the corner of the skullcap away from his ear. Dried blood glued the bandage to his head. He tugged a bit and felt needles of pain prickle his scalp. This was going to hurt.

Ah, shit, he thought. It's like doing a Band-Aid, just way bigger. He took a deep breath and ripped.

His head felt like it caught fire. The room turned white. He screamed an embarrassing, high-pitched shriek and sagged against the counter.

The pain abated. He opened his eyes. His head looked like it belonged in a monster movie. His hair was gone. He noticed that no stubble had sprouted the last two days. He resigned himself to the idea that it never would. Thick, red wounds crisscrossed his head, stitched together with black thread and in some places metal staples. The stitching looked like it barely contained the raw, crimson valleys of damaged skin. Crusts of dried, yellow pus lay here and there. He turned the left side of his head toward the mirror. One swollen spot along an incision by his left ear looked like an enormous zit with a head of pus just below the skin's surface. That couldn't be good.

He flipped open the tiny scissors, took another deep breath and jabbed the pustule. Pain pieced all the way into his skull. The pustule exploded with enough force to splatter the mirror. Tiny, black flecks flinched inside the yellow ooze as it dribbled down the mirror and across Jimmy's reflection.

He rinsed his head, every drop of water a pinprick of pain, then patted it dry. He didn't leave any blood on the towel, which he took as good news, especially since he didn't have any fresh bandages. Even if he did, he wasn't going to wind them around his head one-handed. He was going to have to face the world as part Frankenstein's monster, though, the way the rest of the world was looking, he'd probably fit right in.

Then again, what would it matter? He'd be making people see him as Michael Quinn, no matter what shape his head was in. But he'd need to see that person first, implant that hypnotic suggestion. What if there were more than one or if the person snuck up on him?

Suddenly, he was less worried about his head and more worried about his arms. His injuries might garner sympathy, but his infection might get him killed. He imagined the uninfected would start killing the infected first and pondering cures later.

He rifled through a few drawers until he found makeup. A layer of foundation and an assortment of powders later, he'd covered his uncast arm against discovery by casual inspection. That would be a start.

He opted to finish dressing out of Michael's side of the room.

A quick ransacking of Quinn's study yielded Jimmy a handsome return. Like all rich bastards, he had a stash of cash in one drawer, close to ten thousand bucks, by Jimmy's quick estimate. A printed itinerary on the desk listed the flight times and Miami hotel for Katie Quinn, confirming the trophy wife's location. The laptop on the desk was password protected, with the password taped right under the keypad. His financial sites were conveniently bookmarked. The guy had millions. Or now Jimmy had. Assuming the missus wasn't going to pop back up from Florida—and who would while this infection thing raged? Jimmy would make this a comfortable place to stay for as long as he could.

First, he wanted to put his newfound superpower to good use, at least a good use for him. He had a long list of people who deserved some payback, people who'd kicked him while he was down. They needed to be on the receiving end of a bit of that. His broken arm demanded one person rise to the top of that list.

He picked up the phone on the desk and dialed. His bookie answered.

"Ray-Ray, it's Jimmy Wade… Yeah, well I'm out of the hospital. Noticed you didn't send flowers… Yeah, do me a favor. Tell Mozelle I have his money. He can pick it up at my apartment."

Jimmy hung up. The funny part was he really did have Mozelle's money, and more. Mozelle wouldn't see a dime of it, though. Mozelle would be getting something ever more special.

Chapter Twenty

Jimmy rubbed his sweating palms together as he waited. The plan seemed a lot better from the comfort and distance of Quinn's Belle Pointe retreat. Now, sitting in the shadows of his dingy apartment, Jimmy second-guessed his previously brilliant idea. He'd fooled the gardener, and he'd probably fooled the cop. That really wasn't much of a track record. And he was certain the penalty for failure here would be death.

He shifted on his cheap vinyl recliner. The duct tape on the armrest stuck to his cast and made a ripping sound as he moved. Daylight only lit the one-room apartment outside his recliner's shaded alcove.

A heavy knock at the door broke the silence.

"It's open," Jimmy said. His voice cracked.

The door swung open. K-Dogg stood alone in the hallway and checked the apartment.

Jimmy hadn't expected Mozelle himself to collect. He'd send K-Dogg instead. So far, so good.

"I'm back here," Jimmy said.

K-Dogg squinted at the shadow. "You think you gonna make me walk all the goddamn way there? I oughta break your other damn arm."

Jimmy concentrated on the one picture he wanted K-Dogg to see, and sent it out. Pain rippled back and forth across his brain. K-Dogg entered the apartment. Jimmy stood and stepped out of the shadows.

K-Dogg saw him, stopped in the center of the room and looked confused. Then his expression turned scared and apologetic.

"Mr. Mozelle? What are you doing?"

Jimmy closed his eyes. "I told you to come here."

"Yeah, to collect from that asswipe Wade."

"No, to pick me up and bring me back to the warehouse."

"No, I remember—"

Jimmy sent out a mental audiotape of an imaginary conversation between Mozelle and K-Dogg.

"Yeah," K-Dogg said, "I'm here to pick you up, to take you back to the warehouse."

"Then what are we waiting for?"

"Nothing, sir."

Jimmy followed K-Dogg back to Mozelle's big, black SUV. He embedded the false memory of K-Dogg's conversation with Mozelle even deeper as they walked. He added a warning about Jimmy Wade, about how dangerous he was, how crazy.

Jimmy slid into the backseat. His last trip here had been rife with terror. This time he was thrilled.

His enthusiasm melted a bit as he watched suburban Long Island roll by outside the SUV's window. Traffic was light. Looting had spread like herpes. Cops stood uneasy watches in patrol cars parked by banks and pharmacies. The world outside the Belle Pointe enclave had descended into disaster damn fast.

By the time they arrived at the warehouse, K-Dogg was on edge with a healthy dose of Wade-implanted paranoia. They left the vehicle.

"Wait here outside," Jimmy said as he entered the warehouse.

Jimmy's pace slowed as he passed rows of crates and boxes. His hands began to shake. The pain and terror of his last experience here threatened to return and overwhelm him. He clasped his hands together and took a deep breath. This time, he'd be the one in control.

Mozelle sat in his swivel chair, a fresh cigar shoved in the corner of his mouth. One of his steroid-abusing bodybuilders in a white muscle shirt stood to one side. The thug wore his black hair in a retarded sumo-style topknot. Mozelle looked up from his laptop screen. He raised his head to look imposing, an impossible feat with his receding chin.

"Well, well. Look what the cat dragged in. I sent K-Dogg to get your money, not you."

"I decided you rated a personal delivery."

Mozelle pulled his cigar from his mouth and pointed at Jimmy's misshapen head. "I ain't sure that's the best look for you. And what happened to your arm? Had an accident?"

Jimmy bit his lip. "Yeah, it's dangerous out there."

Jimmy turned to the Neanderthal at the side of the desk. He sent him a picture of a swarm of tarantulas crawling up his legs.

The goon's eyes went wide. He screamed in fear and swept his hands up and down the legs of his pants to scatter the invisible spiders' advance.

Jimmy's brain felt a size too big for his skull. He tweaked the hallucination so the creatures covered Mozelle, the table and the upper half of the room.

"What the hell's wrong with you?" Mozelle asked his bodyguard.

The bodyguard screamed again and ran out a side door. Jimmy wondered how long he could keep the connection going, how far he could send his psychohypnotic suggestion. He severed the link. The pain in his head eased. Bigger fish to fry.

"It's just you and me, Mozelle," Jimmy said.

Mozelle pulled a flat-black 9 mm from his desk drawer. He pointed it at Jimmy. "Not for long, jackass."

"That's my plan."

K-Dogg ran in through the front door. "What's all the screaming about?"

Jimmy painted K-Dogg a mirror-image switch. Jimmy stood there as Mozelle. Mozelle sat at the desk, gun in hand looking like Jimmy.

"Look out!" Jimmy yelled. "Wade's got a gun!"

Mozelle looked confused. He turned to K-Dogg. His pistol wandered to follow his gaze. K-Dogg pulled a gun from the small of his back and took a fast bead on Mozelle. He fired three shots in quick succession. Mozelle's chest opened up like three blooming roses. The impact blew his rolling chair back from the desk. His pistol clattered against the concrete floor. He slumped backward in the chair, arms out to his side, dead still.

The gunshots drew Mr. Top Knot back in through the side door. Jimmy's head felt like it was going to explode. He cut the Mozelle/Jimmy images and painted the returning thug like a cop, in K-Dogg's mind. K-Dogg ripped two more rounds into his fellow bodyguard. Top Knot dropped to the floor like a sack of rocks.

Jimmy snapped off K-Dogg's suggestion. The throbbing pain in his head eased. He nearly dropped to his knees in relief. K-Dogg looked from Mozelle to the bodyguard and back in complete confusion.

"What the hell…"

Jimmy's plan to have K-Dogg kill Mozelle and then get his memory wiped had spun a bit out of control. Then another, bolder idea stepped up to the plate.

Jimmy took a deep breath and summoned up one more scenario in his head. Top Knot killed Mozelle, so K-Dogg killed Top Knot. The guy was probably crazy from the plague. He watched K-Dogg's look of bewilderment as once again what he thought had been true was replaced by yet another alternate version. Jimmy patted K-Dogg on the back.

"You saved my life, dude. Good work."

K-Dogg looked around the room like he'd just awakened from a dream.

Jimmy walked over behind Mozelle's desk. He rolled the corpse aside. The heel of his shoe crushed Mozelle's fallen cigar. He sent K-Dogg a stream of reinforcing false memories as he spoke.

"It was always Mozelle's plan that I succeed him, so no point in waiting, unless you have any objections."

The images of Jimmy Wade, ruthless killer, had apparently done their job in K-Dogg's confused mind. "No, no, sir."

Jimmy pointed a thumb at Top Knot on the floor. "Let's clean up this mess." He kicked Mozelle's chair in Top Knot's direction. "Get rid of these bodies."

"The usual way?"

"Yeah, sure." *Whatever that meant.*

K-Dogg slung Top Knot over his shoulder with impressive ease and took him to another part of the warehouse.

Jimmy slid Mozelle's laptop closer. He updated the password to EATMEMOZELLE. He flashed through spreadsheets and email. Mozelle had a network of bookies that K-Dogg and a few other muscleheads collected from. The business nearly ran itself. Good work if you could get it. And Jimmy just got it.

He sagged against the corner of the desk. His brain felt like it was going to explode. He'd learned a few things here. Sending suggestions hurt like a son of a bitch, though he was pretty sure he could embed more complex memories today than he could with the gardener and cop yesterday. He was also certain that he could only tune in to one person at a time. For example, he could not have simultaneously convinced Mozelle and K-Dogg that the other was a mountain lion.

But he didn't need to. With the right false memories and background information, people would function on autopilot. K-Dogg and company follow the leader. Once convinced Jimmy was the leader, all Jimmy had to do was direct the wolf pack.

Jimmy smiled at his last twenty-four hours. He'd acquired a nice house, a new identity and a high-paying job. The world might be going to hell, but everything in his vicinity was coming up Jimmy.

Chapter Twenty-One

The explosion jolted Dr. Samuel Bradshaw out of a sound sleep. He jumped from his cot and ran to the expansive panoramic window at JFK's former gate C70. The faint dawn light illuminated a tiny cloud rising from the earth outside the western perimeter fence. Inside the perimeter, a Humvee raced to the site like a workman running to plug a leak in a dam.

"Infiltrator," said a soldier who stood outside the window. The night-shift guard looked a bit weary. "We laid a minefield around the perimeter yesterday. Put up big warning signs. The infected don't seem to care. Boom. Splat. Two went up on the east side last night."

"How do you know they were infected?" Samuel asked.

"Uninfected people aren't crazy enough to walk into a minefield."

The soldier walked off to continue his rounds.

The terminal's central shops were closed and locked, save the fast-food location that had been converted into a makeshift mess facility. The rest of the terminal had been stripped near bare, seats unbolted and dumped outside in a pile on the tarmac, with only the booth tables left as places to sit and eat. With no window treatments, the sunrise would awaken every one of the dozens here. No problem there. They all had plenty to do.

Outside, shivering soldiers in shorts and T-shirts assembled on the Terminal 4 ramp in the dusky chill. All wore surgical masks. They expanded their ranks into a wide box formation and began to chant-count as a sergeant led them in exercises. Across the ramp, four pilots in olive-drab flight suits preflighted two attack helicopters.

Samuel noted that it was all army outside and nearly all civilian inside. From what he could gather last night, doctors, nurses and technicians filled this terminal. The military had taken over Terminals 4 through 8, the ones closest to the perimeter. However, his terminal had been organized with military efficiency. The restrooms were clean, MREs and bottled water sat stacked by the former souvenir shop, cots and bedding were abundant.

Stacks of clean scrubs lay ready for use. Vanessa hadn't exaggerated when she said the CDC had made contingency plans.

The smell of percolating java drifted through the terminal. Others started to stir under the twin alarm clocks of the rising sun's glare and the summoning scent of coffee. Deep within the fast-food shop, lights clicked on and metal clattered against metal. Samuel's first day at the Kennedy compound began.

By 8:00 a.m., he'd seen his new workspace. The Terminal 2 wing had been cleared and turned into a sealable lab stocked with first-class equipment. One by one, he met the team he was to lead—several younger doctors and three times as many support technicians. Everyone seemed half his age or less. They brimmed with unbridled motivation. If he'd had this crew and equipment in his African polio work, he marveled to think what he could have accomplished.

Vanessa joined the group in the makeshift lab. The room went silent.

"With Dr. Bradshaw joining us," she started, "this will be the last morning meeting I personally lead. My old *bosi daktari* will lead you from here. All of you are Long Islanders, volunteers working to cure friends and families. About a third of you are also new today, so let me start with what we've learned so far, based on our findings and limited research from Atlanta. The disease is viral. Experimental transmission rates through even trace body fluids have a near 99-percent rate."

A few team members gasped. Samuel cursed to himself. Nothing he'd ever worked with had been that communicable.

"Worse, so far we've left it on smooth, nonporous surfaces like marble, and it hasn't died yet. After days.

"Atlanta confirms that the closest pathogen to this is polio. That's Dr. Bradshaw's area of expertise, and why I'm so thrilled to have him here. Dr. Petty, last night you were summarizing our case studies. Your results?"

A young, skinny man in oversized scrubs adjusted his black-plastic glasses and read from an iPad. "The onset infection presents as sepsis, with darkened veins and a high fever. This initial stage may last minutes or days; it may spread quickly or perhaps stay dormant. We aren't sure." He sighed. "In fact, the really maddening thing about the disease is the varying impact it has after infection. I can't derive a trend. Each person's reaction is different. Especially in the window between the initial physical manifestation and the final stage of raging bloodlust. Some patients seem to recover and mentally blossom in the interlude."

Samuel remembered Gwen had begun writing poetry again before she'd gone mad.

"The variety of reported activities is pretty broad," Dr. Petty continued. "Anecdotally, people claim that the virus stimulates whatever section of the victim's brain was already gifted. But that's wholly subjective."

"How long does that phase last?" one of the technicians asked.

"If it happens, from minutes to hours," Dr. Petty said. "But the middle stage of infection is always the same. A kind of furious, sociopathic mental state accompanied by enormous strength. During Stage 3, the mind of the infected still hums along. Rational thought, the ability to plan and technical skills are all still working. The infected don't just blindly want to kill others, they plan to kill others."

He swiped through a few pages on the iPad. "Here, a police officer reloaded her weapon and hit her targets. In another instance, a construction worker drove his bulldozer through several buildings. The infected are the most dangerous kind of crazy."

This dovetailed with what Samuel had seen with Brenda. She'd been livid with homicidal rage, but rational in her assault. Perhaps the virus hadn't restored her legs as he'd thought. It may just have hypercharged what little muscle control she had left. He wouldn't know until he could examine her.

He caught himself thinking of Brenda in such a detached, clinical way. Was this a defense mechanism of his subconscious? He shook the thoughts from his head and mentally brought himself back to the meeting.

"Eventually the insanity wins out," Dr. Petty said. "Again, there's no telling how long that will take. At Stage 4, the bloodlust conquers reason, and the infected are just like wild animals. The virus itself isn't fatal, but the violence at this stage often is."

"Are there any reports of physically regenerative side effects," Samuel asked, "along with the mental ones?"

Dr. Petty shook his head. "No."

"Would that support your theories?" Vanessa asked.

Theories? A terrifying inadequacy bubbled up inside of him. They expected him to already have theories?

"I'm just asking questions, checking out paths we might otherwise ignore, even if they go nowhere."

Dr. Petty raised an eyebrow in an inquisitive arch and then continued reading.

"The Stage 3 and 4 infected bite. A lot. It's as if the virus knows that's a direct route to propagation, and drives the person to it. It also explains the drive for violent contact, where blood could mix with blood."

"What do we know about Stage 5?" Samuel asked. "After they die and their body explodes?"

A petite woman with dark hair swept into a bun raised a hand halfway in the air. "I'm Dr. Reed. I've been working on that. When body temperature drops, the virus undergoes a metamorphosis into an airborne spore. That mode stays toxic for hours, days depending on conditions. In Stages 3 and 4, the transmissibility rate is based on how much crazy the infected can spread around, how many people they can contact. At Stage 5, the transmissibility rate goes exponential."

"St. Luke's was full of exploded bodies," Samuel said.

Dr. Reed flipped through some pages on a legal pad. "I think that was from artificial resuscitation. The charge from a set of paddles to attempt to restart the heart might put the virus in hyperdrive. It's definitely stimulated, not destroyed, by electricity."

Samuel wrung his hands. Could they seriously tell every physician on Long Island to not cardiostimulate a patient whose heart stopped? Would doctors accept a patient's death, rather than risk stimulating an early onset of the virus?

"I'm leaving the team in your hands, Dr. Bradshaw," Vanessa said. "For the sake of safety, as of midnight last night, all of Atlanta's samples have been destroyed. The risk of infection has to be kept to the island. Atlanta will continue to track the disease and run the data. But when it comes to the research, it's all on you people in Terminal Two now."

She paused. "One last thing. A temporary security measure is about to be announced. All bridges, tunnels and ferries exiting Long Island are about to be closed. Inbound lanes will still operate with suspended tolls, but anyone crossing back to Long Island will not be permitted to leave the quarantine zone. I've made arrangements for your immediate families to join us here at JFK after a brief isolation time and a medical exam outside the perimeter."

The group let out a slow exhale.

Quarantine zone? The entire island? Samuel had tried and failed to set up small quarantine zones in rural areas, a hamlet or a few blocks of a bigger town. Keeping people out wasn't too hard when word got around, but keeping people in was damn near impossible. Quarantining Long Island, with over seven million people on it? How could it be done?

"So your work is now even more important," Vanessa said. "Until you have an answer, this island won't integrate back into the rest of society."

She left the room. All eyes went to Samuel. It felt as if a great weight accompanied them.

"All right," he said. "Yesterday, I brought in samples from St. Luke's Patient Zero. Let's compare that strain to something from today and see where this thing is going. Most of you have been in here, but I've been out there. It's not pretty, and if we don't get a solution going, it's going to turn grim in a hurry. Seven million people depend on you."

The groups dissolved back to their workstations. Samuel stepped over to the window and stared out across the deserted runways. He closed his eyes and rubbed his temples.

Seven million people did depend on all of them, but one person depended just on Samuel. He needed a vaccine for the masses, but he needed a cure for Brenda, and by some miracle, before she crossed into Stage 4 and complete insanity.

Chapter Twenty-Two

Melanie's morning had been frighteningly normal in many respects. Aiden was up and dressed at his normal time. She brewed coffee. He counted his cereal squares. She needed those little bits of normal.

Everything else under this thin, fragile surface was completely sideways. Outside the condo complex, sirens were more common than ever, audio reminders that the unseen world beyond the wall wasn't what it used to be. All the local stations had gone to twenty-four-hour news coverage, and all the news was grim. She turned it off after about three minutes.

By some stroke of luck, she'd gotten through to Charles's cell phone from hers. Charles had been up all night trading futures on foreign markets. He promised to be home tonight. That would make everything better.

She tapped into her Socialize network long enough to see it reeked of panic. Mothers relayed rumors as if they were facts. Conversation chains covered pages. Everyone had nightmarish stories to share.

But when Melanie scanned these stories, she noticed that none of the terrible tales included encounters with the infected. They were all about encounters with the panicked populace, like her wild ride back home from Aiden's school. Even the pyromaniac kids at the school weren't infected, just displaying the dysfunction that got them into Brock Academy.

Maybe things weren't as bad around her area as they were in some of the hot spots, like Port Jefferson. Perhaps the disease had burned itself out. She forced on a little smile and tried to believe.

Whatever was going on, she was going to have to get some food. Today was her normal shopping day, so the pantry was pretty bare except for the stray cans of odd vegetables that seemed to have been there since before Aiden was born. Charles would be home soon and they'd need food for three. Plus, it seemed like a good idea to lay in a reserve. She convinced herself that the knee-jerk public panic of yesterday had probably blown over.

"Aiden!" she called. "We're going shopping."

She pulled her car up to the Cedar Knoll gate. Mickey the plumber stood guard with Paul's rifle. He tapped on her window and she rolled it down.

"You really need to go out there?" he asked.

The view of the street was narrow through the gate's bars, but what she could see looked calm, near deserted. It seemed people were following the government's advice and staying home.

"Just a quick trip for food," she said.

He shook his head, stepped away and pressed the remote control. The gate lurched to the right. Halfway across, it stopped, made a loud grinding noise and then fully opened.

"Here we go," she said, more to herself than Aiden.

She pulled out and joined a few other cars on the street. Early Sunday-morning traffic during Friday-morning rush hour instilled an apocalyptic creepiness. A few police cruisers passed by on patrol. The officers gave her long, hard looks through their windshields.

She turned down the next street. The King Kullen parking lot was nearly full. Two tractor trailers butted up against the dock doors at the building's side, probably restocking after yesterday's sell-off. She found a spot at the end of a row. A cop leaned against the hood of a police cruiser parked front and center.

Several people stood in line outside the main door. A man exited, pulled his bags from his shopping cart and passed the cart to the woman next in line.

Melanie sighed with relief at the sight of this orderly process. Yesterday's panic seemed to have subsided. Rational thought, thank God, had prevailed.

Aiden was out of the car as soon as she shut down the ignition. He liked the supermarket. The well-marked aisles, the rows of uniform cans and boxes, the repetitive shopping pattern always starting on aisle 1. It all appealed to his need for order and familiarity.

Melanie enjoyed the little retail oasis. This location had gone upscale recently and always had organic produce. Employees cooked free samples. She'd brought her reusable shopping bags.

A few minutes' wait later, the cart exchange ritual made it to them. She tossed her bags in the foldout seat, and they entered the store. The usual treacle of music came from the ceiling speakers, but an air of tension stretched amongst the shoppers. None shopped at the usual languid, browsing pace. All moved like they had a mission in mind.

"A reminder, shoppers," a voice said from the ceiling speakers, "there's a fifty-dollar limit, and no more than two of any specific item."

Two women passed Melanie, and she caught part of their conversation.

"…and they had to put that item limit on. People were hoarding, items like diapers and baby formula. People without babies! They were waiting for a black market to start."

The idea of people's first thought being profit made Melanie furious and disgusted. Then she realized that her husband wasn't doing anything much better. He was just doing it at a higher level and reaping a higher reward.

Aiden followed her at his regular side of the cart, hands shoved in his pockets, eyes glued to the floor. Melanie turned to skip aisle 1, unwilling to burn any of her fifty-dollar limit on the snack-food items there.

Aiden grabbed the cart. He froze in place. He let loose a low, rumbling moan. He started a rapid rock from the waist up. Other shoppers backed away.

"Aiden honey, no, we don't need anything in that aisle. We just need a few things, and people are waiting to get in."

The pitch of Aiden's cry increased. He pulled the cart back toward aisle 1.

These were the times when the autism made her boil. Aiden's wake-up rituals, his food fixations, the communication difficulties—all of these she could plan for and manage around. But sometimes she had to do the simplest thing differently, just a quick diversion that in preparenting days she would not have thought twice about, or something like this, where speed was critical. Aiden's disorder turned it into a time-sucking production. She usually caught herself before she snapped and, either way, always felt guilty afterwards. This time she caught herself. She steered the cart to the right.

"Okay, up aisle one we go. But quickly!"

She pushed the cart forward at a brisk pace, steering around other shoppers. Aiden kept up alongside, hands back deep in his pockets. Melanie formed a mental list of what they needed. Fresh food topped the chart, though canned options were cheaper and more stable. She was surprised to see the huge gaps in the snack-food facings. Seriously? That's what people stock up on? Potato chips?

The third aisle ended at dairy. She grabbed one of the last gallons of milk. On the way up the next aisle she passed an employee restocking canned goods. He was about sixteen, pimples protruding through a sparse little beard. He shot her a jittery, quick inspection and went back to filling the shelf.

She felt sorry for the stock boy for letting those news reports get him so paranoid.

She selected some canned tuna and a smattering of vegetables Aiden could tolerate. The aisle ended at the checkout stands. Four of the five were open, none staffed by the usual distracted teen girls. Department managers ran the registers.

A tall, old man at the closest register unloaded three tins of canned ham. Melanie recognized him by sight, one of the unnamed regulars. His long, gray hair, usually brushed straight back and sprayed stiffly into place, swept down across the right side of his face. The cuffs of his long-sleeved shirt hung unbuttoned and flapped with each trip from his cart to the register conveyor.

The meat department manager, a rotund fellow that looked every inch the part, watched from the register. His pristine butcher's whites made him look a lot like the Pillsbury Doughboy.

"Sorry, sir, but there's a limit of two on any item," he said.

"Screw your goddamn rules," the old man said without looking up from unloading his cart.

The manager's face reddened in frustration. He reached out for one of the canned hams.

"Sir, I'll just set it aside here and have one of the girls—"

In a flash, the old man whipped a rusty box cutter from his shirt pocket. He snapped it open and pinned the manager's wrist to the conveyor with his free hand. The old man swept the blade into and up the manager's exposed forearm. It rent the skin and revealed bright-red muscle.

The next woman in line screamed. The manager's hand went limp and he stared in shock at his splayed skin. Blood ran onto the conveyor like spilled tomato soup. The old man flipped the blade in his hand and made a backhanded slash at the manager's throat.

At first it appeared the old man missed. Then a thin, red line appeared across the manager's thick neck. Blood dripped and then poured from the widening gash. It ran down and stained the front of his whites like a wide, cherry bib. He gagged and raised his free hand to the wound.

The old man spun to face the crowd in the store, who by now stared at the scene in disbelief. The old man raised the wet, crimson knife above his head. His sleeve slid down and exposed a thin arm crisscrossed with black veins. His red eyes had the look of the crazed.

"Anyone else say I can't have my goddamn ham?"

The woman next in line fainted. The other managers rushed to the meat manager as he dropped to the floor like dead weight. Screams filled the air and shoppers ran in all directions, most straight past the open registers, with their carts.

Throughout the store, the human spirit broke. The remaining shoppers went wild, cramming their carts with whatever was nearby. The sounds of a scuffle broke out several aisles over.

Aiden crouched down between the cart and a display of canned spaghetti. He rocked on his tiptoes, hands over his ears.

Melanie gripped the cart's handle. She wanted out of this chaos. She wanted her son out of this chaos. She still needed food, the food here at the tip of her fingers. But she couldn't join this melee stealing from the store she loved, from the owner she knew.

But as infectious as the disease outside the store was, the panic inside was worse. It twisted itself around her brain and squeezed. Her adrenaline surged, her heart raced. She surrendered to anxiety's call. She whipped open her recycled bags and swept so many cans of who knows what into them that the bags threatened to burst. She clean-jerked the sacks off the ground with both hands.

"Aiden! We're going. Now!"

Aiden sprang to his feet. But instead of running straight through the bank of registers, he did a U-turn. He ran up aisle 4, a tiny sparrow fighting the jet stream of escaping humanity.

"Aiden! No!"

He had to finish the store route. She followed him. The bulging bags weighed down her arms and threw her off-balance. She barely kept her son in sight. Her bags bounced off carts racing in the opposite direction. One enormous fleeing patron shoved her back into a display of paper towels.

With one aisle down and two to go, she swung around and joined the flow towards the big glass windows at the store's front. A traffic jam of carts blocked the exit. The cop outside noticed the commotion and headed to the front door. No sooner had he left his cruiser than a shirtless man with a back full of bulging, black veins jumped in the front seat and slammed the door. The cop whirled around and sprinted for his car. The cruiser's rear tires spun a cloud of white smoke, and the car blasted away through the parking lot.

The cop stopped running. He reached for the mic at his shoulder. A man in an old camouflage army coat casually walked up behind them. He pulled out a .45 revolver and shot the cop in the back of the head. The muzzle blast blew the officer's hat off and the bullet exited through his face in a spray of blood and brains. The officer dropped to the ground face-first. The attacker reached down, pulled the cop's gun and TASER from his belt, and walked off, calm as if he'd scooped up a bit of trash from the lot.

The gunshots raised a new, higher scream inside the store. More people surged for the exit. A huge can of beans crashed through one of the big glass windows, and the crowd surged through the opening.

The aisles were nearly empty save a few slow looters. Melanie turned and chased Aiden up the next-to-last aisle. She slid around the corner a foot behind him at the turn for the last aisle.

A beefy black man with an inside-out T-shirt and sagging denim pants straddled three cases of beer on the floor. He held an aluminum bat up over his shoulder like he was waiting for a pitch. Blood ran down from the tip to the handle and across his dark-veined hands, as if it bonded him to the weapon. At his feet lay a lifeless corpse in a leather coat, a slick of brains and blood beneath his smashed head. The batter's bright-red eyes narrowed as he saw Aiden coming at a run.

"Now you think you gonna take my damn beer, kid? Nobody taking my damn beer."

"Aiden!" Melanie screamed.

Aiden didn't react, not to his mother's cry, not to the killer's threat, not to the gruesome corpse on the white linoleum. He just ran straight down the aisle to finish the route and use the door beyond. He closed with the murderous batter. Melanie shrieked and chased him, her heart pounding with fear.

The infected man raised his weapon high and stepped into the swing like he was going for the fences. Aiden's head entered his strike zone. The bat came around with a whoosh.

Aiden's heel squished a chunk of brain. He slipped and fell backwards. Like a perfect sinker pitch, his head dropped just below the bat's arc, and the killer missed his target. His backswing smashed the glass cooler case behind him. Aiden landed on his back in the puddle of blood with a thick splat.

Melanie charged, every watt of maternal protective instinct burning bright. Before the killer could react to his miss, she swung the heavy bag of cans up and around like an underhand pitch. It caught the man under the chin and lifted him off the floor. The bag split. Cans sprayed like hail. The batter's head snapped back with a crack. His bat flew down the aisle. He landed on his back, still.

Melanie turned to her son, but Aiden was already up on his feet. He passed her, hell-bent for the front of the store. Blood soaked the back of his shirt through to his skin. He'd scooped up the bat and now dragged it behind him.

"Aiden!" She followed him.

The front of the store was deserted. A pile of shopping carts clogged the exit, and jammed open the automatic doors. Aiden stopped short of the train wreck and stared. He started to wail.

Melanie knew he was lost. One way in, one way around, one way out. As far as his coping mechanism was concerned, no other escape existed. Melanie stopped in front of the shattered window.

"Aiden honey, this way. We can go out this way."

A gridlock of escaping cars filled the parking lot. Bystanders on the street pointed with great excitement at the store then headed for it at a run. The looting she'd just seen was going to be child's play compared to what was coming.

"Aiden! It's blocked. Hurry, this way!"

Aiden rocked back and forth. Melanie's blood pressure spiked.

"Goddamn it, Aiden, now!" she screamed.

Aiden shuddered and then ran to her. She led him through the smashed window. They ran for the car. A crowd surged past them to the store.

Melanie realized she still gripped the shredded empty bag she'd used to deck the killer. She let it flutter to the ground behind her and grabbed her car keys. She chirped the locks open. They practically dove into the car from both sides. She hit the Lock button.

Encased in steel and glass, she regained a small sense of security. Insulation muffled the sounds of the looters. The familiar smell of the Febreze she used to freshen the seats filled her head. She exhaled and realized she'd been holding her breath.

Her son sat in the seat behind her. He clutched the bat across his chest, hands up and crossed to opposite shoulders. The upright handle tapped the door glass in time with his short, rapid rocking. He'd locked his seat belt. Blood stained the upholstery of the seatback behind him.

"We're okay, honey. We're okay. We're going home now. Everything's going to be all right."

She started up the Ford. Something loud crashed inside the supermarket. The street outside the market was clear. She dropped the car in reverse and punched the gas pedal. The car rocketed backwards out of the lot, across the curb and into the street. She screeched to a semi-stop, threw the car into drive. She floored the accelerator. The tires chirped, and she headed for home. A siren wailed a few streets over.

She didn't even check the rearview mirror. Cops giving traffic tickets were a thing of the past, and might be for a very long time.

Chapter Twenty-Three

Melanie pulled into the Cedar Knoll driveway. Mickey gave her a frustratingly long visual inspection, as if he hadn't just seen her leave. She pounded the Ford's horn. Mickey shot her an irritated look and hit his remote. The gate rumbled and shuddered open. She drove in faster than she'd ever dared before.

When she parked the car, Aiden didn't get out with her. The acts were almost always simultaneous, if Aiden didn't actually beat her to the front door and the familiarity of home.

Melanie opened his door from the outside. He sat clutching the bat across his chest. He stared straight ahead.

"C'mon, honey," she said. "It's safe here. We have a wall, a gate and a locked door on our condo."

Touching him would be out of the question, but she thought she could probably slip the bat out of his arms. She reached up and grabbed the handle.

Aiden wailed and jerked the handle back against the doorframe. Melanie yanked her hand away just in time to miss having it crushed. Aiden popped off his seat belt and scrambled past her. He cradled the bat like a baby and did a quickstep version of his odd, stilted walk to the front door.

The seat he left behind carried a bloody stain the perfect shape of Aiden's back.

Melanie remembered the transmission method for this disease. Any body fluids.

She ran to the front door. "Aiden take off that shirt for Mommy before we go inside. It's dirty."

Aiden didn't move. He gripped the bat so tightly that his knuckles turned white.

"Aiden, you have to get rid of that shirt. It may make you sick. Like the man in the store. Then we'll go inside and get clean."

Aiden slipped the bat down between his legs. Melanie had to stop herself from yanking it away. There was blood on that as well. Damn it. Well, one thing at a time.

Aiden pulled his shirt off over his head. Blood smeared his back in a wide, wine-colored stain. He dropped the shirt on the ground and picked up the bat again. Melanie opened the front door.

"Right to the shower, now."

Aiden went straight to the bathroom. He closed the door behind him, and the shower water began to run.

Melanie tucked the top of her shoe under the shirt and flicked it onto the grass. Was the blood from the victim, not the bat-swinging lunatic? Was the victim even infected? Did any of it get on her shoe? How long would it stay toxic? Her paranoia grew. She'd clobbered the wild man with that sack of cans. Had any of his blood or spit or sweat touched her? How much did it take to get infected?

She took a deep breath, stepped inside and locked the door. She couldn't let herself panic. Even a common cold didn't pass from person to person that easily. She couldn't lose it now. She was home safe, just like she'd told her son.

One shower later, Aiden was in a clean set of clothes. He'd set the bat by the front door. He occupied himself in front of the television where a DVD had blessedly replaced the never-ending stream of bad news. Melanie called Charles.

The background office chaos still reigned as he answered.

"Charles, thank God. When are you coming home?"

"After the markets close and we evaluate our positions. I'll be home before eight."

"Eight? Can't you get home earlier than that? There was a riot at King Kullen. Aiden was almost killed."

"Aiden? Why isn't he in school?"

"The schools are closed! Remember? I had to pick him up early yesterday?"

"Right, right. I remember. Closed like the state schools." His voice became muffled as he ordered someone to make a transaction with Purina stock. "Okay, Mel, look, I'll get home as soon as I can. I cleared a month's salary in four hours today. This panic is a boon! Can you check that my pinstripe suit is back from the cleaners? We have big meetings tomorrow, and that's my most conservative one."

"Uh, sure. You know that —"

"Great, I gotta go. See you tonight."

The line went dead. She stared at her phone. The cleaners? Didn't he realize what was going on here? People were killing each other over cases of beer and canned ham. What difference did dry cleaning make?

She wasn't about to go to the dry cleaners. She wasn't driving her car through that gate again without Charles at her side.

That reminded her that the backseat of the car remained a toxic stew of someone else's blood. Who knew how infectious that could be?

She checked that Aiden was still enthralled by the television. She grabbed two yellow gloves from under the kitchen sink, a green scratch pad and a gallon of bleach from the laundry room.

When she got outside, the faint smell of something burning seem to drift on the air. Not the comforting smell of wood in a fireplace, but the sharper smell of melting plastics and blazing gasoline. Smoke rose over the condo wall from about a mile away. The volunteer fire department's alarm sounded. She wondered if they would answer the call.

She threw open the back door of the car. At closer inspection, the bloodstain on the seat had much more definition, the outline of her son's small back for certain, but also his shoulders and arms down to midbicep. The same impression he left on his bed each morning. Then, it was an afterimage of his peaceful rest. Now, it was the ghost of the near-fatal supermarket encounter.

A chill ran up her spine. What if the burgundy blot wasn't an afterimage, but a precognition, a harbinger of worse things to come for Aiden? The stain seemed to seethe with the virus, to bubble and steam and prophesize her son's inclusion in the psychotic world of the infected.

She pulled on her yellow gloves and unscrewed the bottle of bleach. She splashed it on the cloth seatback, as if beating back the virus's advance. Unsatisfied, she upended the bottle and poured. She wanted to hear the virus scream in agony beneath the disinfecting waterfall. Bleach puddled on the seat bottom.

She tossed the half-full bottle aside and grabbed the scratch pad with both hands. Bending in, she dug at the stain, scrubbing hard enough to rock the seat on its mounts. The bleach turned into a bubbling white foam under the pressure. She scrubbed faster. The foam turned pink, then red. Her hands disappeared beneath the lather. She imagined herself squeezing the life out of the virus, crushing it, exploding it in the soup of toxic bleach, keeping it forever from her son.

Her arms burned. She pulled her hands away. Strips of cloth and nuggets of foam cushion coated them. She wiped away the covering bubbles. She'd shredded the seat down to the plastic back.

She stood straight, and leaned back against the open door. Her spine creaked. She remembered how upset the little fender dent had made her, how worried she'd been about Charles's reaction. Now she'd just destroyed her beloved car's interior. She scooped out a handful of melting seat foam, tossed it on the ground with a splat and felt nothing but victory.

Chapter Twenty-Four

Minutes after the quarantine announcement that afternoon, the four counties on the sunrise side of the East River had a new name emblazoned in the banner at the base of every newscast, printed in the headline of every tristate paper. It displaced the top trending search in every social media. Q Island. Every government news release on the quarantine contained the word *temporary*, an adjective completely ignored.

Email on Q Island had turned worthless as the Internet bogged down to a glacial pace. Even with a landline, it took Melanie two hours of attempts to get anything other than a fast busy signal before she finally got in contact with her husband again.

"Charles, you need to come home," she begged. "The island's been sealed off."

"That's only half-true," he said. "Only outbound traffic is temporarily closed."

"Well, we need you inbound. The world is on the edge of crazy here. There're infected people and crazy mobs. You need to be here."

"Don't worry. The condo walls are high, the entrance is gated."

"Big deal! Paul shot one of the infected as he tried to scale the gate yesterday."

"Paul the loner? The deer hunter? Good for him. It's about time he stepped up and joined the group."

Melanie grimaced at how out of touch Charles had become so quickly. "Join it? He's leading it. Him and his deer rifle."

"Hon, it sounds like you're in a safe place. You just need to ride this storm out a day or so until everything comes under control."

"Alone?"

Pause. Traders made whooping noises in the background.

"Look, Mel, let's view this rationally. In the last two days, I've racked up a pile of commissions and moved myself into the next bonus bracket. A month of this, and I'll pay off our condo and buy a house to boot. If I cross the East River, which I would do on foot, mind you, with no train service now, I'll never get back."

"You can work from home," Melanie said. "God knows you've done it enough on late nights and weekends."

"Internet lines are overloaded on the island. Besides, there's too much happening, too fast, right here, live. By the time word filtered out there to me, whatever opportunity would be snapped up by someone here. Seconds are worth millions."

"You must be kidding! You're going to leave me and your son here alone?"

"Melanie, you have everything you need. A safe place, food, water, a roof. You have access to the checking account, and I'll make sure it stays topped off."

"Whoa, whoa. You just said you thought this would last a day or two. How long do you *really* think this will last?"

"I don't know, I'm just thinking worst-case…"

"No, you *do* know." She couldn't keep the panic from her voice. "You're connected to every news outlet, every source of information in the world in your little castle there. What do you know?"

"Nothing. Nothing at all." Keys on a keyboard clicked next to the phone. "Look, I just transferred another thousand dollars from our money market account to checking. I'll deal with the surrender fees later."

"A thousand dollars couldn't have bought a can of tuna when the King Kullen went to hell. We don't need money; we need—"

"Hon, I have to go. There are pharma stocks hitting new highs. I'll call you back in an hour."

Click.

Melanie just stood with the dead phone to her ear. The silence turned to an annoying beep and then a recorded voice giving her instructions on hanging up the phone. She clicked it off and threw it against the couch.

"You bastard!" she screamed.

From his bedroom, Aiden let loose a mournful, terrified howl. Melanie cringed at having let her frustration get the best of her. She ran to Aiden's room.

Her son sat backed into the corner beside his bed. Papers surrounded him on the bedcovers like they were laying siege. His knees were tucked up to his chin, eyes wide in panicked terror; his hands covered his ears over the hood of his red sweatshirt. He wailed and rocked so hard his head bumped the wall.

She rushed to him, dropped to her knees and slid to the edge of the invisible protective space Aiden let no one violate. The last few inches between them felt like a thousand miles.

"No, Aiden," she whispered, soft and soothing. "It's just Mommy yelling at nothing. Everything's taken care of. We're safe."

The last two words barely got past her lips.

Frustration boiled inside her. She longed to calm, to comfort her son, to envelop him in the maternal warmth that her mother had given her when she'd been frightened as a child. What kind of mother could she ever be, unable to deliver that simplest act of human compassion?

But there was more to her longing. She needed to feel his warmth just as much, to relish the beat of the heart she'd created thumping against her skin, to sense his warm breath across her chest. She had to be reassured that through him life had continuity, that through him a part of her would survive. She feared she'd never know that sensation.

Aiden's rocking slowed. His howl subsided to a hum. Did his panic burn itself out or did her presence here make a difference? She had to hope it was the latter.

Drawings covered the papers that littered Aiden's bed. He'd probably been working on them before her shouting disturbed him. She couldn't make them out, a hodgepodge of irregular stick figures in one, something that maybe looked like a car in another. One scene might have been them at the beach, but that was probably just her wishful thinking.

She clenched a fist in frustration at the thought of Charles not coming back home. Maybe home could come to him instead. She and Aiden might be relatively safe behind these walls, shielded by whatever defense forces Lord Paul was able to muster, but they'd be a lot safer with the East River between them and the infected. She and Aiden could be at a bridge in no time, with traffic as light as it was. They weren't infected. Her husband was on the other side, so was a steady supply of her son's medication. Surely, whoever was guarding the crossing would understand and make that compassionate exception.

"Aiden," she said, "we're going to meet Daddy."

Chapter Twenty-Five

The authorities had taken quick steps as soon as Q Island had been declared. News radio broadcasted a long list of closures, not just bridges and tunnels, but entire sections of highways leading to them. Melanie had planned on crossing the Throgs Neck, the closest span. But the Cross Island Parkway was closed to all but military vehicles heading to Fort Totten, which overnight had expanded and commandeered the surrounding parks and the Clearview Park Golf Course. She opted for the Whitestone Bridge instead.

The expressway had light traffic for that time of day. In the bright sunlight, with the open spaces around the superhighway, she could almost forget that the world was going down the drain. A few ambulances screamed by, a couple of police cruisers with sirens blaring, but on the whole, it seemed like a weekend afternoon.

The radio declared the Whitestone Expressway was closed, so Melanie resorted to surface streets off the LIE. She planned to come up parallel to the expressway and park in the neighborhood beside the bridge. She piloted the Ford north on 150th Street, toward the East River and the bridge.

As soon as she hit the surface streets, her mood darkened. Traffic thinned to near nothing. The close-packed houses gave her a claustrophobic sense. Winter's skeletal trees added no color to the endless rows of drab little houses. Vigilant, suspicious faces peered from windows. Here and there, civilians carrying a hodgepodge of weapons stood wary guard along the cracked sidewalks. She never saw a cop.

She rolled into the Whitestone neighborhood adjacent to the bridge. It had turned into a parking lot. Cars ahead of her drove as far forward as possible, stopped and disgorged their occupants. A stream of individuals made their way northwest toward the distant towering spires of the Whitestone Bridge. They carried backpacks, pulled suitcases, pushed strollers. It reminded Melanie of the parking lot at Jones Beach in the summer, everyone unloading the day's gear and heading for the water. But this crowd replaced a beachgoer's jaunty expectation with a sense of grim determination, sprinkled with desperate hope. Melanie pulled into a curbside spot under a *No Parking* sign.

"Out we go, Aiden."

He'd beaten her to the draw and was already halfway out the door. His red Superman backpack hung low from his shoulders. His sweatshirt hood hung back over it, the tip bisecting the big S logo. She pulled her roller board bag out of the Ford's rear hatch.

They followed the group, like two insects trusting in the collective consciousness of the rest of the swarm. Individuals became a loose band, then coalesced into a pack as the surrounding streets funneled them closer to the bridge. The crowd rumbled with the sound of parents hushing confused or complaining children, but no one spoke between groups, as if no energy could be expended, save that in the pursuit of the escape they all dreamed lay just in the distance.

One street dead-ended at the Whitestone Expressway, just shy of the bridge entrance. The chain-link fence lay cut open and peeled back like the skin of an onion. The crowd squeezed through and joined a human mass on the other side. A sea of people packed all six lanes of the on-ramp. The group stretched back at least a half mile from where Melanie stood. They were surprisingly silent.

At the end closest to the bridge, a red Dodge Ram pickup sat facing the river. Its off-road suspension raised it up so high that the man in the bed stood above the shoulders of even the crowd's tallest. A large American flag hung limply behind him, its staff duct-taped to the truck's rear window. The man in the bed wore a white dress shirt, sleeves cuffed, and a loosened yellow tie. He spoke through a black megaphone that coincidentally matched the plastic of his thick-framed glasses.

"Now, we are gathered here with a simple request," he said. His voice echoed across the crowd. He had a slight Hispanic accent. It seemed that Melanie was catching him midspeech. "We only ask for what we have always had, what most of you were born with, what the rest of you immigrated for. Freedom."

A cheer rose from the nearby crowd. At the far end, those who could hear shouted summaries of his speech to the rest.

"We are not infected." He slid his sleeve up past the elbow and raised his tawny arm in the air. "We are clean. We want to stay that way. We don't ask for housing, we don't ask for food, we don't ask for transportation. We just ask for the freedom to go be with our families and friends on the other side of this river."

Another cheer arose, louder this time.

"Now, follow this truck. Women and children up front. Peacefully. We're going to pass through this illegal and immoral barricade, and join our fellow citizens on the other side." He started a chant. "Free-dom! Free-dom!"

The crowd followed suit, and the thunder of "Free-dom" rolled outward and up the bridge. The Ram fired up with a low diesel rumble, like an enraged bull, and spat a puff of black smoke. It began a slow uphill roll to the bridge. The American flag caught the breeze off the river and snapped to full display. The crowd followed, aligned along an invisible border behind the rear bumper. Strollers led the slow-motion charge.

Across the river beckoned the welcoming green expanse of Ferry Point Park and, farther west, the towers of New York City, where Charles and safety awaited them.

"C'mon, Aiden. Daddy's on the other side of that bridge."

Melanie and Aiden joined the march forward.

Up ahead, halfway to the bridge's tower, simple yellow NYPD sawhorses blocked all the lanes where the great steel cables sprouted from the ground to meet the first of the two main towers. A single police car sat across the lanes, roof lights flashing a red-and-white warning. Two cops in surgical masks and heavy blue-nylon jackets stood behind the sawhorses. Across the front of each sawhorse was stenciled *POLICE LINE—DO NOT CROSS*.

The Dodge closed on the barricade. One of cops spoke into the mic on his shoulder. They both retreated to the cruiser and took a defensive position behind the open front doors.

"Turn around and disperse!" one cop shouted through the squad car's speaker. He had a thick city accent. "The bridge is closed. None of you are gonna be allowed into the Bronx. Trust me! Go home."

"Nice and slow," the man in the pickup coached the crowd through his bullhorn. He broke into a broad smile. "These are city cops, our city cops. They won't turn us away." He turned back to thepolicemen. "We are your family members, your neighbors. We are not infected. These are women and children! Show some compassion!"

The truck closed to within yards of the barricade. Fear crossed the cops' faces. They ducked inside the cruiser and slammed the doors.

"This is your last warning!" the cop broadcast. "Do not cross the barricades!"

The crowd sensed victory. All that stood between them and salvation were a few thin wood planks on metal legs. The chant of "Free-dom!" resounded louder.

The crisp breeze off the river sent a chill, a good chill, down Melanie's spine. The whitecaps on the water sparkled in the sunlight. This was going to work. Aiden kept pace beside her, apparently willing to endure the close quarters of the crowd for the reward that lay beyond the bridge's final span.

The police cruiser's rear tires spun in a cloud of smoke, and the car screeched in reverse up the bridge. It disappeared down the other side of the apex.

The Ram rolled over and flattened two sawhorses. The surging crowd tossed the others to the ground. The barricades near the bridge's edge went sailing over the side and into the river. At the sight, cheers rose up from back in the crowd. The tense faces of the lead ranks split into smiles. Tentative steps transformed into strides. The shining Dodge crested the bridge's apex, Old Glory flying proudly behind the cab. As the marchers began the downhill march, their chanting died on their lips.

Two rows of gray-concrete barricades covered the bridge exit. A main battle tank clanked forward to fill the central gap the retreating police cruiser had used to escape. MRAP armored personnel carriers held a position on each flank, with turret guns trained on the bridge. Soldiers in chemical protective suits and gas masks lined the barricades, aiming a nasty assortment of automatic weapons at the crowd. A few yards before the barricade, a red, spray-painted line spanned the width of the bridge.

"No problem," the man in the truck reassured the crowd. "Our cops, our soldiers. American soldiers don't fire on American citizens. We are all one nation, under God. They'll see we're no threat."

A voice rang out across the bridge, twice as loud as the police had been. "This is Colonel Barient of the United States Army. Do not approach the barricades! Withdraw to the far end of the bridge and return to your homes. We are authorized to use deadly force to protect the nation from the virus."

Melanie didn't like his tone. His resolve sounded worse than steely. He sounded perfunctory, as if he had to get this little disclaimer out of the way so he could unleash a murderous fusillade with a clear conscience.

"Aiden, move to the edge of the bridge." She sidestepped them over.

"Continue forward," the man in the Dodge exhorted the crowd. Turning back to the barricades, he left the megaphone to balance on the roof of the Ram. He reached down and tore his shirt open down to the waist.

"Look at me!" he shouted, loud enough the soldiers could hear. "Look at us! We're not infected. We're clean. Check us if you want. There are women and children here, separated from their families."

The crowd continued to surge forward. Aiden moved to the bridge's wall. He cringed as passing people bumped into him. Melanie's heart broke at the massive self-control he was displaying under conditions that had to be torture. She moved to his side, hung on to the bridge barrier's edge and placed herself as a shield against the advancing crowd. Aiden flattened himself into the pocket of calm she created.

"This is your last warning!" the colonel announced.

"Soldiers, the world will see your compassion!" the man in the Ram called out. "Inspire them all, and do the right thing!"

The front tires of the Ram touched the red line. The tank's cannon fired. The barrel belched white smoke and the massive armored vehicle rocked back from the impact.

The shell couldn't miss. It burrowed straight through the Ram's chrome-trimmed grill. It exploded, and the cabin became a fireball. The blast seemed to dismantle the truck from the inside. Doors, fenders, glass—all blew out from the central explosion. The shirtless man in the back disintegrated.

On cue, the rest of the soldiers opened up. The hail of gunfire cut the crowd down like threshed wheat. Hot lead ripped arms and legs from bodies. Strollers splintered into a thousand pieces. Glowing tracer rounds pierced luggage, and the impact blew clothes around like a textile snowstorm.

A round tore the head off a large black woman in a sweat suit standing right in front of them. The force sent her flying back into Aiden and Melanie, pinning them to the ground and saving their lives. Rounds thudded into the protective mass of their unintended savior.

In the shock and awe of the fusillade, the first-row victims died before they could react. The crowd paused, stunned, unable to process what they'd just experienced. Then came the scream. A high-pitched, collective wail rose up from the crowd, a screech that could only be born of absolute panic. The mob turned about as one and ran.

Weapon fire raked the retreating crowd. More victims dropped like dead leaves. Inside the panicked pack, people tripped, fell and were trampled to death.

Underneath the dead woman, Aiden could take no more. Despite the bulk on top of him, he kicked and screamed and twisted to get free. His head slammed into Melanie's nose. She heard it crack and saw stars. Blood gushed down across her mouth. She covered Aiden's mouth with her hand and stifled his screams.

The gunfire petered out amidst someone shouting "Cease fire!" over and over. A final bullet zinged by and shattered the concrete abutment above them. A deafening silence replaced the thunder of guns. The previously invigorating breeze blew the sharp smell of spent gunpowder across the bridge. Muttered comments of shocked despair rose up from the ranks behind the barricades as the weight of their actions settled upon the soldiers' shoulders.

Her heart pounded in her ears. All she could think of was getting her son out of this pile of bleeding corpses. The killers at the end of the bridge might gun her down for trying, but she wasn't staying here. She released her grip on her son. He began to scream again. With both arms and legs, she heaved. The dead woman rolled off them. The hazy smoke of burnt cordite fogged the bridge deck.

"Aiden! Run back to the car! Now!"

He needed no prompting. He was up on his feet in an instant. Melanie leapt up behind him, instinctively shielding him from the soldiers' gun sights, for whatever that might be worth.

The downed marchers lay across the bridge like a lumpy, half-dead carpet. The moans of the living began to rise in the silence. A few bodies stirred. Aiden ran back down the bridge as fast as his strange upright posture permitted, which now seemed like slow motion. They trampled across the bodies, tilting on unsure footing in the slick, soft piles.

She tried not to think about the hundred weapons trained on her back, the cannon that could vaporize her and her child. She focused on her son, the back of his backpack stained with blood and flesh she prayed was not his own. She had to get him over the bridge's apex, out of the soldiers' line of fire. She had no time to relish the irony of Q Island feeling like a safe harbor.

A shot rang out from behind the barricades. A few feet ahead of Aiden, the chest of a body on the ground erupted in blood.

"Stand down, goddamn it!" someone yelled from behind. "They're running away, for Chrissakes!"

Farther up the bridge, the bodies became scattered. The wounded dragged themselves back to Queens, leaving smudged blood trails on the concrete. Melanie followed Aiden step for step as he jump-navigated the minefield of the dead and dying. They traversed the bridge's apex and accelerated on the open, downhill run.

The escaping marchers had knotted into a mass at the on-ramp, as the limited access onto the expressway from the neighborhoods meant limited egress off. Aiden stopped short of the tail end of the pack to catch his breath. Melanie knelt before him. His chest heaved in great, jagged breaths.

"Aiden, are you okay? Are you hurt?" She inspected him head to toe. A couple of scratches. A red patch on his neck that would become a splendid bruise later. His clothes were a bloody mess, but none of it seemed to be his. She gave thanks to God, followed by a prayer that none of the blood was infected.

Screams erupted from the mob on the on-ramp. The unmistakable blat and grind of chainsaws wound up. People at the back of the pack reversed course and began to run toward Melanie. Down below her, a clear circle formed in the mob along the expressway, like a drop of soap repelling oil on water. In the open space, several men with whirling chainsaws gave chase to the terrified masses. Despite the cold, the sawmen were all shirtless. Gray veins wove an evil pattern on their chests.

The mob surged back up the bridge. Kids slipped from between burdened adults and raced ahead of the group. Behind them, women clutched infants, all wide-eyed and terrified. Shrieks rang out from the base of the ramp as a chainsaw's buzz slowed and resurged after slashing a victim.

Aiden froze in place. Melanie grabbed him by the backpack and dragged him against the bridge railing. The children at the leading edge of the surging crowd recrossed the bridge's apex. Gunfire erupted from the north ramp soldiers. Little bodies turned into pink mist.

The approaching chainsaws amplified from buzz to roar. Arterial blood sprayed over the heads of the crowd like rain. Raw, blind panic filled the faces around Melanie. One woman just locked in place, her infant clutched to her breast, her eyes staring out at nothing.

Another volley raked the crowd to the north. The oily smell of the chainsaw exhaust mixed with the gunpowder. One way or another, everyone on this bridge was about to die.

On sheer maternal instinct, Melanie picked Aiden up by the nape of his backpack and his rear belt loop. She launched him over the side toward the East River below. Then she climbed up on the railing and dove after him.

Chapter Twenty-Six

The drop seemed to take forever. She watched Aiden hit the water first, damn near facedown, with a slap that made her cringe. The river drew him under. The surface's swirling currents raced up to greet her.

She straightened her legs, breathed deep and covered her nose. She still hit the water so hard she felt her ankle twist in a decidedly wrong direction. She stifled the scream that pain demanded. Her body sank like an anchor. The ice-cold river made her heart skip a beat. She snapped her eyes open. Feet away, Aiden drifted down into the gloom, lifeless.

She was on him in two panicked strokes. She reached and her fingers grazed his sinking collar. The top of Aiden's head passed into darkness.

Her lungs screamed for air. Every impulse in her quickly cooling body commanded that she swim for the diminishing light.

She dove into darkness.

Absolute blackness enveloped her. She saw nothing, but felt everything. Everything important, everything cherished, everything worth anything floated ahead of her. Some maternal sonar pinged that the only thing that made life worth living was just inches away. Air bubbles spit through her lips as her body demanded oxygen. Water pressure squeezed her skull like a vise. Her head spun.

Better to not surface at all, she thought, *than to surface alone.* She gave one more kick.

Her outstretched fingertips touched cloth. She gripped, turned and kicked for the dim light above. Another stream of bubbles slipped past her lips. Kick. Kick. Aiden's numb weight threatened to drag her back into the deadly darkness. Survival instincts begged her to let him go. Cloth slid against her numbing fingers.

She tightened her grip. One more weak kick. The light brightened. Her lungs overruled her clenched jaw. She belched a mass of bubbles into the river. Water rushed in. Salty, fetid, poisoned. She choked.

Her head broke water. She spit out a mouthful of rank water and sucked in a deep lungful of the crisp winter air. She pulled Aiden to the surface. He didn't move.

The current had dragged them downstream, but closer to Q Island's shore. She rolled onto her back, tucked her arm around his chest and kicked for land. Just as she was certain her numb legs would fail, they scraped the river bottom. She stood up on a tiny riverbank hemmed by houses. The cold froze her to the marrow. She shuddered as she dragged Aiden ashore and laid him down on the sand.

Her son's face was concrete gray, his lips a pale blue, his chest still.

CPR. He needed CPR. She tried to remember the routine. She couldn't focus. Her body shivered violently, out of control. The edges of everything went black. She was going into shock.

No, no, she thought. *I have to save—*

A man appeared from one of the houses. Fuzzy and indistinct, but she was certain it was a man. He started to run toward her.

Her head swam. Was he infected? Was he a criminal? Whatever he was, he wasn't touching her son.

She tried to stand, and the world spun like the view from a merry-go-round. She dropped to her knees. In a last desperate act, she draped her body across her son. She looked up to see the blurry face of a man in glasses staring down at her. She tried to shout at him to get away. Before she could form the words, she passed out.

Chapter Twenty-Seven

Melanie awakened and squinted against the light. She smelled coffee. She was relaxingly warm, in a bed, under a thick comforter. She was also naked.

She screeched and sat up, the comforter pulled close to her. She was in a bedroom decorated for a little girl, in pink with Disney princess pictures on the walls. Visions of being some twisted serial killer's stand-in daughter filled her head.

The door to a hallway stood open. She jumped up with the comforter wrapped around her, sprang for the door, slammed it shut and locked it.

A tentative little knock sounded at the door. "Hello?"

Melanie threw her back against the door to brace it closed. "Where am I? Where's my son?"

"Calm down, missy." The man's voice wavered. He sounded old. "You're in my house. I found you on the beach. Your son's here in the living room."

"Where the hell are my clothes?"

"They were soaking wet. You were turning hypothermic. I had to take them off. I wasn't happy about it, but you would have shorted out the electric blanket."

Melanie checked the bed. An electric blanket lay on the mattress, the yellow Power light illuminated.

"There are some sweats there by the bed for you to wear while your clothes dry."

"I want my son!"

"He's right here. Please, put something on, come out and take care of him."

Dressing at someone's command did nothing to diminish her serial-killer vibe. But she had to see Aiden. She slipped on the dark-blue sweats, a shiny-polyester style long out of fashion for anyone. She zipped up the top.

"Okay," the man said. His voice sounded far away. His accent was lifelong New Yorker. "My name's Eddie Maretti. I've stepped back into the kitchen. You just go into the hallway, you turn right, and the living room is right there. Your son's on the couch. There ain't no one home but me. Please go to him."

Melanie grasped the doorknob and paused. If he were a serial killer, she'd already be dead. If he was as old as he sounded, he wouldn't be a rapist. She scanned the room in vain for a decent defensive weapon. Nothing. Why couldn't this be a boy's room with a dartboard or a hockey stick?

She eased open the door onto an empty hallway.

"I'm in the kitchen, pouring coffee. Go on in. You're safe."

She entered the hallway. At the end, a leather couch backed up against a living room wall. Aiden lay on it under a pile of blankets, eyes closed. She ran to him, all concern about her own safety forgotten. She went down on her knees beside the couch and placed a finger to his neck. A strong, steady pulse throbbed at her fingertips. His chest rose and fell beneath the blanket, another electric model. Relief washed through her.

"See, no cause for alarm," Eddie said.

A counter with a two stools separated the modest kitchen from the living room. Eddie leaned against the counter on the far side. He was well past retirement age, with a full head of short, silver hair. He wore a brown cardigan. A cup of coffee steamed in his hands. Owlish, wire-rimmed glasses framed soft-brown eyes.

"When we came out of the river," Melanie said, "he wasn't breathing. I thought he was dead."

"Almost, but not quite. A little CPR dragged him back to us. You were pretty close yourself, young lady."

"We were lucky you found us."

"Ain't every day someone washes up at my house. But luck had nothing to do with it. That shooting gallery on the Whitestone got my attention damn fast. Did they fire a damn cannon? I was watching from the backyard when you and the boy went over the side. Lucky you weren't a little farther up the bridge. The height of the fall woulda killed ya."

"Then we're lucky, after all. My name's Melanie. This is my son, Aiden. We were trying to cross the bridge to get to my husband in Manhattan."

"That ain't gonna happen. Nothing crosses the Williamsburg in either direction now. The Throgs Neck is open for inbound traffic, but, big surprise, there ain't many takers."

"The river's not that wide. If we could find a boat, even a rowboat…"

"No chance. I've watched from here. Police boats, helicopters and even civilian auxiliary vessels patrol the river. They turn back anyone making the attempt. I even heard a few warning shots making a more persuasive argument. Those guys on the uninfected side of that river are scared."

"So are we."

Two helicopters thundered overhead in the direction of the bridge. The living-room bay window framed the bridge and the river. The gaudy logos of two local news stations covered the helicopters' fuselages. They joined two others hovering over the bridge. Smoke rose from the span's north side.

"Now what?" Eddie said.

He flipped on the television with the remote. The wide screen flared to life. At this point, channel selection was irrelevant. All local stations were all news, all the time. An aerial view of the Whitestone filled the screen. Orange flames leapt from a mound on the span. A small front loader scooped bodies from the roadway, crawled forward and dropped them on the pyre. The driver wore a gas mask.

The anchor cut in, "...and the military is wasting no time burning these bodies to keep the infection from crossing the East River. Again, we want to emphasize that no one from Q Island even came close to crossing the bridge. The military repelled the infected mob that tried to storm the barricades."

"We weren't infected!" Melanie said. "Those were healthy women and children, cut off from their families, like we were."

"Looks like the government covering their asses, or stoking public fear, or both."

The screen flicked over to other aerial footage. Several shirtless men with chainsaws chased a crowd through the neighborhood near the Williamsburg Bridge.

"In this footage," the anchor said, "taken just beforehand, you can see the infected terrorizing the few healthy residents still in the area."

"That happened afterwards," Melanie said. "We wouldn't have been on that bridge with the infected."

Aiden awakened with a start. Melanie waved at Eddie to mute the television. She leaned back outside Aiden's panic space. Aiden looked around in fear.

"It's all right," Melanie said. "We're safe here with Mr. Maretti."

Aiden scurried back to the far corner of the couch with the electric blanket bundled around him. The beginning of a wail slipped through his lips.

"Aiden, everything's fine. I'm right here. We're safe."

Eddie looked on with concern. "That dunk in the water did him some damage."

"No, this is normal. He's autistic."

Eddie eyed him like a science experiment. "Yeah? I've heard of kids like that."

"Could I get his clothes? He'll feel much better with his familiar clothes on."

"Sure, sure. Ought to be dry by now."

Eddie left and returned with a warm bundle of clothes, red sweatshirt on top. "Fresh from the dryer."

Melanie realized drying their clothes would have taken some time. The clock read after 4:30 p.m. They'd been asleep awhile. She took the clothes and Aiden to the bedroom, where they both got dressed. He calmed considerably wearing his own clothes. She led him back to the living room. Eddie passed her a steaming cup of coffee.

"Eddie, I can't thank you enough, but we need to get back home."

"Not now you don't," he said. "Curfew's at five. If the infected don't get you, the cops and soldiers have orders to shoot on sight. You gotta wait 'til morning."

She'd planned on being in Manhattan tonight. A stranger's house wasn't on her agenda, no matter how nice the stranger seemed.

"We can't impose. We'll take our chances."

"You took your chances today and nearly died," Eddie said. "And you aren't imposing. I'm whipping up macaroni and cheese. Ain't a boy alive can turn down mac and cheese. Am I right?"

Outside, the sun already tickled the tips of the city skyline. The Ford was blocks away, if she could find it, and then it was probably gridlocked into place. Based on her bridge experience, everyone would be trigger-happy out there, military and civilians. Not to mention the Chainsaw Trio could be anywhere. And Aiden did love mac and cheese.

"Deal," she said. "But we leave at dawn."

Eddie broke into a smile. "I'll add hot dogs to the mac to celebrate."

Eddie continued cooking, and Aiden settled down to look at the books on the living-room shelves. He grabbed a coffee-table book on African animals and began to page through it.

Melanie took stock of the living room. The furniture was a decade out of style but near showroom-new. Pictures of Eddie and other family members filled the walls, many of him with a striking brunette, including a wedding picture with him in a Navy uniform circa 1960.

"Eddie, does your wife live here with you?"

"Not anymore." His disembodied voice floated in from the kitchen. "She passed away just before I retired. Our daughter moved to sunnier climates, and it's just me standing fast to repel all boarders." He exhaled. "Guess that's literally what I'm doing, now."

"You were in the Navy?"

"Pumped fuel aboard the *USS Kankalee* for years, then pumped fuel for CanAm Oil until a few months ago. Mary Ellen used to say I was just a one-trick pony when it came to work."

"Have you spoken to your daughter, let her know you're okay?"

"We traded some emails. My granddaughter was worried. She's about the same age as your boy. That room you woke up in was fixed up for her visits, just so you don't think I'm some weirdo."

Rotor noise sounded outside. An Apache attack helicopter flew low, under the Whitestone and upriver. The setting sun tinged the sky red. Melanie though about her and Aiden's narrow escape.

"Where would the infected get chainsaws anyway?" she said.

Plates clattered in the kitchen.

"Looted from the mall, no doubt. The place was ransacked this afternoon."

"See, that's terrifying. The infected are still thinking human beings, able to make a plan to steal a chainsaw, get gas and mix the oil, all just to kill people. Zombie movies used to terrify me. But I'd take the walking dead over these people any day."

"The news is pretty sparse with the details," Eddie said as he walked in balancing three plates of mac and cheese with a fork sticking out of each one. An embarrassed look crossed his face. "Oh, sorry. I'm so used to eating alone in front of the TV I just forgot I have a kitchen table."

Melanie waved off his idea. "No time to stand on ceremony. The world's falling apart, after all. Aiden?"

Her son took his plate, and the three of them dug in. The TV played on, a montage of silenced news anchors, talking head guests and clips that should have been in some "found footage" movie.

"Like I was saying," Eddie said, "the news is pretty vague. But the so-called experts believe that the virus attacks and destroys specific parts of the brain, I don't remember the fancy names. A switch gets thrown, and every evil fantasy just blasts on through with no filter. And they do it with superhuman strength."

"Lucky us to find a bunch of guys with a chainsaw fantasy."

"And as long as everyone's fantasy meshes, the infected will cooperate for a common goal."

Aiden scraped the last bit of cheese from his plate and returned to his book.

"Does he speak at all?" Eddie asked.

"No. He's physically capable, he just chooses not to. But he understands everything going on around him, trust me. He just interprets it differently than we do. He also doesn't like being touched. It was a good thing he was unconscious after he hit the water. He probably would have drowned before he let me pull him ashore."

"But you're his mother."

"That doesn't matter to him."

Eddie scratched his chin. "That must be so hard for you."

Melanie was taken aback. She realized that what this stranger just said her husband had never thought to say. He'd always been quick to say how Aiden's condition affected him or their finances, but how it affected her... She shifted the subject.

"This house might not be the safest," Melanie said. "Other houses are real close, there're no fences between them. There're a lot of windows people could break through. The river blocks one escape route."

"Ain't you the little strategist?"

"Getting trapped on the bridge changed my perspective. Our condo is better. There's a wall, we have armed residents, well, at least *one* armed resident, on patrol. We aren't getting across the river, so we'll head back there. You saved our lives, and we owe you. Why don't you come with us?"

Grainy cell phone footage of assaults by the infected played across the television screen in silence. Eddie pushed a slice of hot dog around in the cheese on his plate.

"You know, I appreciate the invitation. I really do. But this has been my home for almost four decades. Mary Ellen and I picked it out, raised our daughter in it and burned the mortgage right there in the backyard. I've got a view of the river, and the garden grows damn good tomatoes. I've lived enough of life here that I ain't interested in living any more of it somewhere else. No offense, please."

"I understand. We'll need to leave in the morning though. No offense."

Eddie smiled. "None taken at all. Gives me an excuse to make waffles in the morning. If your boy eats mac and cheese, he eats waffles."

Melanie doubted husband Charles knew any of his son's favorite foods. "Aiden will eat every one you make."

Chapter Twenty-Eight

Melanie awoke to a room that glowed orange.

She'd slept on the floor of the princess bedroom, Aiden on the bed, both fully dressed, not from a lack of PJs as much as from fear of a midnight catastrophe. That fear that now came to fruition. The air smelled of smoke. The unmistakable flicker of flames lit the window from outside.

She jumped to her feet and parted the curtains. Two houses on the block burned like giant tiki torches, belching smoke and flame into the night sky. Triumphant whoops and hollers echoed outside. Shadows skittered back and forth, backlit by the blazes. The streetlights were dark. The clock in the room as well. No electricity.

A car pulled up in front. A man hung out of the passenger window with a Molotov cocktail in his hand. He lit the rag at the bottle's end. Flame rippled up the hanging cloth fuse. The firelight illuminated the gray web across the attacker's face. His blood-red eyes sparkled. He wound up like a major leaguer and hurled the burning bottle straight at Melanie's window.

The flickering rag cut a flaming arc through the darkness. Melanie ducked. The bottle missed the window and shattered against the exterior's dry cedar shingles. Flames erupted along the facade. The pitcher whooped in victory as the car squealed away down the street.

Instantly, the window glass went hot. Aiden snapped awake, took one look at the window full of flames, screamed and ran for the hallway. Melanie scooped his shoes off the floor and followed.

Aiden cut right for the living room, but she cut left for the master bedroom. She banged on the door.

"Eddie! Wake up! The house is on fire!"

Eddie yanked open the door as he put on his glasses. His hair was a mess, but he was fully dressed. Apparently Eddie hadn't felt that secure either. "Where?"

"Firebombed out front by some of the infected," she said.

Eddie checked the fire from his bedroom window. Flames already blazed up to the roof and across the asphalt shingles. "Damn. We ain't putting that out. Time to abandon ship. Where's Aiden?"

"Already up and moving."

"Out the kitchen door, go!"

They ran down the hall. The sound of the kitchen door slamming shut punctuated the crackle of flames outside. Melanie entered the kitchen and caught sight of her son leaping from the back porch into the darkness.

Eddie paused and stepped into the living room. He gave his head a sad shake. He pulled his wedding picture off the wall, popped the photo from the frame and shoved it in his shirt. Melanie went out the kitchen door. Eddie followed her into the night. She stopped at the edge of the long-harvested tomato garden.

"Aiden!" she called. "Come here now!" Under her breath she added, "There's no time for this."

The air was thick with the acrid smell of smoke. The indirect light from the blazes gave the yard a hellish, otherworldly glow.

Eddie came up beside her. "Where's your boy?"

"Here, somewhere. You'd better get your car out of the garage before the fire reaches it."

"Car? I live in Queens. I haven't owned a car in twenty years."

"Well, I have one. Somewhere along 150th. We'll find Aiden and—"

Aiden's scream pierced the air from the side of the house, a shriek of utter panic. Melanie ran to him without thinking.

Fire had consumed half Eddie's roof. The next-door house burned as well and the blaze lit the space between them in an eerie, dancing illumination of orange and gray. A man, arms and face awash in infected veins, held Aiden by the collar, a foot off the ground. He was one of the Chainsaw Triplets from the afternoon. Aiden screamed and kicked, but the infected man's arm never wavered, solid as the Statue of Liberty holding her torch. In his other hand he held a hand ax. Blood coated the blade all the way to the handle.

"Hey, kid," the man said, "you ever wonder what you'd look like with no legs? Let's have some fun."

"Let go of my son, you bastard!" Melanie screamed.

The man turned to Melanie, eyes crimson with infection. "Well, on second thought, I think Mommy will be a lot more fun."

With the barest flick of his wrist, he tossed Aiden across the yard. The boy landed on the grass and balled up into a whimpering fetal position. The attacker bolted straight for Melanie.

She took him on armed with nothing but fury. It wasn't enough. He grabbed her by the neck and threw her to the ground. Pinning her by her collapsing windpipe, he wedged himself between her legs. His eyes burned like hot coals.

"I'm about to show you a real good time, sweetheart."

She reached up with both hands and grabbed his arm. It felt hard as steel. She choked out a curse. His face was bare inches from hers. A bead of sweat dripped from his nose onto her forehead. She closed her eyes.

Something crunched, like metal on concrete. The man broke the grip on her neck. She opened her eyes. A metal tomato stake entered one of the man's ears and exited through the other. Blood and bits of brain dripped off the pointed end. He slumped over to her right. Eddie stood above her, panting.

"Score one for the old guy," he said.

"I'm really starting to owe you," Melanie said.

She rubbed the spittle off her forehead. Eddie gave her a hand up, and they went to Aiden. He was moaning and rocking at the edge of the light.

"Aiden honey, it's okay now. The man's…gone. No one's going to hurt you. We are safe now."

Aiden kept rocking and moaning, as if in a trance.

"We need to find your car fast," Eddie said. "This place may be crawling with the infected. And nothing's going to stop this fire from spreading unless the fire department shows up in force, and I ain't counting on that. We'll carry him. Just pick him up."

"That won't work. I can do this. Give me a minute."

Eddie scanned the shadows around the yard. "We ain't got a minute."

Melanie cursed that the familiar items she'd packed for just this occasion were blasted to bits on the Whitestone Bridge. She knelt as close to his ear as she dared.

"Honey, don't think about here, think about home, think about your room. As soon as you get up, that's where we're going, behind the tall, safe walls."

Down the street, a car exploded in a ball of flame. A round of cheers followed.

"Honey, as soon as you get up, we are gone. Think about your room, your bed, your big, soft comforter. Focus on that."

Aiden's moaning slowed. She began to sing, "Angels in heaven, look down on the child, perfect and lovely, tender and mild. Shepherds that evening, tending their flocks, kneel without pain on nettles and rocks."

"You're singing a Christmas carol?" Eddie said. "Now?"

Melanie cut him off with a curt hand chop and continued, "The rams and the ewes, surround him in awe, first to acknowledge our Savior and Lord. Wise men who travel, came from afar, guided by faith and the light of a star."

Aiden stopped moaning and went still. His breathing returned to normal.

"C'mon, honey. We're going home right now."

Aiden stood up. His eyes flicked around the scene like a cornered animal.

"All right, Eddie," Melanie said. "We're following you. Let's get out of here."

Eddie took them through a backyard maze of fences, skirting burning houses until they could return to 150th. Cars there were parked everywhere. Several were flipped on their sides, awash in the smell of spilled gasoline. Without the streetlights, the already homogeneous vehicle designs looked exactly the same, with all the colors washed out to the same gray.

They crouched and scrambled along the east side of the street where Melanie knew she parked. At a distance, many cars offered optimism that they were hers, only to prove otherwise. Hope and despair, hope and despair. She could hit the panic button on the remote and fire off the lights and horn, but how many infected would that little aural flare attract?

Up ahead, a house looked familiar. Three holly trees lined the front yard. She remembered walking by them right after she got out of the car. She looked four cars down and found the Ford.

"There it is!" She ran to her car with Aiden and Eddie right behind. She got beside it and her heart fell.

The rear tire was slashed.

Chapter Twenty-Nine

Jimmy Wade smiled at his inheritance from the late, great Mozelle. He propped his feet up on the edge of the desk. The empire he'd acquired exceeded his wildest expectations. With the proper suggestions, the accountant laid bare the operation. The bookie business was just a fraction of it. Drugs were a real cash cow, run in from the Atlantic and churned through phony pharmacy records.

Running the show wouldn't be too hard. K-Dogg and a few other lieutenants kept the rank and file in line. Jimmy just needed to keep middle management in line. His new appearance, with an otherworldly head of red scar tissue and sutures, worked in his favor.

As for controlling the rest of the world, Mozelle had left him some excellent presents. Who knew where the old man was planning on unloading the warehouse's stash of AK-47s and shoulder-fired RPGs. That little nugget of info died with Mozelle. He sure wasn't planning on using them himself. That kind of firepower flash on Long Island would bring in the Feds. Of course, that was before the Feds created Q Island. Law enforcement was spread thin as butter on toast, and most of it seemed to be busier keeping everyone on the island, instead of keeping everyone on the island safe. Jimmy would be keeping the military hardware to himself.

Jimmy gave the future of his new business a quick assessment. The quarantine was going to cut into drug supply. The reinforced security around the island would sever any smuggling routes, or triple the price of anyone still daring the mission. Medicines were still going to come across the bridges, though. The island was in enough trouble without a few million housewives going through Xanax withdrawal. Small-timers were going to target the pharmacies. Jimmy wasn't small-time anymore. He'd go for the distribution center.

Even he was amazed at how easily he assumed the control and understanding of Mozelle's operation. Since he escaped the hospital, he'd had a clarity of thought he'd never experienced before. What the world called infection he deemed enhancement. Ideas clicked faster, concepts had sharper edges. He cut through to answers quicker.

Now he understood the root of so many of his life's frustrations. Struggling at school, trying to learn electronics at that trade college, the frustrating failure of trying to work that stolen laptop—all those things were just beyond his grasp, as if he'd been allowed to the cusp of understanding, but no further. Now it all came easily. Mozelle's ledgers were self-explanatory. The organizational structure made intuitive sense. The rationality of hitting a distribution center just jumped out at him.

So this was how it had always been for smart people? He'd never called himself stupid before, but in hindsight, he had been. This blessing of a virus had boosted his brain in more ways than just supercharging his power of suggestion.

K-Dogg approached the desk. He had an RPG slung over one shoulder. Jimmy dropped his feet and sat up in his chair.

"Ready, Boss. You sure you wanna do this? Mozelle, he didn't never get his hands dirty."

"Another reason Mozelle isn't in charge anymore," Jimmy said. "Let's roll."

He'd reconned the DC himself that day. It was one of several buildings inside a light industrial park with one entrance. The National Guard apparently didn't want the hassle of managing every building's security, so one Humvee covered the DC entrance, with a few soldiers around the perimeter. Enough security to keep the average felon at bay. Luckily, Jimmy had become way above average.

Jimmy's convoy of three rolled through the industrial park entrance at 2:00 a.m. Two pickup trucks carried his muscle while an unladen semi-tractor followed. Once in the gate, the trucks doused their lights. They crept back towards the DC from two different directions. The semi parked by the gate.

Jimmy rode in the backseat of one of the trucks, with an enforcer riding shotgun. K-Dogg lay low in the bed behind them. The truck rolled silently into view of the DC.

Outside, a soldier leaned back against the wall by a dock door, bobbing to an iPod. His helmet hung on top of his rifle barrel. The Humvee sat dark in front of the main entrance. Two glowing cigarettes swayed in the shadowed front seats. The turret machine gun pointed at the sky, unmanned.

Jimmy rapped twice on the pickup's rear glass. K-Dogg popped up with the RPG at his shoulder. He aimed at the Humvee and fired.

The round whooshed from the launching tube. The bobbing cigarettes paused. The round buried itself in the Humvee's windshield, and the vehicle disintegrated in a ball of fire.

Before the stunned guard at the side of the building could react, the enforcer in the passenger seat peppered him with a spray from his AK. A similar burst of fire sounded around the other side of the building. The DC was theirs for the taking. The driver of the pickup keyed a walkie-talkie and called the semi driver, Juno, to swoop in and hook up to the trailer in the first dock door.

Jimmy's crew stormed the DC. The place was deserted, as he'd expected. His men went straight for the huge cage that held the prescription pharmaceuticals. No point in trying to corner the market on Metamucil.

In a display of macho overkill, a rifle barked and shot off the cage door locks. The first dock door rolled up to reveal an empty trailer. The men began a pharmaceutical relay to fill it.

Jimmy probed their minds as they worked. "Reading" them would have been a stretch of a description. He more "sensed" them, felt their emotions, sort of gauged their thought process the way someone measured engine power by reading a tachometer.

None of these guys revved very high. His enlightening infection brought an amazing revelation. Criminals were stupid. Compared to the rate at which his own mind now raced, the men around him crawled. Their emotions came across as brightly colored, but with indefinite edges. Strong, but unfocused. Combined with low-rpm reasoning, they made decisions that more often than not handed them the short end of the stick. It was no wonder they ended up where they did.

The men shuttled around the warehouse like worker bees. Jimmy realized he'd been one of those bees a week ago. He'd been the victim of his own string of bad decisions, an endless loop of repeating the same mistakes. His farthest horizon had been the next day; his primary objective, short-term happiness, even if it came from the neck of a bottle or from a needle's tip. But not now. The infection, Q Island's scourge, was his savior.

Two shots sounded outside the building.

"Goddamn it," Jimmy said.

He went out through the front door. K-Dogg wasn't at his post. A few flames licked at the corpse of the Humvee. Out in the parking lot, the semi sat backed up, but not attached to the empty trailer. One of the infected lay dead on the ground, sporting the filthy coat and the matted, greasy hair of the long-term homeless. He held the semi's detached passenger-side mirror in his hand. K-Dogg stood a few feet away, weapon still trained on the dead man.

"Mofo came running up here," K-Dogg explained as Jimmy approached. "Went all apeshit on the truck. Juno couldn't even get out and hook up."

Two more shapes came running from out of the shadows. Two more homeless, both infected. Jimmy'd heard that gunshots would draw them in, that the rage in them craved the combat the gunfire promised.

K-Dogg spun around, raised the AK and sprayed a burst in their direction. Both of them jerked at the bullets' impacts and crumpled to the ground.

Jimmy looked up into the semi. Juno's fat face stared out the passenger window, wide-eyed and white with fear.

"What the shit are you waiting for?" Jimmy shouted. "Hook that goddamn truck up before I leave you out here as bait for these things!" He kicked the infected corpse at his feet.

Juno scrambled down and began to hook up the trailer. Jimmy smiled. Juno's fear of him trumped his fear of the infected. Ironically, they were one and the same.

The AK had ripped the corpse at Jimmy's feet. An exit wound through the chest on the right had left a gaping hole and a puree of smashed, blackened organs. A second round had creased the side of its head and left a rift, like the bullet had parted its hair all the way down through the skull. A pink-and-red stripe of exposed brain ran the length of the wound's valley.

Jimmy had been squeamish all his life. The sight of blood made him woozy, the slightest scrape made him cringe. As a kid, his older sister had once taunted him with used tampons until he vomited. The sight of this exploded creature at his feet should have had him doubled over, hurling dinner on the asphalt.

But he didn't feel that way at all. No, he'd slipped past that mile marker for indifference and traveled almost to pleasure. The sight of the wounds sparked something akin to attraction. Some part of him, perhaps the part conditioned to revulsion, set off a warning bell that this feeling, however ill-defined, stood on the far side of wrong. He shook his head and made himself look away. He had no time to sort through another minor change the infection had wrought.

Jimmy reentered the DC. The crew had cleaned out the secure area and now were packing the rest of the trailer with anything that fit.

Gunfire sounded outside again.

"Finish it up!" Jimmy yelled.

The men dropped whatever they had in their hands, grabbed their weapons and ran for the exit.

Outside, the parking lot had sprouted the infected. They came at a run from the darkness, now better dressed, of all ages. No longer just the homeless from the nearby patch of woods, these were local residents, definitely drawn to the action.

K-Dogg had retreated to the main doors. A spent magazine lay at his feet. He slapped a fresh one into place and mowed down a row of attackers on the left.

The semi fired up with a throaty roar. The lights snapped on and spotlighted several infected sprinting toward the truck. Gears ground as the truck lurched away from the dock.

The men poured out of the DC and split into two groups for the pickups. K-Dogg covered Jimmy as they entered the first truck's cab.

The second group didn't make it to theirs. Halfway there, the truck rumbled to life with one of the infected behind the wheel. The high beams lit. The men flinched and halted in the light. The truck blasted forward and crushed two of its former occupants under its wheels.

The third man raised his rifle and sprayed the cab as the truck passed. The windshield shattered. The driver slumped over. The pickup made a sharp right as the dead driver's weight yanked the wheel over, hard. The truck careened across the lot and smashed into the side of the DC.

The lone gunman had no time to relish his victory. One of the infected jumped him from behind. It wrapped an arm around his neck and squeezed so hard the gunman's head popped off like the cap off a longneck. A gusher of blood coated the infected. It didn't react. The headless corpse slumped to the ground.

K-Dogg punched the accelerator, and his truck's rear tires sent up twin plumes of burnt rubber. The semi rumbled by, and the pickup fishtailed in behind it. What was left of the crew scrambled for sanctuary in the pickup's bed.

The infected kept coming. The semi accelerated like a wallowing hippo. The open rear doors swung back and forth, and bits of the bouncing cargo within tumbled out like escaping prisoners. Jimmy's pickup, caught behind the lumbering truck, couldn't get out of second gear.

One of the infected sprinted up and grabbed the trailer's swinging door. With its abnormal strength, it levered itself up and leapt into the trailer's open rear. It began to shuffle through the contraband.

"Goddamn it, no," Jimmy whispered.

The infected in the trailer began to toss uninteresting cartons out the rear. One bounced off the pickup's hood. Jimmy dodged behind the dashboard.

"Screw this shit," K-Dogg said. He pulled a pistol from beside the seat, hung it out the open window and sent two wild shots into the trailer. One exploded a case of white pills into a pharmaceutical hailstorm. The infected turned to face them, fury in its glowing, ruby eyes.

Someone in the pickup's bed screamed. The infected came on fast from both sides. One raced up from behind and tore the tailgate off in a shriek of twisting steel. It jumped in the bed, bit the nose off one of the crew and threw him forward against the cab. The bed erupted with wild gunfire.

Panic lit Jimmy up like a Christmas tree. His survival demanded he bail out of this rolling coffin. Only the unknown terrors in the shadows kept him from pulling the handle.

The creature in the trailer dropped its pilfered box. Up like a sprinter, in two steps it launched itself into the air through the open, swinging doors. It landed on the truck's hood with a thud. Its pallid face pulsed with a mass of charcoal veins. It gripped the edge of the hood with one hand and brought the other down and through the windshield with a crash. A bloody hand shot through the shattered glass and writhed between the front seats.

Jimmy shrank into the corner of the cab, filled with his fear, but even more paralyzed by the waves of panic he sensed coming from the men around him. Every one of them believed that in seconds, they would all be dead. And they were right.

Jimmy grasped at a straw. In rapid succession, he touched each of his men's minds. He left one simple thought.

You are invincible.

The panicked shouts died down. A rifle butt crushed the face of the infected at the tailgate. It flew back into the darkness. Punches dislodged two more from the sides.

K-Dogg jammed on the brakes. The infected on the hood flew forward onto the asphalt. K-Dogg hit the accelerator. As the infected rose, the truck's bumper crushed its skull.

In the rear, wild fusillades turned into disciplined, three-round bursts. Infected on both sides of the truck disintegrated. The semi had finally made speed and pulled out of the industrial park onto the main road. The pickup accelerated, skidded out the entrance and passed the truck to take the lead on the empty street. Victory whoops rose up from the survivors in the bed as they high-fived each other.

Jimmy exhaled for what seemed the first time in minutes. A cannonade of pain thudded inside his head. That little round robin of mental manipulation had stretched him to the limit. He sniffed and ran his finger under his nose. Blood smeared his knuckles. Dark flecks peppered the red.

He slammed the dashboard in frustration. That goat screw had just cost him a vehicle, some of his crew, but, worse, some of his automatic weapons with the other truck. The infected were a handful one-on-one, but gathered in an outnumbering pack, they'd be unbeatable.

He'd need a better base of operations. Mozelle's warehouse retreat was great cover from the prying eyes of the cops, but wouldn't be any more defensible from an assault by the infected than that DC. Where was a castle when you needed one?

He knew where.

"Keep heading north," he said to K-Dogg. "Tell the truck to follow."

Chapter Thirty

K-Dogg pulled up to the closed security gate at Belle Pointe. The semi rolled up behind them and stopped with a whoosh of the air brakes.

The guard had been upgraded from lame caretaker security to a uniformed off-duty cop. He stepped out of the shack with the haughty cop look Jimmy had always hated. Then the cop saw the well-armed thugs in the pickup bed. Color drained from his face, and he stepped back. The guard reached for his pistol.

K-Dogg pointed his automatic out the window and fired point-blank. The bullet entered the cop's forehead and vaporized the back of his skull. The impact drove him back through the shack's open door and onto the floor.

"Mitch," Jimmy shouted out the window. "Take the guard's place until relieved. Borrow his uniform. He won't need it. No one who's not one of us gets in or out without my permission."

"Right, Boss." One of the crew, in a Giants NFL jacket, hopped out and hit the button to open the gate. He grabbed the cop by the feet and dragged him out of the shack.

Jimmy directed K-Dogg to his new residence, the former home of Michael Quinn. They stopped in front.

"Nice place, Boss," K-Dogg said.

"Welcome to our new home," Jimmy said. He got out and met the men as they leapt out of the bed. One of them, Sal Bonano, stayed behind.

Sal was a runty little guy. Blood soaked his T-shirt. His jacket was wound around his right hand. Sweat plastered his hair down the sides of his terrified face. One of the other men aimed an AK at Sal's chest.

"What's the deal?" Jimmy said.

The man pointing the AK answered without taking his eyes off Sal. "Damn thing bit off his finger back there. He's infected. He's gonna turn."

"Boss, it ain't that way," Sal pleaded. "I'm cool. I feel fine. I didn't catch nothing. On my mother's grave!"

Jimmy pressed the barrel of the AK toward the ground. "Let's stay calm here. Come on down, Sal."

Sal hopped off the open end of the truck, his face a mixture of relief and anticipation. The rest of the crew took two steps back. Jimmy pointed to the gardener's house. The occupant had disappeared the day Jimmy arrived.

"All of you go bed down in there tonight. We have a lot to do in the morning." He laid a comforting hand on Sal's shoulder. "Sal, you come into the main house with me so we can get that hand taken care of properly."

"Thanks, Boss. You'll see. I'm fine."

The crew trudged off to the gardener's house. Sal turned to the main entrance. K-Dogg shot Jimmy a look like he was insane. Jimmy winked and with a jerk of his head gestured at K-Dogg to follow them inside.

Once inside, Jimmy flipped on the lights for the main foyer.

"Say, Boss," Sal marveled, "this place has class."

"Sedate him," Jimmy said over his shoulder to K-Dogg.

Like a striking snake, K-Dogg had Sal in a sleeper hold in a split second. Sal struggled, gasped and then went limp.

"Tie him up in the living room where I can keep an eye on him. And I don't need to emphasize how important it is that he be tied tight."

"You think he'll turn?"

"I'm counting on it."

Chapter Thirty-One

Tamara threw down her bedcovers and wadded them up around her feet. Her damaged eye throbbed like a Metallica bass line. She'd broken down, followed her doctor's orders and given herself a day of medicated rest. But each time she drifted off into a drug-muddled sleep, she saw all of St. Luke's horrors: the close-up of Gwen Albritton piercing her eye with the needle, the massacre on the ward floor, the attack in the morgue. If bed rest was supposed to make her feel better, it was a dismal failure.

She rolled over and sat up in bed. She looked at the clock and moaned. Two thirty in the morning was no time to be awake.

Mallow whimpered. The German shepherd had spent the night against her legs in the bed. He'd never done that before, always staying outside the door all night until called. If he hadn't been a dog, she'd have thought that he sensed her pain and that he knew nothing fixed that like a warm body.

She gave his side the kind of happy little openhanded pounding only a big dog could absorb and enjoy. "That's a good boy, Mallow."

Mallow thumped the bed with his tail. She left the room and he followed, a factory of joyful panting.

Do-it-yourself medicine was a fool's game, but it was the only one she could play right now. She entered her bathroom, flicked on the light, downed a painkiller and prepared for the worst. She hadn't ventured a look at her eye since Doc Bradshaw's less-than-encouraging observation at the St. Luke's ER.

She unwound the bandage on her head. The pad of gauze over her eye was dirty, but it wasn't bloody or yellow. That meant the stitches were holding, the eyeball healing, at least on the outside. Halfway home.

She removed the pad and angled her head to the bathroom mirror. Her swollen left eyelids blazed a dull red. She touched them. Hot. *Damn.* It could be infection, or it could just be healing combined with being under that insulating bandage.

The moment of truth would be when she pried open her lids. The downside of being a nurse was a full understanding of the myriad poor possible outcomes. Corneal scarring, hyphema, iridodialysis, posttraumatic glaucoma, uveitis cataract, blah, blah, blah. She'd already blown off half of the bed-rest recommendation, and that hadn't helped her odds.

She gripped the lashes on her closed eye with her fingertips. She could feel the two lids swollen together. She counted down. Three, two, one.

She released her lashes. She rationalized that it was too early to tell if her eye had gotten better. But deep down, she knew that it wasn't too early to know if it had gotten worse. And she could definitely wait on that one.

No she couldn't.

She gripped her lashes again. She put her face close to the mirror. She parted her lids ever so slightly, gasped and let them snap closed.

Her dying eye was the color of dirty dishwater.

She chastised herself for getting up and checking, then for not staying in bed initially as ordered, then for letting her guard down so Gwen could stab her in the eye in the first place. This was all screwed up, and there were a dozen ways from Sunday she'd made it worse. She pounded her fist against the wall. Mallow yelped and ran into the living room.

"Aw, crap." Now she'd scared the poor dog.

She followed him into the living room and coaxed the cowering shepherd out from under a corner table. A neck scratch and a belly rub later, all was forgiven. A piece of paper lay on the floor near the front door. She gave Mallow a final thump, grabbed the paper and read it.

Guess you're out. Couldn't get a text through. I've taken Aiden to try to cross into Manhattan to be with Charles. Just letting you know so you don't worry when we aren't around tomorrow. Call you from the other side.
Melanie

"You've got to be kidding me." She couldn't believe Melanie could be that naïve, thinking that someone would look at her and her son and say, "Okay, we'll break quarantine for you, just don't tell anyone." She imagined Melanie and Aiden, standing on a bridge somewhere, talking to—

A bridge! Wasn't there something on the news earlier about a bridge? A riot... something?

She went to the kitchen counter and awakened her snoozing laptop. The Internet response was dial-up-level slow. The first few national and international news sites she tried would not connect. Then she surfed to a local TV news site. A report read that a swarm of the infected tried to rush the Whitestone Bridge. Soldiers and police repelled the assault, bodies burned immediately. The mainland was safe.

But were Melanie and Aiden?

The Whitestone would have been the bridge they took, the closest one they could approach, one that crossed to near Manhattan. If only she'd been coherent enough to answer the door and stop her friend from being so clueless…

She almost headed right out the front door, but remembered what a mess her eye looked like. If she wanted any hope of recovery, she needed to keep it under wraps. She rebandaged her eye, careful not to put pressure on the swollen eyeball within. She cringed at her sloppy, half-blind handiwork. First-year nursing students bandaged better.

Still in the sweatpants and tank top she'd slept in, she went outside to Melanie's door. The cold night air gave her an instant chill. The condo's lights weren't on, but whose were at this hour? She banged on the door with her fists.

"Melanie! Melanie!"

A light came on, but from another condo.

"Melanie! Answer your door! It's Tamara."

From around the corner ran Paul Rosen in a T-shirt and gym shorts. He snapped his Winchester to his shoulder. The flashlight taped to the side shined in Tamara's eyes as he put her in his sights. "Tamara?"

She paused midslam and looked at him. "It's Melanie. I think she—"

"Step away from the door, Tamara." His voice was cold as ice. The rifle barrel didn't move a millimeter. "Do it now."

More lights flicked on in surrounding condos.

"What the hell is wrong with you, Paul? Melanie is…" She understood. "Wait, I know what this looks like. I'm not infected. I'm just checking if Melanie and Aiden came home."

"Then step away from the door to the center of the walkway and go down on your knees."

She raised her hands, stepped over and dropped to her knees. Paul approached, pausing only when the rifle barrel was inches from her. The flashlight's beam played up and down her arms as the rifle barrel traced an outline of her body. The flashlight aimed at her face. She pinched her eyes shut. The cold barrel lay against her cheek and pushed her face into profile. The barrel slid down between her breasts and hooked her tank top. It pulled the shirt low enough to expose her nipples. Anger flared. She was about to grab the barrel when it pulled back. Her top bounced back up into place. Paul clicked the flashlight off.

"Sorry, Tamara. People called me. You were out here screaming. All day people watch the infected screaming on the news. What's the first thing they think of?"

Tamara got to her feet. "Well, I'm not infected, am I?"

"She's okay," Paul called to the surrounding condos. "Go back to sleep. Everything's under control."

Tamara stood and pulled her tank top fully into place. Now wasn't the time to school Paul on his little privacy invasion. "Melanie and Aiden went to try to get to Manhattan. The closest bridges would have been the Throgs Neck or Whitestone Bridge. With the insanity that went down on the Whitestone, I'm afraid for them."

"Maybe they're spending the night with someone else in another condo. Let's check that she did leave. C'mon."

Paul led her to the security room off the main building. He unlocked the door and led her in. An enormous flatscreen television took up most of the wall. The television monitor was broken into six screens, each with a different view of Cedar Knoll: main entrance, outside the dayroom, a few angles between buildings, one covering the street in front of the main entrance.

Paul went to a keyboard and small monitor at the desk below the big screen. He selected Main Entrance from a drop-down screen and typed in yesterday's date and noon for the time. Then he clicked on a Rewind button.

The top-center box of the screen, the view of the main entrance, flipped from night to day. While the live feeds still looked like five tiny movies playing at once, the recorded version only seemed to save a frame every few milliseconds. The action moved herky-jerky, like some cheap 1960s stop-motion cartoon. Outside the gate, the front bumper of a car appeared on the right; then the next frame only captured the rear bumper on the left.

Paul hit a Fast Forward key. Shadows crawled across the pavement to new positions, but the gates never moved. Then a vehicle flashed through the gate at warp speed. Paul rewound a few minutes and played it back at normal speed. Melanie's Ford Escape rolled up, paused as Mickey opened the gate and sped off.

"And she's still out there," Tamara said.

"And we're in here, safe," Paul said. "She chose to leave. She knew the risks."

"Well, we need to find them. They didn't make it across the bridge."

"We don't know that they made it off the bridge, or if they ever got on it, or if they decided to stay at Aunt Tillie's in Bensonhurst. A night ride out there would be suicidal. If the infected didn't get us, some gang would."

Tamara let her silence admit he was right. Paul stood up and put a hand on her bare shoulder. She flinched away.

"If she calls for help, we'll get her," Paul added. "We take care of our own."

Great idea, Tamara thought, if there was a way for Melanie to call.

Chapter Thirty-Two

To the north, flames lit the night sky where Eddie's house once stood. The sound of roaring engines and muffled smaller explosions rolled by Melanie as she crouched in the shadow of her immobilized SUV. It lay like a crippled animal, canted down against the slashed tire. Aiden crouched beside her, knees tucked up to his chin. His eyelids drooped with exhaustion. Eddie peered over the hood and down the street.

"Hell, we probably couldn't get out of here anyway," he said. "The whole street's a damn parking lot."

"We need a safe place," Melanie said. "Do you know anyone around here?"

"Not this far south."

Desperation overtook her. "If we knock on some doors, I'm sure someone will let us in."

Eddie crouched down beside the deflated tire and looked at her over the top of his glasses.

"Seriously? Would you let strangers into your house in the middle of the night? More like they'd shoot us dead right through the front door. And I wouldn't blame 'em."

He was right. It might be different in the daylight, where people could see they weren't infected, but in the dark...

"Then we'll just hide in the car for a few hours until the sun comes up. The tint is too dark to see through at night."

"It beats sitting out here at the mercy of the infected or getting shot by a homeowner."

Melanie pulled out her remote, but paused with her thumb over the Unlock button. When she hit it, the car would chirp, the lights would flash, the headlights blaze. Anyone nearby wouldn't miss it. Using the key would be worse, setting off the alarm.

"Eddie," she said, "when the locks pop, you climb in the backseat and get low." She turned to whisper in her son's ear. "Aiden honey, you're going in the back hatch. Lie down and relax. It'll be safe. Here we go."

She held her breath and squeezed the remote. The locks thunked open. The confirming chirp sounded deafening. The dome light lit the interior like a lighthouse beacon. The headlights seemed to illuminate the entire neighborhood.

Melanie hit the remote's Tailgate Open. The back hatch crawled skyward. Aiden skittered to the rear of the car and slipped in before it was half-open. Melanie followed her son and pulled the cargo cover over the rear area. Aiden tucked in on his side and slid back into the corner.

"We'll go home in the daylight," she promised and slammed the hatch shut. The *Escape* nameplate flashed by.

Eddie climbed into the back. Melanie ran around and dove through the passenger door. With one hand, she threw the dome light Off switch, with the other she reached over and twisted the headlight switch from Auto to Off. The exterior lights died. She locked all four doors and slid down into the passenger-seat footwell.

No one said a word. They just listened for the feared arrival of the infected, the shout of the crazed, the bang of an explosion, the smash of glass.

Nothing happened. Melanie peered over the dash. The streets and yards remained empty. She exhaled and leaned back against the door.

"Not too shabby, Mellie," Eddie whispered from the backseat.

"So far so good," she said.

"If I can ask," Eddie said, "what the heck happened to this seat back here? It smells like Clorox."

"I'll tell you later."

The rumbling hum Aiden made as he slept buzzed under the rear cargo cover. She thanked God that her son could still drop off to sleep in a second. A few minutes passed, and she began to relax.

"What was with the Christmas carol you sang to your son back there?" Eddie said.

Eddie's soft, deep, disembodied voice in the darkness gave her comfort, made her unafraid to open up.

"By Aiden's second year, the autism was unmistakable. He couldn't communicate, so all we got were his panicked moans. We couldn't figure out yet what things set him off. It was around Christmas, and he was having the worst reaction to something. Then that carol came on the radio, and he calmed down. I don't know if it was the words or the melody that soothed him, but it worked some magic. Then next time the song came on, he wasn't in a fit, but it still seemed to relax him. Well, this is like parents of an average child discovering the pacifier. I don't want to burn its power out, so I only use it in the worst-case scenarios."

"I'd say this qualifies. He sure dropped off to sleep quick."

"Once he's out, he'll sleep through a hurricane. Waking up in a strange place won't go over well, though."

"He seems smart. People must think he's retarded because he doesn't speak."

"Not too many people understand Aiden."

"You seem to, and you're the one that matters most. He'll end up okay."

She mulled that comforting thought, leaned against the passenger seat cushion and drifted off to sleep.

A distant smash of glass awakened Melanie. She jerked upright and banged her head against the dashboard. The Escape's interior had a yellow glow. Relief at dawn's arrival turned to dread as she realized the color was too orange for sunlight. A quick glance over the dash revealed that two houses across the street were ablaze.

Somewhere outside the car, two men exchanged frenzied shouts. More glass smashed, closer this time.

"Mellie, wake up," Eddie said.

"I'm up."

Eddie's head periscoped up from the backseat far enough to see out the window. He ducked back down.

"Can't see nothing. The fire's come closer, though."

The shouting match picked up in volume, though not in clarity. Melanie's watch said there was at least an hour until daylight. That seemed like forever. If she and Eddie just stayed low, and if Aiden stayed asleep…

Feet from the car, a chainsaw ripped to life. A shiver went up Melanie's spine. The passenger seat flexed as Eddie tensed up on the other side. A low moan sounded from the cargo area.

"Aiden honey," she whispered, "everything's fine. Go back—"

The chainsaw revved. Aiden howled. The cargo cover kicked up out of its brackets as he beat against it. The silhouette of Aiden's head popped up in the back.

"Aiden, no!"

Another round of shouts. Automatic weapons rattled. Bullets pinged through the

Escape's front fender. Melanie ducked on instinct and covered her head. Aiden's howl rose into a shriek. The roaring chainsaw dropped back to idle, then stopped. Over Melanie's head, someone yanked on the locked door handle. Her heart stopped.

A gloved fist banged on the window. "This is Sergeant Salas, US Army! Unlock the doors and show me your hands!"

Melanie and Eddie sat up, hands in the air. In the car's confines, Aiden's screams seemed to pierce Melanie's skull.

"We're not infected!" she yelled. "My son's just scared. Don't shoot us!"

"Slowly step out of the car, passenger side, hands up behind your head."

Melanie and Eddie slipped out the passenger-side doors. Sgt. Salas stood in full combat gear, looking through night-vision goggles on his helmet. He wore a surgical mask. Two other soldiers flanked him. All three had their rifles trained on the Ford.

Sgt. Salas flipped up his goggles, let his rifle drop to the side and stepped forward. He played a penlight across Melanie's eyes and around her exposed skin. He did the same to Eddie. He seemed satisfied.

"Ma'am, please quiet your son before we get swarmed out here."

Melanie went to the rear of the car. She popped the back hatch. The volume of Aiden's screams dropped as soon as he saw her there. She talked him down and brought him out in front of the soldiers. Sgt. Salas went to check Aiden's eyes. He flinched back and away.

"He won't let you touch him," Melanie said. "He's not infected. If he were infected, we wouldn't have him locked in the car with us."

Sgt. Salas seemed to mull that over a moment. "We are evacuating this area, everything north of 25A." He spoke into a mic that hung down from an earpiece. "Block secure. Pick up three for return to Bay Terrace."

A two-and-a-half-ton Army truck plodded down the street. Canvas covered the open back and a V-shaped snowplow pointed from the front. With a crash of glass and a crunch of metal, it plowed aside any vehicles blocking the street. It lurched to a stop. The soldiers escorted Melanie, Eddie and Aiden to the rear. A half-dozen civilians sat in the shadows of the musty canvas cover, silent, shell-shocked. The three climbed up and joined them.

Dawn broke across the horizon. The big truck rumbled eastward toward the rising yellow sphere. Two NYFD pumper trucks passed going in the other direction.

"Looks like they'll fight the fires with daylight and the Army behind them," Melanie said.

"A little late, as far as I'm concerned," Eddie answered. He stared out the back of the truck at nothing in particular.

Melanie had lost the Ford, but poor Eddie had lost everything. She rested her hand on his knee. She wanted to say that everything was going to work out fine, but didn't think she could pull it off convincingly. She said nothing.

Spreading daylight revealed a neighborhood from nightmares. Cars and houses had been looted. Fires smoldered here and there. Clothes and paper littered the yards. Melanie wondered how much of this was done by the infected and how much wasn't.

A few minutes later, the truck stopped outside the Bay Terrace Shopping Center. The rising sun glinted off triple spirals of concertina razor wire that ringed the property. Soldiers ordered them out of the truck. Many of the dazed passengers moved off like sleepwalkers.

Inside the wire, people milled about the parking lot, stretching and shaking off the morning cold. Cases of MREs and bundles of bottled water sat under a green canvas tent in the parking lot's center. A row of upwind porta-potties sent an unwelcome fragrance over the area.

The three joined the line at the entrance. Two people with Red Cross armbands gave each of them a cursory inspection for infection. A soldier at a table typed in names and Social Security numbers into a laptop. Eddie reached the soldier at the table first.

"What is this place?"

"Temporary holding, sir, for everyone living north of 25A. After the bridge incident yesterday, any nonmilitary personnel in the area will be shot without warning, starting at noon."

Nothing about this place looked healthy to Melanie. "How long is temporary?" she asked.

The soldier shrugged. "You got two choices. In here with us…" he pointed south over their shoulders to a loose line of people with suitcases walking down Bell Boulevard, "…or out there with them."

"Eddie, you can't stay here. We're sure not staying here. You saved our lives. Come home with us."

"No, I couldn't. Got nothing to offer to pay my way. I'll be fine here."

Melanie pulled him aside and whispered in his ear, "Look at the quick exam they gave us before letting us in. They aren't screening out the infected very well. Half the people could be carrying the virus and minutes away from being sick."

She stepped away from him and turned to the soldier. "We'll pass."

"Those people walking out there are crazy," the soldier said. "Heading home is suicide unless you've got someone this side of the river we can call to pick you up."

Melanie's eyes lit up. "Get me to a phone so I can get us a ride out of here."

Chapter Thirty-Three

Melanie couldn't think of a more welcome sight. The Knoll's open-topped Jeep Wrangler jerked to a stop in front of the Bay Terrace entrance. Tamara jumped out and headed for the guards. Her one unbandaged eye searched the perimeter. Every muscle was tense, her lips stretched tight. Two perimeter guards leveled weapons in her direction.

Melanie waved. "Tamara!"

Tamara caught sight of her. She smiled with relief.

"Aiden, Eddie, they're here! C'mon." Melanie shooed them both out the front gate, where Tamara was already in a heated discussion.

"We don't want to get in; we're here to get someone out." Tamara caught sight of Melanie between the shoulders of the two guards. "Her, in fact."

"Yes, yes. She's here for us," Melanie said.

"Ma'am, there's no guarantee of your safety out there," one soldier said. "And we will not let anyone who leaves return. Too risky."

"They won't be coming back," Tamara said. She noticed Eddie. "Wait, who's this?"

"He's Eddie," Melanie said. "He saved our lives at least twice. The infected burned his house to the ground. He'll stay with me."

Tamara reached over and shook Eddie's hand. "Any friend of Melanie's is a friend of mine. Welcome to Cedar Knoll. Let's get out of here."

They walked back to the Jeep. Paul sat in the driver's seat of the Jeep. Mickey Reynolds sat in the rear cargo area with a smaller caliber rifle. Paul stood up and scowled as the four approached.

"Whoa, whoa, who the hell is this?"

"This is Eddie," Melanie said. "He saved our—"

"No way," Paul said. "We're not taking in strangers. We'll have a hard enough time supporting ourselves."

"You aren't Noah," Tamara said, "deciding who gets on the ark. Melanie can have anyone she wants stay in her condo." To Eddie, "Jump in the backseat."

Eddie stepped forward and looked Paul in the eye. "I'm old, but I'll pull my weight, count on that."

"The hell he will," Paul said. "What do we need with another old man in the complex?"

"Here's a better question," Tamara said. She put her hands on her hips. "What will you do without a nurse in the complex? Eddie here comes home with Melanie, or the three of them, and me, will just stay right here under the protective wings of the US Army."

Melanie bit her lower lip. There was no way she wanted to stay here, no way she wanted Aiden to stay here. If Paul called Tamara's bluff...

Paul gripped the top of the Jeep's windshield. His face turned red, his knuckles white.

"Paul," Mickey ventured, "we gotta prepare for every eventuality, right? A nurse is gonna come in handy."

"Drive home without us, Paul," Tamara said. "See how fast the residents jettison you when they see you'll abandon people out here."

Paul looked about ready to erupt. He clenched his teeth and dropped back into the driver's seat. "Get the hell in."

Eddie climbed in with Mickey. Mickey gave Eddie a curt nod. Tamara took the passenger seat. Aiden and Melanie sat in the back.

Paul dropped the Jeep into gear and drove into the rising sun. Melanie had a clear view of his steaming-mad profile. Tamara had humiliated him.

She had a feeling that payback was going to be hell.

Chapter Thirty-Four

K-Dogg had the crew hard at work first thing in the morning. A series of calls had gathered the remaining members of Mozelle's little crime family to the Quinn estate. By noon, they had searched and cleared the remaining twenty homes in Belle Pointe. Half were empty; the rest, the men emptied. Cooperative residents were escorted to the gate and expelled. The less cooperative found that the phrase "over my dead body" was the worst possible choice of words. A few women provided some vital, involuntary stress relief for the crew before their execution.

Juno drove the emptied trailer downtown and returned with the weapons stash. Those toys gave the perimeter guard along the Belle Pointe fence line military-grade firepower. The design of the slat fencing at the south end of Belle Pointe was deemed a bit more decorative than functional. The men took great pleasure in reinforcing it. They delivered vehicles from the plundered houses to the fence and rolled them on their sides to create an irregular wall of steel. One or two cringed at the losses, but most made a game out of tipping the Bentleys, Rollses and Audis into position.

Little of this interested Jimmy. Nothing outside his living room was as important as what was within. Sal Bonano sat on the marble floor in a puddle of urine, bound to a pillar. Several bedsheets wound around him like a mummy's wrap, pinning his arms to his sides. A tourniquet at the wrist had stopped the blood flow to his missing finger. He'd lose his hand that way, but that would have been the least of his worries if he'd been conscious and able to worry.

Jimmy sat a few feet away on a couch. He'd spent the night watching the disease progress, the fever climb, the veins darken. The news reported that there was no predicting how long the infection took to take full control of the victim, but the direct infection from a bite wound seemed to give it a good head start. Nine hours in and old Sal was engulfed.

About three hours ago, Sal's eyes had fluttered open for the first time since K-Dogg had closed them. He'd seemed completely rational, healthy. Jimmy probed his mind, and it registered normal, maybe a bit more disciplined than normal, though he didn't have a baseline on Sal for comparison. Sal begged to be released, asked about his ex-wife and son. Jimmy lied and said they were in Belle Pointe, waiting for him. After forty-five minutes, Sal faded out. His head slumped to the side, his breathing went shallow.

Jimmy had been preoccupied (a more truthful definition might be panicked) during the assault by the infected at the DC. He didn't try to deflect them with one of his new Jedi mind tricks. But he would now, in a controlled environment, like a scientific trial.

At ten minutes to noon, Sal's eyes snapped open again. This time they were red, irises the color of garnet, the whites bloodshot. His face contorted in a crimson rage.

"Let me out of this! Now, you son of a bitch!"

Sal had struggled to no avail against the binding sheets during his first awakening. This time he was different. His strength had increased by a factor large enough that he could move within the binding sheets. Deep within the wrappings, something tore.

Jimmy wasn't going to have as much time as he'd hoped for his little experiment. He leaned forward and tried to make eye contact. But Sal's head weaved back and forth as he shifted hard within the bindings. Jimmy closed his eyes and probed.

Searching the infected's brain was like touching the edge of a boiling tornado. Blinding fury raged as the predominant emotion, though a host of other bitter passions eddied around its edges. Reason had been sent off to Oz.

Jimmy tried to plant a memory in Sal. So great was the furious rush of thoughts and emotions that he couldn't insert the message. It was like trying to stick something through the spinning spokes of a bicycle wheel. The attempt made his head bang like a gong.

"You are so dead," Sal screamed. "When I get free, I'm going to rip your head off and shove it up your ass!"

Another tear sounded inside the bundle of sheets. Jimmy tried one more probe.

Another failure. It was as if his thought ricocheted off into space. Another spike of pain shot through his head.

The next, louder tear in the fabric whelped a long rip along Sal's shoulder. He bellowed in victory.

Jimmy reached between the couch cushions and pulled out a pistol. He aimed at Sal's head and fired. The bullet entered just above his left cheek. Red and pink splattered the pillar. Sal's head hung to one side, limp, his red eyes wide open.

That same strange feeling from the night before swept through Jimmy. His usually weak stomach lay completely calm. Even without his inherent squeamishness, this gruesome scene should have repulsed him on a basic human level. But not only did he not feel the impulse to avert his eyes at the grotesque reshaping of Sal's head, he found he couldn't stop staring. He felt a longing, a comfort in this twisted human wreckage bound up in bedsheets.

He laid the gun on the couch and approached Sal on his knees. With two fingers, he turned Sal's head to face him. Death clouded the corpse's fading pink eyes. He pushed the head back to the side. The gaping exit wound at the rear of the skull made it look like a cracked egg. Pink brain matter and bright-red blood ran down the back of his neck.

Jimmy touched a chunk of brain with his finger. He scooped it up and rubbed the spongy mass between his fingertip and thumb. A cavern opened up within him, a void that demanded to be filled, that screamed for him to take action. His mouth watered.

Alarms sounded in his psyche. Ancient taboos hardwired into the species awakened from their slumber in the shared consciousness of man. What he was thinking, what he was feeling, was horribly, disgustingly wrong.

But the warnings were as distant thunder. The craving drowned out all other thoughts. Undeniable demand buried the roiling revulsion. Drool hung from his lips. His taste buds tingled, aglow with anticipation.

He popped the piece of brain into his mouth.

Ecstasy burst within him. No taste had ever been as sweet, no sensation as fulfilling as the flavor the tiny morsel delivered. He held it there, crushed against his upper palate with his tongue, to savor every bit of its essence before he swallowed. He sucked in a great breath through his mouth and nose. The sweet sensation snaked straight into his mind.

He swallowed. His fingers darted into the hole in the corpse's skull and dug out another larger chunk of occipital lobe. He shoved this in his mouth and swallowed without chewing. His body shivered in delight. In an uncontrolled frenzy, he pulled chunk after chunk of soft tissue from the skull, mashed it into his mouth and swallowed. In seconds he scraped the skull empty.

Jimmy fell backwards against the couch and sighed. His bloated stomach rolled across his belt. Hands greasy with blood lay limply in his lap. He wiped his chin against his sleeve and left a rich-red slash.

The headache that had plagued him since his resurrection was gone. In its place was a new level of clarity, a new surge of mental strength, a new sense of amazing superiority. The craving he could not define had finally been satiated.

He wondered if this was what it felt like to evolve.

Chapter Thirty-Five

Samuel woke up at midnight. In his medical opinion, three hours of sleep really wasn't adequate. But his body didn't listen.

Insomnia was part of the process. When he'd been in Africa doing fieldwork, he was up nearly around the clock for the entire trip. There was too much to do in too-little time, and the promise of an answer always called from just around the next corner. He slept a few hours each night and then woke up wired, and ready to get back to work.

So now, hours before dawn, he lay wide awake. DNA structures and chemical compounds raced around his brain as he tried to fit them all into a big picture that would yield a cure for the blight of Q Island.

He slipped on some clothes and a jacket, and crept away from the sleeping area. Yesterday he'd been inside the whole day, breathing the terminal's stale, sterilized atmosphere. He needed some fresh air, or at least as fresh as New York City could provide.

The lower level exited to the airport tarmac. He popped open the door. The rush of cold air from outside made his skin tingle. He stepped outside and took a deep, cleansing breath. The welcome marshy smell of the nearby bay was like a tonic as it swept out the terminal's stagnant scent. The residual sleepy fuzziness in his brain melted away.

On his second deep breath, it struck him. The silence. New York City was never quiet, not at any time. Even in the morning's wee hours, subways rumbled by, sirens wailed, reverse-warning horns beeped and dumpsters clanged. Planes screamed by overhead bound for one of the nearby tristate airports. Samuel now stood on what had been the busiest airport in one of the world's busiest cities, and the world stood silent. Streetlights' glows lit the sky on the other side of the airport's fences. Samuel imagined it looked like a ghost town over there.

From over the water rolled the drone of propellers. The sound came closer, but its source stayed invisible. Then the dark bulk of a C-130 cargo plane uncloaked at the end of the farthest runway. Without landing or position lights, it was almost indiscernible in the gloom. It landed with a distant screech of tires. It rolled to the end of the runway, but did not approach the terminal. The two outer engines of the four spun to a stop. The rear cargo door dropped to form a ramp. Dim light spilled from the aircraft's interior. A few airmen stepped out onto the runway, only visible by the blue-green glow of the night-vision goggles on their flight helmets.

Two military cargo trucks drove out from Terminal 4 across the ramp. Their lights were out as well, as if the C-130 had started a trend. They pulled up next to the cargo plane and disgorged a dozen soldiers, all with night-vision goggles. Like ants at work, they formed a ragged, glowing line, and began to shift boxes and crates from the aircraft to the trucks.

It seemed odd that the plane wouldn't taxi up to the terminal. Of course, it was odd that it landed in the middle of the night without lights. There was the possibility that the commanders wanted to spare everyone's sleep by not thundering into the terminal at this hour. Samuel shook his head, unable to imagine that conversation taking place.

As soon as the trucks cleared the runway, the C-130's idle engines roared back to life. The gate cranked up as the plane began to turn and taxi. The crew apparently wanted no extra time sharing space with the newfound virus. The plane was airborne by the time the trucks arrived back at Terminal 4.

Samuel stepped sideways into the shadow of the jetway. No rules kept him from being out here, but the clandestine vibe of the soldiers' actions made him uneasy about being seen.

The trucks stopped at one of the Terminal 4 jetways across from Samuel. The jetway was lowered almost to the ground. Boards made a ramp from the tarmac to its open door. The unloading began. Most of the boxes were nondescript, but Samuel swore he recognized a few of the odder-shaped ones as medical equipment still bearing the manufacturer's shipping labels. One was the same centrifuge he had in his lab, and another looked a lot like a field MRI.

Certainly all that should have been coming to Terminal 2. His first impulse was to walk over and tell the soldiers their mistake. But the same nagging feeling that had backed him into the shadows a minute ago told him he'd better stay there. This was something better addressed in the light of day.

A notice posted by the breakfast line later that morning told Samuel he might not get his questions answered after all.

For security reasons, the ramp and taxiways of the airfield are off-limits to all nonmilitary personnel until further notice. In addition, Terminals 4 through 8 are not to be approached for any reason. Guards are authorized to use lethal force without warning.

People in line wondered about what brought this notice on. They speculated about a new incident along the wire or some kind of reaction to the infected rush on the Whitestone Bridge yesterday. Samuel had his own theory, and it had nothing to do with any outside threat.

"It's a normal security procedure," Vanessa said. She barely looked up from her laptop screen.

Samuel stood alone beside her desk. Sheets acting as makeshift blinds tried in vain to block the low morning sun. Cubicle walls now surrounded her workspace and gave them some privacy.

"Shoot without warning is normal?" Samuel said.

"No, not that. The separation of the military and civilians. They're from two different worlds. They need their rules and structure. You need your freedom to pursue your research whenever needed. They have soldiers on duty three shifts a day that need some undisturbed sack time. It's kind of an oil-and-water thing. I've been in these situations before. It's for the best."

Samuel remained unconvinced.

"Last night, some equipment was unloaded from a cargo plane," he said. "Some medical equipment."

Vanessa's fingers stopped over her keyboard. She looked Samuel in the eye. "How do you know that?"

"I saw it out the window." That sounded better than saying he was out on the tarmac. "After all these years, I know what field medical equipment looks like."

"We have backup equipment," she said. "Some of it came in last night. We aren't going to store it here and clutter the place up. Terminal Four is storage. If any of your equipment breaks down, I want your spare available right away."

"Vanessa, even during our government-backed fieldwork, I don't remember ever having a spare anything."

"Samuel, there's a big difference between now and then. The fate of humanity hangs in the balance here. The full resources of the federal government are at play. Whatever the cost, failure is not an option."

Samuel couldn't help but give her an incredulous look at such an uncharacteristic response.

She broke into a more familiar smile. "Sorry, Samuel. The last week, I think I've been spending way too much time with the military. I can't share everything I know with you, but these steps, the security steps, the organization at JFK, they're all proper. They are what we need to do to beat this thing. Trust me."

Samuel's experience was that when people had to tell you to trust them, it meant you most certainly couldn't.

"No problem. I'll get back to my team."

"Find us a cure, Bosi Daktari."

Samuel returned to his lab. He now had a fight on two fronts, an all-out war with the virus on one side, and some sort of shadowy cat-and-mouse game with the CDC on the other. He'd have to make sure winning the second fight didn't endanger winning the first.

Chapter Thirty-Six

If anyone took the time, they could have watched the latest scene of Q Island's tragedy play out from the sweeping view of Jimmy Wade's new backyard in Belle Pointe.

A convoy of six yellow school buses rumbled downhill and into deserted downtown Port Jefferson. They drove past the piers of moored pleasure boats and into the parking lot of the Port Jefferson Ferry Company.

The big, white ship bobbed against the dock, perhaps the largest victim of the quarantine. The boat's car deck ran along the waterline, and an enclosed passenger cabin made up the second deck. A booth-sized bridge created a third deck from which to con the vessel. A wide, sloppy, red cross painted on the ship's side dripped rivulets of dried paint, as if the cross had been bleeding. The ferry's engines fired up. Gray smoke rolled from its stacks.

The buses stopped side by side. The doors swept open. Men armed with rifles or shotguns stepped off of each bus. They formed a rough skirmish line between the buses and the abandoned town, ready to defend against the infected, or anyone else who tried to stop them.

One man waved an arm signal. The buses emptied. A trail of women and children hustled out the open doors. They bustled and fussed as they popped open strollers, belted in kids and strapped on backpacks. Then they surged up the wide metal ramp and onto the ferry. The half circle of men pulled back to the dock's edge.

The metal ramp began a slow, clunking climb as two chains cranked it skyward. Inside the gearing, something slipped. The chains unspooled and the corrugated ramp slammed down on the concrete dock. The crash of steel on stone rolled out from the harbor and echoed through the desolate streets. The men whirled to face the town at this potential infected call to arms. Safety catches snapped off.

The ramp began a second sweep upward. At two feet off the dock, the drive motor wailed with a grinding, shearing noise. Something snapped like a rifle shot. The ramp stopped moving.

The ship's great engines revved. The water at the stern churned in a soup of green and white. Mooring lines slid from the ship's side, and it inched forward against the incoming current. From openings around the waterline, white bedsheets spray-painted with black letters appeared. Each unfurled and displayed one word, like an old Burma-Shave ad— *Only. Women. And. Children. Aboard.*

One of the men on the dock turned to face the ship. His shaved head glistened in the sun. A long moustache drooped down to bracket his chin. The red logo on his black-leather jacket read *Road Demons.* He gripped his rifle with hands sheathed in studded half gloves. He squinted at the ship and scowled.

A woman ran to the stern. She wore a bright-red sweater. A blue streak ran the length of her long, dark hair. She gripped the rear railing with one hand and held a bundled baby to her chest with the other. She released the railing just long enough to wave.

Road Demon smiled and raised a gloved fist in response.

Gunfire erupted from the town. A wave of the infected surged across the parking lot. Several fired wild shots from pistols as they ran. The rest carried weapons that ranged from bats to metal bars.

The men on the dock didn't dash for the bus, unconcerned about their own safe escape. They dropped to one knee and returned fire. Gaps formed in the front rank of the infected. Replacements filled it. The mob drove forward.

The men got off one more volley. Then the infected surged through and over them. The first rank mauled the defenders, tearing at them with bars and blades and teeth. The rest rushed past to the ferry.

The crowd on the ship let out a collective scream. The ferry's nose dipped as the passengers ran from the endangered stern.

At the dock, three infected in a flat-out run launched themselves at the retreating ferry. The first fell straight into the water. The second landed with the ramp's edge across its chest. It scrambled for a handhold on the slick metal surface and then slipped off into the wake from the ship's spinning propellers. A red patch surfaced in the water and dissolved.

The third one cleared the growing gap with ease. It landed on both feet, arms spread for balance, knees flexed against the impact. It looked up with triumphant blood-red eyes.

Two women rushed the boarder. Before it could rise, one grabbed each arm and swept it back off its feet. It clawed and snapped at the women as they dragged it back, and threw it off the edge of the ramp. It hit the water with a splash and bobbed to the surface.

The women high-fived in victory. Blood seeped from a fresh, curved wound on one woman's arm, the size and shape of a set of human teeth. She noticed then looked in panic at the other woman. The wounded one shook her head in a slow plea for mercy.

The other woman showed none. She lowered a shoulder and without hesitation body checked the wounded woman into the water. The ferry chugged forward. She surfaced, spit a mouthful of seawater and dog-paddled toward shore. The infected who was bobbing a hundred yards behind her swam to intercept.

The ferry sailed out of the harbor, bound for Connecticut, in search of compassion.

Thirty-two minutes later, a black smudge rose from the horizon when the *USS Sailfish* torpedoed the ferry. An armed volunteer civilian flotilla ensured there were no survivors.

That afternoon, squadrons of attack helicopters descended on marinas and harbors along both of Q Island's shorelines. High explosive shells shattered and sank anything that floated. A follow-up wave of drones armed with fléchette rounds raked boatyards into mounds of pulverized fiberglass. The next day, the government recommended that everyone destroy any boats in their backyards to minimize the risk of collateral damage during what were now named remote-immobilization operations.

Part Three
Eradication

Chapter One

Four months later

"Dr. Bradshaw!"

Samuel startled awake as Remy, one of the female lab technicians shook him awake. The terminal was dark. She whispered in his ear with the kind of calm urgency medical personnel mastered early in their career. A glance at his watch told him it was just after 3:00 a.m.

"What is it, Remy?"

"Wanda and Eileen are sick. Very sick. Dr. Reed said to come wake you."

An alarm bell went off in his head. If Reed couldn't handle it alone… If the virus had infected someone…

"I'm following you," Samuel said.

He threw on a pair of pants and followed Remy to the restrooms. Inside the ladies' room, a group of women in pajamas made a semicircle outside the open toilet-stall doors. Dr. Reed knelt in the doorway of one.

"Dr. Reed?" Samuel said.

The women turned at the sound of his voice and parted so he could approach. Dr. Reed blew a stray strand of hair from her eyes. She looked grim.

Eileen sat on the toilet, sweatpants down around her knees. The vivacious, twenty-something blonde looked decades older. Dark, swollen rashes blotched her pale skin. She winced with pain, her eyes clamped shut. Vomit speckled her chin.

"The good news is," Dr. Reed said, "it's not the virus. The bad news is it's something else. She woke up with massive cramps, diarrhea, vomiting. I'd credit food poisoning if it weren't for these black blotches on her skin."

Dr. Reed turned over one of Eileen's hands. It looked like she'd been handling coal.

"Wanda is in the next stall, exactly the same."

The symptoms triggered one of Samuel's memories from one of his African trips.

But that didn't make any sense…

He stepped in and sniffed Eileen's breath. It smelled like garlic.

"Is there blood in the urine?"

"Yes, a bit."

"This woman has arsenic poisoning. I saw it in the gold mines in Congo where they use it to leach out the minerals. But those men suffered from chronic exposure. This is acute." Samuel turned to Remy who stood outside the stall. "Where have these two been tonight?"

"I-I'm not sure," Remy said.

"If we don't find what they were exposed to, more people will end up just as sick, or worse. Where were they?"

Remy caved. "They went over to Terminal Four. They got back hours ago. They met some soldiers there, just to have a little fun."

"Looks like the fun is over. Dr. Reed, get these women to the infirmary. Test the urine for arsenic, but start them both on Dimercaprol anyway as you wait for the results. I'm going to go find the source."

Samuel returned to his bunk. He tossed on a jacket and shoes, and headed straight to the tarmac. No guard stood watch beneath Terminal 4. He'd probably been part of the party committee and might be as sick as the techs.

He opened the door to the terminal's ground floor. Pallets of MREs filled the space. They were the bright-green boxes labeled *Civilian Population Use Only—Not Military Rations*. He thanked God his team didn't have to eat these.

He walked between the pallets to an open space between rows. There sat four chairs around a small kerosene stove. A few bottles of vodka and several open boxes of MREs lay around. Beside the stove sat a large pile of dehydrated coffee packets.

"Idiots," Samuel said under his breath. He picked up a few unopened coffee packets. He shoved them in his pocket then noticed something else. Empty atropine injectors lay under one seat.

The lab techs brought atropine; the grunts stripped the coffee from a bunch of MREs. They concentrated the caffeine from the coffee down to an elephant-level dose for a rush, then followed it with vodka and atropine chasers for the downslide. It didn't get much stupider.

But that little game wouldn't have gotten them poisoned. There had to be something else.

"Don't move!"

Samuel turned. An Army colonel between the row of pallets had a pistol aimed at Samuel's head. Samuel raised his hands.

"This area is off-limits to civilians," the colonel said.

"I'm Dr. Samuel Bradshaw with the CDC in Terminal Two. Two of my technicians were here with your soldiers tonight. They are very sick."

"How sick?" His gun never wavered.

Samuel sensed the colonel knew exactly how sick Eileen and Wanda were, and what they were sick with. The colonel was fishing to find out how much Samuel knew. Something about the colonel's unerring aim said if Samuel mentioned the word *arsenic* it would be the last word he ever said. Instead, he glanced down at the floor. His face curled in anger.

"Oh, now that tears it," Samuel said. "And it explains the nausea, the cramps, everything. May I?"

The colonel didn't answer. Samuel crouched down and picked up a few empty atropine injectors.

"Atropine poisoning," Samuel said. "Atropine is used for allergic reactions or defense against nerve gas. We have a supply on hand, testing it against the virus. It's open to abuse. Those techs are going to be fired for this."

"If they got your soldiers sick, I apologize. Let them sleep off any side effects and they'll be fine."

Silence hung heavy in the air.

The colonel lowered his pistol. "My men were as much to blame as your women. They'll be dragged before the battalion commander, trust me. Sorry about drawing down on you. With infected at the wire constantly, you can't be too careful."

"No problem," Samuel said. "Good night."

Samuel turned and walked out, not shaking his expectation of a bullet in the back. Did the colonel buy his lie, or did he just pretend to buy it? Samuel was way too old to have to play these kinds of head games. Only when the terminal door closed behind him did he dare think he was safe.

As soon as he returned, Dr. Petty met him at the door. Everyone from the medical lab stood around, awake and anxious.

"Dr. Reed called," Dr. Petty said, "and Eileen and Wanda are both checked in. They've started your prescribed treatment. Find anything?"

Samuel scanned the worried, expectant faces in the terminal, faces that looked to him for leadership, for comfort.

"No, nothing. There was an Army colonel there, pretty agitated. He didn't say, but I think his men were sick as well." He turned to the rest of his team. "Whatever those people got into, it's not contagious, and it's not inside our terminal. Stay between here and Terminal One, like we're supposed to, and everything will be fine. Eileen and Wanda are in good hands. Go on back to sleep. You have a busy day in a few hours."

The crowd dispersed into packs of two and three. Samuel touched the coffee packets in his pockets. He turned to Dr. Petty.

"Doctor, I need you to do a spectral analysis for me. And do it quietly."

He pressed the stolen coffee packets into Petty's palm and closed the man's hand around them. Petty stole a peek.

"Instant coffee?"

"Most of it is, probably. Look for something trace, something that doesn't belong. Start with a search for arsenic. Give the results straight back to me."

Petty looked solemn. "You got it."

Dr. Reed came running down the length of the terminal, her face frantic. She saw Samuel and went straight for him.

"They're gone! They came and took them?"

"Who's gone?"

"Eileen and Wanda! A squad of soldiers marched into the infirmary and dragged them off!"

Chapter Two

Samuel charged straight for the infirmary, where two armed soldiers made it clear his company was not requested. They wouldn't even contact their superiors. He realized he wouldn't get any straight answers from the military. He'd have to go straight to Vanessa. She'd get this straightened out in minutes once she returned from Atlanta.

Hours later, he met her as she deplaned from the military transport. Just as he was about to unload on her, she struck first.

"What the hell did you do last night, Samuel? Are you trying to create a rift with the military? They *do* keep us alive here, you know."

"What did *I* do? They kidnapped my sick technicians from the infirmary, out of my doctor's medical care."

Vanessa led Samuel into the terminal, then into a small storage room and closed the door.

"I'm going to do you a favor now and not rip you apart in front of your team. You've jeopardized the entire CDC operation here."

"And how did I do that?"

"Your people broke curfew and fraternized with the military. They stole drugs from our stores, used them to get high and made two soldiers too sick to report for duty."

"So the Army kidnaps them?"

"Holds them as witnesses. They'd be well within their rights to arrest them. As a second favor to you, I talked their colonel out of that."

"Vanessa, those women don't have hangovers, they were poisoned. Probably arsenic. I saw it myself."

"Forgive me if I don't take as gospel your bleary-eyed, early morning diagnosis."

Samuel blinked at her blunt, disrespectful tone.

"Do you have any proof of this supposed poisoning?" she continued. "No, because I had the infirmary tests sent to me and they came up negative."

"Negative?"

"Not a trace."

"But I saw—"

"I don't know what you think you saw, but the women were not poisoned. Arsenic! What is this, the nineteenth century? Your technicians will be released after the military concludes its investigation, unless it's found they should be charged for any of the dozen rules they broke."

The discussion wasn't unfolding the way Samuel had envisioned it. Vanessa was supposed to rally with him against the military.

"The military doesn't want to be here," she continued. "They'd rather man the coastline and keep an open body of water between them and the virus. The only thing keeping them here is us. They'd love to have a reason to pull out of here. Why don't you keep your people from giving them one?"

Someone knocked on the storeroom door. "Dr. Clayton?"

Vanessa lowered her voice. "Keep your people in the terminals. Keep them at work. Find a cure."

She opened the storeroom door. A confused staffer stood there tensed like he was braced for a hurricane. Vanessa blew by him. He followed, with a look of relief.

Samuel leaned back against the wall, stunned. An upbraiding by his former protégée was a big pill. It punctured the bubble of respect he thought she had for him, but, worse, it reset his place in the organization, in the world. He'd thought of himself as the leader here, as he'd been on his African trips. Now he realized how long ago those expeditions were, how old he'd become. He no longer powered the machine. He turned as a cog within it.

Halfway up the steps to the main terminal, Dr. Petty met him. He looked grim.

"Just passed Dr. Clayton and she looked ready to kill."

"She's not going to be much help. Without some proof of the poisoning, she's siding with the military."

Dr. Petty's face fell. "About that…the spectrometer results showed no arsenic."

"They had to."

"I ran it three times. It's coffee."

Another buttress of Samuel's world fell away. Surely, he still recognized arsenic poisoning when he saw it. Didn't he? The military might cover something up, but he couldn't dispute Dr. Petty's honest results. He wouldn't lie. Eileen and Wanda worked for him.

"We'll sort through this later," Samuel said. "Dr. Clayton's right about one thing. We need to find a cure. Let's get back to work."

Chapter Three

Melanie upended the brown pill bottle. The last dose of Risperidone rolled out into her palm. Her heart sank.

She'd worried about this day for months, this day when Aiden's medications would run out. She'd rationalized many reasons not to obsess about an event that may never come; perhaps the quarantine would be lifted, maybe medical services would be expanded, maybe Aiden would get better. Every excuse was more desperate, more ridiculous than the last. Now, the single tiny pill in her hand lay there and mocked her foolish avoidance.

She placed the pill beside the other in Aiden's spoon at the breakfast table and picked up the landline phone. She punched in the number to Charles's new Manhattan apartment. Its rental was an admission that their separation was anything but temporary.

"Your call has been sequenced," the familiar automated voice said. "Please hang up. You will be connected in the order in which you called. Do not place a second call or you will lose your place in this queue."

The cascading failure of cell towers made the once indispensable devices all but worthless, which forced all the traffic through the diminished number of landlines. Two months ago, comm restrictions kicked in to filter the calls, like the on-ramp green lights on California freeways. The callback wait sometimes took hours. By then, Charles would be at work on Wall Street, and no one would answer.

The phone rang. She jumped and snatched it from the cradle.

"Your call has been connected," an impassive recording said. "Thank you for your patience during this emergency. Please hold."

"Hello?" Charles said.

"Charles! Thank God. I was afraid I'd miss you. You were supposed to call me last night!"

"What? When?" Dishes clinked in the background. "Oh, I tried. I never got a callback."

There was always a callback. Eventually. She didn't have time to press the point before their two rationed minutes expired.

"Did you get Aiden's meds?"

"No. They won't write me a scrip without him here. They cracked down on that after the big scam in Westchester. Besides, even if I did, how would I get it to you with the limited mail service? Drugs won't get through. Everything coming into Q Island is screened."

It rankled her that he called their home Q Island.

"I thought that private company, TransGlobal, still shipped," she said.

"I could send the pills to the moon cheaper. And Trans doesn't guarantee delivery anymore. Half the armored-car drivers quit when the infected overran their convoy near Sayville. You'll need to take him to one of the med centers. I've put money in the checking account to cover it."

"Barely," Melanie said. "I had seven dollars in the account last Thursday."

"Well, the rates on a Manhattan apartment aren't cheap, laws of supply and demand hard at work here. Food costs a fortune with all the security delays. Besides, the new funds transfer rules limit what I can send you each week."

A higher-pitched voice sounded in the background. More dishes clinked.

"Who's that in the background?" Melanie demanded.

"What? No one." The phone went silent. When Charles spoke again, all the background noise was gone. "The television was on. Look, I need to get to work. The DAX went nuts last night. We need to clean up a mess of trades. I'll get as much money as I can into your account. I'll get back with you later."

He hung up before she could answer, before she could tell him that his distant attitude wasn't cutting it. In the past four months, their conversations had devolved into businesslike exchanges where Charles sounded like he was speaking to a client. For her, the tone sounded all too familiar. As a child, she'd heard conversations like these a thousand times, every time her divorced parents spoke.

Aiden padded into the kitchen in his pajamas, the Routine's modification since Q Island's schools had closed. He sat down and took his pills.

"Good morning, honey," Melanie said.

Aiden stared down at his empty place setting. Melanie shook her head in sadness at her second frustratingly uncommunicative conversation of the morning.

She opened the cabinet beside the sink and sifted through the lime-green sealed plastic pouches inside. The Emergency Civilian Meals, as the government called them, were versions of the military's Meals, Ready to Eat or MREs. The MRE's dark-brown pouch got a cheerier bright-green color and a *Civilian Population Use Only—Resale Prohibited* message on the outside. The government claimed the overprocessed foods on the inside were fortified with more vitamins for children's needs. The government claimed a lot of things lately.

Q Island hadn't wintered well. Canned and frozen food remained edible for months, but that made no difference when there weren't months of it on hand. The system of dropping over-the-road trailers at the bridges to Q Island and having local drivers ferry them inland didn't last a month. Millions couldn't be supported on what amounted to a semitruck bucket brigade. Fuel ran short, even after most inbound supplies were switched to diesel. Trucks had to survive assaults by the infected, hijacking by criminals and then swarmings by the honest and desperate when the drivers tried to unload. Empty trailers jammed the island in queue for decon washes on the mainland side. When nervous National Guardsmen accidentally blew up the Brooklyn Bridge, that sealed the trucking concept's fate.

Now, Q Island lived by airlift. Cargo planes into JFK, recently cleared MacArthur Airport and a fleet of private and military helicopters brought in food. Every ounce counted, and the math equation became calories per kilogram. No cans, no fresh produce, no refrigerated goods. Emergency Civilian Meals in the bright-green boxes packed a day's worth of calories in a pouch, if you could stand to eat everything in the pouch.

Melanie broke open two packs of potatoes and eggs, added extra water and popped them in the microwave. She checked her watch and the calendar. She had two hours before the rolling blackout hit Cedar Knoll today. She pressed the Start button. Ninety seconds later, she served Aiden. The Routine had swapped shredded-wheat squares for eggs, with only a small outburst. He dove into the reconstructed food as usual.

Did he like the eggs? Or was he just starving? A part of her dared hope that he was doing it for her, so she wouldn't worry about him not eating. More questions his condition never let her answer.

Breakfast complete, Aiden left the table without a word. He took his reading book from the kitchen counter and returned to his bedroom, ready to start their daily homeschooling. The Routine. Always the Routine. A different one under quarantine, but still one had to exist to anchor him in this world that he saw so differently from everyone else.

"Honey, you start reading. I'll be in there in a few minutes. I have one thing to check on." She shook her head at the mixed blessing of not having to admonish him to stay in his room.

Melanie stepped outside the condo. The air was chill, the sky a wall of overcast. The calendar lied about the impending end of winter's gray, the pewter skies turning blue, and gunmetal trees sprouting green. These short, depressing days nurtured no hope of the infection's cure. She went down to the dayroom.

The last four months had transformed Cedar Knoll. Water restrictions doomed the landscaping. Dead grass and dirt surrounded the skeletal remains of once robust bushes. Greasy trails stained the sidewalks between the buildings. Garbage somehow tucked itself into every corner, despite the residents' best efforts to keep the grounds clear. The cars in the lot looked junkyard ready, stripped of tires, emptied of gas, clouded glass coated in winter's dirt.

Razor wire reinforced the top of the condo-complex walls, though Paul never explained exactly how he got his hands on it. Wide metal plates welded across the entrance gates transformed them into near-solid walls of black steel. Mickey Reynolds stood guard at the wall, beside the barred main sidewalk gate to the outside world. A pistol hugged one hip and a rifle hung across his opposite shoulder. A line of unwashed outsiders bobbed on the gate's far side. Some of them clutched laden plastic bags they hoped would be their tickets to treatment.

Melanie opened the door to the dayroom as an older woman exited. A tangle of sparse, gray hair touched the woman's shoulders. Her blackened jacket and pants stank of sweat and urine. Her hand sported a fresh, white bandage. She gave the relative sanctuary around her a longing look. Mickey locked his eyes on her and drew his pistol. She beat a beeline for the sidewalk gate, eyes on the ground. Mickey cracked the gate to let her out, then slammed it shut.

Inside, the front half of the dayroom had turned triage clinic. Tamara stood alone beside a fold-up table covered in a white sheet. She wore a blue scrub top over jeans. A stethoscope draped her neck. Her welcoming smile made an odd juxtaposition with her wide, black eye patch.

"Early riser!" she said. She gave a look of mock disappointment. "You didn't bring any coffee?"

"The line at Starbucks was so long. That woman who just left...her hand...was she...?"

"Bitten? No. Mickey wouldn't let her in if she was bitten. Hell, he might shoot her through the gate. Just a slash wound that earned her some stitches."

"It's good you could help her."

"She lucked out. She brought five jars of honey. That's on Paul's list, so Mickey let her in."

"That's the going rate for medical care?"

"I don't know. It changes daily. If it were up to me we'd treat everyone, worst case first. But I'm not one of the gods with a gun. More important, what brings you down here? Are you two okay?"

"Yes, we're fine. But Aiden won't be soon. I'm out of his meds."

"Mel, I've tried, and I can't get someone to write me a scrip for them, even with me being a nurse and running our clinic."

"I know. I'm not blaming you. I've put it off as long as I can, but I'm going to need to take him in to St. Luke's."

Tamara's smile faded. "We knew you'd have to eventually. The place is pretty intimidating now. And the trip over isn't any Sunday drive."

"Could you come with us? It's a lot to ask, but you know your way around, who to talk to. It's going to overwhelm Aiden and—"

Tamara grabbed Melanie in a bear hug. "Of course I'm going with you."

"Going with her where?"

Paul had stepped in through the dayroom's rear door. An assault rifle hung at his shoulder. He'd grown a goatee over the last month and shed thirty pounds since the quarantine.

"She needs to take her son to St. Luke's," Tamara said.

"No way," Paul said. "We need to have the clinic open."

"And her son needs medication." Tamara's face started to flush.

"And we need the cash and goods that the rabble out there trade for your Band-Aids and aspirin. It helps keep everyone in here fed, in case you haven't noticed."

"Oh, I noticed," she nearly yelled. She took a breath and exhaled. "Look, I need to go to St. Luke's anyway to resupply."

Paul considered it. "Fine. Then Mickey goes with you."

"What? I go to St. Luke's by myself all the time."

"Exactly. And this time you have two passengers that need protection. Mickey goes, or you all stay."

Tamara turned to Melanie. Her eyes blazed, though her voice stayed calm. "Mel, get Aiden and come back here in fifteen minutes."

The air felt like it was filled with gunpowder dust and ready to explode. Melanie nodded and backed out the door to leave the two of them alone.

When the door closed behind Melanie, Tamara whirled to face Paul. "What the hell is your—"

Paul grabbed her by the throat. She choked and her heart missed a beat. He yanked his hunting knife from its sheath and laid the blade across her left cheek.

"You ever question me again like that, and I will carve that remaining eye out like you're a goddamn jack-o'-lantern."

"The kid needs medicine," Tamara choked out.

"He won't die without it. He'll just be even more annoying, and only to his mother."

Paul released his grip. Tamara gagged and backed away.

"Those two hang here by a thread," Paul said. "You think I can't get this crowd to demand they leave? The boy adds no value, and the mother spends all her time taking care of him. The two of you brought that old man Eddie into the condos, another waste of space. Melanie hasn't paid her fees in two months. I let everyone in on that, and where do you think she stands?"

Tamara would have killed the authoritarian jackass that very moment if the half-dozen power-drunk men who followed him wouldn't exact retribution against her and Melanie. Melanie had enough on her plate, so whatever dark designs Paul might be drawing, she needed to shield her best friend and Aiden from them. The last thing Melanie needed to know was that Paul was out to get her.

"So," Paul said, "you and Mickey get them to St. Luke's and back during your resupply run. And stop screwing with me, or I'll find a way to get by without Melanie, her freak kid, a geezer, and one pain-in-the-ass nurse."

Paul stalked out the front door. He slipped his knife into its sheath as the door closed behind him.

Tamara imagined slipping that knife into him instead. As one trained to heal, the thought made her feel surprisingly good.

Chapter Four

"C'mon, Aiden. Tamara's waiting for us."

She tried to hurry him down the sidewalk to the main entrance. He had his hood up, his eyes cast to the ground. But he'd reacted much better about going to St. Luke's than she'd expected. She'd explained why, and he seemed to understand. Melanie knew how to see when he did, by his positive reactions, by grabbing his coat to go somewhere, by filling his backpack, mostly by not panicking at the prospect of change.

The Jeep idled at the sidewalk's end. The Jeep had become the de facto Cedar Knoll vehicle. Rugged and reliable, small and maneuverable in the littered streets, it more than made up for its inhospitable open-air setup. Tamara sat in the driver's seat, a Yankees ball cap pulled low across her brow. An open red cooler sat in the rear cargo area. Aiden climbed in the back.

Melanie gripped the edge of the doorframe. Her pulse kicked into high gear. Her knees felt weak.

"You okay?" Tamara said.

"Yeah. It's just that I haven't been outside the gate since…well, the last time I was in this Jeep was when you picked us up."

"I'll get you there and back safely. I know a good route. The guards let me in without stopping. It'll be fine. Before you know it, we'll be home with a month's supply of Aiden's meds."

Tamara exuded contagious self-assurance.

Aiden stared a hole in the driver's seatback headrest. He fiddled with the strings of his hoodie. Was he scared, resigned, indifferent? Did he feel guilty for being the cause of this trip, or was he happy that the medicine that gave him a hold on reality was close at hand? Melanie wished she knew. She slid into the seat next to him.

Paul and Mickey approached from the dayroom. They passed the rear of the Jeep on opposite sides. Paul stopped beside the driver's seat and stared down at Tamara.

"Slide over."

Tamara shot him a look of mixed anger and confusion. "I thought Mickey was going with us."

"Change of plans." His eyes filled with menace. "Slide. Over."

Tamara gripped the wheel then shot a glance at Melanie. She sighed with a growl and slid into the passenger seat. Paul dropped into the driver's seat and wedged his rifle between the seats, barrel against the windshield.

Melanie sat down in the backseat like the whole Jeep might explode from the tension up front. She needed to ask Tamara what in God's name was going on. Just much later.

Mickey rolled open the gate. The line of people outside had vanished when the clinic closed, and now the street was deserted. Paul started the Jeep.

"We're one big, happy Cedar Knoll family," Paul said. "Out for a little drive. Maybe we'll get ice cream on the way back." He bent the rearview mirror for a view of Aiden. "What do you say, boy? Want to stop for ice cream?"

Aiden shrank back in his seat. He ducked his head. His hood drooped forward and cast his face in shadow. Melanie kicked into mother-grizzly mode.

Tamara cut her off before she said a word. "The gate's open, Paul. Let's go."

Everyone tied on surgical facemasks. Melanie double-checked that Aiden tied his knots tight.

When the gate clanked shut behind the Jeep, goose bumps crawled up Melanie's arms. It was as if a huge pair of scissors had cut her off from the safe little world she'd had for the past four months. The open-top Jeep felt exposed and vulnerable, and, worse, like it put Aiden at greater risk. She slid as close to him, and as far from the vehicle's side, as she could.

She watched, stunned, as the neighborhood rolled by. Furnishings and cars littered the road. Paul never got the Jeep out of third gear. Garbage lay everywhere—papers, cans, bottles. Trash pickup was a thing of the past, which left burning it, as Cedar Knoll did, or tossing it in the street and letting the wind take it. Homes and buildings had two modes, either boarded up and secure, or open and looted. Spray-painted messages provided sad epitaphs on some walls.

Sophie, at Mom's. Find me!

In basement. Do not enter. I am armed.

One gutted building had the phrase *Hope Abandoned* sprayed across the shattered exterior.

Whole blocks of last year's houses were now just charred shells. Paul picked his way through a minefield of open manhole covers and crashed cars. At the street's far edges, people scurried for cover as the Jeep passed, unready to risk their lives in the hope that the four of them were benign. The few they passed were armed. Rifles, shotguns, baseball bats. One man carried a hockey stick studded with knife blades.

"Where are the police, the Army?" Melanie said.

"Defending themselves," Paul answered. "We're our own police out here."

Paul slowed at a large four-way intersection. He crawled the Jeep around a blackened mound in the center. The breeze carried the scent of gasoline and the reek of charred meat, the smell somehow both sweet and innately repulsive. From the mound's edge reached one blackened, withered hand, a gold band seared into the ring finger. The infected were feared in life, but everyone was feared in death. Rumor was every town had a pyre site like this, the common end for infected and uninfected alike.

Melanie worried about Aiden's reaction, but his eyes remained fixed on the Jeep's floor. Thank God. The whole world had become some R-rated horror film, with those under seventeen admitted without parental permission.

Two soldiers staffed St. Luke's security perimeter, aided by some unimposing civilians. They did wave Tamara right in. Lights burned in the hospital main floor, with sporadic lighting on the floors above. A few cars and military vehicles parked by the main entrance. Paul pulled around back to the loading dock where clinics like theirs resupplied with whatever was available.

Paul jumped out, rifle slung on his shoulder, and met an orderly just outside the door. He dropped his mask. They exchanged a quick, low conversation. Paul returned and volunteered to load the supplies while Tamara helped Melanie. It came across more as an order.

Tamara led Melanie and Aiden inside and into the hospital's chaos. She introduced them to Dr. Klein, a petite, harried GP. She took them both into a separate room. Aiden got a rushed exam. Dr. Klein even gave Melanie a once-over. She pronounced them fit and handed Melanie a baggie full of Risperidone. Plastic bottles had become quaint as homespun quilts. Dr. Klein obviously cared, and just as obviously didn't have the time to. Melanie thanked her as she shuffled them out the door. Tamara was waiting.

"Looks like the doc hooked you up," she said.

"Two months' worth. But I feel like a street addict picking up pills in a baggie."

"Let's get home," Tamara said.

At the loading dock, Paul and the orderly were deep into another furtive conversation. It broke off as soon as they saw the women approach. Aiden wandered over to look into an open ambulance. Melanie followed him as Tamara headed for the Jeep.

The orderly dropped back into the warehouse. Paul met Tamara at the Jeep. Three small boxes sat in the cargo area beside the closed red cooler.

"What's this?" Tamara said. "Where're the usual supplies?" She turned to the warehouse. "Hey, orderly! Where the hell—"

"That's what they've got," Paul said. "They got shorted, we get shorted. Shit rolls downhill."

Tamara ran to the back of the Jeep. "What about Ms. Reifler's insulin?"

She popped open the cooler. Three vials of insulin sat on a thin bed of ice.

"We got that," Paul said.

Tamara reached for a battered, unlabeled box. Paul jabbed the butt of his rifle between her and the box. "That one's not your concern."

"Medical supplies *are* my concern."

The rifle butt slid the box out of her reach. "Your concern should be getting the three of you back home," Paul whispered. "The state may think the boy would be better served in their care, with his disabilities and all. At least held for observation here. Should I ask?"

"You've really mastered being a jackass, haven't you?" Tamara retreated to the passenger seat.

"That's a good nurse."

Melanie and Aiden stepped down from the dock.

Paul smiled without warmth. "Let's get out of here," he said.

Chapter Five

Melanie clutched the baggie of pills to her stomach as she bounced beside her son in the Jeep's backseat. Days, no, months of calm for Aiden rolled between her fingers. A panicked vision of dropping them out the open side of the Jeep flashed by. She tucked them under her shirt and into her waistband.

While they were in the hospital, the warm sun had vaporized the clouds. Blue sky stretched to both horizons. If she looked up past the damaged and abandoned homes, she could imagine the change of seasons arriving, the lengthening days. Flowers would bloom. Fresh vegetables would grow. Certainly, this year, a vaccine…

The Jeep turned a corner. Paul stood on the brakes, and Melanie slammed into the back of the front seats.

"Son of a bitch!" Paul said.

Two cars that had earlier been on the side of the road now pivoted to block it. The Jeep slid to a halt with inches to spare.

"Damn it!" Paul threw the Jeep into reverse. He hit the gas, but all four tires spun in place. A film of oil covered the road.

Five infected rushed out of the buildings on both sides. Four months of hell had turned their clothes to rags. Their eyes burned bright red within filthy faces. A bat, a board, a shovel—all five brandished some kind of weapon.

Paul stood between the front seats and tossed his revolver in Melanie's lap. It landed hard and heavy. He snapped his rifle to his shoulder and aimed to the right.

"Shoot something!" he shouted.

Melanie lurched back and looked at the gun like it was a coiled snake. She hadn't ever fired a gun, hadn't ever even held one. Her family had a storied antigun tradition.

Tamara crawled across into the driver's seat. She punched the accelerator. The Jeep slid left as the whining, spinning tires pivoted the vehicle in place. Gray smoke billowed from the wheel wells. Tamara made a frantic hand-over-hand spin of the wheel to try to regain control. The infected closed to within yards.

A rifle shot cracked by Melanie's ear. She jumped, and the pistol leapt up off her lap. To the right, the chest of one of the infected exploded, and it dropped to the ground. The pistol clattered to the floor of the Jeep.

Chunk-snap.

A spent brass shell whizzed by Melanie's head. Another roar of the rifle made her cringe. The shot went wide. One of the infected reached the Jeep.

Aiden screamed. He ducked down into the footwell. A blazing-eyed woman on the left reached for him with emaciated, scaly arms. Her lips curled back in sadistic pleasure to reveal rows of rotting teeth. She laughed in victory and snagged Aiden's coat with her long, broken nails.

Melanie reached for the pistol. It slid out of her grasp. The woman yanked Aiden up from the floor. He shrieked.

Melanie found the butt of the gun and grabbed it. She swung it up and pulled the trigger as the barrel cleared her son's rising body. The gun barked and jerked nearly out of her hands.

The bullet whizzed an inch past Aiden's head. It tore the ear off the infected woman. Her head whipped to one side. She screamed in pain. She spun back around, her face a mask of uncontrolled fury. She bared her teeth and plunged them through his sweatshirt and into Aiden's shoulder.

"NOOO!" Melanie pulled her son forward with one hand. She jammed the revolver into the infected woman's eye and pulled the trigger. With a muffled report, the back of the woman's head exploded.

Paul fired two more rounds at the infected to the right in quick succession. The Jeep found traction and spun to face sideways in the road.

In a final act of defiance, the dead woman would not release Aiden. Her jaws clamped his shoulder; her hand, his arm. She slumped back along the side of the Jeep. With the added weight, Aiden's sweatshirt slid through Melanie's grasp.

Melanie slammed the pistol butt against the woman's skull. The dead woman's legs caught under the Jeep's spinning rear tires. The Jeep jerked and bucked as it made her corpse bounce like a landed fish. Clouds of choking, greasy smoke enveloped the Jeep's rear in a fog.

A pair of grungy, tattooed arms pierced through the smarmy veil as another infected man reached into the Jeep's cargo area. His fingers grazed Melanie's hair.

Up front, two infected mounted the Jeep's front bumper. Paul swung the rifle inches from the head of one and fired.

Tamara slammed the Jeep into first gear. The wheels reversed direction and shot the woman's corpse back under the Jeep's rear. The body swept the back attacker off his feet. His hands disappeared back through the smoke. The Jeep lurched forward and ran over both of the infected to the front with a bone-crushing pair of cantilevered twists. Paul grabbed the upright windshield for support.

Melanie pulled her screaming son down to the floorboards. The pistol slipped from her hand and bounced on the steel floor. She whispered a prayer and pulled his sweatshirt away from his shoulder.

Blood seeped from two crescent-shaped bite marks. A tooth protruded from one, twin roots pointing at her in defiance.

Melanie's whole existence seemed to evaporate. Every struggle, every purpose, every breath she'd ever taken now seemed pointless as a black pool of denial filled her. A 99-percent transmission rate. This could not be happening.

She pulled the tooth from her son's skin. He'd turned near catatonic from the shock and sensory overload. He shivered and whimpered on the floor.

"Are you okay?" Tamara shouted across her shoulder over the screaming engine. "Is Aiden okay?"

Melanie yanked his sweatshirt back up over the wound. "Yes, we're fine."

Paul glanced down and did a double take. "Did that bitch bite him?"

"No," Melanie said. She straightened Aiden's sweatshirt and pulled his jacket up to his neck. "I got her first."

Paul looked hard past Melanie at Aiden's shoulder. Melanie moved her head over to block his view. The Jeep hit a rut, and Paul bounced up and down.

"Sit the hell down before you fall out," Tamara said.

Paul took his seat and scanned ahead of the Jeep. Melanie shielded Aiden from anyone's view and pulled back his sweatshirt. Tiny, black lines, like thin charcoal etchings, radiated from his wounds.

As far she was concerned, the infection had just killed two people.

Chapter Six

As soon as they were back in the condo, Melanie hurried Aiden straight to the bathroom.

Eddie came out of his bedroom. "Mellie, you made it back. Did you get the—"

Melanie slammed the bathroom door shut on Aiden and turned to Eddie. "Aiden's sick. Seems like the flu or something. You'd better not expose yourself."

Eddie cast her a suspicious look. "You're exposing *yourself*."

Her words came out rapid-fire. "I'm his mother. At your age, the flu turns to pneumonia in no time. Let's take no chances. You should spend the night at Tamara's."

"Whoa, Mellie. Ain't that a bit drastic. So the boy's got sniffles—"

"Damn it, Eddie." She had no time to finesse her half-baked line of crap. "It's my house, my son. Go to Tamara's. Stay with her tonight."

The hurt look on Eddie's face broke her heart. She took a deep breath. This was for his own good. He couldn't stay here through what she had planned.

"Well, all right," he said. "I'll tell Tamara Aiden's sick, have her come over—"

"NO! Do you think I can't take care of my own son? I've been doing it long before you came along. Both of you just stay away. I'll let you know when he's better. Now go. NOW!"

Eddie shrank under the assault. Melanie gritted her teeth and choked back the apology that begged to be spoken.

"All right then," Eddie said.

He shuffled out the front door. Melanie locked the door and twirled the key in the upper deadbolt. She left it in the cylinder so no key could slide into the other side.

On the Whitestone Bridge, Aiden had been able to tolerate the pressing crowd, to fight back the panic and confusion, and keep a tenuous grip on the edge of the reality everyone else shared. She imagined the struggle for him to ignore every impulse his body sent and trust that the vision of the world his mother explained was the truth, no matter how he saw reality unfold. It was as if someone tried to convince her to keep her hand in a pot of boiling water, no matter what pain she thought she felt, no matter the gut-churning stink of boiling flesh assaulting her senses. She knew she couldn't do it and ached for her son during the times when he could. She prayed now would be one of those times.

She entered the bathroom. Aiden sat on the closed toilet. She rushed to him. He didn't recoil, didn't shy away. Without prompting, Aiden whipped off his sweatshirt. The poison had moved fast. His shoulder was a mass of black veins, the skin around them tinged yellow. Aiden rarely looked her in the eye, but he did now, and not with his familiar impassive, blank stare. His cheeks were flush. His eyes burned with longing and one unmistakable demand.

Help me.

And Melanie felt helpless. In the time of her son's greatest need, she was about to fail.

Beads of sweat formed on his reddening brow. Melanie pulled the laser thermometer from the counter drawer. She aimed the beam at his head—101.2 degrees.

Dammit.

"Aiden honey, get in the tub."

Aiden stripped off the rest of his clothes. She checked him as he stepped over the edge and sat in the tub. She found no other injuries, but the swelling twin crescents on his shoulder were more than enough.

Aiden sat against the cold porcelain without a shiver. Naked, his thin body looked so frail, as if a decent breeze might reduce him to pieces, like a spindly tower of sticks. Melanie's heart fell. What response could one so defenseless muster against the alien invader in his bloodstream?

She threw a washcloth in the sink and blasted it with cold water. From the medicine cabinet, she pulled a bottle of hydrogen peroxide. She knelt beside her son. She'd never seen his eyes so wide.

"Honey, this won't hurt, it just bubbles. You remember?"

She spun the top off the hydrogen peroxide and poured it across his shoulder. It splashed wild in her shaking hand. Aiden flinched. The twin arcs bubbled like volcanic vents.

This pseudotreatment served no purpose. The killer was loose. She rationalized Aiden wouldn't know that, that this common conduct for a cut would ease his mind. Then she wondered if she did it more to ease hers, to convince herself that she was doing something. She draped the cold, white washcloth across his blazing forehead. His eyes rolled up and back. He leaned against the back of the tub. She set the stopper and turned on the tap. Cool water splashed around her son's feet. He didn't flinch.

"Sit tight, honey. Don't move."

She ran to the kitchen counter. Weeks' worth of mail lay piled at one end. She rifled through the stack. Envelopes and ads hit the floor as she searched for the one missive she was certain—she hoped she was certain—she'd seen and ignored earlier in the week. It was an odd color, a red or a purple...

She uncovered an orange pamphlet and clutched it in triumph.

Symptoms of the Paleovirus read the cover. Doctors had at least named what they could not cure.

Tamara had given it to her, something she'd picked up with the medical supplies. Melanie practically ripped the cover off opening it. She flash-read the disease's normal progression.

Infection.

Darkened veins, lightened skin.

Fever.

Hallucinations.

Hallucinations? she thought. *Aiden sees the world through some sort of fractured kaleidoscope already. What would his hallucinations be like?*

Then there was the possibility of a brief return to what looked like normalcy. It might last minutes, it might last hours. In red, underlined letters, the pamphlet warned her not to be fooled. The disease never cured itself. Ever.

Then came the rage. Eyes red as rubies. Unbelievable strength. An unquenchable desire for destruction.

She flipped the page, and then the next. Not a word about treatment. Just a list of ways to...damn...to kill the victim. Slash the carotid artery, a plastic bag over the head, an instantly fatal gunshot wound, aiming diagram thoughtfully provided.

She threw the pamphlet across the room. It hit the wall and exploded in a flurry of separate sheets that fluttered down to the floor. Before she killed her own son, she'd...

...die.

And without Aiden, what difference would it make if she did die? Her husband wouldn't mourn one minute.

She returned to the bathroom. Aiden lay passed out in the tub. The damp cloth she'd left on his head was bone dry and stiff. Water had risen to his waist. His tiny chest heaved with each uneven breath. Charcoal veins spread like poison ivy across his left side. As she reached for the washcloth, radiant heat hovered beneath her palm. She didn't need to check a thermometer.

She closed the bathroom door and locked it. The water level rose to cover his bony knees. She sat on the tub's edge and dipped the washcloth in the water. She caressed his shoulders with the cloth. Clear water drizzled down his chest like spring rain.

She remembered washing him like this in the kitchen sink when he was just a year old. So long ago, yet still it was just yesterday.

He seemed so small, so fragile. She ran her fingers through the silky curls of his hair. She'd spent a lifetime only touching her son as he slept. She loved him no less for his condition; in fact, she loved him more, empathized with how he was trapped within the confines of his perception of the world. So many people, especially Charles, had urged her to abandon Aiden, to leave her damaged son in the hands of others, in the hands of professionals. She was more likely to amputate her own arm.

She laid the damp cloth across his forehead and turned off the tap. She placed her hand on his scrawny, white chest and felt his heartbeat. He couldn't hear her, but she started to sing anyway, "Angels in heaven, look down on the child, perfect and lovely, tender and mild."

She hadn't abandoned him then, she wouldn't abandon him now. He'd sleep and then awaken, either by the grace of God as Aiden, or without it as something else. That something else would respond to her as his mother, or she'd die trying to make it. They'd leave this condo as mother and son, or never leave it at all.

Chapter Seven

Jimmy Wade rubbed his palms together as he watched the raiding party's return. Two SUVs bracketed a commandeered U-Haul as it rolled through Belle Pointe's front gate. Sheet metal covered the wheel wells and replaced the windows on the SUVs. Gun slits ran the length of each rusting steel plate. Haphazard graffiti plastered the sides of the U-Haul, and the logo now read *HAUL ASS*. The caravan pulled to a stop past the guardhouse. A dually diesel Ford pickup grumbled awake and pushed a rolling, reinforced school bus back across the opening in the wall.

K-Dogg went straight to the rear of the U-Haul and rolled up the door. The truck's cargo was like an animal arriving to be butchered. Nothing inside went to waste, everything found a purpose. Pallets of green MREs covered one side. The other side held cases of beer, looted silverware that Blacksmith Bob would smelt, jewelry for Levinson to appraise and a sack of mixed prescription drugs Doc Pharma would sort through. Runners waited to divide the spoils and ferry them off to new homes.

The lead SUV had a few women in the back, destined for a short, painful career servicing the new lords of Belle Pointe.

Neither vehicle interested Jimmy. He went straight to the rear SUV, a battered, old Dodge Durango with a hemi wedged between the fender wells. The men around it parted as he approached. Jimmy had implanted fear in all of them, but his appearance iced the cake. Over the months, his head had healed into a hairless, red lump of shiny skin, riven with a mass of Frankensteinesque, white scar stitching. He'd grown a devilish goatee to accentuate his evil persona. It appeared to work.

He opened the driver's door. A scared, sweaty little Korean driver looked at him with wide eyes from the gloom.

"I got one for you, Boss. Kind of a fighter."

Jimmy nodded. "Down to the house."

He closed the door in the driver's face, grabbed the roof rack with his long-healed left arm and stood on the running board. He banged twice on the roof, and the SUV headed for the former home of Michael Quinn.

The SUV backed into the open, empty garage. Jimmy hopped off. The little Korean man jumped out of the driver's door, made a haphazard, deferential bow and beat a hasty exit back up the long driveway. Jimmy hit a switch on the wall, and the garage door rolled shut. As everywhere on Q Island, the power still flowed most of the time, though residents gave up on paying bills months ago.

He pulled a TASER from a wall charger and double-checked the power level. He went to the rear tailgate of the SUV and grabbed the handle. He probed the mind inside the vehicle.

Thoughts swirled in a chaotic hurricane. Rage, frustration, pain, hunger. Snippets of torture, arson, murder. Whether these were fantasies or experiences, Jimmy could not tell. Over the last four months, he'd become more adept at reading the infected. His probes no longer bounced off the churning mass of red-tinged fury inside each skull. He couldn't implant anything, couldn't control them. Not yet.

A headache like a lump of molten lead plopped into the base of his skull. He cut the telepathic tether. He'd learned when to stop before the migraines and nosebleeds began.

He jerked open the door. A reinforced cage filled the SUV's cargo area, with metal bars welded to the stripped-down interior. On the floor lay a woman in her forties, arms and legs hog-tied behind her. She was probably attractive once, when the rags she wore were still clothes, when her greasy mass of hair still met a stylist's hands, when the gray spiderweb of veins across her face still pumped red blood. Her eyes burned like two lasers. She hissed at Jimmy.

He nailed her with 50,000 volts. She went rigid, then unconscious.

He untied her bindings and dragged her into the house. He'd become accustomed to the house's smell, that thick, humid stench of human decay that filled every corner. Even K-Dogg stopped setting foot in the place, always meeting Jimmy in the front driveway, not even on the porch. Jimmy didn't mind the privacy.

Michael Quinn had no doubt designed his living room to entertain, and the spacious area could host a dozen visitors at once. Jimmy preferred a guest list of one. The couches and entertainment center lay piled in one corner. In the room's center, a heavy, upright chair sat bolted to the floor. Leather belts liberated from Mrs. Quinn's closet hung from bolts on the arms, legs and back. Jimmy flopped the woman into the chair and strapped in her limbs. The final, thicker, padded strap went across her mouth and bound her head to the back of the chair.

The woman roused from her TASER-induced stupor and crossed straight to boiling rage. She yanked against the bindings, bit into the mouth strap like a dog on a chew toy. Her fingers and feet writhed. After months of victims, and a few mishaps, Jimmy had fine-tuned the chair to perfection.

Jimmy laid his palm on her forehead, like some tent-revival preacher.

"Thanks for involuntarily volunteering," he said. He closed his eyes. "Hmm. I sense you are…troubled."

The woman screamed and cursed into the gagging belt. Rage stoked her eyes.

Jimmy laughed. "Great news! All your troubles will soon disappear. And you get to be a part of human evolution."

Jimmy mocked the woman, but over the past few months, he'd come to believe what he said. His heightened mental capabilities had spawned amazing new perception. So many things finally fit. Effects became tied to causes, individual trees became forests. This plague was the next step in the stymied path of human transcendence. It had not only raised him from the pool of ignorance he'd wallowed in his whole life, it had elevated him above the others, above *all* others. He would not have been given the psychic power to command the rest of humanity if they were not inherently inferior.

Jimmy stepped to the china cabinet against the wall. From a drawer, he pulled a Dremel tool, a small, handheld, battery-powered drill. Instead of a bit, it sported a small cutting disk. Blood splattered the drill in multiple layers and colors. He gave the trigger a quick squeeze. The cutting wheel spun to life with a high-pitched whir and then ramped back down. He stood behind the woman in the chair. He wound the crown of her hair into a knot in one hand. The unctuous mess slipped against his fingers. He gripped tighter and raised her hair straight up.

"Full-disclosure time. This is going to hurt for a minute, I won't lie to you. But then you'll pass out from the pain. I mean, most likely. Only one guy stayed conscious through the whole procedure. So the odds are in your favor. Try to stay still so I can get a clean cut."

He revved the tiny drill to full speed. It whined like a killer bee. The woman screamed until her face burned cherry red.

Jimmy held her hair aloft and touched the blade to the side of the woman's head, just in front of her hairline. The blade sliced through skin and sent a mist of blood into the air. The motor revved down as it bit into skull bone. The drill bucked. Jimmy tightened his grip. Then he began to scribe a horizontal line around her head.

The woman's wails of pain would no doubt have sounded inhuman without the muffling strap, one of the reasons Jimmy had reinforced it. There was an art to this work, and distracting screams made for sloppy results. As he guided the drill over her right eyebrow, she met his expectations and passed out. He could finish in peace.

The drill cut past her left eyebrow. Pulverized bone chips fluttered down across her face like snowfall. A thin curtain of blood followed the path of the blade as it circumnavigated her head. It ran down and covered her face like a shimmering, red shroud.

Jimmy finished his buzzing lap of her skull. The spinning blade cycled up to full speed as it joined the slot where it had started. He snapped off the drill and tossed it aside. With a reverential finesse, he pulled her hair up with an almost-dainty pressure. Membranes tore, and the lightest of suction released with a tiny pop. Jimmy cast the woman's skullcap aside like he'd uncovered a pot of boiling pasta. He cupped her ears in both hands and stared down, smiling.

The pink brain mass pulsed and quivered. In the way that his first foray into brain consumption had been instinctual, so had this newer method. For while the flaccid brains of the dead had given him satisfaction, the throbbing brains of the living gave him power. The electrical charge of the firing neurons danced on his tongue. The living, supercharged virus in his victim joined with his, and the power of his mind surged so rapidly that it felt like his head would burst.

The experience was glorious.

They lasted quite a while, these volunteers. Jimmy saved the autonomic function area for last, to better enjoy that sensation of devouring the living. To think that he used to cringe at the idea of sushi.

A near-sexual blast of excitement hit him like a sirocco. He bent down and, like bobbing for apples, bit off a chunk of brain matter. He swirled it in his mouth, savoring the flavor, the texture, the symbiotic essence of the woman and the virus that shared her body. He swallowed and quivered with pleasure as the brain matter slid down his throat.

Moments or maybe hours later, he finished. Blood and brains coated his face from the nose down. He gripped the chairback for support, woozy from the receding rush. He fumbled with the straps and unbound the corpse. He dragged it by the wrists into the living room.

Other bodies lay on the floor, across furniture, piled in corners. Shattered, empty skulls spoke of the victims' last moments alive. Black dust coated their exploded chest cavities. Spores darkened the walls like fireplace soot.

Jimmy dropped his nameless dinner by an end table. He staggered over to the remains of yesterday's meal. Had it been a man, a woman? Jimmy couldn't remember. The lifeless, gray face and glassy, faded eyes contrasted with its swollen, quivering stomach. He sat beside it, legs crossed in a lotus position, awaiting the enlightenment about to come. He placed his hands on the edge of the distended belly. His fingertips tingled.

The corpse's stomach burst open. A deadly fog of spores filled the air. Jimmy closed his eyes, breathed deep and welcomed more of his brothers into the fold.

Chapter Eight

The morning briefing with Vanessa and the rest of the department heads at JFK Terminal 1 wasn't as humiliating as Samuel expected. Vanessa didn't mention a word about the arsenic allegations. The military didn't mention his nurses' security breach. On the way back to Terminal 2, Dr. Petty met Samuel.

"Dr. Bradshaw," Petty practically whispered, "I need to talk to you."

Earlier, Petty had appeared strained, worried, nervous. Samuel followed him to a secluded spot on the side of Terminal 1.

"When Eileen and Wanda got sick," Petty said, "you asked me to check some coffee samples for arsenic. I didn't find any trace of it."

"My diagnosis must have been wrong."

"The more I thought about that, the less likely I thought that was," Petty said. "I reran the samples and found something that gave me chills. Not arsenic, but inorganic arsenic."

"What's inorganic arsenic?"

"Someone synthesized a compound that looks harmless until ingested. Once inside, the digestive process strips away some of the elements and leaves arsenic behind, but not just conventional arsenic. This stuff has receptors that probably quadruple its absorption rate. Organic arsenic eventually passes through the urine. Not this stuff."

"If that was true," Samuel said, "everyone on Long Island who ever drank the coffee would already be dead."

"No, those idiots boiled it down and concentrated it. To get a buzz, they did months' worth of coffee in minutes. Taken slowly, over time, this toxin would give someone conventional, aggressive arsenic poisoning."

"Any chance this compound occurred naturally?"

"There isn't even a chance it occurred accidentally. It was specifically engineered."

The wheels turned in Samuel's head. He didn't like the direction they took.

"The list of organizations with the resources to do that is one-name long," Samuel said. "The U.S. Government. Coincidentally, the source of the food."

"But what's the point?" Petty said.

"The poisoning would be hard to diagnose," Samuel said. "Especially at a distance. Arsenic attacks multiple organs. Some people would have kidney failure, some the liver, it all depends. In the Q Island chaos, with isolated people dying unrecorded, who'd put that puzzle together? Even if they did, acute poisoning like this only shows up in urine tests, not hair or fingernails. But with the burning of the dead, no tests would be likely at all."

"Poisoning coffee seems kind of hit or miss."

"I'll bet everything's poisoned, the whole meal. That's why they have the green boxes; that's why they all only go to Q Island."

"Jesus. Why do that?" Petty said.

"We've seen how this thing mutates. Maybe the CDC has determined it can't be controlled."

"But we're getting closer to a cure," Petty said.

"But maybe not close enough," Samuel said. "Have you shared your results with anyone?"

"No."

"Don't. We need to be certain before we tell anyone. Those with families on the island will be panicked. Tonight, I'll liberate a few samples from Terminal Four for more testing."

"You mean *we'll* liberate a few samples," Dr. Petty said.

"It might be dangerous."

"Apparently so's eating the food."

Chapter Nine

Melanie awoke with a start on the cold bathroom floor. She'd fallen asleep sometime during the night. She pulled herself up by the bathtub's side.

The tub was empty, save a few inches of water in the bottom. The white washcloth floated in it like a dead fish. The bathroom door yawned open. Tiny, wet footprints traced a glistening path across the tile.

Her mouth went dry.

She rose. With silent steps, she crept down the hallway. She'd seen the infected, knew what to expect. She felt defenseless, exposed. The idea of grabbing a knife from the kitchen occurred. She ignored it.

She entered the dining room. Aiden sat at the table, back to her, in a T-shirt and underpants. Several sheets of paper lay spread out across the tabletop. His right arm swept up and down in broad strokes as he ran a crayon across the page. His head bobbed in time with his arm, like a mechanical toy.

Melanie sighed in relief. The rage hadn't set in. Everything she'd read, seen or experienced said the infected were universally, unstoppably violent. She crept forward a few steps.

"Aiden, how are you?"

She didn't expect an answer. She just wanted to keep from startling him. She came up behind him and rested her hands on the top of his chairback. She looked past him at the papers on the table. Her jaw dropped.

These weren't Aiden's usual stick-figure specials. These were art executed in crayon. A bluebird in three dimensions, in perfect scale, spread wings colored with seamless shading and shadow. Another picture showed Jones Beach at low tide, an almost impressionistic take, with the sand as a perfect mixture of browns and white. Beside that lay one of Aiden's school on a bright spring morning, roses blooming along the walkway.

She stepped past her son and picked up the bluebird picture. Even close up, it looked amazingly realistic.

"Aiden honey…" she turned to her son, "…this picture is beautiful."

Aiden paused and looked up at her. She jerked and shredded the bluebird in half. Aiden's eyes were a deep, rich red. The black veins covered his face like the road map of Hell. But that face was as impassive as ever, with no hint of the fury that drove the infected. He spun the picture in front of him around and slid it toward her. He began a new picture without waiting for her reaction.

The drawing was Aiden's eye view of the attack on the Jeep. The crazed, infected woman had ahold of the side of the vehicle, teeth bared, red eyes filled with hate.

The clarity of these pictures meant one of two things. Either Aiden's autism-tinged view of the world wasn't any different from her own, or this virus had rewired his perception into all the normal receptors. Whichever was right, the virus had turned her son into an artist.

A key scratched at the blocked deadbolt lock in the front door.

Crap, Melanie thought. This was the last thing she needed. Didn't she tell Eddie that she'd let him know when to come back?

Three knocks on the door.

"Mellie? You up and awake?"

"Eddie, I told you I'd let you know when Aiden wasn't contagious. Go back to Tamara's."

"Melanie! Come over to the door now." Tamara's voice this time, in her toughest no-nonsense tone.

Double crap. She told Eddie not to bring her over here. Couldn't that old man follow any directions? Melanie went to the front door.

"Eddie, I told you not to drag her over here. I don't need any help."

"He didn't come to me," Tamara said. "I was on my way to the dayroom and rousted the old coot from a sound sleep on your porch. He gave me some line of BS about Aiden having the flu and how you told him to leave."

"Well, I don't want him sick. Aiden's probably contagious."

Tamara's voice hushed, and it sounded like she'd put her mouth up against the crack in the door. "What Aiden's contagious with isn't the goddamn flu. He was bitten yesterday. Now you let us in, or I'll take a rock to your window, and we'll both come in that way."

Melanie sighed and flipped the deadbolt. She opened the door. Tamara and Eddie entered. Melanie closed the door and locked it. Tamara had a messenger bag over her shoulder.

"Where is he?" Tamara asked.

"In the dining room."

"Restrained?"

"No. He's normal."

"He can't be normal," Tamara said.

"He's better than normal. C'mon."

They entered the dining room. Aiden sat at the far end of the table, drawing a picture with fierce intensity. The crayon bent to an unnatural angle in his fingers. Melanie slid his other drawings to their side of the table and spread them out.

"Whoa! That's some artwork," Eddie said.

"How long has he been like this?" Tamara said.

"Hours probably. I fell asleep beside him in the bathroom last night, woke up, and he was in here being Rembrandt."

Tamara took a laser thermometer from her messenger bag and tested Aiden—98.7 degrees.

"Aiden, can you look at me?" Tamara asked.

Aiden looked her in the eyes. Tamara did a double take. Aiden rarely looked even her in the eyes. Aiden's eyes were red, but not with the earlier fire of the infected, more a rose color.

"Can you pull up his shirt for me?" Tamara asked.

Melanie came up behind Aiden. "I'm just going to raise your shirt for a moment. No one's going to touch you."

She raised his shirt to his chest. He flinched and squirmed. Blackened veins made a twisted tapestry of his skin. Tamara nodded and Melanie dropped his shirt then pulled Aiden's collar away to expose the red, swollen bite marks. Tamara directed Melanie back to the living room with a flick of her head. Eddie followed them.

"Well, he's infected," Tamara said. "But he isn't displaying a fully symptomatic response. I had a patient at St. Luke's who came out of her sickness into a creative state like this for about half an hour. But she went into the rage phase like everyone else."

"But Aiden's been this way for hours," Melanie said. "So he's not going to turn like she did, right?"

"I wish I could tell you that. Everyone responds at different rates to this virus. It could still happen."

"Then you two need to leave," Melanie said. "Just in case."

Eddie sat down on the couch with a thud. "Don't know about the two of you, but I'm staying."

Tamara smiled and joined him. "Well if he's staying, I'm certainly staying."

She pulled a syringe and a vial from the messenger bag and filled the syringe with a clear liquid. She placed it on the coffee table.

"And in case things go south, I'll administer a tranq."

"And if things go smooth," Eddie said, "I'll take her up on the shot, just so it doesn't go to waste."

"No, I can't put all of you at risk," Melanie said.

"You aren't," Tamara replied. "We are."

Melanie sighed with relief and sat beside Eddie on the couch. Aiden walked in, placed a finished drawing on Tamara's lap and walked out. She gave it a quizzical look.

"I could place the other ones," Tamara said. "But who's this a picture of?"

She placed the picture in the center of the coffee table. The likeness was a man with no hair and a horrible set of scars that crisscrossed the top of his swollen head. Blood coated the lower half of his face and dripped from a close-cropped goatee.

In rough letters along the bottom it read *BAD MAN*.

In Belle Pointe, Jimmy Wade jolted up in bed. A buzz saw of a headache wrenched him wide awake. Visions filled his head. An apartment, a Jeep, a man with a deer rifle, a nurse with an eye patch. He moved past the cascading images and swam upstream to the source. He sensed a mind of such profound clarity that he actually gasped.

He'd touched many minds these past few months, blindingly smart, hopelessly stupid, chaotically infected. But never one like this. One with such power, one that possessed the same duality as his own—infected by the virus yet not mastered by it.

The link broke. Jimmy lurched backward as if the connection had been a rubber band and had snapped. His head howled worse than it ever had. Blood trickled from both nostrils.

His hunger announced itself. This one he felt, this...boy...was a prize, the answer. The piecemeal improvements he'd felt with each dose of infected brain paled in comparison to what this future volunteer offered. In one meal, he'd have the power to master the uninfected and the infected. He'd receive deliverance from the skull-splitting headaches.

He'd complete the evolutionary path. Homo sapiens would become Homo superior.

Somewhere on Q Island, a second survivor of the paleovirus lived. Just not for long. Jimmy could practically taste this boy's brain already.

Chapter Ten

Aiden made it through the day unchanged. The disease neither advanced nor retreated. His eyes remained rose-colored, most of his skin stayed streaked with gray. Tamara monitored his decidedly stable vitals. That evening, she briefed Eddie on injecting Aiden with the paralytic if it became necessary, and went home for a few hours' sleep. After everyone turned in, Melanie went insomniac waiting for her sleeping son to rise like a vampire in the night, but he slept soundly.

Tamara completed another checkup the next morning. Aiden passed with flying colors. The three adults met in another room afterwards.

"Look, I've seen how fast this disease progresses," Tamara said. "While I'm no expert, I can say that by now, the virus has done its worst. There's no organ it hasn't touched, no blood cell it hasn't contaminated. I don't think he's going to get any worse."

"But that's different from getting better," Eddie said.

"Yes. But it's a start. I think the underlying factor for Aiden's autism is giving him a high level of immunity, whatever that factor is."

"No one knows for sure," Melanie said. "Doctors confirmed he had autism, but could never tell us why. And he's not just immune to the infection." She pointed to a sheaf of drawings on the coffee table. "He's improved by it. He's not fully functional, but he's taken small steps, like looking people in the eye for a moment or letting you put the blood pressure cuff on his arm today."

"Aiden might be able to get doctors a step closer to a cure," Tamara said. "We just need to get him to the right doctor."

"Someone at St. Luke's?"

"Not hardly. The docs there are all triage and patch up, short on everything. The guards outside would take one look at Aiden's symptoms and shoot him on sight."

"Hell, anyone would," Eddie said. "The whole island is in better-safe-than-sorry mode."

"Exactly," Tamara said. "He needs to go where the research is being done. And Doc Bradshaw is in a position down at JFK to get him there."

A way out of this nightmare for Aiden? Melanie was sure this idea would end up being too good to be true. "Can you get in touch with him?"

"I can go on a run to St. Luke's this afternoon. They have a dedicated landline to the CDC site at JFK. I might need to wait awhile, but if Doc Bradshaw knows it's me, I'll get through. But until I can arrange for a ride, Aiden needs to stay inside, away from open windows."

"No problem there," Melanie said. "Finally, autism works in my favor."

Melanie spent the rest of the morning in a combination of creeping terror and joyful anticipation.

At midday, a knock sounded at the door. Tamara was preparing for her run to St. Luke's. Eddie was on his shift monitoring the security cameras. Tamara checked the peephole.

Paul stood on the porch, deer rifle over his shoulder, new Kevlar vest cinched tight, pistol slung low at his hip. He carried a white bag.

"Melanie, it's Paul. Open the door."

Crap. Paul was about the last thing she needed.

"What do you need, Paul?"

"Tamara sent some medication over for Aiden."

"Just leave it there. I'm not decent."

"Melanie, I'm not leaving prescription drugs out on the porch where kids walk by. Throw on something, and open the damn door."

Damn. Tamara should have known better than to send Paul over here on an errand. He'd probably volunteered and wouldn't take no for an answer.

She rushed back to the dining room table where Aiden had a picture of a marina about half-finished. "Aiden honey, into the kitchen. Now. And be quiet."

Aiden dropped what he was doing without looking up, and stepped into the kitchen.

Melanie ran her fingers through her hair, took a deep breath and opened the door a few inches. "I'll take that—"

Paul shouldered the door open and barged in.

"Paul!"

The gentle giant she once knew was gone. He surveyed the room with a predator's gaze.

"People are worried, Melanie. No one's seen you or your son ever since we came back from that infected ambush. There's some concern about your boy."

Melanie planted herself between Paul and the kitchen. "My son is fine. He's autistic, and he's happier inside in his room. Which should thrill you, one less person to worry about being out by the wall."

"Then you won't mind if I check on him just so I can put everyone's fears to rest."

"Get out of my house. You leave me and my son alone!"

"Aiden! Come on out here and let me see you."

"Get out now!" Melanie marched up to Paul and slammed her palms against his chest. He didn't flinch. For the first time, she realized how big he was, how much leaner he'd become these past few months. She looked up into a face like stone.

Like lightning, Paul grabbed a handful of Melanie's hair and yanked. Her scalp caught fire, and she shrieked.

"Hey, kid, come on out. Your mom needs you."

Melanie started to yell for her son to stay away. Paul gave her hair another yank, this time so hard she fell to her knees. She yelled again.

"Now, boy, there you are," Paul said.

Melanie looked into the kitchen from the corner of her eye. Tears blurred her vision. Aiden's face peered out from the doorway, eyes rose-red, neck a fan of gray veins.

"Son of a bitch!" Paul said. He released Melanie and drew the pistol from his hip. "Goddamn kid's infected! I knew that bitch bit him!"

"No!" Melanie reached up and wrapped her hands around the pistol. She tried to tug it away from pointing at her son. "He's safe, he's immune."

"No one's immune." Paul cocked the hammer.

Melanie wedged a finger under the hammer. "No, he's normal. He just looks infected. Aiden, come out, honey."

Aiden stepped out from the kitchen. He raised his shirt to show the extent of the infection.

"I'll be damned," Paul said.

"Aiden honey, go to your room. Stay there."

Aiden scampered off down the hall. Melanie looked up into Paul's eyes and saw him processing what had just happened.

"Who else knows about him?" Paul said.

"No one, I promise," she begged. "Just leave him alone. He's not dangerous. He's been this way for days. I'll keep him inside. No one needs to know."

Paul whipped the pistol up and out of her hands. "Are you nuts? I'm going to let one of the infected live inside the walls? Once people know what's going on in here, they'll throw the both of you over the wall."

"No, no! Please, I'll do anything. Don't hurt my son."

Paul's stoic face gave birth to an evil, lascivious look. Melanie felt like she'd just walked herself off a cliff. Paul slid his pistol back into its holster.

"As long as you're down there, I think we could come to an arrangement. I might become too satisfied to speak."

A bulge in Paul's pants began to swell. He grabbed the side of her head with one hand. Panic swept through Melanie like wildfire. Paul unzipped his pants and exposed himself, hard and pulsing.

"Little spoiled housewife," Paul said. Disdain dripped from his words like sludge. "Your only job is to keep your man happy. You oughta be a pro at this."

Paul gave her no chance to react. He grabbed her head with both hands and jammed himself into her mouth. She gagged. Tears streamed from her eyes. She barely caught a breath between the violent penetrations as he yanked her head up and down. She tensed to bite him. A vision flashed of her son with a bullet hole in him. She stopped herself.

"How's a real man feel?" Paul hissed.

Melanie was seconds from passing out. Paul gripped her head tight as a vise. He climaxed. He kept her head in place until she swallowed. Then he cast her aside. She collapsed against the wall, violated, sobbing, humiliated.

Paul zipped himself back into his pants and sniffed. "Yeah, I think that once a day for that ought to keep me quiet as a church mouse. Maybe twice on Sunday." He looked down to the end of the hallway. "See, kid. Take a lesson. That's how it's done."

Melanie's heart dropped into an abyss. She spun around. Aiden stood at the end of the hall, eyes wide, jaw open, face white.

"Aiden!" Her scream came out as a croak from her bruised throat.

Aiden ran into his room and slammed the door.

Paul opened the front door. He pulled the key from the top deadbolt and pocketed it. "I'll just let myself in next time. Until tomorrow."

He slammed the door. Melanie scrambled to her feet and staggered down the hallway to her son's room. She put her hand on the knob and paused.

What would she say? How could she explain?

She had no answers. She slumped against the wall and slid down to the floor. Whatever hell the world seemed to be minutes ago, it was now infinitely worse. An impenetrable darkness enveloped her mind. She curled into a ball and began to cry.

Chapter Eleven

A tornado of negative emotions raged within Melanie in a dark, swirling mass. Shame, guilt, anger, frustration, depression. How had she let herself get into that situation? Why didn't she fight? What was wrong with her?

Her stomach churned, and she remembered with horrifying disgust what she'd been forced to ingest. It felt like a vile, cloying creature inside her, an evil emissary gloating over her debasement. She scrambled for the bathroom. She dropped to her knees over the toilet just in time to spray a torrent of vomit into the bowl.

She heaved a second time. The third was a dry, agonizing attempt to rid herself of every drop of anything Paul's disgusting seed had touched. The forced expulsions left her body exhausted. She slipped back onto the floor and rested her head against the cool porcelain tank. No puking purge had ever been so satisfying.

Her tears had stopped, replaced by blinding fury, fury not with herself, the victim, but at Paul. That power-hungry bastard dared enter her home and assault her? That worthless shit who otherwise couldn't get a woman to touch him?

Anger kick-started her back to life. She popped to her feet and turned the water in the sink on full blast. She rinsed twice with mouthwash, the second time swallowing it to slay anything of Paul that might still be hiding inside of her.

She was done. Done with letting a jackass like Paul push her around. Done with being a doormat for her cheating, absent husband as well. That prick should have been back with his family at the first sign of trouble, not setting up a Manhattan apartment. She needed to pull her head out of the sand and see the world as it really was.

She grabbed a washcloth and scrubbed her face clean with water two degrees under scalding. It felt wonderful.

Then there was Aiden. She'd been humiliated in front of him, degraded in the most base way. All his life, she'd tried to put herself in the best light, worked hard to be a model parent. In those minutes he watched her assaulted, how much of that had been erased?

And now this was his introduction to sex. He didn't even need to know about sex for years, but his first contact with it was seeing his mother raped in their own house. Was that going to scar him? How could it not? The poor boy already had the deck stacked against him. Now, isolated from his father, his first view of male sexuality was this? That was the kind of autobiographical excuse serial rapists offered at their trials.

Another wave of wrath deluged her. She almost tore the washcloth in half, then threw it in the tub.

She left the bathroom and paused outside Aiden's door. She took a deep, cleansing breath and tried to leave her anger there in the hallway. She added one more breath for good measure.

She entered Aiden's room. He sat against the headboard of his bed, knees tucked up with his oversized spiral drawing pad against them. He was sketching in it with a pencil. Her heart melted, the way it always did when she watched him draw. She sat at the foot of his bed.

"Aiden honey, you saw something pretty rough in the hallway. Paul did something no one should ever do to someone else."

Aiden continued to draw. His face betrayed no reaction. She wanted so much to have some idea if she was getting through to him, if he understood anything she was trying to say.

"I want you to understand that I'm all right. In fact, *we* are all right. Bad things happen, but good things follow. You'll be out of here soon and in a better place."

Aiden gave no response. He just kept drawing. She rationalized that was better than him rocking back and forth with his eyes closed and his hoodie up. She shifted her weight on the bed to get up.

Aiden flipped the cover to his drawing pad closed. He reached down underneath his bed and pulled out the aluminum bat from the supermarket riot. Melanie hadn't noticed it missing from where she'd stashed it in the hall closet.

Aiden's eyes stayed locked on his bedspread as he laid the bat beside him. He flipped it end over end so the grip faced Melanie. With two fingers against the endcap, he slid it forward until the knob just touched Melanie's leg.

Melanie's jaw dropped. Tears welled in her eyes. In nine years, this was the closest thing she'd ever had to a conversation with her son, the closest thing to any interaction greater than her telling and him doing something vaguely in response. There was no question that he understood and empathized with her.

She held herself back from ruining this moment by throwing her arms around him and sending him screaming down the hallway. She slid the bat back his way. He needed his talisman of defense. She'd make her own.

"Aiden honey, you hold on to this for both of us. You sit tight here and draw all you want to."

Melanie went straight to the kitchen. She hovered a finger over a block of kitchen knives, then extracted the midsize blade. She turned it until the light shimmered on the sharp cutting edge. She'd spent a lot of time with these blades and a whetstone. Charles demanded sharp knives for carving. Now, so did she.

She placed the knife on the counter and pulled an emergency meal from the cabinet. She emptied the pouch, folded it in thirds and then bound the edge of the makeshift sheath with duct tape from the junk drawer. She slipped the knife into its new home. She smiled.

She reached down and tucked the sheath into her sock. A quick wrap of tape around the top bound the knife to her calf. She slipped the leg of her jeans down over the knife's handle.

She wasn't going to be a victim again. Not of Paul, not of anyone. There were a thousand things uncertain about the future on Q Island. But one wasn't. She and Aiden were going to survive.

If Paul, however, even darkened the doorway of her condo again, it would be his last visit anywhere.

Chapter Twelve

Tamara and Mickey sat in the Jeep, her on the passenger seat, he in the cargo area. She fumed at the company, but after the narrow escape from the infected's ambush, Paul decreed her days of solo drives to St. Luke's over.

Tamara checked her watch for the hundredth time. Paul was late. Normally, she wouldn't sweat being a few minutes behind, but with no idea how long it would take to get through to Doc Bradshaw, she'd hoped they'd be ahead of schedule today.

Paul finally appeared from between the buildings. His step had an uncharacteristic swagger.

Great, she thought. Like he wasn't jackass enough, now he had to add being extra full of himself. Just her day.

One of the other volunteer guards exited the rec center. He traded Paul his deer rifle for a short submachine gun and three extra magazines. Paul stuffed the magazines in his pockets. Mickey had graduated to an assault rifle with a grenade launcher strapped underneath. The last month, Cedar Knoll had seen a firepower upgrade for some reason. No one asked where the weapons came from. Everyone was just happy to feel safer. The guards had even trusted Tamara with a pair of 9 mm pistols today. No one wanted to underestimate the infected again.

Paul took the driver's seat. Mickey stood up in the cargo area and loaded a round into the grenade launcher. Tamara squirmed with a combination of hatred and disgust as Paul sat down. The idea of moving to the backseat crossed her mind, but she wanted the best view once they hit the streets.

"You two ready?" Paul said.

"I was born ready," Mickey said.

"How's Melanie holding up," Paul asked Tamara. "After the attack and all?"

"Uh, pretty good." Paul hadn't ever asked about anyone's mental health.

"Is her son doing okay?"

"Absolutely."

"So you've seen him? He isn't out much."

"Sure, I saw him last night. Fit and happy."

Paul nodded and started the Jeep. "Just seeing where everyone stands."

The guard rolled open the gate, and they headed for the hospital.

Once inside St. Luke's, Tamara arranged for the medical supplies and went to the bank of phones set up in the front office. Her eye patch had become her ID and now garnered her unquestioned access, like a handicapped decal getting a good parking spot. She checked the contact list on the wall and dialed the CDC at JFK. An automated menu got her to a human being in Research. He asked her to wait. He'd see if he could find Doctor Bradshaw. The Doc picked up a few minutes later.

"Tamara?"

"Hey, Doc, the one and only."

"How's your eye?"

"You know how it is. Not all patients make it."

Pause. "I'm sorry."

"I'm short on time. I have someone here who needs your help. Remember Melanie's son, Aiden?"

"The boy with autism?"

"Right. Well, he's immune. He's infected and normal, only showing some external signs. Internally, he's fine. In fact, better than fine, like Ms. Albritton was temporarily."

"That would be a major breakthrough. Can you get him here?"

"No way, roads are completely unsafe. Can you get the military to come get him?"

"For an example of immunity? NASA would send a rocket."

"He's at Cedar Knoll. I'll need transport for him and his mother, a package deal."

"Of course. I'll get you out of there with them."

Temptation screamed for her to accept. She considered the little Cedar Knoll clinic and the long line that formed for it each day.

"Sorry, Doc. Your expertise is in one spot, mine's in another. I can't provide a lot out here, but what I can provide goes a long way. Just take good care of them."

"Absolutely. I'll call your cell when I have the details arranged."

"Cell service is down."

"Not for the CDC. Just keep them both safe until then."

They said goodbyes and Tamara felt, for the first time in a while, hopeful. Melanie and Aiden safe, and a shorter path to a cure. Maybe there was something to having spring in the air after all.

As she made her way back to the loading dock, a gunshot rang out. Shouts echoed down the hallway. Several scared people bolted past her. She drew one of her pistols and sprinted through the loading-dock doors.

Three heavily armed men held at gunpoint a group herded into a corner. Paul and Mickey stood among them, disarmed and arms raised. The men with the guns weren't military or even paramilitary. They looked more like a cross between a motorcycle gang and street thugs. Tamara ducked behind some boxes and peered through a space between the columns. One of the staff doctors in a white lab coat spoke to someone out of her field of view.

"Whatever you want, just take it. But we're a hospital. We treat the sick. It's them you're stealing from."

"We're not looking for drugs," the offstage leader said. "We're looking for a patient. A boy, a very special boy who's been infected but hasn't gone psycho."

"There's no one like that anywhere. Everyone goes to Stage 3."

"I expected that kind of evasive answer. Let me clarify your thinking."

The speaker stepped up next to the doctor. Goose bumps rippled up Tamara's arms. The bald, scarred head, burning eyes and devil's goatee. He was the man Aiden drew, the BAD MAN.

The scarred man stared into the doctor's eyes. The doctor moaned. Panic spread across his face. He swatted at invisible creatures swarming around his head.

"Get them away, get them away from me!" the doctor shouted. His voice cracked with fear.

"They'll leave when you tell me where the boy is."

"There's no boy like that! Not anywhere. Go check!"

"I plan on it." He closed his eyes, and nodded his head towards the flailing doctor.

"Ahh! My eyes!" The doctor reached for his face. "They're in my eyes! Get them out!"

The doctor clawed at his eyes. He gouged both completely out then tore at his nose and mouth. He ran off the edge of the loading dock, hit the ground and went unconscious.

The scarred man told one gunman to watch the hostage group. He took two others with him to search the hospital.

Tamara ducked back out the door and made a break for the lobby. She ran out the front door. A collection of patients and staff huddled in the parking lot. Two scummy-looking men stood guard at the main entrance, beside the dead bodies of the security detail. An SUV layered in homemade armor blocked the driveway.

"Damn," she said to herself. "How many times am I going to have to escape from this hospital?"

She had to get back to Cedar Knoll, to warn Melanie about the danger that awaited them, the danger Aiden had somehow foretold.

A new fear surfaced. Had anyone overheard her conversation with Doc Bradshaw? If the man with the scars questioned everyone the way he did that poor doctor, that secret wouldn't last long.

Doc Bradshaw needed to pull a rabbit of a rescue out of his hat, and soon. She cut across the side parking lot and out onto the main road.

Chapter Thirteen

Eddie hadn't lied when he vowed to earn his keep at Cedar Knoll. Melanie and Tamara had brought him in. The rest of the residents couldn't have been happy about that, so Eddie knew to pull his weight. He was too old to walk guard duty, but he could do it virtually and monitor the security cameras, ready to warn those on guard if necessary.

Over the past few months, Eddie had absorbed all the Cedar Knoll lore. The days before the virus, the day after, Paul Rosen's rise from quiet nobody to community king. He realized that sitting here he had the power to do more than hear about that fateful day.

On the main control screen, a box read *REWIND TO* with a space beneath for a date and time. He punched in the date of the last pre-apocalypse condo meeting. He typed in noon as the time. All the camera views reset.

In playback mode, the system delivered a choppy playback of a limited number of saved frames. In one view, a car moved up the street outside the Knoll in stop motion ten-foot increments. It disappeared from that view and reappeared on the main gate camera. He watched Paul wave it in. This clean-shaven Paul looked much heavier and much more slovenly than Eddie had ever seen him. It was hard to believe Q Island had improved anybody. He recognized Tamara as the driver. She and Paul had a brief conversation.

A camera view inside the rec center had the most action. The pictures winked. Dozens of people magically appeared outside the dayroom and filed in, seemingly disappearing from frame to frame. In the main-gate view, Paul stood a slouchy guard with his Winchester slung over his shoulder.

The legendary infected gate-crasher appeared on the street-scene camera. He sagged against the outside condo wall several times as he video-jumped his way down the street. He didn't have the late, crazed stage of infection like Eddie had seen in the homicidal people the last night in his neighborhood. This man looked like he was still in the early stage—sick, feverish, weak. He passed close to the camera and looked up at it. In that freeze-frame second, his eyes still shined clear, not late-stage red.

Eddie knit his brow. The man disappeared out of frame.

The man reappeared in the main-gate camera view. Paul brought his rifle to bear. The man gripped the gate's bars with one hand and reached through with the other, palm outstretched. The little movie didn't need a soundtrack to confirm that the poor wretch was begging for help.

Paul waved him back with a few motions of his rifle then looked right and left around the condos. He opened the gate with his remote control. The infected man smiled in relief and raised his hands as if in thanks to God. He entered through the gate. Paul leveled his weapon at him. The man stopped. The gate closed behind him.

This wasn't the story he'd been told about how Paul had fended off a crazed assault.

Fear spread across the victim's face. In the next frame, his mouth hung open, his hands stretched out above him, palms up in surrender. The following frame came up white, overexposed by the Winchester's muzzle flash. Eddie held his breath.

The scene came back into focus with a hole in the victim's chest and a spray of blood and organs exiting his back. In the next frame, the man was on his knees, a second gaping hole above his breastbone. The third frame appeared, and the man lay facedown on the ground.

Paul unclipped his hunting knife from his belt, dropped the sheath in his pocket and lay the knife by the victim, his hand outstretched in submission now co-opted to appear to attack.

Eddie knotted his fingers together so tightly his knuckles popped. Paul hadn't hesitated in planting that knife on the victim. There was no remorse, no fear, no panic at having committed a mortal sin. The victim's framing happened so quickly it had to be part of Paul's plan from the moment he opened the gate. Perhaps it was worse; perhaps Paul had made the plan long before he opened the gate, even long before the virus landed on the shores of Q Island. Paul had spent a lot of time making material preparations for the apocalypse. Who knew what mental fantasies had accompanied them?

Eddie's first instinct was to bolt and tell Melanie what he'd found. He stopped himself. He couldn't leave the surroundings unmonitored. With Paul and Mickey gone, the guard staff was at minimum. He also needed time to think through a plan, a way to get the word about his findings out to everyone before Paul could erase all traces of his murderous deceit. At worst, he needed a plan to get his three friends here out if he couldn't expose Paul.

The two ladies had saved him from the infected. He'd save them from the rest.

Chapter Fourteen

"He's not here, Boss," K-Dogg said.

Three hospitals and three disappointments didn't make Jimmy Wade's mood any better. From their positions around the hospital loading dock, the rest of his crew watched for his reaction. A bolt of pain flashed through his skull. He gritted his teeth. "Are you sure?"

"Shot a nurse on each floor to motivate the rest to give him up. None did. Maybe he ain't in a hospital."

"No, his parents would have brought him in as soon as he was bitten. That's what parents do."

Jimmy held off adding that he could feel the boy was close. The farther west they drove, the stronger the sensation, the greater the hunger inside him grew.

"Boss, it's late," K-Dogg offered. "Gotta move, we going to get back in daylight. Not a total loss, we did score that."

K-Dogg pointed to a large plastic container on the dock. They'd uncovered this decidedly nonmedical shipment of crystal meth in the back of a Jeep.

"Not the point," Jimmy said. It had taken hours to get this far west, and that was without any resistance from military patrols. He'd pushed the limit of what he could accomplish without traveling at night. "Damn it. Load up what you can from the pharmacy. We'll leave in ten."

K-Dogg pointed to the group under guard in the corner. "And them?"

"Have as much fun as you want, but leave them all dead. It'll spread the word we mean business about the boy."

"You got it, Boss. Hector?"

K-Dogg gave the thug guarding the group a chopping hand motion across his neck. Hector racked the slide of his shotgun and smiled.

"Whoa, whoa!" a man in the group shouted. "I can help you."

The outburst, and the wave of panic he sensed with it, caught Jimmy's attention. He approached the hostages. The tall man who'd shouted worked his way through the group with his hands raised. At the crowd's edge, Hector shoved his shotgun barrel under the man's chin and brought him to a halt.

"I can get you who you're looking for," the man said.

A rounder, anxious little man scurried up beside him. "Paul, what are you talking about?"

"Shut the hell up, Mickey," he said over his shoulder. Back to Jimmy he said, "I can take you right to him. Depending on what's in it for me."

"For starters," Jimmy said, "Hector here blows your head off if you don't."

"Might do that even if I do," Paul said. "The kid's in a secure area. My secure area. Fenced and guarded. The guards aren't much, but you'll take casualties in an assault. I can fix that, for a price."

Jimmy liked how cool this guy was under pressure. He sensed Paul's confidence now, instead of panic. "And what might that price be?"

Paul lowered his hands. "The military and cops get weaker every day. This island is going to end up in the hands of the strong. I want a place in that organization. And…" he pointed to the plastic container on the dock, "…I bring a nice crystal meth business with me as an added bonus."

"Paul?" Mickey whispered in shock.

"Wake up, Mickey. We need to get on the winning side."

Paul was selling out someone in his group and dealing homemade poison. Jimmy couldn't ask for two better scumbag bona fides. "So what can you do for me?"

"Your men arrive at midnight. I rearrange the guards and open the gate. You are in and out with the kid in no time. Leave me a few men I can trust to help me on the dirtier side of my business, and you end up with ten percent of it."

"That kind of help is worth thirty percent," Jimmy said.

Paul tapped a finger against Hector's shotgun barrel under his chin. "You have a knack for negotiations. We got a deal."

Minutes later, Paul and Mickey rolled out the front entrance of St. Luke's in the Jeep. Mickey, silent since the loading-dock betrayal, turned to him as soon as they passed Jimmy's guard that glared at the entrance.

"Jesus, Paul. What the hell? What kid were you talking about back there?"

"Melanie Bailey's weird kid. He's some kind of half-infected mess."

"No shit? Damn."

The setting sun turned the empty streets red. Paul wheeled the Jeep around a series of abandoned, torched cars. Mickey adopted as contemplative a look as the plumber could muster.

"But, jeez, that guy with the scars and his crew are hardcore scum."

"In case you haven't noticed, the meek aren't about to inherit the Earth."

Paul turned the Jeep left, down the street they'd been ambushed before.

"Paul, we can't let them into Cedar Knoll. We can't give up our own people." Mickey gave the street a look of fearful recognition. "Hey, why are we going this way?"

Paul pulled up and swung the Jeep sideways at the ambush point.

"You're right," he said. "*We* can't let them into Cedar Knoll. But *I* can."

He pulled his pistol and blasted Mickey's right foot. The shot echoed between the buildings. Mickey screamed and grabbed his ankle. Paul pivoted in his seat and kicked Mickey out into the street. The plumber hit the asphalt like a sack of flour. His rifle lay in the backseat. Paul spun the wheel left with his free hand.

"Survival of the fittest, Mick," he said. "And you just aren't ready to do what it takes. I'll brag about your brave defense of me to everyone. Either they shot you when we escaped the hospital or we were attacked by the infected. I haven't decided yet."

Several of the infected, drawn by the gunshot, stepped out of doorways. At the sight of Mickey writhing on the ground, they came at a run.

"Looks like a party starting to honor our new hero," Paul said. "I'll leave you to it."

"Paul, no!" Mickey's eyes bulged. "You can't leave me here!"

Paul stomped the gas. The Jeep spun its tires and sped away down the street. In the rearview mirror, Mickey jumped up on one foot, face white with terror, and hopped away from the advancing infected. He left a splattered blood trail across the road.

Paul thrummed his fingers against the steering wheel and wished he had some decent music for the CD player. This turn of events couldn't have worked out better. His BJ of the Day appointment with Melanie wouldn't go on forever anyhow. Melanie would blab about the encounter to the one-eyed nurse eventually. Women were like that. Then Tamara would become an even bigger pain in the ass.

Then again, maybe that bitch wouldn't find her way home from the hospital. That would make two tragic Cedar Knoll heroes in one day.

Everyone saw Q Island as a death sentence. Paul saw it as his resurrection. He'd gone from the ignored gnome to the dungeon master of Cedar Knoll. Just as it seemed he'd played that as far as it would go, Fate dropped another opportunity in his lap, the chance to expand his meth trade, become part of the island's rising power and, in time, perhaps become the rising power himself.

All he had to do to make this dream come true was roll open a gate at midnight tonight.

Chapter Fifteen

Tamara's trek back from St. Luke's took hours in the gathering darkness, dashing from shadowed hiding place to shadowed hiding place. Pausing, listening, running again. Holding her pistol tight in her defense, at the same time afraid that firing it would bring a swarm of the infected. The eventual sight of Cedar Knoll's front gates across the street nearly brought tears to her eyes.

She spied Cody Stern on guard behind the main gate. The rifle on the sixteen-year-old's slight shoulder looked a size too big for him. He wore a stained New York Rangers jersey. He rubbed the rifle's sling between his fingertips and snapped his head at every tiny sound. If she could keep the nervous kid from shooting her first and asking questions later…

"Cody!" she yelled across the quiet street.

Cody unslung his weapon. His shaking hands chambered a round. "Who's there?" His voice had a dismaying squeak to it.

"It's Tamara. For Christ's sake, don't shoot me when I cross the street."

Cody pointed the rifle barrel through a slot in the gate. Tamara popped her head up from across the street. She waved and ran over.

"Paul said you were dead," Cody said. "Said you and Mickey got killed at the hospital."

"Well, I'm not dead yet, so why don't you open this gate and keep that streak alive."

Cody punched the code onto the keypad. The sidewalk gate buzzed open. Tamara jumped inside and slammed it shut.

"Paul thought I was dead?"

"Yeah, said the hospital was overrun by the infected. That they got you and Mickey."

Paul hadn't even told the truth about who overran the hospital, let alone her absence, so she didn't buy that Mickey somehow fell prey to the infected. The Jeep stood parked by the rec center. The man with the scars had let Paul go. That couldn't be good.

"I'd better call and tell him you made it," Cody said. "He'll be relieved."

Relieved wasn't the word that came to Tamara's mind. "Let me go tell him. Don't spoil the surprise."

Cody laughed a refreshing teenage laugh at setting up a prank. "Yeah, that would be too cool. You go for it." He slung his rifle back onto his shoulder.

Tamara hurried off. Her personal clock started ticking. Paul wouldn't be happy she was back contradicting the story he'd delivered. Cody wouldn't call him, but he'd put it in the log. And Paul read the log every morning. Then there'd be trouble. She still carried the two pistols from the Cedar Knoll stash, but they wouldn't be enough. He'd come with company, company ready to shoot first. She made it to her condo and opened the door.

"Mallow!"

The German shepherd came at a run, with an enormous, slobbering dog smile. His wagging tail thudded against the wall. Tamara knelt and hugged his neck as he licked her face.

"C'mon, boy, we have a mission."

She led him straight to Melanie's. Her friend needed to be warned about the scarred man's quest for Aiden.

Tamara knocked on the door. A second too late, she wondered if Paul was already in there.

Melanie checked the peephole. Her heart leapt with joy, and she yanked open the door.

"Tamara, you're alive!"

The two hugged.

"Let's get inside and keep it that way," Tamara said.

Mallow followed them in as she closed the door. Eddie stood in the living room. Mallow bounded over to him for a hug.

"Well, look what the cat dragged in. Damn glad to see you." He knelt and scratched Mallow's head. "And you too, boy."

"Where's Aiden?" Tamara said.

"Safe in his room," Melanie said. "Eddie found out something awful."

Eddie recounted his discovery of Paul's staging of the first attack by the infected. Tamara cursed herself for not catching the details around the victim's medical condition when she'd been so close to the body.

"Paul can't be trusted," Tamara said. "He knew I wasn't dead. At least he didn't see me killed. And the hospital wasn't overrun by the infected. It was some gang of criminals. And I saw *him*."

"Who?"

Tamara went to the pile of Aiden's drawings on the table. She rifled through them and pulled out the picture Aiden had labeled BAD MAN. She held it up to Eddie and Melanie.

"I saw *him*. He was at St. Luke's and he was looking for Aiden. Not by name, but he was looking for a boy immune to the infection. How many of those can there be?"

"Good thing no one outside this room knows about Aiden," Eddie said.

The duct-taped sheath chafed against Melanie's leg. Scenes of Paul's assault flashed before her eyes. She clenched a fist and quelled her rising anger. This wasn't the time to tell these two what happened to her.

"If that psycho somehow finds out Aiden's here," Tamara said, "he's got more firepower than we'll fend off with teenaged boys and old men." She cringed and looked at Eddie. "Sorry, Eddie, no offense."

"None taken. I admit my geezerhood."

"Dr. Bradshaw was going to get the military to get us to the CDC," Melanie said.

"But I haven't heard back from him yet," Tamara said. "And we can't wait. We need to take Aiden there ourselves."

"Now?" Melanie said.

Tamara looked out the window at the darkness. "No, I guess not. Crack of dawn, we go up and out."

"On foot?" Eddie said.

"I'll cover that," Tamara said. "It'll be a risky trip, but we're armed." She pulled one of the pistols from her waistband and handed it to Eddie. "But I don't feel safe here. Do you?"

"I don't trust Paul," Eddie said.

Melanie just shook her head in agreement.

Tamara sifted through the rest of Aiden's pictures.

"Did he draw any more of the man with the scars?"

"No, just that one," Melanie said.

"All the rest of these are from his point of view," Tamara said. "Things he's seen.

Would he have seen that guy somehow?"

"I don't know how. He never leaves the house without me. And I sure would have noticed someone looking like that."

"This infection might have given your son something more than artistic ability," Tamara said.

"All the more reason to get him to the CDC experts," Eddie said.

"Everyone pack a light bag," Tamara said. "We're out of here at sunrise."

Chapter Sixteen

In the shadows under JFK's Terminal 3, Samuel led Dr. Petty to the corner closest to Terminal 4. He pointed across to the area underneath the elevated gates.

"The civilian rations were stored there," he said. "Will a few random packets be enough for inorganic arsenic testing?"

"Now that I know what I'm looking for," Dr. Petty said.

The two soldiers assigned to guard the terminal sat together on a Delta Airlines tug truck at the far end. Their rifles lay across the hood. Cigarettes glowed in their hands. If the officers had upbraided the ranks for the earlier security breach, it certainly hadn't had an impact.

Samuel was about to sneak over to the terminal when, overhead, a big propeller-driven plane lumbered by. He paused and put a hand against Dr. Petty's chest. The plane dropped one wing and rolled 180 degrees for a landing on the runway. Tires chirped as the plane kissed the tarmac. It rolled toward Terminal 5. The two guards ditched their cigarettes, slung their rifles over their shoulders and set off in that direction.

"Here we go," Samuel said.

The two doctors trotted across to Terminal 4. Half the pallets of green civilian rations were gone. An extra-thick layer of plastic shrink-wrap encased the remaining pallets. Each now had a red warning label attached that read:

Civilian Rations Only!
Pilfering these rations takes food from the hungry and is punishable under the Uniform Code of Military Justice.

Some general had signed the bottom in an illegible scrawl.

"All of a sudden," Petty said, "lots of the rations are gone, and the rest get shrink-wrap lockdown. Pretty big coincidence."

Petty unfolded a pocket knife, slit the shrink-wrap and then the box underneath. He pulled out a lime-green MRE bag, tore it open and stuffed the main course and the coffee into his pocket. Samuel went to work on a second packet.

Muffled noises rose from the other side of the terminal. Between Terminals 4 and 5 stood a collection of shipping containers. Lengths of gray PVC pipes and thick bundles of wires ran from the terminal to between the containers. With the poor lighting, it was hard to tell at this distance, but Samuel swore the container doors hosted biohazard labels. No one had briefed him that there were any biohazards on-site outside his lab, and certainly not so close to where his people slept.

A second plane landed at the far end of the airport. Thinking the guards would remain occupied a bit longer, Samuel tapped Petty on the shoulder and pointed to the containers.

"Yeah, what are those?" Petty said.

"We're about to find out."

Samuel led Petty on a sprint to the containers. They did indeed have biohazard labels, as well as two padlocks on each door and warnings not to open. Samuel and Petty slipped into the narrow, shadowed space between two containers. The PVC pipes and wires ran up the center of the grid of steel boxes and branched off to service each one. Samuel caught a heavy whiff of human waste. The containers' thick steel sides muted the sounds, but something definitely stirred within the boxes.

A white tag fluttered from the corner of the front door. It had the same type GPID system identifier they used in the lab. Petty scanned it with his smartphone. The screen flashed red.

"Whatever's in here," he said, "my access codes say I'm not worthy to know about it."

"Try mine—8434751."

Petty punched in the code. The screen filled with information. He let out a slow exhale.

"Holy hell. These records are all military medical. This thing's full of people, infected people."

Something thudded inside the container.

"Soldiers?"

Petty scrolled up the screen. "No, civilians. Prisoners from the Atlanta penitentiary. It gives their dates of infection as three and a half months ago. Jesus, there's a whole list of experiments here they did on them."

"We haven't given them a cure to test yet."

"They aren't testing cures. They're testing limits. Bone strength, gunshot impact, starvation rates. Damn, this is torture."

Petty scanned the tag of the container next door. "This test group started two weeks ago. People infected with a different strain of the virus, and it isn't one we've isolated. It's one they've spliced and created. Jesus, the colonel who made it even has his damn name on it, like some proud papa. They're weaponizing the thing."

"And testing it on prisoners," Samuel said. "Like Nazis."

"Oh no." Petty's mouth dropped as he stared at the screen. He rested a hand against the container. "These people here aren't prisoners. They're Long Islanders. From Lindenhurst. What the hell is going on here?"

Chapter Seventeen

Samuel and Petty made a run for Terminal 3 as a third cargo plane, this time a big jet, landed and rolled up to the runway's far end. The other two planes had their rear cargo doors open. A platoon of soldiers organized equipment for loading nearby.

Samuel left Petty in the Terminal 2 lab to run through any other files he could access, now that the combination of the container's GPID and Samuel's code had let them into the military side of the system. Samuel went over into Terminal 1.

He planned on shaking Vanessa awake and finding out what the hell was really going on at this airport. But on the way to the sleeping area, he saw the light in her office area was on. He barged in without knocking. She glanced up from her desk, looking surprised and tired.

"Samuel? What are you—"

"You need to level with me. I need to know what you've gotten me into. What exactly is going on here?"

"The planes tonight are just routine," she said. She went back to typing. "Military training flights."

"I'm not talking about the planes. I'm talking about shipping containers full of the infected on the far side of Terminal Four."

She stopped what she was typing. "What were you doing over there?"

"What damn difference does it make? Is the military weaponizing this virus?"

"Yes."

Samuel waited for more. "That's it? Just yes?"

"The show's about over here anyway. What do you want me to say? Do you think the CDC alone rates the level of military intervention you see around this island? This was a golden opportunity for a knockout stealth weapon, and they carried enough weight with the President to get approval. Having that technology makes sense."

"Biological weapons are banned," Samuel said. "How could they ever be considered?"

"Do the math. How would we, how would the world, ever match a hundred million Chinese soldiers on the march? How are we going to find a way into remote cells of terrorists along the Afghan border? Bioweapons."

"The virus mutates," Samuel said. "It would be out of control."

"That's why we're engineering it. That's why you were going to provide a cure before we deployed it. But we're almost out of time. We're losing the lease on our little lab here."

"Because you're really poisoning everyone, aren't you? With the food rations."

Vanessa raised an eyebrow. "Well, you've really been jumping into water way over your head. You'll drown swimming out this deep, Bosi Daktari."

"When word of the poison gets out—"

"No one will care," Vanessa said. "They don't care now. Let me tell you what this place looks like to the outside world. Q Island is a leech. A growing number of people are realizing they're supporting families they'll never see again and that they can't afford it. Taxpayers are tired of funding the electric bill for the island through surcharges on their own. Do you know what emergency health care for five million people costs?

"We feed the island all the information it gets. Satellites are blocked, the Internet is so filtered it barely moves. Over the air, radio and TV news comes from duplicate broadcasts that the government creates. You Q Islanders don't know it, but no one's holding telethons and bake sales for you people anymore. The island is a cancerous tumor everyone wishes would just go away.

"So when inorganic arsenic excises that tumor, do you think anyone's going to do any investigation? Not in a million years. We'll blame the plague and get on with our lives. Do you have any idea how many real estate people ask me how long after the last person kicks before the virus dies off? Developers are salivating to get their hands on this place again. Those are the people with money, the ones that count."

"No," Samuel said, "that can't be true."

"Wake up, Samuel. Your head has always been in the clouds doing research, not looking at real-world consequences. Your polio funding died out because people with money stopped contracting the disease. If Bill Gates hadn't stepped in, nothing more would have ever happened.

"When this is over, the country will have a real estate bonanza that'll fuel the whole nation's economy, and we'll have a weapon that will return us to the dominant military force in the world."

"Created using human beings?" Samuel said. "I haven't even tested cures on animals.

I'd never let anyone infect humans on purpose."

"They were prisoners, lifers and scumbags, murderers and child rapists."

"Except for the Long Island civilians," Samuel said.

"Who were dead anyway," Vanessa said. "Do you think anyone will ever be let off this island? No matter what you discover?"

Samuel could barely process this amazing level of betrayal, this coldhearted calculation that left the value of human life out of the equation. What happened to the Vanessa he'd worked with so long ago?

"The planes out there are starting the evacuation," Vanessa said. "Research will continue on a decommissioned carrier at anchor off the Chesapeake Bay. The weaponization team will be there. That immune boy you told us about? We extract him at dawn, and he's coming with us. You and the cure team need to decide if you want to be part of a national solution, or stay behind as part of the problem."

Samuel knew a cure could stop this whole plan. He'd give it to the people on Long Island; he'd share it with the world so the weaponized version was useless. This horrible plot would fall apart at the seams.

But he didn't have the cure. He was close, but he couldn't get the pieces to fit, he needed more time or more brainpower. Vanessa had just told him he was about out of the first of those two.

"Well, Samuel? Are you part of our solution or part of our problem?"

"I have my own solution," he said.

He took off running down the darkened terminal to the exit door. Behind him, keys on the phone beeped as Vanessa dialed for security to detain him. He practically rolled down the stairwell to the emergency exit then burst through the door into the cool, crisp evening.

By tomorrow the lab would be shuttered. And he had a bad feeling that while anyone who didn't join the weaponizing team would be left behind, they wouldn't be left behind alive.

He was about to bet on million-to-one odds. But it was the only bet he could place.

Chapter Eighteen

Tamara had just dropped off to sleep when her cell phone rang. Mallow leapt up from the foot of her bed and barked. In her groggy state, she had trouble recognizing the sound. The phone hadn't rung in months. The caller ID was blocked.

"Hello?"

"Tamara. It's Samuel Bradshaw. Are you awake enough to understand me?"

She sat up straight. "Damn, I am now. Go."

"I have to hurry before I'm discovered or cut off. Soldiers will arrive at dawn to take Aiden. Don't let them and don't bring the boy to JFK. This whole operation here is evil. He'll become an experiment."

"God no."

"It's worse. The government's written off Q Island. Whatever you do, stop eating the government rations. You need to get the boy off the island and into the hands of sane researchers."

"How can I do that?"

"I don't know, but you have to. I have some research here. It's just a few steps from a vaccine. I think I can figure it out, or most of it. I'm going to send it to your phone in a data packet. Between that and Aiden's samples, I'm sure someone can synthesize a cure. Someone not connected with any government agency."

"Even the CDC?"

"Especially the CDC." Doors slammed in the background. "Gotta go."

The line went dead.

Tamara threw on some clothes and tucked the heavy pistol into her waistband. Mallow sat in the doorway with an expectant look on his face.

"You're so lucky you don't understand all this."

Mallow followed her as she ran across to Melanie's condo. She rang the bell a few dozen times until a dazed Melanie answered the door. Eddie squinted at them both from a few feet behind her. He held the pistol with both hands, pointed at the door.

"Eddie, it's me Tamara!"

Eddie lowered the weapon.

"Guys," she said, "we have a problem."

She told them the story of Samuel's call. Melanie sagged at the news.

"Now what?" she sighed.

"Sounds like we need to amscray out of here," Eddie said.

"The bridges that aren't blown up are guarded with shoot-to-kill orders," Tamara said. "I doubt there's anything larger than a rowboat that still floats between here and Montauk Point. Drones patrol the sky. Unless we're going to dig a tunnel, we're not going anywhere."

"There may be another way off the island," Eddie said. "It's a long shot. Not underground. Underwater."

Both women stared at him in anticipation.

"I told you I worked at the CanAm transfer station near Washington Point. We pumped fuel oil from Connecticut into big holding tanks. From there, trucks took it to homes. That pipeline was big, over four feet across. It had to be inspected, repaired, you know, make sure no one hung an anchor on it or whatever. I used to do that every month. In a submarine."

"Really?"

"Yeah. I mean, not a full-fledged submarine like Jules Verne or nothing. More like a crawler. A wide disc with two seats under a plastic bubble. We used to call it Crabby Cathy. It crawled along tracks on the side of the pipeline. We'd flip on these big spotlights and check the pipeline for leaks and whatever. It ain't fast or nothing, but it will follow that pipeline all the way to a place where no one's got this plague."

Tamara leaned forward. "So where's this sub, Captain Nemo?"

"It's mounted on the pipeline where it comes ashore. We had a service shed where we stored Crabby Cathy and the pipeline scrubbers. I thought through this option when I saw Paul wasn't trustworthy. But the plan to go to JFK seemed better."

"It's not better anymore," Tamara said.

"The sub can get all of us out of here?" Melanie said.

"It seats two. I'd need to make three trips, but yeah, sure."

"What happens when we surface on the other side?" Tamara said.

"Nothing. The Connecticut shed is just like the one here. With the pipeline closed from the quarantine, it'll be sealed up and abandoned. No one sees old Cathy arrive or depart. Three trips later, we're all on the other side. Once it gets dark, we sneak out to freedom."

"And we get Aiden into the hands of someone trustworthy," Tamara said, "not some government agency where he could disappear without a trace."

Melanie smiled. "I like this plan."

Mallow thudded the floor with his tail, as if casting his own vote.

"A hundred things might go wrong," Tamara warned. "We need to get out of here. We need to get to Port Washington. We need to get into the shed. This list goes on and on."

"One chance in a hundred is still more chance than we have here," Melanie said. "Saving Aiden might mean saving everyone. Let's launch that sub."

Chapter Nineteen

Samuel hung up the phone, went straight to the Terminal 2 wing. As he'd expected, Dr. Petty was the only one there.

"What did you find out?" Petty asked.

"That all our worst nightmares are true. You?"

"About the same. They're cooking up nasty stuff over there."

"Don't waste time testing the food," Samuel said. "Vanessa admitted it's poisoned. They're going to eradicate the disease and the host at once. The weapons guys are pulling out of JFK starting tonight."

"And all of us?"

"You can turn to the Dark Side and join them or be left behind."

"I love it when all my choices suck," Petty said.

"Do me a favor and grab the notebook by my cot for me?"

"Sure." Petty stepped out of the lab. As soon as he did, Samuel locked the door behind him. Petty turned around. He tried the door. "What are you doing?"

"Look, I'm inches from a solution. We both know that. Some parts don't fit; some things I can't quite wrap my head around. When I was twenty years younger, I'd have flipped this upside down and solved it in no time."

"What are you talking about?"

Samuel booted up the lab computer. All the research was here, all the pieces of the puzzle, all the tests, all the results. They said something. He just needed to listen to them all speak at once to get the message.

Petty pulled a set of keys from his pocket. He slipped one into the door lock.

"Bad idea," Samuel said. He activated the emergency containment system. An alarm wailed. The air circulation stopped. Door seals expanded.

He pulled a glass tube of virus sample from the refrigerator and threw it at the base of the door. It shattered.

"What the hell?" Petty yelled.

A sleepy-looking lab tech stepped up behind Petty, rubbing her eyes. "What's going on?"

Samuel extracted another vial of the virus from the refrigerator. He poured it straight down his throat. The lab tech screamed. Samuel stepped up to the glass wall opposite Petty.

"I've seen what the virus can do, for a while, before it destroys the host," Samuel said. "I need that window, that jump in my ability."

"Not everyone turns ultragifted," Petty said. "Even if you do, you can't think you'll cure this."

"I'll at least get you years closer. And put you years ahead of the weaponizers."

"The virus needs to grow in you," the lab tech pleaded. "It may take days to present."

"I'll help it along," Samuel said.

He went over where an emergency defibrillator hung on the wall. He unbuttoned his shirt.

"Dr. Bradshaw, no!" Petty said. "Jump-starting your beating heart like that might kill you."

"Thanks for not adding 'especially at your age' to that," Samuel said.

He flipped the Charge switch on the defibrillator. The On light turned green. He placed the paddles against his gray-haired chest. The cold surfaces zipped a shiver up his spine. He kept his grip and lay down on top of them so the initial charge didn't bounce them off his chest. On the other side of the glass, Petty led a growing chorus of onlookers demanding that he stop.

He didn't look up. He closed his eyes and focused on what he had to complete, what lay ahead, on the other side of squeezing the triggers.

One. Two. Three.

He squeezed. The world turned to starlight.

Chapter Twenty

At a few minutes to midnight, Paul approached Cody at the main gate. He couldn't have picked a better dupe. The kid was green as a glowstick. He'd been on duty for a while and would gladly accept a diversion.

"So how's it looking, Cody?"

"All quiet out there. One or two infected dudes across the street, but they didn't come this way."

"Good work. Tell you what, go walk the perimeter for me. I'll keep an eye on the gate."

"Something wrong?"

"No, just routine."

"Sure thing."

Cody sauntered off. He stopped and turned. "Hey, great news about Tamara getting back safe, ain't it?"

"What?"

A proud look swept Cody's face. "I checked her in here, let her surprise you at your place. Ain't she lucky she got out alive?"

What the hell? Paul thought. *How could she get back here from the hospital, on foot, through the infected...*

"You bet," he said. "Lucky's the word."

Cody loped off on his fool's errand. Paul fumed. He wondered how much that bitch nurse knew about what happened at the hospital. Probably a lot since she lied about checking in with him when she got back. She probably went straight to Melanie to warn her...

He checked his watch. She was too late, anyway. He walked over and peered out the front gate. K-Dogg stood in the middle of the street. Paul waved. K-Dogg nodded. Paul punched in the access code for the main gate. It rolled aside with a grinding moan.

Three sets of headlights flared to life, and a trio of armored SUVs rolled toward the gates of Cedar Knoll. Paul leapt back out of their way. They fanned out and parked around the main gate. K-Dogg followed in on foot.

Jimmy Wade stepped out of the center vehicle. Paul ran up to him, furious.

"What the hell is this? We agreed to one vehicle, four guys, a quiet extraction."

"I've modified a few aspects of our arrangement," Jimmy said. "We also agreed to a thirty-percent cut. I changed that to seventy."

"Hey!" Cody shouted from way down the perimeter wall. "What are you doing?"

He unslung his rifle and came back at a run. His oversized Rangers shirt flapped behind him like a cape. A monster of a man in a leather vest stepped out of the SUV on the right. He held an AK-47.

"Cody, stop!" Paul yelled.

Cody already had his rifle halfway to his shoulder. The monster man fired the AK one-handed from the hip. A spray of bullets splattered Cody's chest. The impact sent him sprawling backwards. He hit the ground hard and lay still. His rifle struck the pavement and sent an errant bullet zinging into the sky.

Men unloaded from the rest of the vehicles. Fury at his betrayal boiled up in Paul.

"We made a goddamn deal," Paul said. "If you want that kid—"

Paul froze. A whirlwind whipped through his mind. Every memory he held, every thought he had, felt like it was simultaneously unpacked and tossed in the air. Melanie, Aiden, Tamara, Eddie. Jimmy now knew it all. Paul dropped to his knees, stunned"It took every ounce of my self-control to not do that to you in the hospital," Jimmy said, "to keep you cooperative and give me the element of surprise here."

"But...my meth..."

"Like I give a shit about your piddly dope sales. Once I have the boy, I'll have everything."Jimmy turned to K-Dogg. "He lives with his mother in condo 6A. He's here. He's so close I can practically taste him. There may be an old man there with them. I don't care about the adults, but the kid must be brought back alive. Damaged is okay, but definitely alive."

Chapter Twenty-One

K-Dogg fired his submachine gun at the deadbolt on the front door of condo 6A. The lock and doorframe disappeared in a snow of woodchips and metal flakes. He kicked at the door handle, and the door flew open. He stormed in with three men behind him.

Eddie sat up on the couch. The blanket that covered him fell to the floor. He scrambled for his glasses on the end table and then shoved them on his face. He squinted through the crooked frames at the intruders.

"Who are you?"

The three men began to search the house.

"Where's the kid?" K-Dogg said.

"What?" Eddie said.

K-Dogg shoved Eddie back into the couch with the barrel of the gun. Then he stuck it in Eddie's mouth.

"The next words out of your goddamn mouth'll be the kid's location, or you ain't gonna have no mouth left."

The three men returned. "No one's here. No woman, no kid," one said.

K-Dogg pulled the gun barrel from Eddie's mouth. "Well?"

Raw panic filled Eddie's face. "They just left. They went to Tamara's condo."

K-Dogg jammed the gun barrel against Eddie's forehead. It made a deep, red circle. Blood seeped from one edge. Eddie shut his eyes tight. A tear rolled down one cheek.

"Which one?" K-Dogg said.

"T-t-twenty-two," Eddie said "Unit B, s-second floor. Don't kill me. I'm just an old man."

K-Dogg paused then pulled the gun away. "And a pussy of an old man at that."

He spit on Eddie's shirt. Eddie trembled, eyes clamped shut.

K-Dogg waved the men to the door. "You heard him—22B. Go!"

Eddie waited until he was sure the men's footsteps were well down the path outside. He opened one eye. The room was empty. He broke into a smile. He reached under the couch cushion and pulled out the pistol Tamara gave him. He stood and tucked it in his belt. In over sixty years, that was a move he'd only seen in the movies. For the first time since the Navy, he was handling a gun. He'd sent the bad guys on a wild-goose chase. He had a bit of badass left in him after all.

He went to the wall and took down his reframed wedding picture. It looked much worse for the wear from its last evacuation, with two deep creases and a missing corner. He pulled it from the frame, looked at his late wife and smiled.

"Look at us, girl," he said. "I've moved you more in a few months than I did in twenty years."

He folded the picture with religious reverence and put it in his pocket. He left the condo through the rear sliding glass door. He jogged between the other units to the perimeter driveway. Tamara's white Range Rover idled at the curb, lights out. He ran around to the front passenger door and got in.

"And?" Tamara asked.

"Perfect," Eddie said. "They're on their way to the far end of the complex. But once they kick open the door to that empty condo, they'll be back damn fast."

"And we'll be gone." Tamara handed him an open box filled with an assortment of screws and nails.

Eddie turned to the backseat. Melanie sat behind Tamara, Aiden behind him. Aiden had the baseball bat from his supermarket close call between his legs. Mallow panted from the rear cargo area. "You both okay?"

"Thanks to that gunshot warning and you two's quick planning," Melanie said.

Tamara inched the truck up to the edge of the complex. The perimeter drive turned left for the main gate. The three SUVs were parked across most of the road. The front gate yawned open and inviting.

"How we getting past those trucks?" Eddie said.

"I'll nudge one out of the way," Tamara said. She pointed to the big, black brush guard on the front of the Rover. "That's what my ex bought that ugly metal thing for, isn't it?"

She gunned the engine, and the Rover laid rubber. It fishtailed around the corner, and she popped on the lights. Two men raised their rifles and took positions behind the nose of the near SUV. Tamara aimed right for them.

The men realized their danger and fled before getting off a shot. Tamara angled the Rover and hit the nose of the closest SUV. The right headlights died and the brush guard folded as the Rover collapsed the SUV's front wheel. The SUV spun around and opened a clear path to the front gate.

"Dump it!" Tamara shouted.

Eddie poured the contents of his cardboard box out his open window. Melanie did the same. Screws and nails and reinforcing brads from Tamara's storage unit tinkled as they scattered across the black asphalt in the Rover's wake.

The remaining headlight lit up Paul Rosen to the left, on his knees beside one of the SUVs. Tamara fought the urge to trade a clean escape for running him down. She twitched the wheel right. The truck blasted through the open gate.

Gunfire erupted from the condos. Aiden and Melanie ducked in the rear seat. Bullets cracked into the concrete wall behind them. The back window shattered. Mallow barked. The Rover's rear end swung wide as the truck turned right down the main road.

Eddie sat up and looked over the dashboard at the front end of the car. "Looks like you did a little damage to your vehicle."

"You know," Tamara said, "I never really liked this thing anyway."

At the sound of crunching metal, Jimmy came running to the front lot. He arrived just in time to see a Range Rover careen around the corner and disappear in a hail of worthless gunfire. The boy was in that truck. He could feel it, feel that power slip away from him, like the retreating scent of a warm apple pie as someone takes it away from the oven.

"What the hell?" he shouted.

The two men shooting looked at him in abject terror, as if awaiting their execution. Jimmy clenched his fists in frustration.

"Go get them!" he ordered.

The two men climbed into one of the undamaged SUVs. They fired it up and launched it in reverse at the open gate.

Halfway there, twin muffled booms sounded. The SUV swayed as the two rear tires went flat. It skidded sideways. The rear quarter rammed the edge of the open gate in a crash of shattered glass and crunched steel. The SUV stalled.

A sea of sparkling, sharp objects glittered on the pavement beneath the streetlights.

Jimmy cursed under his breath. K-Dogg came running up behind him.

"They ain't here," he panted. "Old man sent us to nothing, now he's gone."

"He went that way, idiot," Jimmy said, pointing out the gate. "Along with the boy. Roll that wreck out of the way and clear a path to the street. They're not getting away."

Chapter Twenty-Two

Samuel's eyes fluttered open. He lay faceup in the lab. He tasted burnt metal. A charred electrical smell like from his childhood toy trains filled the air. He looked at the lab's glass partition wall. The whole team seemed to have their faces pressed against it. He rose to a sitting position.

He expected a cheer from the crowd, a gasp of relief, at least a greeting. He got silence. Their faces all hosted the same emotion. Horror.

He saw his chest had several burns. He must have flopped a few times on the defibrillator. But underneath those burns and across the rest of his chest stretched Q Island's universal sign of imminent death—raised, blackened blood vessels. He smiled.

He stood up. His head swam for a second. His heart labored a bit. His snap diagnosis was some heart-muscle damage. A long-term problem in what for him was now a very short-term world. He staggered over to the glass. No one said a word.

He caught sight of his reflection superimposed over Petty's ashen countenance. His own face was grey with dark veins. His eyes were red as candied apples.

"How long was I out?" Samuel asked.

"Minutes, maybe ten," Petty said. "It progressed fast between your direct dose and the electric shock."

"More to add to our lab notes."

Samuel returned to the computer. He pulled up several files on the virus. He used the lab's unfiltered Internet access to bring up published research on polio and several blood-borne diseases. He thought about how the disease impacted the central nervous system, the temporary enhancements that allowed Ms. Albritton to create poetry and his wife to walk. It occurred to him that the enhancements might not be temporary, just overwhelmed by the desire for violence, the need to stoke the adrenal reaction.

Ideas piled upon ideas, multiple paths of possibilities stretched out simultaneously. The clues came together. The electric stimulation. The sepsis presentation. What all seemed unrelated, he now saw as integral. He could practically draw the viral DNA and describe every function of every rung of the double helix.

"Clear the way!" someone shouted outside the lab. "Goddamn it, I said clear the way!"

Faces scattered from the wall of glass, replaced by the green camouflage of soldiers and the ominous black of automatic weapons. Only Dr. Petty held his position, watching Samuel's every move. A colonel appeared whom Samuel recognized from the encounter under Terminal 4. The officer spun Petty around to face him.

"What the in Christ's name is going on here? Where's Bradshaw?"

Petty pointed through the glass.

The colonel's face went red when he saw Samuel. "He's infected? Get him out of there."

"The room's contaminated," Petty said. "It's sealed."

Ideas came to Samuel faster than he could record them. His fingers flew over the keys. Experiments run, success probabilities estimated, a shift in the understanding of the polio virus, explained in detail and how it fit with this viral outbreak. It was now so clear, as if he'd been trying to make out a distant coastline and suddenly the obscuring fog lifted.

He smiled at the familiarity of how his mind used to work, how it could cut and paste so much together so quickly. Right now, he was doing that and more. He was at full rpm with a turbocharger kicked in.

A box popped up on his screen that read *File Deleting*. A number zipped from *1* to *100* in a split second. The box disappeared and one of his reference files winked out. Another File Deleting box appeared.

"Dr. Petty!" Samuel shouted. "They're in the system. They're downloading our research and deleting it."

"Stop this," Petty said to the colonel. "Without that, he can't finish his work."

"Then someone else will," the colonel said. "Open this door and get him out of there."

"That door opens and we're all contaminated," Petty said.

"Not all of us," the colonel answered. He shouted over his shoulder, "Don protective gear."

The soldiers put their rifles between their knees and whipped gas masks out of canvas pouches strapped to their waists.

On Samuel's screen, two more files disappeared into the ether. His active, unsaved work would be the last thing they could get, but they'd get it. But they couldn't cut his Internet access while they needed it to download his files. At least he hoped not. His fingers flickered over the keys.

The soldiers pulled the masks over their heads, cleared the filters and checked the seals. At the rear, two men with backpack flamethrowers advanced to the glass. The colonel looked like a great insect in his mask, two huge oval eyes in the black rubber. He pulled his pistol from his holster and racked the slide.

"Run!" Petty shouted. "Everybody run!"

The medical staff surged past the soldiers to the exit. The colonel aimed at the glass wall on one side of the door and fired. The wall shattered and a torrent of tinkling glass shards rained to the ground.

The last of Samuel's reference files disappeared. Whatever he'd completed, it would have to be enough.

A second gunshot brought the other glass wall tumbling down.

"Torch it!" came the muffled command from the colonel's protective mask.

Samuel clicked the Email icon. He typed in Tamara's number, the one person he knew he could trust. He reached for the Send key.

Fire bellowed from the flamethrowers like the mouths of twin dragons had been opened. Other soldiers stepped back and shielded their faces. Twin plumes of orange flame raced into the lab from two directions. They rolled in, dual masses of superheated air that consumed every molecule of oxygen in their paths. The air swept up and out of Samuel's lungs a split second before the streams of fire rolled over him from both sides, his fingers still on the keyboard.

Chapter Twenty-Three

Tamara's Rover attracted the infected. They came out of the darkness like dogs to chase the vehicle. Tamara gunned it and outran them. Eddie guided Tamara through the route to the transfer station outside Port Washington.

"We're almost there," Eddie said. "The main entrance is on the other side of town."

Melanie watched the passing ravaged storefronts that lined the street—working shops in the 1940s, emptied by big-box-store competition in the 1980s, resurrected by boutiques in the 2000s. The infection finally had pounded a stake through their collective hearts. Tamara circumnavigated a small crater in the street and let the Rover roll to a stop.

On the left rose a 1950s vintage high school, one of the sandstone monuments towns built in the image of college campuses, with tall-windowed, two-story wings and a central tower that looked like a carillon. Wally and the Beav would have attended in the days when a high school's felony offense was a cigarette in a bathroom stall or a skirt that stopped above the knees.

But the infection had driven the school to another purpose. Blackened plywood covered the first-floor windows. Posted signs read *STAY IN LINE* and *HAVE ID READY*. Coils of concertina wire encased the old wrought iron fence around the perimeter. The front gate hung wide open on one hinge. A main battle tank listed to one side as it blocked the street. One track lay unspooled along the pavement like a dead eel. The turret faced sideways, and the gun barrel drooped toward the asphalt as if the tank finally had succumbed to exhaustion. The corpse of a dead soldier lay half-exposed from a front hatch, his chest exploded and black. Other uniformed bodies littered the front lawn of the school. A shredded American flag hung limply at the flagpole, somehow still lit by a floodlight.

"Damn," Eddie said, "if the infected can take out a tank, we're screwed."

"I think the soldiers took themselves out," Tamara observed. "The gate is broken from the inside. The soldier in the tank was infected. The dead in the yard are all military.

Some of the infected would have died in an assault."

A chill ran up Melanie's spine. "And I bet all the infected soldiers didn't die."

Tamara threw the Rover into reverse. "Get me out of here, Eddie."

"Take the right back there on Buckley Street."

The Rover's tires spun, and Tamara cranked the wheel. The SUV arced backwards. The rear tire rolled over a bump of crumbled asphalt. Several inches underground, a switch tripped.

Five kilos of H6 composition explosive detonated in a fireball. The Rover blew straight up in the air. For a split second, it seemed to hang suspended on the billowing flames. Then it rolled in the air and crashed down on the passenger side. Glass exploded in every direction. The four tires burst into flame.

Melanie hung from her seat belt. Her head buzzed, and the world looked blurry. Beneath her, Aiden lay against the crushed door panel. Blood trickled from his ear.

"Aiden!" Her voice sounded muffled and far away. She reached down for him. Her fingertips grazed his coat. Oily, black smoke from the burning tires invaded the cabin. She choked on the fumes.

A strong hand grabbed her coat from above. A muffled, distant command followed. She looked up into Tamara's face. Blood coated her. Her lips moved. Her words became crisper. "Release your seat belt."

Melanie clicked the release. With Tamara holding her suspended, she swung her feet down on either side of her son. She snapped off his belt and scooped him into her arms. He was still breathing. Tamara opened the door above her. It came off the hinges, and she cast it aside. Melanie raised Aiden above her head, and Tamara pulled him out of the car. Together, they lay Aiden on the ground away from the Rover.

Mallow trotted over and licked Aiden's face. The fur on his right shoulder was damp with blood. Tamara returned to the truck. Mallow bounded after her.

"Aiden," Melanie pleaded. Her hearing had improved. She ran her fingers through his hair. His eyes fluttered open. They sparkled in the firelight of the burning tires. She suppressed a scream of joy.

"Melanie! Help!" Tamara yelled from the side of the Rover.

Aiden nodded to his mother. She ran to Tamara, who stood facing the roof of the toppled Rover.

"Eddie's trapped. We have to flip this thing over."

They both reached down and grabbed the edge of the roof. Melanie pulled. Every muscle from her arms to her calves strained. The Rover rose a few inches then fell back.

"Again!" Tamara said.

A second try sent Melanie's back into torment, with the same results.

The two bent down for a final attempt. A third, smaller set of hands gripped the roof beside hers. Aiden stood there, muscles tensed for the pull. Melanie swelled with pride.

"One-two-three," Tamara said.

The three of them pulled. The Rover rose, hit the tipping point and rolled over onto its burning tires. Melanie yanked at the crumpled passenger door. It lurched open with a scream of shearing metal. She caught Eddie as he nearly fell out of the truck. She pulled him to the ground. He screamed in pain. His pistol clattered to the pavement. Aiden scooped it up. Melanie didn't have time to be horrified.

Mallow barked and shifted to a low growl. They whirled around. An infected soldier in a filthy, blood-soaked uniform aimed a pistol at the four. His other arm flopped at his side, apparently broken. He charged.

Tamara drew her pistol and fired. The shot hit the soldier in the chest. He rocked back on his heels. He fired twice as Tamara fired her second round.

Her bullet hit his head. One of his rounds exploded the Rover's side-view mirror. Tamara grabbed the right side of her face. Blood trickled through her fingers.

"Goddamn it," Tamara cried.

A blood-soaked, second soldier stepped out of the shadows. He carried a knife nearly a foot long. He sprinted in their direction, mouth pulled open in a wicked grin.

Every ounce of anger Melanie had within went to full boil. Paul's assault, that scarred man trying to take her son, her husband's shit treatment of her. Now this infected bastard was going to kill her son and her friends. She shook with rage.

She pulled Aiden's bat from the backseat and charged the soldier. He went straight for her, knife raised high.

In a split second, he was on her. Melanie swung the bat upward and deflected his crude slash with the knife. The blade flew from his hand. Melanie followed through on the backswing, spun around and swept the bat up between the soldier's legs.

Bone crunched and the soldier let loose a high-pitched wail. He dropped to his knees, both hands clutching between his legs. She brought the bat up and crashed it onto the side of his head. The impact made the bat sing in her hands. Blood gushed from the soldier's head, and he dropped to the ground.

Her repressed rage took control. The bat spun like a windmill in her hands, smashing and bashing the soldier's corpse. Blood pounded in her ears and drowned out some faraway noise. The third time it sounded, it broke through. A shout.

"Melanie!"

Melanie paused and looked back at the Rover. Tamara stood there screaming her name. The blood-greased bat slipped from her hands. The head of the soldier at her feet looked like pulped red grapefruit.

Her heart rate dropped back to normal. She went back to Tamara.

Tamara pressed her hand tighter against her own cheek. "We have seconds to get Eddie out of here before every infected in town jumps us."

"Can you walk?" Melanie asked Eddie.

"No. I think my leg's broken."

"Mel, get us to some cover," Tamara said.

Melanie spied a trashed portrait studio across the street. "Over there."

Tamara and Melanie each slung one of Eddie's arms over their shoulders. Melanie led them to the studio at a shuffling run, Aiden right behind them. Eddie moaned with each step. Behind them, a tire on the Rover exploded. Several more infected soldiers appeared on the high school grounds.

The four pushed into the studio through the unlocked door. Mallow rushed past them and sniffed out the room's four corners for danger. Old-fashioned oils of family portraits hung askew on the walls. A sign proclaimed *WE DON'T DO DIGITAL*. The cash register lay smashed on the floor. They lowered Eddie to an open spot. He gritted his teeth and suppressed a scream.

"Oh yeah…" he winced, "…that leg's broken."

Outside, a second tire exploded. Melanie crawled past Aiden, took the gun from him and looked out the window.

"The infected soldiers are milling around the Rover. Two infected civilians just joined them."

"All this noise is like ringing a homicide dinner bell," Tamara said. "Melanie, you're going to need to get Eddie ambulatory."

"Wouldn't you do that better?"

"Not anymore. That bullet got my good eye. I'm blind."

Horror shot through Melanie. She crawled over from the window and inspected Tamara's face in the streetlight's faded glow. Blood-covered flecks of glass were embedded everywhere. Her eyelid was twice its normal size and swollen shut.

Tamara jerked her head from Melanie's hands. "You need to fix Eddie. Go check that leg."

"I'm no nurse."

"No, I am. You're just my eyes and hands. Now, we need to see his leg. Find something to cut open his pant leg."

"I have something." Melanie pulled the kitchen knife from her sock sheath. "Eddie, I'm about to ruin these pants."

"Least of my troubles, Mellie."

Melanie sliced a slit up Eddie's pant leg. The leg lay at an odd angle. She traced her fingers along the edge. The sharp, broken middle of his shinbone pushed up against the skin from the inside. Her stomach went queasy.

"Yeah, it's broken. But not through the skin."

"The leg has two bones, like a chicken wing," Tamara said. "Are they both broken?"

"No, just the big one in front."

"Good. You're going to reset that bone. You're going to grab Eddie's ankle and pull down hard. You'll feel the two parts of the bone come back together well enough for us to splint it."

"And I'm guessing I'll feel it too," Eddie said.

"Hell yeah." Tamara felt her way forward until she reached Eddie's head. She knelt on his shoulders from behind with the back of his head in her lap. "And you're going to have to suck it up, buttercup, or none of us'll make it out of here. It'll hurt a lot less when she's finished."

Melanie's hands began to shake. "I can't do this. You pull, I'll hold him down."

"I can't see what I'm doing. It has to be you, and it has to be done. Without Eddie, Aiden doesn't get off this island. And if you don't hurry, we won't even get out of this store."

Melanie slid around and put Eddie's foot between her knees. She grabbed his ankle. Her heart beat so fast she feared it would burst. "I'm sorry," she whispered.

Tamara clamped a hand over Eddie's mouth. Melanie pulled. Bone scraped against bone inside the leg. Eddie screamed through Tamara's hand. His body jerked a half-dozen ways at once.

"Harder!" Tamara yelled. "Set it!"

All Melanie wanted to do was let go, to stop inflicting pain on her friend. She held her breath and pulled. The fractured bones snapped into place. Eddie's scream reached alto level, and he passed out. Tamara removed her hand.

"Thank God," she said. "Let's splint this before he wakes up."

Wood shattered on the left. Aiden had stomped on a big picture frame and broken it into pieces. He handed the two longest to his mother. She just held them, stunned. She couldn't remember the last time Aiden had done something unasked, let alone something thought out in advance for someone else. He'd also helped roll the Rover unbidden. He began to tear the canvas from the painting into strips.

"I have two sides of a picture frame," Melanie said, "and Aiden is shredding me some canvas."

"Excellent." She detailed how to tie a splint. Melanie followed instructions.

Tamara tapped Eddie awake. "Rise and shine, Eddie."

Eddie moaned.

"Feeling better?"

"Uh, yeah."

"Good, time to leave. Melanie, see if this place has a back door."

Melanie went to the rear of the shop. She pushed the exit door open a crack. Outside was a narrow alley, free of the infected. A little van with the portrait studio logo on the door sat parked between the buildings. A set of keys hung on a hook on the wall by her head. She clenched a fist in victory. The door slammed shut behind her on a heavy spring. When she returned, Tamara was whispering in Eddie's ear. He nodded.

"Not only is there a door," Melanie said, "there's a vehicle with keys."

"Good," Tamara said. She backed away from Eddie and sat up against the wall, facing the studio front door. "You three need to get in it and go."

"Oh no," Melanie said, "we four need to go."

Melanie dropped to Tamara's side and held her hand. Tamara pressed it against her own side. Warm, wet blood seeped from Tamara's rib cage.

"Two bullets found their mark. I'm a nurse. I can feel the damage inside me. One of us is as good as gone. You three need to finish this."

"We all started this. We all need to finish."

"I'll never make it out the door, let alone to the crawler. The only route for all of you to make it is through town and out the other side. Right now the street out there is full of infected looking for trouble. I'll divert them into here and clear you a path."

"No! That's not an option."

"She's right, Melanie," Eddie said. "I need to drive the crawler, or I'd say the same thing, with my leg here. Bad enough you gotta carry one piece of bruised fruit. Carrying two ain't worth the risk."

The third of the Rover's tires exploded. The front of the store glowed a low yellow from the flames. The infected crowd outside had grown to over a hundred.

"But, Tamara, you got us this far…" Melanie said.

"And you'll get the rest of the way. You'll get your son the rest of the way. You're the one who said saving Aiden might save everyone. Now get out of here."

Melanie hugged her and kissed her cheek. "We won't forget you."

Tamara placed her phone in Melanie's hand and forced Melanie's fingers to curl around it.

"Doc Bradshaw's going to send his research files here. Between that and your miracle son, the right people can create a cure."

"Got it."

Tamara pulled out her pistol. "Now, throw some pictures in front of the door. Something with glass." She leveled the gun in the direction of the doorway. "I want to hear what I'm shooting at when they come in."

Aiden tossed a pair of pictures into the doorway.

A tear dribbled down Melanie's cheek. "C'mon, Aiden. We have to go."

Aiden went to the back door. Melanie helped Eddie to his feet and they followed.

Mallow trotted over to Tamara. He licked the side of her face and sat next to her.

"Oh no. You go with them, Mallow."

Mallow whimpered and wagged his tail.

"Hell no. Last thing I need is some dog messing things up around here. Go take care of them. Mel, call this stupid dog."

"Mallow," Melanie said. "C'mon boy. Time for a ride."

Tamara groped around until she touched Mallow's chest. She thumped it. "You heard her. Beat it."

Aiden opened the back door. Mallow whimpered and trotted out behind the boy. The door closed.

"We'll take care of him," Melanie said.

"You'd better," Tamara said. A tear cleared a track through the blood as it ran down her cheek. She sniffed. "You'll hear when I have their attention. Then go."

Melanie hitched Eddie up a bit higher on her shoulder and dragged him out the back door. Aiden already sat in the passenger seat. Mallow sat beside the rear tire. Melanie popped the rear doors and eased Eddie down into the van's cargo area.

The portrait studio door swung to close. At the last millisecond, Mallow darted back through an opening that looked half his size.

"Mallow!" Melanie yelled.

The door slammed shut with a tuft of fur in the jamb.

Eddie slid himself back into the van. Melanie yanked on the handle to the studio door. Locked from the inside. She smiled at how smart that stupid dog really was.

Months of being half-blind hadn't prepared her for the real thing. She sat alone in the dark in a strange place. She'd never known how to do helpless.

She raised the gun and pointed it at her best guess for the front plate-glass window. Dog nails clicked on tile behind her. She released the trigger.

"You damn stupid dog, you'd better not be—"

A warm, wet tongue licked her hand. Tears welled in her eyes.

"That's a good boy, Mallow. You gonna help me kill some bad guys?"

Mallow yipped.

She reached around and hugged her dog. She rubbed her face in his warm fur. His musky scent enveloped her, that same scent she'd smelled on cold winter days when he lay at her feet watching TV, the same scent she awoke to when he snuck into bed beside her during thunderstorms. She thumped his side and pulled away.

"Okay, boy. With a bang, not a whimper."

She raised the pistol and put a shot through the big glass window.

At the pistol's report, Melanie tensed in the van's driver's seat. The sound of shattering glass seemed to go on forever. Then came the fainter crunch of the infected in front of the store, then the trampling of Tamara's early warning system. Mallow barked and growled. A gunshot, another. Something crashed on the other side of the wall.

She imagined Tamara firing blindly at any sound, surrounded by an infected mob. Mallow fighting to keep her safe just one second longer. Melanie couldn't bear it.

Tamara screamed.

Melanie started the van and zipped down the alley. She swung right, and then right again, to pass the portrait studio and head for the pipeline. The road was clear of the infected.

She tried not to look, to avoid the fodder of future nightmares. But she shot a quick glance at the studio. A writhing mass of former human beings blocked the studio door and window. She looked back out the windshield.

"All right, Eddie," she shouted over her shoulder, "which way to the pipeline?"

Chapter Twenty-Four

"Hold it right here," Jimmy said.

The SUV jerked to a stop outside the portrait studio. A platoon of the infected milled about, in and out of the store. They looked up at the headlights of the SUV.

"Clear that space," he ordered.

The SUV's back doors swung open. Two men climbed out toting AK-47s. The infected crowd sprinted in their direction. In unison, the men opened fire. Bullets mowed down the infected, row by row, until none still stood. Gun smoke drifted into the passenger seat and swirled around Jimmy.

Jimmy stepped out. The two gunmen flanked him as he approached the studio. Random single shots rang out as they put bullets into the heads of anything that looked alive. They took up a defensive stance on either side of the shop. Jimmy strode in through the front door. He kicked away some broken picture frames.

Several infected lay on the ground. All dead, save one with a clearly mortal sucking chest wound. At the far end of the shop, the dismembered body of the one-eyed nurse occupied a puddle of blood. To her left lay what looked like a bloody fur coat. Only on closer examination did he see the distorted face of a dog at one end.

Jimmy clenched a fist on frustration. He couldn't have missed them by more than minutes.

The day had been long, and Jimmy still had miles to go before he slept. A pick-me-up was in order, a little something to help curb the insatiable hunger the trail of the immune boy had created.

Jimmy reached down and grabbed the infected man at the neck. His arterial pulse raced against Jimmy's palm. Jimmy bashed his head against the floor once, twice. On the third impact, the skull cracked open like a boiled egg.

Jimmy flicked a chunk of bone out of the way. He reached in, scooped out a handful of warm, wet brains and began to feed.

The boy still lived, and he had one fewer defender. Good news abounded. Jimmy sensed him north of here, but not far north. In that direction, they'd run out of island pretty quickly. They would not be hard to find. And one housewife and an old man wouldn't be hard to kill.

Despair fell heavy as a late winter snow when Melanie saw the CanAm terminal's gate. It lay flat on the ground.

"Eddie, we're too late."

"We don't know that." He peered between the seats from the back of the van. "Take a left up here. Go to the long building at the end."

A mile down the pitch-black road, they came upon a elongated building sheathed in corrugated steel. Dirt caked the few small windows near the roofline. The building extended onto a dock a hundred yards past a rocky beach. Melanie pulled the van up next to the entrance. A rusting combination lock secured the door.

"This is it," Eddie said. "The pipeline hangs a right out there for the main tanks. People used to mistake the place for a gardener's shed."

Melanie helped Eddie out of the back and over to the entrance. The only sound was the rhythmic lap of tiny waves against the stony shore.

"See why I got a house on the shore?" Eddie said. "Between the Navy and here, I just don't know no better. Uh-oh. This ain't good."

Eddie put his finger in a bullet hole in the door. Melanie scanned the rest of the wall. A line of bullet holes peppered the metal about four feet off the ground.

"Well, it's still locked," he said. "So maybe—"

Aiden uttered a panicked moan. He pointed south. A group of the infected stood at the end of the long road. They started a sprint northward.

"Hurry, Eddie."

He spun the dial on the lock. It ground as it turned. He stopped at the final number and jerked down on the lock. It held fast.

The infected were close enough that Melanie could make out their faces. A second group appeared behind the first.

Eddie hopped on his good foot to regain his balance. He banged the lock up and down, and redialed the combination. He gave it a shake and pulled. It popped open. Rust flaked from both sides of the shaft.

Eddie pushed the door open. The building was black as an abyss. Melanie and Aiden followed him in. He slammed the door and threw a huge bolt.

"Wait here."

He winced as he hopped to the left and popped open a breaker box. He threw a few switches. Lights along the ceiling flickered on. Two at the far end popped and went dark. The rest stayed on.

The four-foot-wide pipeline rose up from the sea and down the center of the shed. A large saucer with a set of clear windows straddled the pipeline near the water. Its wheels clamped on rails along the pipeline's side. A bullet had shattered the craft's center window. Two other punctures in the skin stared them in the face.

"No!" Melanie whispered.

Behind them, one of the infected slammed against the door. It flexed on its hinges. Aiden retreated to the end of the pipeline. Melanie grabbed the edge of a desk and shoved it up against the door.

"Crabby Cathy ain't going nowhere," Eddie said.

At the pipeline's end, a long hatch opened to expose a ten-foot-long, double-ended torpedolike device with bristles and nozzles along the outside. As Aiden stared at it, Melanie looked over his shoulder.

"This looks like a weapon," she said.

"Against sludge," Eddie said. "That's the cleaning drone. Only works in the pipeline."

Melanie pulled the pistol from her waistband. She felt ridiculous with the heavy piece in her hand. She didn't know what to do with it, was still a bit afraid of it after a lifetime of anti-gun indoctrination. She handed it to Eddie and began a frantic search of the tabletops and cabinets in the shop for a defensive weapon she could manage.

She picked up a box-cutting knife. If only they were being attacked by boxes. She grimaced and tossed it aside.

"I dunno, maybe..." Eddie winced and let out a low moan. He hopped over to the pipeline on his good leg. He lowered himself to the ground. His body shuddered in pain as his splinted leg touched the floor. "...ouch, yeah. Uh, the cleaning fluid for that drone is flammable as hell. We make some sort of Molotov cocktail..."

"We set them on fire, and we'll probably set the building on fire."

A rock crashed through one of the upper windows. Shattered glass rained down onto the concrete floor.

"We swim out along the pipeline," Eddie said.

"To a beach crawling with the infected? No chance. What about through the pipeline?"

"All the way to Connecticut? It's miles through sludge in the dark. The airborne toxins would kill you."

Outside, the delivery van started up. The engine revved to its limit. Melanie realized she'd left the keys in the ignition. Could the infected drive? If they weren't far gone enough. She'd seen them wield chainsaws.

Tires screeched outside. Then the building shook. Another wail of tires, and the building shook again. Tools and pictures jumped off the wall by the door. A third scream of tires. On this impact, the wall by the door buckled inward.

"This shack won't take that kind of ramming long," Eddie said.

More glass shattered over their heads. The long, black tire iron from the van poked through and cleared the rest of the pane with a circular swirl. The tire iron and one arm poked through the window frame. Then the head of one of the infected appeared. Melanie imagined the creature climbing on the offered backs of its brethren to reach the window. It locked its gaze on Melanie, eyes ablaze. Spittle sprayed from its snarling lips.

Eddie took a bead on the intruder and fired the pistol. Its neck exploded. It slumped over halfway through the window. The tire iron slipped from its lifeless hand. It twirled and hit the floor with a deep ping.

Melanie scooped it off the floor and brought it to the ready at her shoulder . She looked for Aiden. He still stood beside the pipeline hatch. But he'd somehow opened the top half of the cleaning drone. The hatch stood near vertical, like the open hood of a car.

"Aiden, get away from—"

More glass exploded above her. Windows on either side of the corpse in the window frame shattered and sent a waterfall of glass shards sailing down. Two more infected pushed through the openings.

The van slammed into the building again. The doorframe cracked. A fissure of darkness split the wall from top to bottom. Multiple pairs of gray-veined hands reached through and began to rip parts of the wall away to widen the gap. The van's red taillight glared through the lower part of the gap and turned the shop floor the color of blood.

Melanie charged the broken wall. She smashed a hand with the tire iron. Eddie raised the pistol. He trained the sights on one of the infected.

Gunshots sounded. Eddie hadn't pulled the trigger. The infected in the upper windows sagged, lifeless and slid back through to the outside world. Another burst of gunfire erupted from a different direction. Bullets raked the van in a staccato set of pings. Two bullets pierced the wall and zinged by Melanie. She ducked and covered her head. The hands in the wall gap froze and then slithered back into the darkness. Silence reigned.

Melanie exhaled in ecstatic relief. The Army, the police, CanAm security. Someone had come like the cavalry-over-the-hill rescue, and not a moment too soon.

"In the shed!" someone called from outside. "Are you all right?"

"Yes," Melanie shouted. She checked Eddie, leaning against the pipeline with his pistol still trained on the windows above. Aiden still stood staring at the drone. "We're all fine!"

"Even the boy?"

Melanie's heart skipped a beat. No one saw them enter the building except the infected. Who would know Aiden was in here?

She peered through the crack in the wall. Two men in motorcycle leathers held AK-47s at the ready. Between them stood a man with blood coating his hands and the lower half of his bearded face. A man with a bald head covered in scar tissue and stitches. The man from Aiden's pictures.

Chapter Twenty-Five

Another wave of pain shot through Jimmy's head. The world swirled like a flushing toilet for an instant. Blood ran from both nostrils, and he wiped it on his sleeve.

The kid was strong. Amazingly strong. Jimmy had tracked the sensation of the boy all the way to the CanAm gates, then followed the sound of the infected's assault on the building after that. He couldn't read the boy, though. It was like feeling the heat from the sun in the sky and still being unable to look straight at it.

Worse, he could not read and manipulate the others in the building. The boy had dropped some sort of psychic curtain. Jimmy couldn't even tell how many there were. That ability, that raw strength the boy wielded, just whet Jimmy's appetite for him. He'd hoped for control over the infected after eating the boy. Now he was sure he'd have that, as well as untold other powers.

"Good news for you," Jimmy announced from near the frame-shop van's nose. "I'm ready to let you all walk out of there alive."

Melanie peered through the crack in the wall.

Dear old mom was one of the survivors. That was going to add a bit more incentive for the boy to hold out. That wasn't good. And killing her would give the boy a bit more incentive to put up a fight, a fight that might get him killed before Jimmy could do it in his own leisurely way.

"I don't believe you," Melanie shouted.

"All that gunfire you heard," Jimmy said, "that was the sound of me saving your lives. You ought to see the swarm we put down out here. If I'd wanted you all dead, I would have kept shooting until you were."

Another ice pick of pain lanced Jimmy's skull. He grabbed the sides of his head and moaned. He tasted blood as it ran down the back of his throat. This goddamn kid was really starting to piss him off.

"Well, if that's so," Melanie said, "you and your men leave, then we'll leave, and you've kept us alive."

"Not that simple, Melanie, and you know it. Your son is special. He's reacted to the infection differently. The rest die, but he's improved, isn't he?"

Silence. He'd hit pay dirt.

"How do you know that?" she asked.

Jimmy blanked out the hearing of the two men with him. "Because he and I are the same. I got infected and I improved. Your son's destiny and mine are intertwined."

"My son's destiny is to cure the world."

Jimmy stepped halfway down the length of the van. His head reeled as he moved closer to the boy's location. A drop of blood seeped from a tear duct.

"A cure? The world doesn't need, doesn't deserve, a cure. Your son and I are the next stage of the evolutionary process. Would you eradicate Homo sapiens to preserve Neanderthals? When he joins with me, a new, superior species walks the Earth. One who controls the viral and the nonviral, and turns Q Island into paradise."

"I'm not liking the paradise you've made so far."

She wasn't going to see reason. He'd expected as much. He switched his men's hearing back on. He mentally ordered them to opposite sides of the building. The effort felt like it tied his brain in a knot. The two moved off, rifles at the ready.

Jimmy moved to the crack in the wall. The boy's psychic force repelled him like a hurricane's wind. He reached his left hand into the crack to pull the torn steel back for a wider view.

"Think it through, Melanie. Your son—"

A shaft of white-hot pain pierced his hand. He screamed and pulled it back. A broken kitchen-knife blade stuck out from the middle. He gripped it between his teeth, yanked it free and spat it on the ground.

"You goddamn bitch!" he shouted.

He cradled his left hand in his right. So be it. Whether those in the building were dead after he consumed the boy or before, the choice they made really didn't matter. One way or another, in a few minutes, he'd be master of all that surrounded him.

"That's sending a message," Eddie said.

Melanie tossed her end of the broken kitchen knife on the ground and scooped up the tire iron.

"Ain't no dealing with him," Eddie continued. "We need to go down swinging and take that bastard out there down with us."

"I know." Melanie had seen the two men with Jimmy move off in opposite directions. Here they were, an invalid with a pistol and a woman with a tire iron. They didn't stand a chance. Her son still stood beside the drone, staring down at it. He hadn't flinched through the entire assault. She went to his side.

"Aiden honey, you need to get down. It's about to get…"

The inside of the drone was six feet of empty space, a cylindrical coffin, complete with lid.

"You got one hope," Eddie said. "And he's looking at it. The cleaning solvents go in there. The nozzles spray them in the pipeline, the brushes scrub the tube. So it's airtight to keep from leaking."

Eddie crawled over to a panel under the drone. He flicked a switch. A needle on a gauge bounced upward. "The internal battery's got three-quarters charge."

"What are you thinking?"

"We send Aiden to Connecticut. He'll only get what air's in there. But I can send it in return mode instead of scrub mode, to get there faster."

Jimmy's voice wafted in from outside. "I'm going to give you one more chance to do this the reasonable way. I'm ready to come in there if I have to."

"He'll die if he stays here," Eddie said. "I'm sure of it."

Melanie envisioned Aiden in Jimmy's hands. "Okay, we send him."

"You'll both need to go."

"Are you crazy? There might not be enough air."

"Mellie, I've known him for months now. He's afraid of the dark, afraid of closed spaces. He won't get in there without you."

Melanie thought of all the times she had trouble even getting him into the car.

"And then," Eddie continued, "what do you think will happen if he pops up over there and climbs out all alone and infected? Will he be able to explain what's happened? Would anyone listen? Those people over there are the same people who gunned down the Port Jeff ferry survivors. If they even suspect he's come from Q Island they'll kill him, burn him and ask questions later. Forget about it, with his red eyes and black veins. You need to be there."

He was right. She couldn't send him off like Moses in a basket and hope someone enlightened found him down river. She needed to hand him to trusted medical authorities.

Russell James

"But what about you?"

Eddie tapped his splint with the barrel of his gun. "I ain't going nowhere with this. And someone needs to launch the drone. I'll hold 'em off 'til you get safely under the Sound. Once it's on its way, there ain't no calling it back."

Aiden stared into the drone. He rubbed his palms up and down against the sides of his pants. She knew he understood what they were planning. She saw the fear in his eyes. He wouldn't get in there alone. But would getting in there with her, where close contact would be guaranteed, be any more palatable?

"We're out of time, Mellie," Eddie said.

Melanie shook her head in wonder. "How many times are you going to save our lives, Eddie?"

"I'm guessing this will be the last."

She bent down and kissed his stubbled cheek.

"Tell my daughter what happened," he whispered.

"I'll tell the whole world."

Melanie climbed into the drone. The cold metal chilled her back. She slid to the side in a futile attempt to make more room. A single bed had more space. Aiden looked down on her. Beads of sweat glistened on his forehead. His lower lip trembled.

"C'mon, honey. I won't let anything happen to you. It will be a short trip, and then we'll be safe."

"Time's up," Jimmy shouted from outside. "Little pigs, little pigs, let me in."

Aiden climbed in. He stifled a cry of panic. He tried to plaster himself to the far side, but there was no escaping contact. His chest pushed against Melanie's. His racing heart pounded against her breast. His warm, panting breath blew across her neck. She'd felt neither since he was a baby.

Eddie flicked a switch on the console. The cover lowered into place. The last sliver of light winked out. The latch sealed with a click.

A rising wail slipped through Aiden's clenched teeth. He clamped Melanie's waist. She slid her hands around the side of the tube to touch him. She gathered him closer. The scent of his hair brought back memories of those first amazing months of motherhood, when the future was equal parts wonder and terror and the emotion of love had finally revealed its full, glorious maternal self.

She kissed her son's ear and whispered, "Everything will be all right."

Then she began to sing, so low and soft she could barely hear it herself, "Angels in heaven, look down on the child, perfect and lovely, tender and mild…"

Outside the tube, something clicked. A motor whirred.

They launched.

Chapter Twenty-Six

Paul Rosen rolled onto his back and stared up at the sky from the cold asphalt of the Cedar Knoll parking lot. Every part of him seemed to sing its own personal song of pain. The culminating off-key chorus amplified with any movement.

He didn't know it was possible to survive such a beating, though from the feel of it, his survival seemed to still be in question. Jimmy Wade had used the interval before he could set out in pursuit of the Range Rover to have his men express his profound disappointment in Paul's performance. Boots and rifle butts seemed the preferred method of expression.

But the worst was over. Wade and his men had left. And they'd left an armored SUV here, a significant upgrade from the open-air Jeep. He could expand meth distribution from selling at the gate to making deliveries. He'd lost his one-eyed nurse, but she was a pain in the ass anyway. And the good news was she'd taken Melanie, her screwed-up kid and the mooching old man with her. A net gain for the community and two empty condos he could fill for a profit.

All he needed was a little time to heal, to let his cracked ribs knit, to close up a few of these gashes, to set his crushed fingers. Once he told the idiots here how he repelled the invading thugs at high personal risk, they'd elect him emperor for life.

Footsteps fell on the pavement. Cody Stern stepped up beside him. The three holes torn in his shirt revealed that his dimpled Kevlar vest beneath had functioned as advertised.

"Cody!" Paul said. His voice croaked from his bruised throat. "You're alive! Thank God!"

Paul tried like hell, but wasn't sure if his swollen, bleeding face showed the relief he tried to fake, the fear he actually felt or neither. Other association members drifted in. Cody knelt down close.

"Yeah, saved by the vest," he said. "From the scumbags you let in the front gate."

"Let in? They had me at gunpoint."

"Save the lies. The bullets knocked me down, they didn't knock me out. I heard everything that happened. Normally, no one would believe me, but the whole association just saw an interesting video. You were the star."

"Video?"

"Yeah, main-gate surveillance from the first attack by the infected. You remember that day?"

Paul's heart sank. Hadn't he deleted that video? He'd meant to.

"Let me refresh your memory," Cody said.

He grabbed Paul's wrists and yanked his arms up over his head. Pain slicked through both sides of Paul's body, and he screamed. Cody dragged Paul on his back to the open main gate. He passed by blurred faces of Cedar Knoll residents. One old lady spit on his head.

He scraped over an assortment of the screws and nails that had flown out of the Rover's windows. They ripped trails down his back. Cody dropped him near the gate. His skull hit the pavement with a crack.

"See, that first infected dude, you shot and killed him right here. This very spot. Saved us all from major disaster, didn't you?"

"Cody, you weren't there. The guy was viral. You can't see it on the video."

"Oh, yeah I can. Here's what I saw."

Cody grabbed his wrists again. This time he yanked them twice as hard. He dragged him past the open gate and into the narrow space between the gate and the street. He dropped him again and kicked one of his cracked ribs. A sword of pain lanced through his gut. Paul doubled over.

"See," Cody said, "I saw a dude standing here, pleading for help. A dude you baited in and murdered. We've all seen it. We judge-and-juried you, found you guilty of murder. Welcome to the outside. Hope the infected treat you better than you treated one of them."

"Cody! No! Look at me, man. I'm defenseless." The double *S* slurred on forever from his pain-numbed lips.

"So was the dude you killed." Cody spit on Paul's face. "Good luck, jackass."

Cody stepped back through the gate and punched the code into the gate control. The gate ground back closed. It locked with a clang.

"Cody!" Paul could barely raise his head off the concrete apron. "I saved you all! I kept you safe! You'll all die without me!"

Paul rolled over and stared out into the darkened street. He felt naked on this side of the wall. Unarmed, exposed, alone. He knew what lurked out there. Bands of the infected waiting for a call to action, a sound that said "welcome to some excitement". If he was quiet, he could crawl off, hide somewhere, heal enough to get on his feet. Then—

Two rifle shots cracked behind him. Bullets zinged over his head and exploded the side windows of an abandoned car across the street.

"Hey out there!" Cody's voice echoed through his cupped hands. "Play tiiiiime!"

A cheer rose up from the residents who now lined the main gate.

"Oh no," Paul moaned.

Shadows shifted in the gloom across the street. A few infected stepped into the streetlight's glow to investigate. Paul sat up on one hand. They caught the movement and stepped in his direction. Wary at first, then faster as it appeared Paul wasn't bait for a trap, just an inexplicable gift.

Panic gripped Paul as the ragged band of the infected broke into a sprint. One of them was much better dressed than the rest, in clothes that looked near clean. The stout man kicked it into gear and improbably passed the front of the pack before they crossed half the street. His arms were a tangle of blackened veins, his eyes burned like flames. Paul shit himself in fear and closed his eyes.

The sprinting man arrived first. He leapt on Paul's chest. His weight finished the job of snapping Paul's ribs, and punctured his lungs. Hands with a Herculean grip crushed his throat. In the surge of new pain, Paul's eyelids snapped open.

His last vision on Earth was the furious, infected face of the abandoned Mickey Reynolds.

Chapter Twenty-Seven

Jimmy Wade's jaw dropped. Even from outside the building, he could sense the shift, the dissipation of power, the fleeting retreat of the boy from his presence. His men bracketed the building. The boy couldn't fly out through the roof. The building looked something like a boathouse, but no boat had left. But somehow…

Jimmy aimed an AK-47 at the front door and reduced the locks to a ragged mess with a half magazine. He kicked open the door.

A pipeline ran up out of the water through the center of the building. Some kind of damaged underwater vehicle perched on the far end of the pipe. The close end was open at the top; the lower half, empty. An old man with a splinted leg sat up next to the pipeline. He had a pistol, but it lay flat on the floor beside him, under his left palm, pointing away. A tattered, old black-and-white wedding picture lay next to the gun. Jimmy leveled his rifle at the old man.

"Where's the damn kid?"

Eddie pointed a thumb down the length of the pipeline. "On his way to Connecticut."

Jimmy stepped up and jammed the rifle in Eddie's chest, too furious and impatient to concentrate on any mind tricks. "Well, reel him back in."

"Couldn't if I wanted to," Eddie said. "Besides, you wouldn't be here anyway."

"Really?"

Eddie smiled. "By then you'll be blown to halfway across the Sound."

Eddie's middle finger moved to the pistol's trigger. He pulled it. The gun barked. A bullet flew a quarter inch off the ground and straight across the room into a drum of cleaning fluid.

From the outside, for a split second, the entire building took on a rosy, internal glow. Then the expanding fireball blew all four walls and the roof straight out like a disassembled toy house. Crabby Cathy rode the ball of flame on an airborne trip to a final resting place beneath the sea.

Inside, Eddie died smiling. Jimmy Wade, the next phase of the progress of mankind, disintegrated in a state of shock, an evolutionary dead end.

After the blast of initial acceleration, it seemed as if the drone wasn't moving at all. With no way to judge relative motion, no flow of air, no ray of light, only the hum of the drone's passage against the pipeline convinced Melanie they still moved at all.

Aiden quivered in her arms, and she imagined the host of fears he fought in his head, each one enough alone to send him into a catatonic state. But he was hanging on, riding his phobias like a bucking rodeo bull.

The drone casing turned frigid cold as it passed through the depths of Long Island Sound. Condensation prickled the tube. The damp cold soaked into her back and chilled her spine until she shivered. She pulled her son closer and slid her hands between his back and the drone's cold steel.

Time seemed eternal. The stagnant air turned humid and thick. She began to envision every molecule of life-giving O_2 she breathed in, every molecule of poisoned CO_2 she exhaled. She willed her heart rate to slow, her pulse to fade. Anything to use less of the precious, finite supply of oxygen she, but more importantly, Aiden needed.

At this moment, with her son finally, blessedly in her arms, it was all so clear. Whether the fate of Q Island or the fate of the world hung on his safety or not, she would save him before herself. She'd always said she would, as all parents do, but she always harbored a shadow of a doubt. When it all hit the fan, would she be unselfish enough to sacrifice it all for him? Now she knew.

Eddie said it was miles across the Sound. How many? How fast were they travelling? How long had it been? She felt lightheaded. The drone seemed to start a sideways spin, though her brain told her that was impossible.

A rainbow of colors flashed across the drone's interior like multicolored shooting stars. A giddiness drifted down upon her like a flurry of feathers. Despite every element of her dire situation, she broke out in an enormous smile. She stifled a laugh. The world around her turned white and cottony, like clouds with substance.

"Mom?"

It was Aiden's voice, a voice she'd never heard, yet instantly recognized. She looked across a drone interior that had suddenly grown impossibly wide. Aiden looked up at her with a big, toothy grin. His face was clear of the gray scourge. His mop of curly, black hair shined in the bright light that was everywhere, and yet came from nowhere.

"You've been amazing, Mom," Aiden said. He sounded so adult, so certain. "You never gave up on me."

"How could I? You're my son, you're part of me."

"I couldn't show you," Aiden said. He held her hands in his. "But I love you."

Joyful tears ran down her face. "And I love you, Aiden honey."

Aiden smiled. His eyes flashed, not with their new rosy, toxic tint, but like two twinkling stars. He released her hands, and he floated away to be enveloped by the swirling, misty mass.

In her heart, she felt the finality of this moment, the permanence of this parting. But a feeling of bliss still enveloped her, and as the edges of the brilliant clouds turned dark, that joy remained. Like the end of an old-movie serial, the white world shrank, an ever-collapsing circle before her eyes. It diminished until it was just a blazing, white dot, a single star in a galaxy infinitely dark. Then the dot winked out.

Melanie sighed and let go of the only world she knew.

Chapter Twenty-Eight

Bright light.

All the stories told of it, the light at the end of death's tunnel. You had to walk to the light. You had to embrace the light. She sensed the light, the warmth that was just up ahead.

"Angels in heaven, look down on the child, perfect and lovely, tender and mild."

Her heart leapt with joy. Aiden's voice again. Here in the afterlife, in Heaven. Her eyes snapped open. His face hovered inches from hers. A glowing, angelic halo backlit his thick curls.

"Aiden." She exhaled.

He pulled away. Sunlight made her squint. Her eyes adjusted. She looked up at the underside of a corrugated roof. This wasn't Heaven.

She sat up. Her head took a little spin. When it cleared, she saw she was sitting in the drone, in the open end of the pipeline. Morning sunshine streamed in through the upper windows. Aiden stood next to her. It looked like she was back in the building where they left Eddie. But there was no Eddie. And the wall wasn't collapsed. The windows weren't shattered. The toolboxes and tables were in different places. She faced the opposite direction than when she left.

Connecticut!

"We made it?"

Aiden nodded. He reached out a hand to her, a hand still covered with the black scourge of the virus. She took it, and he helped her out of the drone. When she stood up, he did not let go.

She pulled out Tamara's phone. Five bars raced to life. Two newly added files blinked in the lower right-hand corner, one named RESEARCH; the other, CONTACTS.

She walked Aiden over to the window in the door. She wiped a hole in the dirt. The building was in some kind of industrial park. At the end of the block was a bus stop. A few pedestrians walked by, intent on their own destinations. She could see the reflections of her son's rose eyes in the window glass.

"Aiden honey, we're about to change the world."

Acknowledgments

I planted the seed of this story over five years ago and had to stop nurturing it, admitting that the scope and the medical expertise were beyond my skill set. But the Dark Muse wouldn't stand for that excuse and, several novels later, pushed it to the forefront again.

Common writers' advice is to write about what you know, and for me, nothing medical falls in that category. I want to thank Rita Brandon, RN and writer, for her time-consuming answers to all my stupid questions about life as a working nurse. Any medical parts that ring true are due to her. For the parts that don't, blame me and my soon-to-be-revoked poetic license.

Thanks to Teresa Robeson, talented writer and artist, who donated Gwen Albritton's poem.

Fellow authors Janet Guy, Kelly Horn and Belinda Whitney, all beta read the story. Their contributions made it so much stronger. I thank them for it, and so does Melanie Bailey, who wouldn't be who she is without them.

And thanks to my wife, Christy, for demanding that I mount framed book covers on the wall and that I take the time to pursue this strange obsession called writing.

About a week after I finished this manuscript, scientists reportedly dug up a 30,000-year-old virus somewhere in the Siberian wilderness.

Start buying canned food.

Russell James
March 18, 2014

About the Author

Russell James grew up on Long Island, New York and spent too much time watching *Chiller*, *Kolchak: The Night Stalker*, and *The Twilight Zone*, despite his parents' warnings. Bookshelves full of Stephen King and Edgar Allan Poe didn't make things better. He graduated from Cornell University and the University of Central Florida.

After a tour flying helicopters with the U.S. Army, he now spins twisted tales best read in daylight. He has written the paranormal thrillers *Dark Inspiration*, *Sacrifice*, *Black Magic*, *Dark Vengeance*, and *Dreamwalker*. He has two horror short story collections, *Tales from Beyond* and *Deeper into Darkness*.

His wife reads what he writes, rolls her eyes, and says "There is something seriously wrong with you."

Visit his website at www.russellrjames.com and read some free short stories.

Follow on Twitter @RRJames14, or drop a line complaining about his writing to rrj@russellrjames.com.

Two realities. One hope.

Dreamwalker
© *2015 Russell James*

What if you lived in two worlds, and could die in either? Pete Holm can. He is a dreamwalker, able to travel to the realm of dreams, including the devastated world of Twin Moon City, where an evil voodoo spirit holds living souls in terror with his army of the walking dead.

In the waking world, drug lord Jean St. Croix knows only the power of the dreamwalker can stop him, so St. Croix vows Pete must die.

Pete is the only hope to rescue the lost souls in Twin Moon City...unless St. Croix kills him first. Can anyone survive when two realities collide?

Enjoy the following excerpt for Dreamwalker:

Flaming arrows sang by Pete's ears, one so close the heat singed his hair. A quick glance over his shoulder revealed a horde of tribesmen closing fast from the edge of the jungle clearing. They wore animal skin loincloths with bizarre fur patterns. Necklaces of human bones pounded against their tanned chests as they charged. In unison, they screamed like shearing metal and displayed mouths full of tiger shark teeth. The lead savage, face painted white as death, brandished a trident with a man's gaping skull on each tine.

Pete's instant arrival here wasn't the least disorienting. In a flash, his memory gaps filled in. A magic emerald figurine sat heavy in the pouch at his waist. When he and his team took it across the rope bridge over the gorge, the spells the leader had cast over the local villages would be broken.

Three of them were running to the bridge, one man yards ahead and almost there. He was familiar yet somehow nameless, the same late-teen age as Pete, clad in similar khaki shorts and a grimy T-shirt. Sunlight flashed off a tortoise shell shield slung across his shoulder. He reached the anchors of the rickety suspension bridge and spun around. He unshouldered the shield. Wind from the gorge behind him blew his brown hair back across his face. He crouched to defend the rope bridge entrance.

"Pete, hurry!"

Pete instinctively glanced back to check for her. She was right on Pete's heels, her footfalls in sync with his. Her long, blonde hair trailed behind her, a hint of panic in her green eyes. Even mottled with the jungle's dirt, her graceful features were beautiful. That's why she was Dream Girl.

"I'm here," she panted. "Don't wait."

The tribesmen's scream came louder this time as they closed the gap. Another volley of burning arrows cut the air. Several stuck into the suspension bridge planks. Pete hit the bridge at full speed, hands gliding along the gnarled rope railing. The blonde was right behind him.

They were halfway across when Pete heard the scream. He could only get a glimpse past his shoulder, but that was enough. A shield pierced with flaming arrows. A lifeless body on the ground. Men with machetes chopping at the ropes.

"Don't look back," he yelled. "Run!"

The hand railing ropes jumped in sync with the hack of each tribesman's machete. The bridge bounced as they bounded down the last few feet. Pete leapt across the remaining planks and landed on the far side of the gorge. The sickening crack of rotted wood rolled across from the gorge's other side.

Pete whirled around. The log towers at the far end tore from the ground and tumbled into the gorge. Parted twin support ropes flew toward him like snapped rubber bands. The bridge dropped. Dream Girl's determined look turned into shock as the planks fell away beneath her.

"Pete!"

Pete's hand darted out and grabbed her arm. He wrapped his other arm around one log tower's base. Her hand gripped his wrist. It was soft, but strong. She looked up with a smile of relief.

"A bit too close, don't you think?" she said.

Then it all dissolved, that episode over.

Pete Holm spent his nights this way, bouncing from dream to dream. They were usually great adventures, Hollywood blockbusters inside his head as he sailed pirate ships or fought off space aliens. While most people had fuzzy dreams with muddled narratives, Pete dreamed with exceptional clarity. Technicolor hues, exquisite detail, nuanced scents. He'd describe it as more real than reality, if there was someone he'd ever describe it to. And while most people's dreams faded with the advance of consciousness, Pete's remained sharp as high-definition TV.

But the real nightly treats were continuing storylines. His dreams often picked up the next evening where they left off. And while Pete might start *in media res* as his English professor described certain stories, he knew exactly where he was and what he was doing, as if he'd just paused the movie from the night before. Characters rarely made the transition from one storyline to the next, except for Dream Girl, the forever unnamed beautiful blonde with the emerald eyes.

He was always aware that he was dreaming, but knowing that never made it any less real, any more than a pilot in a flight simulator ever felt as if he wasn't flying. He regretted that he lacked control of the dream's outcome, a prerogative his subconscious refused to yield.

In tonight's double feature, he now stood alone in what he had dubbed "The Mansion", a brick antebellum masterpiece, complete with an immense two-story front porch. The house had been with him his entire life, a slowly evolving symbol of Southern graciousness. A warm sense of recognition filled him upon each arrival.

Pete stood at the base of a staircase that rivaled Tara's, stretching to the unfinished second floor. Ornate trim work surrounded each door in the room and the dark wood floor was waxed to a mirror finish. Paintings of places Pete had visited and loved hung on the walls, scenes of Niagara Falls and the backyard of his grandmother's house. The open front doors ushered in a breeze touched with the invigorating scent of fresh-cut alfalfa.

Some things in the mansion changed with each visit; some always remained the same. The second floor never altered, forever a maze of rough framed walls and plywood flooring. Old-fashioned copper stubs of incomplete plumbing poked through the floors and errant pigtailed wires sprouted from the wall studs. Pete had plans for the expanse on the second floor: a room with a pool table, a master bedroom with a veranda, a bathroom with an archaic claw foot tub. One night he would arrive, and the new rooms would be finished.

On the ground floor, hallways snaked away in impossible lengths, promising yet more undiscovered spaces. Through each door, some rooms were familiar, some not. Often, first floor rooms were empty, though they had been furnished in other visits. Pete peered inside a few doors, rediscovering the mansion, finding details his subconscious had added.

Pete entered his favorite room, an elegant sunroom, with three walls and a ceiling of solid glass panels in a wrought iron frame. Potted tropical plants covered the floor, parting to make a path to an open observation area. Daylight blazed down on the white marble floor. On the other side of the glass, a lush green lawn rolled away from the mansion. Pete decided to spend the dream right here, warmed by the sun and bathed in the scents of rich earth and flowering plants.

Suddenly something ice cold blew through him, an Arctic blast that penetrated his clothes, his skin, his soul. He shivered. His stomach clenched in an involuntary knot of fear.

A low rumbling noise rolled across the vast stretch of lawn, like the roar of a distant jet. At the far edge of the grass, a dark, amorphous mass emerged from the trees. The pulsating mix of black smoke and gray substance nosed out into the open. It slithered across the grass like a huge worm and began a slow zigzag up the hill to the mansion.

Pete stepped to the window and gripped the cold iron windowpane. His short, shallow breaths fogged the glass.

The apparition closed on the house. Its bellowing's pitch grew piercing and shrill, sonic steel needles that probed Pete's. He covered his ears.

The creature sharpened into a massive gray snake, a freight train of shifting scales with jagged spikes along its back. The head reared up. A gaunt shadowy face, as misshapen as a Picasso abstract, stared through the window at Pete with empty black eye sockets. Its mouth stretched into a howling oval. The head wore a peaked officer's cap with an indistinct central white logo. Around its neck hung a tarnished medallion on a thick chain. It bore the likeness of two crossed snakes, one dark and one light.

It slithered back and forth across the yard ever quicker, but its gaze never wavered. It remained locked on the mansion, the head swiveling counter to the body movement, always facing the sunroom, always facing Pete.

Pete staggered back from the glass. This was all wrong. He was in *the mansion*. Mansion dreams were never nightmares. What was this thing he summoned that came on the way a killer entered a schoolyard?

The creature turned again and charged the sunroom. The hideous head closed on the mansion. Its ear-shattering shriek pierced Pete's skull. The hairs on his arms stood on end and vibrated in time with the creature's wailing. The white object on the peak of the cap came into focus, a clenched skeletal fist.

Its pit of a mouth opened wider, as if to ingest the house. Windowpanes in the house shuddered from the screaming noise. Pete fell to his knees. His heart slammed inside his chest.

Pete's subconscious reached up, grabbed a hold of the real world, and pulled.

He woke up in his dark dorm room in a cold, soaking sweat. He clenched the edge of the bed and prayed it was really over. His roommate snored. Pete relaxed and slumped back into his pillow. The clock read 4:50 a.m.

This is no way to start the first day of midterm exams, he thought.

PUBLISHING

It's all about the story...

Romance

HORROR

www.samhainpublishing.com

CPSIA information can be obtained at www.ICGtesting.com
Printed in the USA
LVOW07s0001060815

448963LV00006BB/926/P